W9-CIR-459

# THE BEST
# HORROR OF THE YEAR

## VOLUME ONE

# THE BEST
# HORROR OF THE YEAR

## VOLUME ONE

EDITED BY ELLEN DATLOW

NIGHT SHADE BOOKS
SAN FRANCISCO

**First Edition**

ISBN: 978-1-59780-161-4

Printed in Canada

**Night Shade Books**
Please visit us on the web at
www.nightshadebooks.com

*I'd like to dedicate this volume to James Frenkel,*
*packager of* The Year's Best Fantasy and Horror
*for its twenty-one volume run.*

*Also, to my co-editors Terri Windling,*
*and then Kelly Link & Gavin J. Grant.*

Acknowledgements to John Kenny, Frank Ludlow, David Murphy, Eugene Myer, Sheila Williams, Brian Bieniowski, Harlan Ellison, and Charles Tan.

Thanks to Gavin J. Grant for suggesting I approach the editors at Night Shade about spinning off a new best of the year in horror annual.

I'd like to acknowledge the following magazines and catalogs for invaluable information and descriptions of material I was unable to obtain: *Locus, All Hallows, Publishers Weekly, Washington Post Book World,* and *Prism* (the quarterly journal of fantasy given with membership to the British Fantasy Society). I'd also like to thank all the editors who made sure I saw their magazines during the year, the webzine editors who provided printouts, and the book publishers who provided review copies in a timely manner. Also, the writers who sent me printouts of their stories when I was unable to acquire the magazine or book in which they appeared.

And thank you to Jeremy Lassen and Jason Williams for taking a chance on a new best of the year anthology.

# CONTENTS

# SUMMATION 2008

The twenty-one stories and poems included were chosen from magazines, webzines, anthologies, literary journals, and single author collections. One story and one poem were published in single author collections. One story was originally published in a webzine. The authors reside in the United States, Canada, Australia, Great Britain, Wales, and Thailand. Thirteen out of twenty-one stories are by writers whose stories I've never before chosen for a best of the year volume, which is probably a record.

## AWARDS

The Bram Stoker Awards for Achievement in Horror is given by the Horror Writers Association. The full membership may recommend in all categories but only active members can vote on the final ballot. The awards for material appearing during 2007 were presented at the organization's annual banquet held Saturday evening, March 29, 2008, in Salt Lake City, Utah, in conjunction with the World Horror Convention.

## 2007 WINNERS FOR SUPERIOR ACHIEVEMENT:

Novel: *The Missing* by Sarah Langan; First Novel: *Heart-Shaped Box* by Joe Hill; Long Fiction: "Afterward, There Will Be a Hallway" by Gary Braunbeck; Short Fiction: "The Gentle Brush of Wings" by David Niall Wilson; Fiction Collection (Tie): *Proverbs for Monsters* by Michael A. Arnzen and *5 Stories* by Peter Straub; Anthology: *Five Strokes to Midnight*, edited by Gary Braunbeck and Hank Schwaeble; Nonfiction: *The Cryptopedia: A Dictionary of the Weird, Strange & Downright Bizarre* by Jonathan Maberry & David F. Kramer; Poetry Collection (Tie): *Being Full of Light, Insubstantial* by Linda Addison and *Vectors: A Week in the Death of a Planet* by Charlee Jacob & Marge Simon; Lifetime Achievement Award: John Carpenter, Robert Weinberg; Richard Laymon President's Award:

Mark Worthen, Stephen Dorato, Christopher Fulbright.

The Shirley Jackson Award, recognizing the legacy of Jackson's writing, and with permission of her estate, was established for outstanding achievement in the literature of psychological suspense, horror, and the dark fantastic. The inaugural awards were announced at Readercon, held in Burlington, Massachusetts.

The winners for the best work in 2007:

Novel: *Generation Loss* by Elizabeth Hand (Small Beer Press); Novella: *Vacancy* by Lucius Shepard (*Subterranean #7*, 2007); Novelette: "The Janus Tree" by Glen Hirshberg (*Inferno*, Tor); Short Story: "The Monsters of Heaven" by Nathan Ballingrud (*Inferno*, Tor); Collection: *The Imago Sequence and Other Stories* by Laird Barron (Night Shade Books); Anthology: *Inferno* edited by Ellen Datlow (Tor).

The British Fantasy Society announced the winners of the British Fantasy Awards for 2008 at the awards banquet of Fantasycon 2008 in Nottingham, England on September 20.

The Sydney J. Bounds Best Newcomer Award: Scott Lynch; BFS Special Award: The Karl Edward Wagner Award: Ray Harryhausen; Best Non-Fiction: Peter Tennant, *Whispers of Wickedness* website reviews; Best Artist: Vincent Chong; Best Small Press: Peter Crowther, PS Publishing; Best Anthology: Stephen Jones, *The Mammoth Book of Best New Horror 18* (Robinson); Best Collection: Christopher Fowler *Old Devil Moon* (Serpent's Tail); Best Short Fiction: Joel Lane, "My Stone Desire" (*Black Static #1*, TTA Press); Best Novella: Conrad Williams, *The Scalding Rooms* (PS Publishing); Best Novel: The August Derleth Fantasy Award: Ramsey Campbell, *The Grin of the Dark* (PS Publishing).

The International Horror Guild Awards for works from 2007 were announced Friday, October 31, 2008, and posted on the IHG website. Peter Straub, named earlier as the year's Living Legend, was honored in an essay by Stefan R. Dziemianowicz.

Winners for the best work in 2007:

Novel: *The Terror* by Dan Simmons (Little, Brown); Long Fiction: *Softspoken* by Lucius Shepard (Night Shade Books); Mid-Length Fiction: "Closet Dreams," by Lisa Tuttle (*Postscripts #10*); Short Fiction: "Honey in the Wound" by Nancy Etchemendy (*The Restless Dead*); Illustrated Narrative: *The Nightmare Factory*, Thomas Ligotti (Fox Atomic/Harper Paperbacks); Collection: *Dagger Key and Other Stories*, Lucius Shepard (PS Publishing); Anthology: *Inferno*, Ellen Datlow, ed. (Tor); Nonfiction: *Mario Bava: All the Colors of Dark*, Tim Lucas (Video Watchdog); Periodical: *Postscripts*; Art: Elizabeth McGrath (for "The Incurable Disorder," Billy Shire Fine Arts, December 2007).

Judges for this year's awards were Edward Bryant, Stefan R. Dziemianowicz, Ann Kennedy VanderMeer, and Hank Wagner. This was the last year that the award was given.

The World Fantasy Awards were announced November 2, 2008, at the World

Fantasy Convention in Calgary, Alberta. Lifetime Achievement recipients were previously announced.

Winners for the best work in 2007:

Life Achievement: Patricia McKillip and Leo & Diane Dillon; Novel: *Ysabel* by Guy Gavriel Kay (Viking Canada; Roc); Novella: *Illyria* by Elizabeth Hand (PS Publishing); Short Story: "Singing of Mount Abora" by Theodora Goss (*Logorrhea*); Anthology: *Inferno*, Ellen Datlow, ed. (Tor); Collection: *Tiny Deaths* by Robert Shearman (Comma Press); Artist: Edward Miller; Special Award, Professional: Peter Crowther (PS Publishing); Special Award, Non-Professional: Midori Snyder & Terri Windling (Endicott Studios Website).

## NOTABLE NOVELS OF 2008

*The Resurrectionist* by Jack O'Connell (Algonquin) is the author's fifth novel, and as with his previous ones his lucid prose easily carries the reader into realms of the phantasmagoric. The story begins with a man taking a job at a very special clinic, hoping that the doctors there can miraculously help his comatose son, who is a patient. A second strand of the story follows the adventures of a group of circus freaks on the run from hostility and discrimination—a graphic novel series the man's son loves. The third strand involves a motorcycle gang, one of whose members has infiltrated the clinic. The strands tenuously come together to create a moving finale.

*Sharp Teeth* by Toby Barlow (Harper) is a werewolf novel told in verse, but don't let that scare you away. It's free verse, not rhyming, and the book is wonderfully gripping, in part due to the compression of language. Go and read it, you'll not be disappointed. Highly recommended.

*The Gargoyle* by Andrew Davidson (Doubleday) is a dark, offbeat love story about the deepening relationship between a male, ex-porn-star hideously burned in a terrible accident, and a brilliant sculptor of gargoyles who claims to have been a reincarnated nun from the middle ages where they were lovers. The woman (who most people in the novel believe is mentally ill, but is quite obviously not, to any fantasy reader) tells wonderful stories within the overarching story of their love to both entertain and teach the recovering man. Not really horror— although there are horrific descriptions of the accident that maimed the man and other dark bits— but always absorbing.

*The Man on the Ceiling* by Steve Rasnic Tem and Melanie Tem (Discoveries) is an expansion of the multi award-winning novella by the Tems, published in 2000. A kind of fictionalized family memoir, their story is told in sections by each of them. It is imaginative, harrowing, moving, and always thoughtful about transmuting one's life experience into fiction and how that reflects back onto the creator. The book doesn't really add to the brilliance of the novella, but for those who missed that gem this is a worthwhile substitute.

*The Ghost in Love* by Jonathan Carroll (Farrar, Straus) is about a man who should have died, but didn't. There's a glitch in the system, so he's still around, but he's got a ghost who lives with him (although he doesn't realize it). The ghost—which can manifest as anything it likes, including a fly—is in love with the dead guy's ex-girlfriend. The Angel of Death is not happy. And of course, as in almost all of Carroll's novels, there's a dog.

*Severance Package* by Duane Swierczynski (St. Martin's Press) is a clever, violent, fast-moving romp that, if the reader stops to actually think about it, makes very little sense. An executive invites his key personnel to a mysterious Saturday morning meeting in the office and then offers them poison-laced juice to drink—or face a more violent death. Why does he want to kill them and will anyone get out alive?

*Infected* by Scott Sigler (Crown) is an sf/horror thriller about a series of horrific homicides committed by seemingly normal, happy citizens. The story alternates between the governmental and medical teams tracking down and studying the plague, and a newly infected victim and his efforts to rid himself of what's ailing him. Entertaining, but with large plot holes that hopefully will be plugged in the sequel, titled *Contagious*.

*Sway* by Zachary Lazar (Little, Brown) miraculously projects the reader into the lives and minds of some of the prime movers of the sixties: underground filmmaker Kenneth Anger; Brian Jones, Keith Richards, and Mick Jagger of the Rolling Stones; and would-be rocker/Charlie Manson follower Bobby Beausoleil. By doing this, Lazar creates something that reads almost like a memoir of the era that started with love and promise, culminating in darkness, with the murders of Bobby Kennedy and Martin Luther King, the Manson killings, and the near-riot at the Stones' concert at Altamont. The voices are so authentic-sounding, it's as if the author is channeling his characters.

*The Shadow Year* by Jeffrey Ford (William Morrow) is a satisfying expansion of Ford's novella "Botch Town," creating a sharp snapshot of growing up on Long Island, New York, in the early 1960s. Two brothers and their young sister investigate mysterious occurrences in the neighborhood, partly with the help of the sister's seemingly preternatural powers of detection. The adult narrator looking back at a dark year in his family's hometown, never intrudes on the story and the characters are so realistic that it's almost painful to read about them. Highly recommended.

*Pandemonium* by Daryl Gregory (Del Rey) is an impressive first novel that's a dazzling mix of science fiction, fantasy, and horror. In an alternate reality, archetypical "demons" appear on earth in the mid-1950s, possessing ordinary citizens. There are faint echoes of O'Connell's *The Resurrectionist* (mentioned above). A young man who was possessed by such a demon when he was a young boy has been troubled ever since, believing that the demon never left. His voyage of self-discovery is traumatic and moving.

*The Man in the Picture* by Susan Hill (Overlook Press) is a well-packaged little hardcover novella. It's an absorbing ghost story of spurned love, vengeance, and a mysterious painting, but like Hill's more famous *The Woman in Black* (adapted into a long-running play), its ideal readers are those unfamiliar with the classic ghost stories of the last century and a half. For most everyone else, there's nothing remarkable about Hill's work.

*Ghost Radio* by Leopoldo Gout (William Morrow) is a marvelous prose debut by a Mexican graphic novelist about a call-in radio host with a strange and tragic past who becomes caught up by the true ghostly experiences that his callers reveal. Haunting, and with short, snappy chapters, fast-moving.

*Let the Right One In* by John Ajvide Lindquist (Quercus) was originally published in Sweden in 2004. It came out in the United States and the United Kingdom in 2007, and the movie based on the novel was released in 2008. I saw the movie first and although I ended up enjoying the movie more than the novel, the novel is also quite good. Oskar, a bullied twelve-year-old, lives with his divorced mother in a housing complex, just outside Stockholm. Mysterious neighbors move next door, heralding several brutal murders in the area. Oskar meets one of the new neighbors, Eli, a 200-year-old vampire child as lonely as he is. There are some nice touches as their relationship develops. And there are also some terrific scenes indicating what happens when a vampire doesn't follow its own kind's rules, such as when it enters a dwelling uninvited. Both novel and movie do a terrific job of depicting pre-teen loneliness and the cold, bleak Swedish winter.

*The Sister* by Poppy Adams (Knopf) is a subtle first novel of psychological suspense narrated by a fascinating voice. Virginia and Vivian are sisters who are unexpectedly reunited after almost fifty years, when Vivian returns to the family home in Dorset where her Ginny has lived alone for decades, continuing her father's work as a lepidopterist. The return of the vivacious and selfish Vivian churns up memories and causes a major upheaval in the measured ordered life that Virginia has constructed for herself.

*Rain Dogs* by Gary McMahon (Humdrumming) is the author's first novel, although he's written some fine short stories over the years. A rain dog is a dog that cannot find its way home because its trail has been washed away by the rain. This definition serves as the epigraph for the short novel, and perfectly describes the plight of the two main characters. An ex-con returns home, hoping to redeem himself in the eyes of the wife and child he left behind in the aftermath of the violence that sent him to prison. A broken, battered woman who can see ghosts returns to the family she fled two decades ago, sensing that she has unfinished business to attend to. A third, and possibly most important "character," is the never-ending rain plaguing the area. A deluge of Biblical proportions has been brought forth by the inadvertent actions of a grieving woman, unleashing a supernatural power that cannot be controlled. As the storylines converge, the importance—and sometimes poison—of familial relationships is brought into sharp focus.

*The Graveyard Book* by Neil Gaiman (HarperCollins) is a charming yet scary coming-of-age story about an orphan brought up by the ghosts in a graveyard after his family is murdered by a mystery man. It's got enough nastiness to scare the pants off kids (the intended audience) and should also be thoroughly enjoyed by older readers. (It won the Newbery Medal and the Hugo Award).

## ALSO NOTED

This is not meant to be all inclusive but merely a sampling of dark fiction available during 2008.

The paranormal romance subgenre is booming with unending variations of vampires, werewolves, witches, and ghosts. Here's a mere sampling of some of the vampires novels: *The Darkness* is the newest in L. A. Banks's (St Martin's Press) vampire Huntress series; *Chosen* by P. C. Cast and Kristin Cast (St. Martin's Press) is the third in a series of young adult vampire novels. *The Bleeding Dusk* by Colleen Gleason (Signet Eclipse) is the third in a series about a family of vampire slayers. *The Mark of the Vampire Queen* by Joey W. Hill (Berkley Heat) another series entry. *Midnight Reign* by Chris Marie Green (Ace) is the second book in a vampire series. *The Vampire of New York* by Lee Hunt (Signet), an 1860s murder mystery involving Dracula. *Dark Wars: The Tale of Meiji Dracula* by Hideyuki Kikuchi (Del Rey), translated from the Japanese, is about Dracula in 1880 Japan. *Vampire Interrupted* by Lynsay Sands (Avon), about a vampire training to be a private investigator. *The Ravening* by Dawn Thompson (Love Spell) is part of a historical vampire romance series. *The Undead Kama Sutra* by Mario Acevedo (Eos) is the third in a vampire mystery series. *Blood Colony* by Tananarive Due (Atria) is the third installment of her Living Blood series. *Midnight Rising* by Lara Adrian (Dell) is a vampire romance. Even Aunt Dimity, of the cozy mystery series by Nancy Atherton, gets into the act with *Aunt Dimity: Vampire Hunter* (Viking). *Staked* by J. F. Lewis (Pocket) is a first novel about vampires and werewolves. *Breaking Dawn*, another in the *Twilight* series by Stephenie Meyer (Little, Brown). *Every Last Drop* by Charlie Huston (Del Rey), fourth in the series about a vampiric private eye. *Brides of the Impaler* by Edward Lee (Leisure) is the first vampire novel by the prolific author. *The Dracula Dossier* by James Reese (Morrow) is about Bram Stoker's investigation of the Jack the Ripper murders in London, and using them later for inspiration in writing *Dracula*. *Vampire Zero* by David Wellington (Three Rivers Press), the third book in this continuing series. *Yellow Moon* by Jewell Parker Rhodes (Atria) is the second of the Marie Laveau mystery series. *Blood Noir* by Laurell K. Hamilton (Berkley) is sixteenth in the Anita Blake series. *Vamps: Vampire American Princesses*, *Vamps: Night Life*, and *Vamps: After Dark* by Nancy A. Collins (HarperCollins) introduces the creator of the Sonya Blue vampire series to the young adult market with the first three books of a new series. *From Dead to Worse* by Charlaine Harris (Ace) is a new entry in the Sookie Stackhouse series. *A Dangerous Climate*, a new Count St. Germain novel by Chelsea Quinn Yarbro (Tor).

Other supernatural creatures are far less prevalent than vampires but still popular: Werewolves: *The Accidental Werewolf* by Dakota Cassidy (Berkley Sensation). *Night Life* by Caitlin Kittredge (St. Martin's) is the first book in a series about a werewolf cop. *Howling at the Moon* by Karen MacInerney (Ballantine) is the first novel of an urban werewolf trilogy. A new werewolf series by L. A. Banks debuted with *Bad Blood* (St. Martin's). *Ravenous* by Ray Garton (Leisure) is about an infestation of werewolves in a small California town. *The Wolfman* by George Pekearo (Tor) is about a werewolf who trains himself to only hunt and kill those who are evil. It was the first novel by a young writer whose life was cut tragically short and died before the book's publication.

Witches: *The Outlaw Demon Wails* (Eos) is sixth in the series about a witch who is a private eye. *Witch Blood* by Anya Bast (Sensation) is part of a series. *The 5ᵗʰ Witch* by Graham Masterton (Leisure) about an LA detective embroiled in a struggle against an international crime czar who uses a witch to enable him to take over LA. *Fathom* by Cherie Priest (Tor) is about an evil water witch who hopes to awaken mankind's long-sleeping enemy.

Demons: *Beast of Desire* by Lisa Renee Jones (Silhouette Nocturne) is a romance about demon hunters. *The Devouring* by Simon Holt (Little, Brown), a young adult novel about a girl confronted by demons that feed on fear. Another novel about creatures that feed upon fear is Mary SanGiovanni's *Found You* (Leisure), the sequel to *The Hollower*.

Ghosts: *Ghost of a Chance* by Kate Marsh (Obsidian) is the first book in a series featuring a ghosthunter. *The Wicked Dead*, the young adult series about ghosts by Stefan Petrucha and Thomas Pendleton, continues (HarperTeen). *Seer of Shadows* by Avi (HarperCollins) is a young adult ghost story taking place in 1872. *Ghost Walk* by Brian Keene (Leisure) is about a haunted Halloween attraction.

Zombies, despite all the hype of 2007, seem to have died down in popularity, judging by the tiny number of novels published last year. *Soulless* by Christopher Golden (Pocket/MTV Books) is about what happens when a séance held in Times Square somehow summons up the living dead. *Empire* by David Dunwoody (Permuted Press) with the Grim Reaper as a hero, destroying zombies wherever he goes. *Blood of the Dead* by A. P. Fuchs (Coscom Entertainment), first in the Undead World trilogy.

Some other odds and ends in the novel category: Stephen King had a big new novel out, *Duma Key* (Scribner) and so did Dean Koontz with *Your Heart Belongs to Me* (Bantam). Stephenie Meyer's first adult novel, *The Host*, was published by Little, Brown. *Orgy of Souls* by Wrath James White and Maurice Broaddus (Apex) was a short novel as was Ray Garton's *The Folks 2: No Place Like Home*, followup to his early short novel *The Folks* (Cemetery Dance). *The Midnight Man* by Simon Clark (Severn House). *Coffin Country* by Gary A. Braunbeck (Leisure), which is a prologue to his Cedar Hill series and includes two reprinted Cedar Hill stories. *Johnny Gruesome* by Greg Lamberson (Bad Moon Books). *The Academy* by Bentley Little (Signet). *Night Children* by Kit Reed (Tor). *The Economy of Light* by Jack Dann (PS) about a retired Nazi hunter called in by authorities to identify what is thought to be Mengele's body in Brazil. *Night Work* by Thomas Glavinic, translated from the German by John Brownjohn (Canongate), is about a man who wakes up to find the world deserted. Starts off well but loses steam about halfway through. *Contagious* by Scott Sigler (Crown) is the sequel to *Infected*, reviewed above. *The Casebook of Victor Frankenstein* by Peter Ackroyd (Chatto & Windus) is another retelling of Mary Shelley's *Frankenstein*. The always reliable Patrick McGrath's *Trauma* (Knopf) is about a psychiatrist trying to manage his own demons. *The Suspicions of Mr. Whicher* by Kate Summerscale (Walker) is the fictionalized re-creation of an infamous case of child murder taking place in 1860 and Scotland Yard Detective-Inspector Jonathan Whicher who attempted to solve it.

## ANTHOLOGIES

2008 was a disappointing year for original horror anthologies with a few exceptions noted below

*The Werewolf Pack*, selected and introduced by Mark Valentine (Wordsworth Editions Ltd.) provides a good historical overview of the subgenre with seventeen werewolf stories. Four are contemporary tales, with three original to the volume. The originals by Gail-Nina Anderson, Steve Duffy, and R. B. Russell are very fine contributions to the canon, with Russell's and Duffy's both reprinted herein. From the same publisher, *The Black Veil and Other Tales of Supernatural Sleuths*, selected and introduced by Mark Valentine, has another seventeen stories, four published for the first time. The reprints are by William Hope Hodgson, Arthur Machen, A. F. Kidd, editor Valentine, and others. The strongest originals are by R. B. Russell and Rosalie Parker. The publisher presents both anthologies so that it appears that editor Valentine wrote all the stories—the front jacket doesn't identify him as the editor and the table of contents has story titles with no individual authors. Very odd.

*Shades of Darkness* edited by Barbara and Christopher Roden (Ash-Tree Press) is the fifth volume of original fiction in the series and it's excellent. The stories are varied and literate and although the anthology started a little slowly for me, most of the stories are good, and several are better than that. This is one of the best original horror anthologies of the year. Stories by Glen Hirshberg and E. Michael Lewis are reprinted herein.

*Subterranean: Tales of Dark Fantasy* edited by William Schafer (Subterranean Press) is a beautiful hardcover with stunning cover art by Dave McKean, featuring eleven new stories, all of them good. The best of the darker ones are by Joe R. Lansdale, Caitlín R. Kiernan, Rachel Swirsky, William Browning Spencer, and Darren Speegle. The Spencer and Lansdale are reprinted herein.

*Exotic Gothic 2* edited by Danel Olson (Ash-Tree Press) is a worthy follow-up to the editor's first, mixed reprint and original anthology. *EG2* has all new stories taking place all over the world. The most notable were those by George Makana Clark, Barbara Roden, Nicholas Royle, Nancy A. Collins, Edward P. Crandall,

Christopher Fowler, Reggie Oliver, Tia V. Travis, and Robert Hood. The Royle is reprinted herein.

*The New Uncanny: Tales of Unease* edited by Sarah Eyre and Ra Page (Comma Press) makes great use of Sigmund Freud's 1919 essay listing eight uncanny tropes, "irrational causes of fear deployed in literature." The editors sent the original essay to fourteen writers and asked them "to respond directly and consciously, in any way they wished, with a new story." At least five of the stories use dolls or doubles as their central image. Many of the stories are quite good, making this for me, one of the best original horror anthologies of the year.

*The Second Black Book of Horror* selected by Charles Black (Mortbury Press) was very good overall, with only a few clunkers. The strongest stories were by Mike Chinn, Rog Pile, Steve Goodwin, writing partners L. H. Maynard and M. P. N. Sims, Daniel McGachey, and Gary McMahon. *The Third Black Book of Horror* selected by Charles Black also came out in 2008 with good stories by Mike Chinn, Paul Finch, David A. Riley, Craig Herbertson, Joel Lane, Gary McMahon, Paul Newman, and Rog Pile.

*Gaslight Grimoire: Fantastic Tales of Sherlock Holmes* edited by J. R. Campbell and Charles Prepolec (Edge) is a thoroughly entertaining anthology of eleven new stories that likely would have had Holmes turning over in his grave (if he existed), as he loathed any hint of the supernatural, and always solved his cases rationally. But despite this, you the reader can enjoy them. Those I liked the best were by Barbara Roden, M. J. Elliott, Martin Powell, Chris Roberson, J. R. Campbell, Kim Newman, and a collaboration by Chico Kidd and Rick Kennett.

*We Fade to Grey* edited by Gary McMahon (Pendragon Press) has five non-theme dark novelettes and novellas by British writers. Simon Bestwick's "The Narrows" a very powerful, frightening sf/horror story, is reprinted herein.

*Bound for Evil: Curious Tales of Books Gone Bad* edited by Tom English (Dead Letter Press) is a hefty, entertaining anthology of sixty-five stories about nasty, demented, or overly influential books and the people who love or obsess over them. It's a good-looking limited edition hardcover tome of almost eight hundred pages, with half the stories original to the volume, and of those, at least eleven are notable. Illustrations by Allen Koszowski.

*The Second Humdrumming Book of Horror Stories* edited by Ian Alexander Martin (Humdrumming) is the follow-up to last year's promising anthology and it doesn't disappoint. All fifteen stories appear for the first time and some are quite good, particularly those by Christopher Fowler, Davin Ireland, Michael Kelly, Sarah Pinborough, Simon Strantzas, John Travis, and Conrad Williams. Unfortunately, the press ceased publishing.

*Desolate Souls*, the souvenir anthology of the World Horror Convention 2008 held in Salt Lake City, Utah, was edited by Mark Worthen and J. P. Edwards (Bones & Casket Press). Thematically related in its use of the desert and other desolate areas around SLC, the anthology includes reprints and originals. The best originals were by Scott Edelman, Linda Addison, and Cullen Bunn.

*Unspeakable Horror: From the Shadows of the Closet* edited by Vince A. Liaguno and Chad Helder (Dark Scribe Press) contains twenty-three stories featuring gay and lesbian characters, with many of the stories revealing the negative consequences of remaining in the sexual closet. There were very good stories by Lee Thomas, Sarah Langan, C. Michael Cook, and Livia Llewellyn.

*The Undead: Headshot Quartet* edited by Christina Bivins and Lane Adamson (Permuted Press) has four zombie novellas by John Sunseri, Ryan C. Thomas, David Dunwoody, and D. L. Snell. The most ambitious one is Snell's, about a man who awakes in a zombie-filled alley with no memory but the power to create objects out of nothing.

*Hell in the Heartlands* edited by Martel Sardina and Roger Dale Trexler (Annihilation Press) features sixteen new stories by Illinois writers. There are notable stories by S. C. E. Cooney, Nikki M. Pill, and a particularly good one by Richard Chwedyk.

*Dark Territories* edited by Gary Frank and Mary SanGiovanni (GSHW Press) is part of an annual anthology series showcasing stories by members of the Garden State Horror Writers. All fifteen stories take place in New Jersey and twelve are published for the first time.

*Like a Chinese Tattoo: Twelve Inscrutably Twisted Tales* (DarkArts Books) features four writers with three stories each, most originals. Contributors are Cullen Bunn, Rick R. Reed, David Thomas Lord, and J. A. Konrath. The strongest entries are the novellas by Bunn and Konrath.

*The Living Dead* edited by John Joseph Adams (Night Shade Books) is an almost five-hundred-page anthology of thirty-four zombie stories (one, a brand new novella by John Langan) including stories by Clive Barker, Laurell K. Hamilton, Stephen King, Neil Gaiman, Poppy Z. Brite, and others.

*Read by Dawn, Volume 3* edited by Adèle Hartley (Bloody Books) has twenty eight new stories, too many of which are thin on character and seem to unfold with no rhyme or reason. However, this volume is a definite improvement over the earlier two volumes in the series, and there are notable stories by Scott Stainton Miller, Samuel Miner, Peter Gutiérrez, Rebecca Lloyd, Joel Sutherland, Ryan Cooper, and Jamie Killen.

*Blood Lite* edited by Kevin J. Anderson is published under the aegis of the Horror Writers Association and has twenty-one stories of humorous horror. The stories that best accomplish this difficult task are by Janet Berliner, Lucien Soulban, Nancy Kilpatrick, and Jim Butcher.

*Sins of the Sirens: Fourteen Tales of Dark Desire* edited by John Everson (Dark Arts Books) presents 20,000 words of original and reprinted fiction by four writers: Loren Rhoads, Maria Alexander, Mehitobel Wilson, and Christa Faust. Some good stories here.

*Houses on the Borderland* edited by David A. Sutton (British Fantasy Society) features six very dark novellas, all inspired by William Hope Hodgson's classic novel, *The House on the Borderland*.

*Horror Library, Volume 3* edited by R. J. Cavender (Cutting Block Press) has thirty original stories, the best of which were by Stephen Couch, Lisa Morton, Kurt Dinan, A. C. Wise, and Michael C. Cook.

*Traps* edited by Scott T. Goudsward (DarkHart Press) has twenty-eight stories, the best by Del Howison, P. D. Cacek, J. M Heluk, and Nancy Kilpatrick.

*Deadlines: An Anthology of Horror and Dark Fantasy* edited by Cheryl Mullenax (Comet Press) has twenty stories, two reprints.

*Ghost Stories* edited by Peter Washington (Knopf) is a new hardcover volume from the Everyman Library series featuring stories by Jorge Luis Borges, Eudora Welty and Vladimir Nabokov, Ray Bradbury, and others.

*Erie Tales: Tales of Terror From Michigan* presented by the Great Lakes Horror Association and edited by Bob Strauss is the group's first anthology in a planned annual series.

*And Soon…the Darkness* edited by David Byron is a NVF Magazine publication (Turner/Maxwell Books) with seventeen stories.

*The Mammoth Book of Best New Horror 19* edited by Stephen Jones (Robinson): Contained twenty-six stories and novellas, a summary of the year, a necrology, and an index of horror booksellers, organizations, small press publishers, and other useful information. For perhaps the first time in many years the volume covering 2007 did not overlap at all with the *Year's Best Fantasy and Horror*.

*Poe's Children: The New Horror, An Anthology* edited by Peter Straub (Doubleday) is a strong anthology of dark fiction but has nothing to do with Edgar Allan Poe. What it is, is Straub's appreciation of writers not especially known for their horror but who write it brilliantly. Writers such as Elizabeth Hand, Jonathan Carroll, Kelly Link, Dan Chaon, and Brian Evenson. Also, the seasoned writers who have continuously produced excellent dark work for years, those such as Ramsey Campbell, Stephen King, David J. Schow, Thomas Ligotti, Melanie Tem and Steve Rasnic Tem, and M. John Harrison. The stories by these and the other thirteen authors chosen to represent the field in all its glory may cause disagreements, but the stories are all worth reading and isn't that what any anthology should be about?

## MIXED-GENRE ANTHOLOGIES

*Clockwork Phoenix: Tales of Beauty and Strangeness* edited by Mike Allen (Norilana Books) is the first volume of a projected annual non-theme anthology of all original fantasy fiction. This volume of eighteen stories has a few dark ones, the best by Leah Bobet, Ekaterina Sedia, and Laird Barron. *The Ghost Quartet* edited by Marvin Kaye (Tor) features four entertaining new stories by Brian Lumley, Marvin Kaye, Tanith Lee, and Orson Scott Card. *Hotter than Hell* edited by Kim Harrison (and Martin H. Greenberg, credited on the title page, not the cover) (Harper) is a paranormal romance anthology with lots of hot sex and a bit of horror. Twelve stories, with the best of the darker ones by Tanya Huff and Keri Arthur. *D.C. Noir 2: The Classics* edited by George Pelecanos (Akashic Books) features reprints by Langston Hughes, Richard Wright, Russ Thomas, Ward Just, Elizabeth Hand, Pelecanos himself and other writers not as well-known. *Manhattan Noir 2: The Classics* edited by Lawrence Block (Akashic Books) features reprints by Joyce Carol Oates, Jerome Charyn, Donald. E. Westlake, Barry N. Malzberg, Edgar Allan Poe, Edith Wharton, editor Block, and a host of other well-known writers. *Unusual Suspects: Stories of Mystery and Fantasy* edited by Dana Stabenow (Ace) features all original stories on the above theme. The best darker stories were by Sharon Shinn and Laurie R. King. *Cone Zero: Nemonymous 8* edited by D. F. Lewis (Megazanthus Press) is the editor's continuing experiment in oddly structured anthologies. This one seems to require contributors to use the term "cone zero" somewhere in their story. Four are simply titled "Cone Zero" and two use that phrase in addition to other words. There's not even an introduction to explain the meaning or purpose of Lewis's little game. For this issue, instead of holding the contributor's names back from readers until the next issue of the series, the editor supplies all the names but doesn't reveal who wrote which story. Five of the fourteen stories are both dark and notable. They're by Dominy Clements, A. J. Kirby, Sean Parker, Eric Schaller, and S. D. Tullis. *Voices* edited by Mark S. Deniz and Amanda Pillar (Morrigan Books) focuses on the history of a hotel's rooms from 1928-2008 and contains original stories by Robert Hood, Gary McMahon, Martin Livings, and others. *Better off Undead* edited by Martin H. Greenberg and Daniel M. Hoyt (DAW) contains original stories about vampires, haunts, zombies, and mummies but the tone is unusually light. Despite this, there were notable darker stories by Jay Lake, Kate Paulk, and Devon Monk. *Alembical: A Distillation of Four Novellas* edited by Lawrence M. Schoen and Arthur Dorrance (Paper Golem) features four speculative fiction novellas, including a powerful nightmarish future America envisioned by Jay Lake and a moving ghost story by James Van Pelt. *Dreaming Again* edited by Jack Dann (HarperVoyager, Australia/ Eos, US) follows up Dann's previous non-theme anthology showcase of Australian voices (co-edited with Janeen Webb) the World Fantasy Award-winning *Dreaming Down-Under*. The second volume is hefty, and there are good darker stories by Trent Jamieson, Lee Battersby, Simon Brown, Sara Douglass, and Terry Dowling. *Writers for Relief* edited by Davey Beauchamp (Dragon Moon) does something I've never seen a publisher do before: It misspelled one of the two big name contributors' names every place it appears, including on the Table of Contents and under the title of his story. The anthology has a few horror stories in it. *The Del Rey Book of Science Fiction and Fantasy* edited by Ellen Datlow (Del Rey) featured several dark stories, including those by Margo Lanagan, Nathan Ballingrud, Anna Tambour, Richard Bowes, and Laird Barron. The Lanagan and Barron are reprinted herein. *Istanbul Noir* edited by Mustafa Ziyalan and Amy Spangler (Akashic Books) has three good darker stories by Takan Barlas, Sadik Yemni, and Müge iplikçi. *Writers of the Future, Volume XXIV* edited by Algis Budrys (Galaxy) has three notable dark stories by Ian McHugh, Sarah L. Edwards, and Al Bogdan. *Fast*

*Ships, Black Sails* edited by Ann and Jeff VanderMeer (Night Shade Books) is an entertaining mixed-genre bag of pirate stories. The best of the darker stories were by Conrad Williams, and the collaboration by Elizabeth Bear and Sarah Monette. *Killers* edited by Colin Harvey (Swimming Kangaroo Books) is a good dark crime anthology with notable stories by editor Harvey, Eugie Foster, Philip J. Lees, and Lee Thomas. *The Lone Star Stories Reader* edited by Eric T. Marin (LSS Press) showcases fifteen varied stories originally published on the website between 2004 and 2008. *Otherworldly Maine* edited by Noreen Doyle (Down East) combines twenty-one reprinted and original science fiction, fantasy, and dark fantasy stories about Maine by Mark Twain, Stephen King, Elizabeth Hand, Gardner Dozois, Edgar Pangborn, Steve Rasnic Tem, Gregory Feeley, Melanie Tem, and others. *Scary Food: A Compendium of Gastronomic Atrocity* edited by Cat Sparks (Agog! Press) is more weird and occasionally disgusting than scary but still, it's a fun little book with entries by Gillian Pollack, Anna Tambour, Stephen Dedman, Margo Lanagan, Lee Battersby, and other Australian writers. *Wilde Stories 2008: The Best of the Year's Gay Speculative Fiction* edited by Steve Berman (Lethe Press) includes some horror, including stories by Lee Thomas, and collaboration by Joel Lane and John Pelan. *Wastelands* edited by John Joseph Adams (Night Shade) reprints twenty-one post-apocalyptic stories by writers including Stephen King, Octavia E. Butler, Jonathan Lethem, George R. R. Martin, Nancy Kress, and others, plus an original by John Langan. *The New Weird* edited by Ann and Jeff VanderMeer (Tachyon) attempts to define what just might be un-definable—a mode of literature practiced by a diverse group of writers of science fiction, fantasy, and horror who (sometimes) appear preoccupied by the grotesque in their fiction. Some of the writers have been publishing for decades: Kathe Koja, M. John Harrison, Clive Barker, Michael Moorcock, Thomas Ligotti, and Paul Di Filippo, to name just a few of those whose work is included. The problematic argument of "the new weird's" difference from slipstream and/or literary cross-genre fiction aside, there are some very good stories, novel excerpts, and essays.

## COLLECTIONS

*The Bleeding Horse and Other Ghost Stories* by Brian J. Showers (Mercier Fiction) is an attractive-looking little hardcover of seven original stories, adapted by the author from the regional tales of Dublin and its environs. Some of the stories are very creepy, and the book has a gorgeous dust jacket by Scott Hampton and lovingly rendered black and white interior illustrations by Duane Spurlock.

*Mr. Gaunt and Other Uneasy Encounters* by John Langan (Prime) debut showcases only five stories, all novelettes or novellas, with one new novella. Langan's work is influenced by his work in academia and his interest in the literature of both Henry James and M. R. James. I'm especially fond of Langan's novella "Mr. Gaunt," but all his stories are worth reading. His fine story notes are illuminating to readers who want to know "where did you get that idea."

*Other Voices* by Andrew Humphrey (Elastic Press) is the second collection by this talented writer. This one, introduced by Eric Brown, contains twelve stories, all but one reprints from such venues as *The Third Alternative, Crimewave, Midnight Street*, and *Bare Bone*, and at least half of them received honorable mentions in the *Year's Best Fantasy and Horror* series.

*A Thread of Truth* by Nina Allen (Eibonvale Press) is an impressive first collection by a writer whose stories I've admired in the magazines *Supernatural Tales* and *Dark Horizons*, and in the anthology *Strange Tales*. Its eight stories are a combination of dark fantasy and dread, mystery, and the occasional barely fantastical. Six appear for the first time in the collection, which came out mid-2007. (first seen in 2008)

*Hell Is Murky* by John Alfred Taylor (Ash-Tree Press) is a very pleasurable first collection of twenty strange tales published between 1978 and 2007 in venues as varied as *The Twilight Zone Magazine, All Hallows, Space and Time*, and *Asimov's Science Fiction Magazine*. Four of the stories are original to the collection.

*Rope Trick: Thirteen Strange Tales* by Mark P. Henderson (Ash-Tree Press) is the author's first published fiction book. The best of the stories are subtle, mysterious, and well-told ghost and haunted house tales, a few lead the reader into a tantalizing maze that unfortunately trails off. All but three of the stories included are previously unpublished.

*Coffin Nails* by John Llewellyn Probert (Ash-Tree Press) has several new stories among the eighteen in the book. Probert is excellent at creating tension but for me, some of the endings falter, which is a shame. The author provides an entertaining introduction to the volume and afterwords for each story, explaining its genesis.

*Scattered Ashes* by Scott Nicholson (Dark Regions Press) collects the best of the author's short stories published between 1998 and 2008, with three originals. Nicholson writes in a variety of tones and voices and this is a good introduction to his short work. One reprint appeared in *The Year's Best Fantasy and Horror: Twentieth Annual Collection.*

*Glyphotech and Other Macabre Processes* by Mark Samuels (PS Showcase 4) has eleven stories, and is the author's third collection. It contains some of Samuels's more recent stories, including one I originally published in *Inferno* and one reprinted in *YBFH #19*. Two stories appear for the first time. With an introduction by Ramsey Campbell. The striking jacket art is by Jason Van Hollander.

*Ghost Realm* by Paul Finch (Ash-Tree Press) showcases nine new stories and novellas featuring hauntings from around Great Britain. These stories have something in common with most of Finch's stories: rough, thoroughly unlikable men who are prone to violence (the women are usually victims of their mates' stupidity/insensitivity). Singly, the stories are often very effective, but all together, in a collection, the oppressiveness can be overwhelming.

*Worse Than Myself* by Adam Golaski (Raw Dog Screaming) is the first collection by someone who up to now, has been better known for his editorship of *New*

*Genre Magazine* than his short fiction, but this collection of literary supernatural fiction should change that. The reprints were originally published in *Supernatural Tales* and *All Hallows*, and in original anthologies from Ash-Tree Press and Tartarus Press. Six of the eleven stories appear for the first time and although a few founder, most are very good. This trade paperback is the perfect opportunity to check out Golaski's work. "The Man from the Peak" is reprinted herein.

*The Autopsy and Other Tales* by Michael Shea (Centipede Press) is a gorgeous, over-sized, illustrated volume of twenty-one of the author's best stories and novellas, including some of my favorites: the creepy Lovecraftian *Fat Face* and the novella *I, Said the Fly*. The book reprints all eight stories from *Polyphemus*, published by Arkham House in 1988. Laird Barron has written an introduction to Shea's work. Also included is one story published for the first time.

*The Ghosts of Kerfol* by Deborah Noyes (Candlewick Press) is a tour de force by a writer best-known as the editor of two excellent young adult horror anthologies: *The Restless Dead* and *Gothic!* Retelling the Edith Wharton ghost story "Kerfol," about the murder of a French aristocrat in the seventeenth century from the point of view of a servant girl, Noyes then adds four new ghost tales, all of which take place in the unlucky house over the next four centuries.

*Just After Sunset* by Stephen King (Scribner) is this prolific author's first collection since 2002 and has thirteen stories published between 1977 and 2008, with "N," a very good novelette, appearing for the first time. With an introduction and story notes by the author.

*The Number 121 to Pennsylvania* by Kealan Patrick Burke (Cemetery Dance) contains fourteen stories, novellas, and a screenplay of one of the novellas. One novella and the screenplay appear for the first time.

*How to Make Monsters* by Gary McMahon (Morrigan Books) has fourteen stories about monsters, most human or produced from human fear or anger. Half of the stories appear for the first time.

*Slivers of Bone* by Ray Garton (Cemetery Dance) is the long-delayed hefty collection of thirteen stories (including two new novellas) by the author best known for his novel about vampire truck-stop hookers, *Live Girls*.

*Halloween and Other Seasons* by Al Sarrantonio (Cemetery Dance Publications) is the author's third collection and contains eighteen stories published between 1979 and 2007.

*H. P. Lovecraft: the Fiction* (Barnes & Noble), part of the B&N Library of essential writers, is a huge volume collecting all his stories in one volume for the first time. It has sixty-eight stories,.

*The Strange Cases of Rudolph Pearson* by William Jones (Chaosium) is a clever and entertaining collection of ten interrelated stories of Lovecraftian fiction with the framing device of a manuscript of "cases" left by a professor of Medieval studies at Columbia University. Four of the "cases" were previously published.

*Haggopian and Other Stories: Best Mythos Tales,* Volume 2 by Brian Lumley (Subterranean) collects twenty-four more of the author's Lovecraftian stories.

*The Horror Stories of Robert E. Howard* (Del Rey) has sixty-one stories, poems, and story fragments. Introduction by Rusty Burke and illustrations by Greg Staples.

*Brimstone Turnpike* edited by Kealan Patrick Burke (Cemetery Dance) features five novellas by Thomas F. Monteleone, Scott Nicholson, Mike Oliveri, Harry Shannon, and Tim Waggoner connected by interstitial material written by the editor. In each story, the main character meets an old man at a ruined gas station on a deserted highway, and is given a gift.

*Shadows and Other Tales* by Tony Richards (Dark Regions Press) is the British author's first U.S. collection and covers the globe with the twenty-one horror stories, two published for the first time. *Passport to Purgatory* also by Tony Richards (Gray Friar Press) occasionally overlaps with *Shadows and Other Tales* but most of the fifteen reprints cover different territory.

*Voices from Hades* by Jeffrey Thomas (Dark Regions Press) is a collection of stories loosely related to the author's novel *Letters from Hades* published in 2003. Here are seven stories (two published for the first time) about dead people who have been consigned to Hades.

*Experiments in Human Nature* by Monica O'Rourke (Two Backed Books), one of the few female proponents of extreme horror, has included an interesting mix of twenty-three stories, four published for the first time.

*Other Gods* by Stephen Mark Rainey (Dark Regions Press) collects sixteen stories published over the past twenty years, with one new story included.

*Degrees of Fear and Others* by C. J. Henderson (Dark Regions Press) features twenty stories and vignettes, two published for the first time, many inspired by Lovecraft.

*Skeleton in the Closet and Other Stories* edited by Stefan Dziemianowicz (Subterranean) is the second volume in the Reader's Bloch collection and contains a lot of his earlier stories originally published in the pulps.

*Gleefully Macabre Tales* by Jeff Strand (Delirium Books) showcases thirty-two of the author's mostly humorously grotesque horror stories. Most of the stories are very brief, some are gross (they were entries in WHC gross-out contests). This is most definitely taste specific. It's got appropriate jacket art by Alan M. Clark.

*The Garden of Ghosts* by Scott Thomas (Dark Regions Press) is a charming collection of eighteen brief ghost stories, all published for the first time. Most are more poignant than horrific but there are a few good scares here.

*Inconsequential Tales* by Ramsey Campbell (Hippocampus) includes twenty-four stories never before collected—and two never before published. Campbell provides an introduction explaining the inspiration for each story in the volume.

*Queen of the Country* by d. k. g. goldberg (Prime) has fourteen horror stories (two, never before published) by the late author, who succumbed to cancer in 2005.

*Beneath the Surface* by Simon Strantzas (Humdrumming) is the debut collection by an expert in British urban ennui. Of the twelve stories, seven appear for the first time.

*Tales of the Callamo Mountains* by Larry Blamire is a self-published collection of thirteen stories of Western horror by a filmmaker and sometimes actor that's better than most self-published books, and I recommend that readers seek it out.

*Mama's Boy and Other Dark Tales* by Fran Friel (Apex Publications) has fifteen stories, a few published for the first time.

*The Diving Pool* by Yoko Ogawa, translated by Stephen Snyder (Picador) contains three novellas tinged with darkness by a multi-award-winning Japanese writer.

*Peripheral Visions* by Paul Kane (Creative Guy Publishing) collects twenty-one stories (three appearing for the first time) of dark fantasy and horror by this British writer.

*Ennui and Other States of Madness* by David Niall Wilson (Dark Regions Press) has sixteen diverse stories (two new) and an original novella—the collection includes Wilson's Stoker Award-winning story "The Gentle Brush of Wings."

*Black Pearls: A Faerie Strand* by Louise Hawes (Houghton Mifflin) is a young adult collection of seven dark, retold fairy tales.

*Necronomicon: The Best Weird Tales of H. P. Lovecraft*, Commemorative Edition edited and with an afterword by Stephen Jones (Gollancz) with illustrations by Les Edwards.

*Sredni Vashtar: Sardonic Tales* by Saki (Tartarus Press) collects thirty-one weird and macabre stories and one novel by noted satirist Hector Hugh Monroe, known by the pen name, Saki. Mark Valentine's introduction gives the reader a glimpse of Saki's life, and explores possible influences on his fiction.

*The Triumph of Night and Other Tales* by Edith Wharton (Tartarus Press) includes the preface to her collection, *Ghosts*. In it, she bemoans the literal mindedness of some of her readers who ask how a ghost "could write a letter or put it in a letterbox." The book includes fifteen stories, all those that first appeared in *Ghosts* and four that were published elsewhere.

*A Natural Body and a Spiritual Body: Some Worcestershire Encounters with the Supernatural* by J. S. Leatherbarrow (Ash-Tree Press) is a new edition of a twelve-story collection originally published privately in 1983. The Ash-Tree edition contains the original twelve ghost stories plus a previously uncollected story, a preface by the author, and an introduction by James Doig.

*Tedious Brief Tales of Granta and Gramarye by Ingulphus* (Arthur Gray) (Ash-Tree Press) with ten stories and one poem, is intended as the "true" history of Jesus College's Everlasting Club, whose members were sworn to meet annually on All Souls' Day. The stories were originally published between 1910 and 1919 in two Cambridge magazines under the pseudonym Ingulphus but then were collected by a publisher and their author revealed to be Arthur Gray, Master of Jesus College.

## MIXED-GENRE COLLECTIONS

*Unwelcome Bodies* by Jennifer Pelland (Apex Publications) is this promising writer's debut collection, and features eleven, mostly dark science fiction stories, three published for the first time. Her best work terrifies in its brutal depiction of future possibilities, but I personally would welcome a little more subtlety. *Crazy Love* by Leslie What (Wordcraft of Oregon) showcases seventeen, mostly darkly edged stories. *Bull Running for Girls* by Allyson Bird (Screaming Dreams) is a promising debut with most of the twenty-one stories appearing for the first time, some very good. *Islington Crocodiles* by Paul Meloy (TTA Press) is a marvelous introduction to this talented author's work, most of which were originally published in *The Third Alternative*. Meloy's stories are sometimes science fiction, sometimes crime fiction but what they all have in common is his sharp, precise language and a very dark tone. Of the ten stories, three appear for the first time. *Summer Morning, Summer Night* by Ray Bradbury (P.S./Subterranean Press) contains twenty-seven old and new stories, all set in Greentown, Illinois. *Midnight Call and Other Stories* by Jonathan Thomas (Hippocampus Press) debuts a new voice with twenty-five stories, most published for the first time, several quite dark. *Creeping in Reptile Flesh* by Robert Hood (Altair Australian Books) contains fourteen stories (three previously unpublished) of science fiction, fantasy, and horror. *Voices from Punktown* by Jeffrey Thomas (Dark Regions Press) collects eleven more stories set in the terrifically vital, violent, and imaginative world created by Thomas. Two of the stories are new. *Sheep and Wolves* by Jeremy C. Shipp (Raw Dog Screaming Press) is a mix of the dark and the absurd, with the author taking a little too much delight in creating surrealist images at the expense of developing memorable characters and a story. But it's an interesting first collection. *Wild Nights!* by Joyce Carol Oates (Ecco) is a collection of five novellas about the last days of Edgar Allan Poe, Emily Dickinson, Mark Twain, Henry James, and Ernest Hemingway, each written in the author's style. *Masks* by Ray Bradbury (Gauntlet) features fragments of a never finished novel called *The Masks* written in the mid-1940s. There are also six previously unpublished stories written between 1947 and 1954 ranging in length from two pages to twenty pages. This is a fascinating view into the imagination of a master. *Fourtold* by Michael Stone (Baysgarth Publications) contains four novellas about war, magical powers, and grotesqueries. The book has a foreword by Garry Kilworth. *Where Angels Fear* by Ken Rand (Fairwood Press) is the first of two volumes of the collected short fiction by Rand, who died in 2009. Included are thirty-four sf/f/dark fantasy stories, of which thirteen are appearing for the first time. *The Loved Dead and Other Tales* by C. M. Eddy, Jr. (Fenham Publishing) is a collection of thirteen stories ranging from horror to mystery by a friend and sometimes collaborator of H. P. Lovecraft. Some of the stories are reprinted here for the first time since their original publication in the pulps. Edited and with an introduction by Jim Dyer. *The Wall of America* by Thomas M. Disch (Tachyon) includes twenty stories by the late author published between 1981 and 2008 in venues ranging from *The*

*Magazine of Fantasy & Science Fiction, OMNI* Magazine, and *Interzone* to *Playboy* and *The Hudson Review. The Best of Michael Swanwick* by Michael Swanwick (Subterranean) has twenty stories from throughout this master craftsman's career including several award winners, some quite dark. With an introduction by the author explaining the origin of each story. *Little Creatures* by Michael McCarty [and Special Guests] (Sam's Dot) has twenty-five brief stories, eleven published for the first time. Some of the stories are sf/horror. *Pump Six and Other Stories* by Paolo Bacigalupi (Night Shade) is the first collection of this lauded young science fiction writer, several of whose short stories are tinged with horror. The ten stories included were published between 1999 and 2008 (one original to the collection). One, "The Fluted Girl," was reprinted in *The Year's Best Fantasy and Horror 17. City of the Sea and Other Ghost Stories* by Jerome K. Jerome (Ash-Tree Press) is best known for his comic novel *Three Men in a Boat* and this is the first book collecting all his ghost stories, humorous and horrific in one volume. With an extensive introduction about the author and his work by Jessica Amanda Salmonson. *Pretty Monsters* by Kelly Link (Viking), aimed at the young adult market, contains nine stories, several award winners—and all but one previously published. At least a few of the stories are darkly tinged. Australian artist Shaun Tan has created wonderful black and white decorations. PS reissued a beautiful boxed set of the classic Ray Bradbury collection alternately titled *The Day It Rained Forever* and *A Medicine for Melancholy*. There is a lot of overlap between the two volumes, but some stories only appeared in one or the other. Both books have different jacket covers and endpapers by Tomislav Tikulin. Jonathan Eller introduces *A Medicine for Melancholy* and Caitlín R. Kiernan introduces *The Day It Rained Forever*. Some of Bradbury's most memorable stories appear here, including the two title stories, "The Wonderful Ice-Cream Suit," and "Perchance to Dream." The books also contain the story illustrations that originally accompanied them in their first magazine publications. *The Drowned Life* by Jeffrey Ford (Harper Perennial) consists of sixteen science fiction, fantasy, and dark fantasy stories published between 2002 and 2008, two appearing for the first time. Ford's got a prodigious imagination and always seems keen to push the limits of dream logic. *The Best of Lucius Shepard* (limited edition includes a trade paperback titled *Skull City and Other Lost Stories* (Subterranean) is a retrospective of eighteen stories and novellas—or twenty-nine with the extra book—ranging from very early work like "The Taylorville Reconstruction" to his recent award-nominated novella "Stars Seen Through Stone." Oddly, for a project that should be very special, nowhere in either book is there anything other than the stories: no introduction, no commentary by Shepard or anyone else. Nor is there a first publication page.

## JOURNALS, NEWSLETTERS, MAGAZINES, AND WEBZINES

I feel it's important to recognize the work of the talented artists working in the field of fantastic fiction, both dark and light. The following artists created art that I thought especially noteworthy during 2008: Cameron Gray, Newel Anderson, Lydia Burris, Sarah Xu, Minouk Duin, David Leonard, Ben Sowards, Dave Leri, Luke Ramsey, Donna Kendrigan, Andrew McKiernan, James Birkbeck, Vincent Chong, Steven Archer, Victoria Alexandrova, Jason Levesque, Jason Van Hollander, Saara Salmi, Will Koffman, Daniele Serra, Jane Chen, Brian Smith, Eleanor Clarke, Hendrick Gericke, Vincent Sammy, Pierre Smit, Kobus Faber, Laura Givens, Brad Foster, Dora Wayland, Chrissy Ellsworth, Keith Boulger, Carrie Anne Baade, Fatima Asimova, K. J. Bishop, Eric M. Turnmire, Sandro Castelli, John Picacio, Tim Mullins, Wayne Blackhurst, Steve C. Gilberts, Rodger Gerberding and Suzanne Clarke, Aunia Kahn, Zak Jarvis, Kiriko Moth, Bartlomiej Jurkowski, John Stanton, Harry Fassl, Sean Simmans, Dean Harkness, David Migman, Travis Anthony Soumis, and David Gentry.

There's an enormous annual turnover in small-press magazines, and most rarely last more than a year or two, so it's difficult to recommend buying a subscription to those that haven't proven their longevity. But I urge readers to at least buy single issues of those that sound interesting. Most magazines have web sites with subscription information, eliminating the need to include it here. The following are, I thought, the best in 2008.

Some of the most important magazines/webzines are those specializing in news of the field, market reports, and reviews. *The Gila Queen's Guide to Markets*, edited by Kathryn Ptacek, emailed to subscribers on a regular basis, is an excellent fount of information for markets in and outside the horror field. *Market Maven*, edited by Cynthia Ward, is a monthly email newsletter specializing in professional and semi-professional speculative fiction market news. Ralan.com is *the* web site for up-to-date market information. *Locus*, edited by Charles N. Brown, Liza Groen Trombi, and Amelia Beamer, and *Locus Online*, edited by Mark Kelly, specialize in news about the science fiction and fantasy fields, but include horror coverage as well. The only major venues specializing in reviewing short genre fiction are *The Fix* (http://thefix-online.com/), *The Internet Review of Science Fiction* (www.irosf.com/), and *Locus* but none of them specialize in horror. *Dead Reckonings: A Review of Horror Literature* edited by S. T. Joshi and Jack M. Haringa and published by Hippocampus Press is a fine review journal focusing on contemporary work while also considering the classics. In addition to the reviews, it includes the regular column "Ramsey Campbell, Probably." The first issue of *Studies in the Fantastic* edited by S. T. Joshi announces its intention to "provide a useful forum for scholars of various disciplines to probe the history, theory, and historical significance of weird fiction, ranging from the analysis of specific authors and works to broader cultural issues raised by the popularity and dissemination of the genre." Issue #1 contains articles by John Langan, George M. Johnson, Joshi, and others, plus original fiction and original and classic poetry. *Wormwood:* Literature of the Fantastic, Supernatural and Decadent edited by Mark Valentine brought out two issues in 2008, with articles by Peter Bell on Robert Aickman's work as an anthologist, Joel Lane about Fritz Leiber's taking the supernatural tale out of the countryside and into the industrial city, Mike Barrett's overview of Michael McDowell's fiction, Douglas A. Anderson's attempt to resurrect Alexander Crawford, an almost forgotten author of four novels, the ongoing series by Brian Stableford about the decadent world view, and other interesting items. The journal also runs a "late reviews" column covering rare fantasy and supernatural literature, and Camera Obscura, covering recent but possibly overlooked books. *Lovecraft Annual* edited by S. T. Joshi and published by Hippocampus Press is a journal devoted to H. P. Lovecraft. The second, two-hundred-plus-page issue has meaty articles on Lovecraft and his work, plus reviews. A must for anyone seriously interested in Lovecraft's work. *Dissections* edited by Gina Wisker, David Sandner, Michael Arnzen, Al Wendland, and Lawrence Connolly put out two online issues in 2008, with articles about the evolution of the heroine in horror film, the evolution of zombies and other pertinent subjects. Poetry is also featured on the website.

Friends of Arthur Machen is a worldwide society aiming to "promote a wider recognition for Machen's work." Members receive the semi-annual *Faunus: The Journal of the friends of Arthur Machen* edited by Mark Valentine and Ray Russell. The eighteenth issue was published in 2008 as an attractive cloth-bound limited edition. It contains material by Machen and critical essays on his work. The Ghost Story Society was formed in 1988 to provide admirers of the classic ghost story with an outlet for their interest, and membership of the Society now numbers more than four hundred worldwide. The Society offers members an opportunity to exchange thoughts and ideas through regular publication of its journal, *All Hallows*, which now averages two hundred pages per issue and contains fiction, articles, and letters concerning ghost stories past and present.

A Ghostly Company, a literary society devoted to the ghost story in all forms, was created in 2004 to take up the slack left by the Ghost Story Society, which moved to Canada. It sponsors regular meetings and informal gatherings in the U.K. (foreign members welcome).

The British Fantasy Society has existed for over thirty-five years in order to promote and enjoy the genres of fantasy, science fiction, and horror in all its forms. Members receive a copy of *Prism*, the organization's news magazine, with book and games reviews, an events column, and the occasional article. They also receive the dark fantasy fiction magazine, *Dark Horizons*, and all BFS special publications. The two issues of *Dark Horizons* brought out in 2008 were the last edited by Peter Coleborn and Jan Edwards, and featured especially good fiction and poetry by Joel Lane and Karl Bell plus interviews with Charles de Lint and Terry Pratchett. *New Horizons* edited by Andrew Hook is a new, sister publication to *Dark Horizons*, and will be publishing fantasy. The first issue had interviews with writer Tony Richards and publisher of Eibonvale Press, David Rix.

Horror Writers Association is a useful organization that exists to "promote and protect the careers of professional horror writers and those seeking to enter their ranks, while at the same time using its best endeavors to raise the profile of the horror genre in the publishing industry and among readers in general." There are three levels of membership. The organization gives out the annual Bram Stoker Awards for Superior Achievement.

## MAGAZINES

*Rue Morgue*, edited by Jovanka Vuckovic, is a monthly media magazine covering horror in all its bloody glory (with the still photos to prove it), but in between the gore there are often thoughtful articles and columns. In 2008 the magazine did major features on *Sweeney Todd*, with an interview with director Tim Burton, a history of the various theatrical productions, and an article about the London neighborhood in which Sweeney supposedly flourished. One issue was dedicated to vampires, showcasing the brilliant Swedish *Let the Right One In* by interviewing both the director, Tomas Alfredson, and the author of the novel, John Ajvide Lindqvist. Another issue was dedicated to celebrating the fiftieth anniversary of *Famous Monsters of Filmland* and its creator Forrest J. Ackerman.

*Fangoria*, edited by Anthony Timpone, is a monthly media magazine covering both big and small budget horror productions, the grislier the better. It features columns on film news, DVD releases, video games, and books. All monsters all the time. And guilty of bad punning throughout. The articles are less varied and lightweight compared to those in *Rue Morgue*.

*Video Watchdog*, a bi-monthly edited by Tim Lucas, is one of the most exuberant film magazines around, and is one of my favorites, because I'm usually inspired to watch or re-watch at least one movie they review in every issue. The magazine is invaluable for the connoisseur of trashy, pulp, and horror movies and enjoyable for just about everyone. In 2008 there was a lengthy article about the long-running Doctor Who series, a profile and overview of George Méliès, the early filmmaker, and his work. The magazine runs regular columns by Ramsey Campbell and Douglas E. Winter.

*Weird Tales* edited by Ann VanderMeer continues to reinvent itself with attractive and quirky cover art and design and some lively nonfiction. During 2008 there were interviews with China Miéville, cartoonist/animator Bill Plympton, and Mike Mignola, the creator of *Hellboy*. The March/April issue ran a fun feature of mini profiles of "the eighty-five weirdest storytellers" in honor of the magazine's 85th anniversary. The weird ones range from Laurie Anderson, Andy Kaufman, Penn & Teller, and Shirley Jackson to J. G. Ballard, Franz Kafka, Andy Warhol, and the Coen Brothers. The stories I enjoyed best in 2008 were by John Kirk, Matthew Pridham, Calvin Mills, Sarah Monette, Karen Heuler, Kelly Barnhill, Cat Rambo, Ramsey Shehadeh, a collaboration by W. M. Pugmire and M. K. Snyder, and a novella by Michael Moorcock.

*Cemetery Dance* edited by Robert Morrish is way behind its schedule with one issue, a Charles L. Grant tribute, published two years after his death, and most of the book reviews over two years old. This is not promising—there was also only a single issue published in 2007. In 2008's #58, there were interviews with

Stephen Graham Jones, T. E. D. Klein, David Morrell, and Robert Masello, plus written tributes to Grant and a reprint of one of his stories. The original stories in the issue were a mixed bag, with the most interesting by Sarah Monette, Karen Heuler, and Ian Rogers. The publisher promises to get back on track in 2009.

*Black Static* edited by Andy Cox brought out six excellent issues in 2008, with most of the fiction good to excellent—twenty-two stories received honorable mentions—plus a generous number of movie and book reviews and some author profiles. Daniel Kaysen's "The Rising River" is reprinted herein.

*Supernatural Tales* #14 edited by David Longhorn was an excellent issue, with very good stories by Simon Strantzas, Tony Lovell, C. E. Ward, and Stone Franks. This is a British magazine that could really use your support if you enjoy weird supernatural fiction.

*GUD (Greatest Uncommon Denominator Magazine)* edited by Kaolin Fire, Sue Miller, Julia Bernd, and Debbie Moorhouse publishes twice a year. It's a perfect-bound magazine that looks like an anthology and contains fiction and poetry with good-looking cover and interior art. The spring issue was darker than the two issues from 2007, and contained notable stories by Kirstyn McDermott, Jeff Somers, Paul Haines, and good poetry by Kristine Ong Muslim and Samantha Henderson.

*Shroud* edited by Timothy P. Deal is a new bi-monthly magazine publishing dark fiction and featuring interviews with author Brian Keene and dark artist Mike Pucciarelli. There are also book and movie reviews. The best fiction was by John Mantooth, Curtis Bradley Vickers, Maura McHugh, Tim Waggoner, Ken Bruen, and Tom Piccirilli.

*Not One of Us* edited by John Benson continues to publish unusual, often dark fiction. There were two issues out in 2008, a special one-off called *Home and Away*, and the first in a planned annual series of chapbooks, *Follow the Wounded One* by Mike Allen. The best dark stories and poems were by Shane Nelson, Amanda Downum, Sonya Taaffe, and Karen R. Porter.

*Dark Discoveries* edited by James R. Beach is meant to be a quarterly, but so far has only been published twice a year since 2005. Original fiction, reviews, interviews. There was a very good story by Tim Lebbon in #11.

*Something Wicked* edited by Joe Vaz is a very promising science fiction and horror quarterly now in its second year, being published in South Africa. There was some fine dark fiction by Michael Bailey, Inge Papp, Widaad Pangarker, Paul Marlowe, Tauriq Moosa, Ian R. Faulkner, and Jonathan C. Gillespie.

*Midnight Echo* issue 1 edited by Kirstyn McDermott and Ian Mondis will be a semi-annual showcase for dark fantasy and horror, with a revolving team of editors, and published under the auspices of the Australian Horror Writers Association. However, submissions are open to everyone. The strongest stories in the first issue are by Deborah Biancotti, Paul Haines, Martin Livings, and the World Fantasy Award-winning British writer Robert Shearman. There will be a series of interviews with new Australian writers in each issue.

## MIXED-GENRE MAGAZINES

*Realms of Fantasy* edited by Shawna McCarthy is a bi-monthly that sometimes publishes dark fantasy and occasionally even horror. In 2008 there were notable dark stories by Margaret Ronald, Graham Edwards, and Sharon Mock. The Edwards is reprinted herein. The magazine features a regular, always erudite column on "folk roots," plus book and movie reviews, and a gallery of beautiful samples of fantastic art with text by Karen Haber. *Zahir* edited by Sheryl Tempchin is published three times a year. The spring issue had a minimal amount of horror in its seven stories but the summer issue had notable dark fiction by Matthew David Brozik, Sarah Odishoo, and Daniel Brugioni. *Postscripts* is a well-designed quarterly published by Peter Crowther and edited by Nick Gevers. 2008 saw the publication of very good dark stories by Paul Jessup, Eric Schaller, John Grant, Sarah Monette, R. B. Russell, T. M. Wright, and William Alexander. *Fictitious Force* edited by Jonathan Laden is a quarterly magazine of "speculative fiction," encompassing science fiction, fantasy, and occasionally horror. The best horror in 2008 was by Aliette de Bodard. *On Spec* edited by Susan MacGregor, Barb Galler-Smith, Diane L. Walton, Robin S. Carson, and Barry Hammond continues its run as the most prominent Canadian sf/f/h magazine with notable dark stories by Claude Lalumière, Daniel LeMoal, Tyler Keevil, and Lisa Carreiro, and a charming fantasy by Kate Riedel. The LeMoal is reprinted herein. *Borderlands*, the Australian magazine edited by Stephen Dedman, had strong dark fiction in 2008 by Simon Brown, Lyn Battersby, and Shane Dix. *Aurealis* edited by Stuart Mayne is a long-time fixture in Australia with mixed-genre fiction. Although the copyright page of #40 says 2007, the issue actually came out in 2008 with seven stories, a science article, and book reviews. The best of the darker stories were by Adam Browne, Nathan Burrage, and Paul Haines (also published in issue #2 of *GUD*). *Space and Time* edited by Hildy Silverman is a quarterly mix of science, fiction, and horror prose and poetry. During 2008, there were good dark stories and poetry by Jennifer Crow, Gordon Linzner, Laurel Hickey, Kevin Brown, Kendall Evans, Day al-Mohamad, and Doug Russell. *Albedo One* edited by John Kenny, Frank Ludlow, David Murphy, Roelof Goudriaan, and Robert Neilson published two issues in 2008, neither with much horror, but there was a strong dark story by James Steimle. *Talebones* edited by Patrick Swenson is a well-produced perfect-bound digest-sized magazine that showcases science fiction and dark fantasy stories and poetry. There were two issues in 2008, with notable dark fiction by Julie McGalliard and Lon Prater. *Andromeda Spaceways Inflight Magazine,* edited by an Australian cooperative, published six issues in 2008. In addition to its fiction, which is mostly sf/f, there are reviews and interviews with Australian luminaries. There were good darker stories by Tessa Kum, Penny-Anne Beaudoin, Cat Sparks, Kent Purvis, Sarah Totten, and Henry Loïc. *Shimmer* edited by Beth Wodzinski regularly publishes a variety of good fiction, including some dark material. There were notable darker stories in the spring issue by Tinatsu Wallace, M. K. Hobson, Joy Marchand, and Angela Slatter. The Art issue, specially edited by art director Mary Robinette Kowal, asked four writers to produce fiction inspired by the art selected for the issue. There was an especially good dark story in this issue, also by Slatter. *Crimewave 10* edited by Andy Cox returns after skipping a year, and the new issue is excellent, with consistently strong stories, especially those by Simon Avery and Daniel Kaysen. *Midnight Street* edited by Trevor Denyer brought out two issues in 2008, with reviews, poetry, interviews, and notable dark fiction by Simon Bestwick, Andrew Humphrey, and Joel Lane. *The Magazine of Fantasy & Science Fiction* edited by Gordon Van Gelder often publishes dark fantasy and sometimes publishes horror. In 2008, there were strong darker stories by Albert Cowdrey, Scott Dalrymple, Laura Kasischke, John Kessel, Stephen King (also in the King collection), Ted Kosmatka, Marc Laidlaw, Rand B. Lee, Richard Mueller, M. Rickert, James Stoddard, and Steven Utley. *Asimov's Science Fiction* edited by Sheila Williams occasionally publishes dark fantasy and in 2008 included good ones by Carol Emshwiller, Peter Higgins, Derek Künsken, Tanith Lee, Ian R. MacLeod, Lawrence Person, S. P. Somtow, and Elizabeth Bear (charming and not horrific but Lovecraftian).

The best webzines publishing horror in 2008: *Chizine* edited by Brett Alexander Savory, Sandra Kasturi, Gord Zajac, and Hannah Wolf Bowen had some fine dark fiction and poetry by David Tallerman, Brenta Blevins, Mia Nutick, Lon Prater, Mildred Tremblay, Michael R. Colangelo, An Owomoyela, and a collaboration by Nick Mamatas and Tim Pratt. *Strange Horizons* showcases reviews and nonfiction columns and essays in addition to fiction. The fiction is edited by Susan Marie Groppi, Jed Hartman, and Karen Meisner and in 2008 there were good dark stories by Tina Connelly, Haddyr Copley-Woods, and Kris Dikeman. *Orson Scott Card's Intergalactic Medicine Show* edited by Edmund R. Schubert, while better known for its science fiction and fantasy, had strong dark work by Scott Emerson Bull, John Brown, Alethea Kontis, and James Maxey. *Apex Science Fiction and Horror* edited by Jason Sizemore is a monthly online webzine with consistently readable fiction. There were notable horror stories by James Walton Langolf, Andrew C. Porter, George Mann, Mary Robinette Kowal, William T. Vandemark, and Lavie Tidhar. *Apex's* print edition published good dark stories by Lavie Tidhar and Ryck Neube and featured Angela Slatter's informative essay about variations of "Little Red Riding Hood." Heather Shaw and Tim Pratt produced two issues of their little magazine *Flytrap*, and although most of the stories weren't dark, there *were* a few standouts by Greg Van Eekhout, M. Rickert, and Catherynne M. Valente. *Lone Star Stories* edited by Eric T. Marin runs an interesting mix of material and in 2008 had a notable dark story by Samantha Henderson, and good dark poetry by Elizabeth Bear and Elizabeth Hand. *McSweeney's 27* edited by Dave Eggers had a facsimile notebook by Art Spiegelman, a small book titled *Lots of Things Like This*, created to accompany an art show and consisting of art from the show, plus a book of fives stories and one very effective suspense novella by Stephen King.

## POETRY MAGAZINES, WEB SITES, AND CHAPBOOKS

*Star*Line, the Journal of the Science Fiction Poetry Society* edited by Marge Simon is a long-running bi-monthly poetry magazine. There was a good dark poem by JoSelle Vanderhooft. *Mythic Delirium,* edited by Mike Allen, publishes two issues a year. In 2008 there was strong dark poetry by Jeannine Hall Gailey, Sonya Taaffe, Jessica Paige Wick, Gemma Files, and Jacqueline West. *The Magazine of Speculative Poetry* edited by Roger Dutcher is published twice a year. In 2008 there was an excellent dark poem by JoSelle Vanderhooft. *Dreams and Nightmares,* edited by David C. Kopaska-Merkel, has been publishing two or three issues annually since January 1986.

*Signs & Wonders* by Jennifer Crow (Sam's Dot) is a collection of over forty poems, all published previously. Crow's horror poetry has consistently received Honorable Mentions from me over the years. With illustrations by Marge B. Simon.

*A Guide to Folktales in Fragile Dialects* by Catherynne M. Valente (Norilana/ Curiosities) is a must buy for anyone interested in dark fantasy poetry. Valente is one of the field's most talented poets and prose writers and this collection, with gorgeous cover art by Connie Toebe and lush, thought-provoking poems by Valente, is a perfect introduction to her poetic work. All but two of the poems are reprints. *The Phantom World* by Gary Crawford (Sam's Dot) has thirty poems, all previously published. *Holy Land* by Rauan Klassnik (Black Ocean) contains over fifty tiny poems, each only a few powerful lines long. More than half appear for the first time. *The Journey to Kailash* by Mike Allen (Norilana/Curiosities) is an excellent new collection by one of the best cross-genre poets in the genres of fantasy and dark fantasy. Ten of the more than sixty poems appear for the first time. *The Nightmare Collection* by Bruce Boston (Dark Regions Press) contains a good variety of this master poet's work, including a few appearing for the first time. *Outgrow* by Stella Brice (Art Club Press) is an impressive collection of thirty-nine ferocious reinterpretations of fairy tales. *Dwarf Stars 2008* edited by Deborah Kolodji and Stephen M. Wilson (Science Fiction Poetry Association) presents the best speculative poems of ten lines or less from 2007. Included are a few horror and dark fantasy poems. *The 2008 Rhysling Anthology* edited by Drew Morse (Science Fiction Poetry Association) features ninety-six science fiction, fantasy, and horror poems considered the best of 2007 by the members of the association. This is the thirty-first Rhysling volume and it's used by members to vote for the best short and best long poems of the year. *Virgin of the Apocalypse* by Corinne de Winter (Sam's Dot) has fifty-six poems, all but nine published for the first time. *Spores from Sharnoth and Other Madnesses* by Leigh Black-more (P'rea Press) contains forty-five fantasy and horror poems. *Clark Ashton Smith: The Complete Poetry and Translations, Volume 1: The Abyss Triumphant* and *Clark Ashton Smith: The Complete Poetry and Translations, Volume 2: The*

*Wine of Summer* edited by S. T. Joshi and David E. Schultz (Hippocampus Press) represents an impressive achievement by Smith and by the editors, as they've included almost one thousand poems (about three hundred previously unpublished) written over fifty years and have made textual corrections by consulting the original manuscripts.

## NONFICTION

*Shadows over New England* by David Goudsward and Scott T. Goudsward (BearManor Media) is a very entertaining guide to places (real and imaginary) in New England that have been the inspiration for horror stories, novels, and movies. *Taboo Breakers: 18 Independent Films That Courted Controversy and Created a Legend* by Calum Waddell (Telos) analyzes eighteen titles that Waddell believes pushed boundaries and used shock tactics to sell tickets. Even if you haven't seen some of the movies, the descriptions are so detailed that you get the idea. There are interviews with the directors, writers, and occasionally actors. Some of the movies included are *Blood Feast*, *Night of the Living Dead*, *Cannibal Holocaust*, *Coffey*, and *The Plague Dogs*. *Stephen King: A Primary Bibliography of the World's Most Popular Author* by Justin Brooks (CD) has over nine hundred entries and covers all of King's published and known unpublished works from 1959 to the end of 2005. *The New Annotated Dracula by Bram Stoker*, edited and with a foreword and notes by Leslie S. Klinger (W. W. Norton), is a joy to behold. The book is massive, with over six hundred pages rich with material including the original 1897 text of the novel, annotations, illustrations, and photographs. Also included are an introduction by Neil Gaiman and a lengthy article on the context of *Dracula*.

*The Dead Travel Fast: Stalking Vampires from Nosferatu to Count Chocula* by Eric Nuzum (St. Martin's Griffin) explores the vampire in pop culture. *Dark Banquet: Blood & the Curious Lives of Blood-Feeding Creatures* by Bill Schutt (Harmony), in which a zoologist takes readers on a voyage into the world of some of nature's strangest creatures—the sanguivores—those that subsist on blood. *Hammer Film Scores and the Musical Avant-Garde* by David Huckvale (McFarland) explains "how Hammer commissioned composers at the cutting edge of European musical modernism to write their movie scores, introducing the avant-garde into popular culture." With illustrations. *The Bedside, Bathtub & Armchair Companion to Dracula* by Mark Dawidziak (Continuum) is a relatively brief (188 pages) but dense guide for the non-expert aficionado. *Spirits and Death in Niagara* by Marcy Italiano (Schiffer) is a guide to the supernatural and macabre in the towns of Niagara Falls and Niagara-on-the-Lake on the Canadian-US border. *Shock Festival* by Stephen Romano (IDW) is an illustrated history of one hundred and one of the strangest, sleaziest, most outrageous movies you've never seen—because they're imaginary. With hundreds of exclusive, never-before-seen original movie posters and memorabilia items (of the non-existent films). *A Halloween Anthology: Literary and Historical Writings Over*

*The Centuries* by Lisa Morton (McFarland) has twenty-seven entries including poems, short stories, excerpts from books on folklore, Irish and Scottish folk tales, and a one-act play. *Horror Isn't a 4-Letter Word: Essays on Writing & Appreciating the Genre* by Matthew Warner (Guide Dog Books) collects columns originally written between 2002 and 2007 for *horrorworld.org* and the *Hellnotes* newsletter. *The Monster Hunter in Modern Popular Culture* by Heather L. Duda (McFarland) surveys books, films, television shows, and graphic novels showing the evolution of the monster hunter from white, upper-class, educated male to everything from a vampire to a teenage girl with supernatural powers. *Videodrome: Studies in the Horror Film* by Tim Lucas (Millipede Press) celebrates the twenty-fifth anniversary of the Cronenberg film. Movie expert and publisher of *Video Watchdog*, Lucas has interviewed cast and crew, including exclusive, never-before-published interviews with Cronenberg, provides commentary and analysis of the film, and over sixty black-and-white and color photographs, many never before seen. *The Great Monster Magazines: A Critical Study of the Black and White Publications of the 1950s, 1960s and 1970s* by Robert Michael "Bobb" Cotter (McFarland). *Zombie Movies: The Ultimate Guide* by Glenn Kay (Chicago Review Press) provides a chronological listing, with summaries and reviews, for more than two hundred and fifty films released from 1932 to 2008. *Zombie CSU: The Forensics of the Living Dead* by Jonathan Maberry (Citadel) seems like the perfect companion volume to the *Zombie Survival Guide* of several years ago, covering the history, culture, and science of zombies. It also analyzes how an actual zombie epidemic might play out in the real world. *Hazel Court Horror Queen: An Autobiography* by Hazel Court (Tomahawk Press) is lavishly illustrated. *Arts of Darkness: American Noir and the Quest for Redemption* by Thomas S. Hibbs (Spence) is a critical examination of noir and neo-noir films through the lens of spiritual journeys and religious redemption. *Dreams and Nightmares: Science and Technology in Myth and Fiction* by Mordecai Roshwald (McFarland). *A New Dawn: Your Favorite Authors on Stephenie Meyers' Twilight Series* (Ben Bella) edited by Ellen Hopkins and Leah Wilson has thirteen essays and is available only through Borders. *Horror Panegyric* by Keith Seward (Savoy Books) has a critical essay on the Lord Horror novels of David Britton plus excerpts from those novels. *The Vampire Hunter's Handbook* by Raphael Van Helsing (Pavilion) is an illustrated guide/diary about vampires. *Metamorphoses of the Werewolf: A Literary Study from Antiquity Through the Renaissance* by Leslie A. Sconduto (McFarland). *American Exorcist: Critical Essays on William Peter Blatty* edited by Benjamin Szumskyj (McFarland) collects thirteen essays on Blatty's work. *A Hideous Bit of Morbidity: An Anthology of Horror Criticism from the Enlightenment to World War I* edited by Jason Colavito (McFarland) collects reviews and essays showing how the critical reception to horror evolved during that period. *Silver Scream: 40 Classic Horror Movies Volume One 1920-1941* by Steven Warren Hill (Telos) is a dense, compact guide covering early horror movies including *The Cabinet of Dr. Caligari, Nosferatu, Frankenstein,* and *The Devil Bat*. Each movie is covered in detail, with a description of the plot, highlights, memorable quotes, lowlights, goofs, trivia, cast and crew, music, the movie's context in film history, changes that shaped the production, and video availability, critical words—the author's opinions, and another perspective—introducing "guest" reviewers for each film. *Haunted Heart: The Life and Times of Stephen King* by Lisa Rogak (St Martin's/A Thomas Dunne Book) is a biography of the writer, with eight pages of black-and-white photographs. *Dissecting Hannibal Lecter: Essays on the Novels of Thomas Harris* by Benjamin Szumskyj (McFarland) examines all five of Harris' novels, including *Black Sunday*, his first, oddly prescient novel about terrorism. *Book of Souls* by Jack Ketchum (Bloodletting Press) is a short collection of personal essays by the author, providing insight into his fiction. *Essential Solitude: The Letters of H. P. Lovecraft and August Derleth* (Hippocampus Press) is a two-volume set edited by David E. Schultz and S. T. Joshi. The first volume covers 1926–1931 and the second 1932–1937. The introduction provides context for the hundreds of letters, which are annotated by the editors. *The Book of Lists: Horror* by Amy Wallace, Del Howison, and Scott Bradley (Harper) has an introduction by Gahan Wilson and includes everything from the top six grossing horror films of all time in the United States (adjusted for inflation) and the eight worst monster movie costumes to eight memorable quotes from horror writers. *The Fly at Fifty: The Creation and Legacy of a Classic Science Fiction Film* by Diana Kachmar & David Goudsward (BearManor Media) celebrates *The Fly* by including profiles and interviews with many of those connected to both adaptations of the original story—which is itself included and well worth reading. *Bram Stoker's Notes for Dracula: A Facsimile Edition,* annotated and transcribed by Robert Eighteen-Bisang and Elizabeth Miller (McFarland), is a fantastic book that provides insight into the choices Stoker made in the creation of his masterwork. The notes, photographs, and newspaper clippings reproduced in the book are housed in the Rosenbach Museum & Library in Philadelphia. *Flowers from Hell: The Modern Japanese Horror Film* by Jim Harper (Noir Publishing) provides an absorbing primer for newcomers to its subject, covering the past twenty-five years worth of movies leading up to the most recent crop of Japanese horror films. The book is broken down into chapters covering specific types of horror movies and some of the genre's most influential directors. *Maps and Legends: Reading and Writing Along the Borderlands* by Michael Chabon (McSweeney's Books) collects fifteen essays and reviews by Chabon about such subjects as M. R. James's ghost stories, Philip Pullman's Dark Materials trilogy, golems, and Cormac McCarthy's *The Road*—this last essay referencing previous post-disaster novels by John Christopher, John Wyndham, J. G. Ballard, Roger Zelazny, Richard Matheson, and Walter M. Miller, Jr. *Servants of the Supernatural: The Night Side of the Victorian Mind* by Antonio Melechi (William Heinemann) covers the keen interest and experimentation with mesmerism and spiritualism that even the learned exhibited during the Victorian era. *Yokai Attack!: The Japanese Monster Survival Guide* by Hiroko Yoda and Matt Alt with illustrations by Tatsuya Morino (Kodansha International) is a *seemingly* serious guide to the traditional Japanese creatures that do men harm, separated into chapters covering ferocious fiends, gruesome gourmets, annoying neighbors, the sexy and the slimy, and the wimps. Each chapter gives the name of the monster, where it can be found, how to identify it, and how to survive an attack. *Basil Copper: A Life in Books* compiled and edited by Stephen Jones (PS) is a marvelous combination memoir/biography of a living legend of horror with photographs of Copper and his friends over the years, articles by him, and bibliographies of his prose and media work. Also included is the previously unpublished teleplay of Copper's adaptation of M. R. James's ghost story, "Count Magnus." *The Monster of Florence* by Douglas Preston with Mario Spezi (Grand Central) is a riveting true crime investigation of a series of brutal, unsolved murders committed over a period of decades. Preston and his family move to Florence in 2000, the dream of a lifetime, and he becomes fascinated with the unsolved crimes (one of which took place in the olive grove next to his home, years before). He joins forces with journalist Mario Spezi and together they dig deeper into the failed investigation, finding themselves facing bizarre accusations by the police.

## CHAPBOOKS AND OTHER SMALL PRESS ITEMS

*KRDR: Welcome to the Ether* (Earthling Publications) features three new stories by Peter Atkins, Glen Hirshberg, and Kevin Moffett with interstitial material by Atkins and Hirshberg. The chapbook is the physical manifestation of the readings that the three writers gave in California during the month of October. *The Shallow End of the Pool* by Adam-Troy Castro (Creeping Hemlock Press) is an unbelievable yet intriguing story about a warring, formerly married couple who have each taken one twin to raise and rigorously train to fight to the death once the children are old enough. Cemetery Dance publishes a chapbook story series and in 2008 brought out *The Lost* by Sarah Langan, about a young woman who is literally disappearing from her own life. *Overtoun Bridge* by Bev Vincent, a ghost story about a bridge from which dogs have jumped to their deaths for over thirty years. *Tanglewood* by Ronald Kelly is about a guy with a marriage going sour whose car breaks down when he takes a short cut through the woods. *Bone Harvest* by James A. Moore is about two unlucky amateur botanists who venture into a unique wood in which something resides that's even more dangerous than the weird plants that grow there. *Triptych: 3 Tales of Terror* by Michael Kelly and Carol Weekes (Undertow Publications) has two reprints, and an original about suburban ennui that's not at all horrific. *Redemption Roadshow* by Weston Ochse (Burning Effigy Press) is a tautly written story about an Arizona Highway Patrolman who begins noticing the crosses and shrines dotting the side of the road commemorating loved ones who have died in car accidents. When he hears about the "long cool woman"—a woman in a coma since she was a child who purportedly can speak with the dead along the road, he finds himself burning for redemption. *Miranda* by John Little (Bad Moon Books) is about a man aging backwards and Miranda is the woman he meets on his journey—with the same condition. Off the top of my head I can think of (obviously) F. Scott Fitzgerald's "The Curious Case of Benjamin Button" and the award-winning story "Morning Child" by Gardner Dozois. I'm also pretty sure there are at least a half-dozen earlier stories with the same MacGuffin. *The Reach of Children* by Tim Lebbon (Humdrumming) is about a ten-year-old boy grief-stricken at his mother's death. His father drinks to dampen his misery and talks to a mysterious pine box under the bed. The boy begins to hear a voice coming from the box, saying things he might not want to hear. Nice job. *Follow the Wounded One* by Mike Allen (Not One of Us) is about a man who is becoming increasingly disoriented by what he believes are hallucinations of being hunted by a giant, blue-eyed being with horns. *The Long Way* by Ramsey Campbell (PS) is about a young boy who loves writing scary stories but hides them from his strict family. The boy must pass a deserted street with one lone house on his weekly trip to and from taking his disabled uncle shopping and one day he sees someone or something that frightens him more than the stories he makes up. It's a lovely hardback book with a fine black and white illustration by Wayne Blackhurst on the cover. *The Gray Friar Christmas Chapbook 2007* presents seven stories by writers who have been published by Gray Friar Press. Four of the stories appear for the first time. *Living with the Dead* by Darrell Schweitzer (PS) is a compelling novella about a town that houses the regularly arriving dead, delivered and deposited by ships in the night and left in piles on the wharf come morning. Grotesque without being frightening but a very good read. *A Dick and Jane Primer for Adults* edited by Lavie Tidhar (BFS) contains ten very brief stories using the children's primer book characters (sometimes along with their dog, Spot). Cover and interior art is by John Keates, and Jeff VanderMeer has written an introduction. Most of the stories are trifles but Conrad Williams's is more than that. *Divagations* by John Maclay (Delirium Books) is a small, attractive hardcover containing six new stories. The book is number five in the publisher's chapbook series. *Suckers* by J. A. Konrath and Jeff Strand (Delirium Books) is a fun, silly story about the adventures of a guy out to find the "correct" spaghetti sauce for dinner and a crazy nut of a private eye hired to rescue a Goth teen from the clutches of wannabe vampires. *Orpheus and the Pearl* by Kim Paffenroth (Magus Press) takes place in a suburb of Boston during the 1920s and is about a female follower of Freud hired to "cure" the ailing wife of a famous research scientist. A common horror trope made new. *Tails of Tales of Pain & Wonder* by Caitlín E. Kiernan (Subterranean) accompanied the third edition of Kiernan's collection *Tales of Pain and Wonder*, and includes seven story fragments from over the years. *Little Graveyard on the Prairie* by Steven E. Wedel (Eclipse) has three stories, two of them reprints. The title story is new, and it's about a lonely, broken former farmer who sees ghosts and is losing his sanity. *Red* by Paul Kane (Skullvines Press) is about a grisly serial killer that turns out to be more than he seems in this fast-paced novella. *The*

*Situation* by Jeff VanderMeer (PS) is an imaginative and surreal oddity about the office from Hell, in the tradition of Eileen Gunn's classic "Stable Strategies for Middle Management," Thomas Ligotti, and Franz Kafka. *Charles Urban's Brutal Spirits* edited by Gary McMahon (The Swan River Press) is presented as a mss found by McMahon, a friend of the late (non-existent?) Charles Urban. It's a clever and nicely creepy tale about a haunted multi-story parking garage. *The Oz Suite* by Gerard Houarner (Eibonvale Press) contains three intriguing stories riffing on the real versus imaginary worlds of the *Wizard of Oz*. One story was previously published, the second two are new.

## ODDS AND ENDS

*Black Box* edited by Shane Jiraiya Cummings (Brimstone Press) is a multimedia follow-up to *Shadow Box*, featuring dozens of pieces of horror flash fiction, most by Australians, plus sound effects and music.

*The Complete Collected Essays of H. P. Lovecraft* edited by S. T. Joshi (Hippocampus) can now be bought as a CD-ROM. The disc includes the five volumes that were previously released in trade paperback. Also included is the complete run of Lovecraft's amateur magazine, *The Conservative*.

*The Sirenia Digest* by Caitlín R. Kiernan is a PDF file emailed monthly to subscribers. In it she always includes a story or vignette or two, an excerpt from a novel-in-progress, and occasionally a guest's story (Sonya Taaffe has contributed fiction on several occasions). You can subscribe by going to Kiernan's website.

*The Nightmare Factory, Volume 2* by Thomas Ligotti (HarperCollins/Fox Atomic Comics) collects graphic adaptations of "Gas Station Carnivals," "The Clown Puppet," "The Chymist," and "The Sect of the Idiot." Ligotti provides introductions. Stuart Moore and Joe Harris adapted the stories and the art is by Bill Sienkiewicz, Toby Cypress, Vasilis Lolos, and Nick Stakal.

*Fantasy Classics, Graphic Classics, Volume 15* edited by Tom Pomplun (Eureka productions) includes work by Lord Dunsany, Mary Shelley, Nathaniel Hawthorne, L. Frank Baum, Clark Ashton-Smith, and H. P. Lovecraft, illustrated by various artists.

*Three Shadows* by Cyril Pedrosa (First Second) is a graphic novel translated from French about a father determined to save his young son's life, despite the three shadows that want to take him away. He takes the child on a journey to cheat fate, encountering pain and ugliness and magic along the way. Dark and moving.

*Where Madness Reigns: The Art of Gris Grimly* (Baby Tattoo Books) is a fun introduction to the grotesque yet charming cartoonish art of this illustrator, which ranges from evil bunnies to a pill-filled Elvis. The book includes samples from a 2007 gallery exhibition and privately owned art that has never before been published.

*The Dangerous Alphabet* by Neil Gaiman and illustrated by Gris Grimly (HarperCollins) is a clever, rhyming pirate journey taken by two children who meet with all types of wicked, ugly, and dangerous creatures beneath the city where they live.

*Sparrow* art book series number six by Rick Berry (IDW Publishing) is a small square hardcover book of a variety of darkly fantastic and sometimes erotic subjects. Berry is best-known for illustrating Stephen King's and Harlan Ellison's work.

*Poe: A Screenplay* by Stewart O'Nan (Lonely Road Books) is a limited edition of O'Nan's so far unproduced screenplay about Edgar Allan Poe's life. With an introduction by Roger Corman, a beautiful black and white frontispiece by artist Jill Bauman, and an afterword by O'Nan explaining why he wrote the screenplay.

*Spectrum 15: The Best in Contemporary Fantastic Art*, edited by Cathy Fenner and Arnie Fenner (Underwood Books), covered the year 2007 and was juried by five fantasy artists. The book continues to be the showcase for the best in genre art—the sheer variety of style and tone and media and subject matter is impressive. The volume was heftier than in the past, having added over twenty pages. John Jude Palencar was honored with the Grand Master Award, and to mark the fifteenth anniversary of the series an award for Best in Show was given to James Jean. Arnie Fenner provided an overview of the political and cultural year plus a necrology. The jury convened in Kansas City all day where they decided on Gold and Silver awards in several categories. This is a book for anyone interested in art of the fantastic, dark or light.

The brilliant Shaun Tan strikes again with his gorgeously illustrated *Tales From Outer Suburbia* (Allen & Unwin/Scholastic), a book of fifteen brief, strange, occasionally dark and always delightful stories. For children and adults.

*A Lovecraft Retrospective: Artists Inspired by H. P. Lovecraft* (Centipede Press) is a massive, beautifully rendered undertaking with a preface by Stuart Gordon, introduction by Harlan Ellison, and afterword by Thomas Ligotti. The book is divided into three sections covering: the early art, created in the 1920s to 1950s and including such artists as Hannes Bok, Virgil Finlay, and Lee Brown Coye; the middle art, created in the 1960s and 1970s including Bernie Wrightson, Harry O. Morris, Stephen Fabian, H. R. Giger; and modern art, including J. K. Potter, John Jude Palencar, Ian Miller, Les Edwards, Bob Eggleton. In all, there are at least eighty-five artists represented, and text by Stefan Dziemianowicz introducing the three sections and some of the artists (except for the entry on H. R. Giger, written by Harlan Ellison). In the back is a section of thumbnails of each piece of art found inside the book, and mini-biographies of each artist. The book is two feet high, with full page illustrations in color and in black and white. Pricey but gorgeous.

# CARGO

## E. MICHAEL LEWIS

I dreamt of cargo. Thousands of crates filled the airplane's hold, all made of unfinished pine, the kind that drives slivers through work gloves. They were stamped with unknowable numbers and bizarre acronyms that glowed fiercely with dim red light. They were supposed to be jeep tires, but some were as large as a house, others as small as a spark plug, all of them secured to pallets with binding like straitjacket straps. I tried to check them all, but there were too many. There was a low shuffling as the boxes shifted, then the cargo fell on me. I couldn't reach the interphone to warn the pilot. The cargo pressed down on me with a thousand sharp little fingers as the plane rolled, crushing the life out of me even as we dived, even as we crashed, the interphone ringing now like a scream. But there was another sound too, from inside the crate next to my ear. Something struggled inside the box, something sodden and defiled, something that I didn't want to see, something that wanted *out*.

It changed into the sound of a clipboard being rapped on the metal frame of my crew house bunk. My eyes shot open. The airman—new in-country, by the sweat lining his collar—stood over me, holding the clipboard between us, trying to decide if I was the type to rip his head off just for doing his job. "Tech Sergeant Davis," he said, "they need you on the flight line right away."

I sat up and stretched. He handed me the clipboard and attached manifest: a knocked-down HU-53 with flight crew, mechanics, and medical support personnel bound for... somewhere new.

"Timehri Airport?"

"It's outside Georgetown, Guyana." When I looked blank, he went on, "It's a former British colony. Timehri used to be Atkinson Air Force Base."

35

"What's the mission?"

"It's some kind of mass med-evac of ex-pats from somewhere called Jones-town."

Americans in trouble. I'd spent a good part of my Air Force career flying Americans out of trouble. That being said, flying Americans out of trouble was a hell of a lot more satisfying than hauling jeep tires. I thanked him and hurried into a clean flight suit.

I was looking forward to another Panamanian Thanksgiving at Howard Air Force Base—eighty-five degrees, turkey and stuffing from the mess hall, football on Armed Forces Radio, and enough time out of flight rotation to get good and drunk. The in-bound hop from the Philippines went by the numbers and both the passengers and cargo were free and easy. Now this.

Interruption was something you grew accustomed to as a Loadmaster. The C-141 StarLifter was the largest freighter and troop carrier in the Military Air Command, capable of carrying seventy thousand pounds of cargo or two hundred battle-ready troops and flying them anywhere in the world. Half as long as a football field, the high-set swept-back wings drooped bat-like over the tarmac. With an upswept T-tail, petal-doors, and a built-in cargo ramp, the StarLifter was unmatched when it came to moving cargo. Part stewardess and part moving man, my job as a Loadmaster was to pack it as tight and as safe as possible.

With everything onboard and my weight and balance sheets complete, the same airman found me cussing up the Panamanian ground crew for leaving a scuffmark on the airframe.

"Sergeant Davis! Change in plans," he yelled over the whine of the forklift. He handed me another manifest.

"More passengers?"

"New passengers. Med crew is staying here." He said something unintelligible about a change of mission.

"Who are these people?"

Again, I strained to hear him. Or maybe I heard him fine and with the sinking in my gut, I wanted him to repeat it. I wanted to hear him wrong.

"Graves registration," he cried.

That's what I'd thought he'd said.

\* \* \*

Timehri was your typical third-world airport—large enough to squeeze down a 747, but strewn with potholes and sprawling with rusted Quonset huts. The low line of jungle surrounding the field looked as if it had been beaten back only an hour before. Helicopters buzzed up and down and US servicemen swarmed the tarmac. I knew then that things must be bad.

Outside the bird, the heat rising from the asphalt threatened to melt the soles of my boots even before I had the wheel chocks in place. A ground crew of American GIs approached, anxious to unload and assemble the chopper. One of them, bare-chested with his shirt tied around his waist, handed me a manifest.

"Don't get comfy," he said. "As soon as the chopper's clear, we're loading you up." He nodded over his shoulder.

I looked out over the shimmering taxiway. Coffins. Rows and rows of dull aluminum funerary boxes gleamed in the unforgiving tropical sun. I recognized them from my flights out of Saigon six years ago, my first as Loadmaster. Maybe my insides did a little flip because I'd had no rest, or maybe because I hadn't carried a stiff in a few years. Still, I swallowed hard. I looked at the destination: Dover, Delaware.

\* \* \*

The ground crew loaded a fresh comfort pallet when I learned we'd have two passengers on the outbound flight.

The first was a kid, right out of high school by the look of it, with bristle-black hair, and too-large jungle fatigues that were starched, clean, and showed the rank of Airman First Class. I told him, "Welcome aboard," and went to help him through the crew door, but he jerked away, nearly hitting his head against the low entrance. I think he would have leapt back if there had been room. His scent hit me, strong and medicinal—Vicks VapoRub.

Behind him a flight nurse, crisp and professional in step, dress, and gesture, also boarded without assistance. I regarded her evenly. I recognized her as one of a batch I had flown regularly from Clark in the Philippines to Da Nang and back again in my early days. A steel-eyed, silver-haired lieutenant. She had been very specific—more than once—in pointing out how any numbskull high school dropout could do my job better. The name on her uniform read Pembry. She touched the kid on his back and guided him to the seats, but if she recognized me, she said nothing.

"Take a seat anywhere," I told them. "I'm Tech Sergeant Davis. We'll be wheels up in less than half an hour so make yourself comfortable."

The kid stopped short. "You didn't tell me," he said to the nurse.

The hold of a StarLifter is most like the inside of a boiler room, with all the heat, cooling, and pressure ducts exposed rather than hidden away like on an airliner. The coffins formed two rows down the length of the hold, leaving a center aisle clear. Stacked four high, there were one hundred and sixty of them. Yellow cargo nets held them in place. Looking past them, we watched the sunlight disappear as the cargo hatch closed, leaving us in an awkward semi-darkness.

"It's the fastest way to get you home," she said to him, her voice neutral. "You want to go home, don't you?"

His voice dripped with fearful outrage. "I don't want to see them. I want a forward facing seat."

If the kid would have looked around, he could have seen that there were no forward facing seats.

"It's okay," she said, tugging on his arm again. "They're going home, too."

"I don't want to look at them," he said as she pushed him to a seat nearest one of the small windows. When he didn't move to strap himself in, Pembry bent and did it for him. He gripped the handrails like the oh-shit bar on a roller coaster. "I don't want to think about them."

"I got it." I went forward and shut down the cabin lights. Now only the twin red jump lights illuminated the long metal containers. When I returned, I brought him a pillow.

The ID label on the kid's loose jacket read "Hernandez." He said, "Thank you," but did not let go of the armrests.

Pembry strapped herself in next to him. I stowed their gear and went through my final checklist.

* * *

Once in the air, I brewed coffee on the electric stove in the comfort pallet. Nurse Pembry declined, but Hernandez took some. The plastic cup shook in his hands.

"Afraid of flying?" I asked. It wasn't so unusual for the Air Force. "I have some Dramamine…"

"I'm not afraid of flying," he said through clenched teeth. All the while he looked past me, to the boxes lining the hold.

Next the crew. No one bird was assigned the same crew, like in the old days. The MAC took great pride in having men be so interchangeable that a flight crew who had never met before could assemble at a flight line and fly any StarLifter to the ends of the Earth. Each man knew my job, like I knew theirs, inside and out.

I went to the cockpit and found everyone on stations. The second engineer sat closest to the cockpit door, hunched over instrumentation. "Four is evening out now, keep the throttle low," he said. I recognized his hangdog face and his Arkansas drawl, but I could not tell from where. I figured after seven years of flying StarLifters, I had flown with just about everybody at one time or another. He thanked me as I set the black coffee on his table. His flightsuit named him Hadley.

The first engineer sat in the bitchseat, the one usually reserved for a "Black Hatter"—mission inspectors were the bane of all MAC aircrews. He asked for two lumps and then stood and looked out the navigator's dome at the blue rushing past.

"Throttle low on four, got it," replied the pilot. He was the designated Aircraft Commander, but both he and the co-pilot were such typical flight jocks that they could have been the same person. They took their coffee with two creams each. "We're trying to outfly some clear air turbulence, but it won't be easy. Tell your passengers to expect some weather."

"Will do, sir. Anything else?"

"Thank you, Load Davis, that's all."

"Yes, sir."

Finally time to relax. As I went to have a horizontal moment in the crew berth, I saw Pembry snooping around the comfort pallet. "Anything I can help you find?"

"An extra blanket?"

I pulled one from the storage cabinet between the cooking station and the latrine and gritted my teeth. "Anything else?"

"No," she said, pulling a piece of imaginary lint from the wool. "We've flown together before, you know."

"Have we?"

She raised an eyebrow. "I probably ought to apologize."

"No need, ma'am," I said. I dodged around her and opened the fridge. "I could serve an in-flight meal later if you are…"

She placed her hand on my shoulder, like she had on Hernandez, and it commanded my attention. "You do remember me."

"Yes, ma'am."

"I was pretty hard on you during those evac flights."

I wished she'd stop being so direct. "You were speaking your mind, ma'am. It made me a better Loadmaster."

"Still…"

"Ma'am, there's no need." Why can't women figure out that apologies only make things worse?

"Very well." The hardness of her face melted into sincerity, and suddenly it occurred to me that she wanted to talk.

"How's your patient?"

"Resting." Pembry tried to act casual, but I knew she wanted to say more.

"What's his problem?"

"He was one of the first to arrive," she said, "and the first to leave."

"Jonestown? Was it that bad?"

Flashback to our earlier evac flights. The old look, hard and cool, returned instantly. "We flew out of Dover on White House orders five hours after they got the call. He's a Medical Records Specialist, six months in the service, he's never been anywhere before, never saw a day of trauma in his life. Next thing he knows, he's in a South American jungle with a thousand dead bodies."

"A thousand?"

"Count's not in yet, but it's headed that way." She brushed the back of her hand against her cheek. "So many kids."

"Kids?"

"Whole families. They all drank poison. Some kind of cult, they said. Someone told me the parents killed their children first. I don't know what could make a person do that to their own family." She shook her head. "I stayed at Timehri to organize triage. Hernandez said the smell was unimaginable. They had to spray the bodies with insecticide and defend them from hungry giant rats. He said they made him bayonet the bodies to release the pressure. He burned his uniform."

She shuffled to keep her balance as the bird jolted.

Something nasty crept down the back of my throat as I tried not to visualize what she said. I struggled not to grimace. "The AC says it may get rough. You better strap in." I walked her back to her seat. Hernandez's mouth gaped as he sprawled across his seat, looking for all the world like he'd lost a bar fight—bad. Then I went to my bunk and fell asleep.

*  *  *

Ask any Loadmaster: after so much time in the air, the roar of engines is something you ignore. You find you can sleep through just about anything. Still, your mind tunes in and wakes up at the sound of anything unusual, like the flight from Yakota to Elmendorf when a jeep came loose and rolled into a crate of MREs. Chipped beef everywhere. You can bet the ground crew heard from me on that one. So it should not come as a shock that I started at the sound of a scream.

On my feet, out of the bunk, past the comfort pallet before I could think. Then I saw Pembry. She was out of her seat and in front of Hernandez, dodging his flailing arms, speaking calmly and below the engine noise. Not him, though.

"I heard them! I heard them! They're in there! All those kids! All those kids!"

I put my hand on him—hard. "Calm down!"

He stopped flailing. A shamed expression came over him. His eyes riveted mine. "I heard them singing."

"Who?"

"The children! All the…" He gave a helpless gesture to the unlighted coffins.

"You had a dream," Pembry said. Her voice shook a little. "I was with you the whole time. You were asleep. You couldn't have heard anything."

"All the children are dead," he said. "All of them. They didn't know. How could they have known they were drinking poison? Who would give their own child poison to drink?" I let go of his arm and he looked at me. "Do you have kids?"

"No," I said.

"My daughter," he said, "is a year-and-a-half old. My son is three months. You have to be careful with them, patient with them. My wife is really good at it, y'know?" I noticed for the first time how sweat crawled across his forehead, the backs of his hands. "But I'm okay too, I mean, I don't really know what the fuck I'm doing, but I wouldn't hurt them. I hold them and I sing to them and—and if anyone else tried to hurt them…" He grabbed me on the arm that had held him. "Who would give their child poison?"

"It isn't your fault," I told him.

"They didn't know it was poison. They still don't." He pulled me closer and said into my ear, "I heard them singing." I'll be damned if the words he spoke didn't make my spine shiver.

"I'll go check it out," I told him as I grabbed a flashlight off the wall and started down the center aisle.

There was a practical reason for checking out the noise. As a Loadmaster, I knew that an unusual sound meant trouble. I had heard a story about how an aircrew kept hearing the sound of a cat meowing from somewhere in the hold. The Loadmaster couldn't find it, but figured it'd turn up when they off-loaded the cargo. Turns out the "meowing" was a weakened load brace that buckled when the wheels touched runway, freeing three tons of explosive ordnance and making the landing very interesting. Strange noises meant trouble, and I'd have been a fool not to look into it.

I checked all the buckles and netting as I went, stooping and listening, checking for signs of shifting, fraying straps, anything out of the ordinary. I went up one side and down the other, even checking the cargo doors. Nothing. Everything was sound, my usual best work.

I walked up the aisle to face them. Hernandez wept, head in his hands. Pembry rubbed his back with one hand as she sat next to him, like my mother had done to me.

"All clear, Hernandez." I put the flashlight back on the wall.

"Thanks," Pembry replied for him, then said to me, "I gave him a Valium, he should quiet down now."

"Just a safety check," I told her. "Now, both of you get some rest."

I went back to my bunk to find it occupied by Hadley, the second engineer. I took the one below him but couldn't fall asleep right away. I tried to keep my mind far away from the reason that the coffins were in my bird in the first place.

Cargo was the euphemism. From blood plasma to high explosives to secret service limousines to gold bullion, you packed it and hauled it because it was your job, that was all, and anything that could be done to speed you on your way was important.

*Just cargo*, I thought. But whole families that killed themselves... I was glad to get them the hell out of the jungle, back home to their families—but the medics who got there first, all those guys on the ground, even my crew, we were too late to do any more than that. I was interested in having kids in a vague, unsettled sort of way, and it pissed me off to hear about anyone harming them. But these parents did it willingly, didn't they?

I couldn't relax. I found an old copy of the *New York Times* folded into the bunk. Peace in the Middle East in our lifetimes, it read. Next to the article was a picture of President Carter and Anwar Sadat shaking hands. I was just about to drift off when I thought I heard Hernandez cry out again.

I dragged my ass up. Pembry stood with her hands clutched over her mouth. I thought Hernandez had hit her, so I went to her and peeled her hands away, looking for damage.

There was none. Looking over her shoulder, I could see Hernandez riveted to his seat, eyes glued to the darkness like a reverse color television.

"What happened? Did he hit you?"

"He—he heard it again," she stammered as one hand rose to her face again.

"You—you ought to go check again. You ought to go check…"

The pitch of the plane shifted and she fell into me a little, and as I steadied myself by grabbing her elbow she collapsed against me. I met her gaze matter-of-factly. She looked away. "What happened?" I asked again.

"I heard it too," Pembry said.

My eyes went to the aisle of shadow. "Just now?"

"Yes."

"Was it like he said? Children singing?" I realized I was on the verge of shaking her. Were they both going crazy?

"Children playing," she said. "Like—playground noise, y'know? Kids playing."

I wracked my brain for some object, or some collection of objects, that when stuffed into a C-141 StarLifter and flown thirty-nine thousand feet over the Caribbean, would make a sound like children playing.

Hernandez shifted his position and we both brought our attention to bear on him. He smiled a defeated smile and said to us, "I told you."

"I'll go check it out," I told them.

"Let them play," said Hernandez. "They just want to play. Isn't that what you wanted to do as a kid?"

I remembered my childhood like a jolt, endless summers and bike rides and skinned knees and coming home at dusk to my mother saying, "Look how dirty you are." I wondered if the recovery crews washed the bodies before they put them in the coffins.

"I'll find out what it is," I told them. I went and got the flashlight again. "Stay put."

I used the darkness to close off my sight, give me more to hear. The turbulence had subsided by then, and I used my flashlight only to avoid tripping on the cargo netting. I listened for anything new or unusual. It wasn't one thing—it had to be a combination—noises like that just don't stop and start again. Fuel leak? Stowaway? The thought of a snake or some other jungle beast lurking inside those metal boxes heightened my whole state of being and brought back my dream.

Near the cargo doors, I shut off my light and listened. Pressurized air. Four Pratt and Whitney turbofan engines. Fracture rattles. Cargo straps flapping.

And then, something. Something came in sharp after a moment, at first dull and sweeping, like noise from the back of a cave, but then pure and unbidden, like sounds to a surprised eavesdropper.

Children. Laughter. Like recess at grade school.

I opened my eyes and flashed my light around the silver crates. I found them waiting, huddled with me, almost expectant.

*Children*, I thought, *just children*.

I ran past Hernandez and Pembry to the comfort pallet. I can't tell you what they saw in my face, but if it was anything like what I saw in the little mirror above the latrine sink, I would have been at once terrified and redeemed.

I looked from the mirror to the interphone. Any problem with the cargo should be reported immediately—procedure demanded it—but what could I tell the AC? I had an urge to drop it all, just eject the coffins and call it a day. If I told him there was a fire in the hold, we would drop below ten thousand feet so I could blow the bolts and send the whole load to the bottom of the Gulf of Mexico, no questions asked.

I stopped then, straightened up, tried to think. *Children,* I thought. *Not monsters, not demons, just the sounds of children playing. Nothing that will get you. Nothing that* can *get you.* I tossed off the shiver that ran through my body and decided to get some help.

At the bunk, I found Hadley still asleep. A dog-eared copy of a paperback showing two women locked in a passionate embrace lay like a tent on his chest. I shook his arm and he sat up. Neither of us said anything for a moment. He rubbed his face with one hand and yawned.

Then he looked right at me and I watched his face arch into worry. His next action was to grab his portable oxygen. He recovered his game face in an instant. "What is it, Davis?"

I groped for something. "The cargo." I said. "There's a... possible shift in the cargo. I need a hand, sir."

His worry snapped into annoyance. "Have you told the AC?"

"No sir," I said. "I—I don't want to trouble him yet. It may be nothing."

His face screwed into something unpleasant and I thought I'd have words from him, but he let me lead the way aft. Just his presence was enough to revive my doubt, my professionalism. My walk sharpened, my eyes widened, my stomach returned to its place in my gut.

I found Pembry sitting next to Hernandez now, both together in a feigned indifference. Hadley gave them a disinterested look and followed me down the aisle between the coffins.

"What about the main lights?" he asked.

"They don't help," I said. "Here." I handed him the flashlight and asked him, "Do you hear it?"

"Hear what?"

"Just listen."

Again, only engines and the jetstream. "I don't..."

"Shhh! Listen."

His mouth opened and stayed there for a minute, then shut. The engines quieted and the sounds came, dripping over us like water vapor, the fog of sound around us. I didn't realise how cold I was until I noticed my hands shaking.

"What in the hell is that?" Hadley asked. "It sounds like..."

"Don't," I interrupted. "That can't be it." I nodded at the metal boxes. "You know what's in these coffins, don't you?"

He didn't say anything. The sound seemed to filter around us for a moment, at once close, then far away. He tried to follow the sound with his light. "Can you tell where it's coming from?"

"No. I'm just glad you hear it too, sir."

The engineer scratched his head, his face drawn, like he swallowed something foul and couldn't lose the aftertaste. "I'll be damned," he drawled.

All at once, as before, the sound stopped, and the roar of the jets filled our ears.

"I'll hit the lights." I moved away hesitantly. "I'm not going to call the AC."

His silence was conspiratorial. As I rejoined him, I found him examining a particular row of coffins through the netting.

"You need to conduct a search," he said dully.

I didn't respond. I'd done midair cargo searches before, but never like this, not even on bodies of servicemen. If everything Pembry said was true, I couldn't think of anything worse than opening one of these caskets.

We both started at the next sound. Imagine a wet tennis ball. Now imagine the sound a wet tennis ball makes when it hits the court—a sort of dull THWAK—like a bird striking the fuselage. It sounded again, and this time I could hear it inside the hold. Then, after a buffet of turbulence, the thump sounded again. It came clearly from a coffin at Hadley's feet.

Not a serious problem, his face tried to say. We just imagined it. *A noise from one coffin can't bring a plane down*, his face said. *There are no such things as ghosts.*

"Sir?"

"We need to see," he said.

Blood pooled in my stomach again. *See*, he had said. *I didn't want to see.*

"Get on the horn and tell the AC to avoid the chop," he said. I knew at that moment he was going to help me. He didn't want to, but he was going to do it anyway.

"What are you doing?" Pembry asked. She stood by as I removed the cargo netting from the row of caskets while the engineer undid the individual straps around that one certain row. Hernandez slept head bowed, the downers having finally taken effect.

"We have to examine the cargo," I stated matter-of-factly. "The flight may have caused the load to become unbalanced."

She grabbed my arm as I went by. "Was that all it was? A shifting load?"

There was a touch of desperation in her question. *Tell me I imagined it*, the look on her face said. *Tell me and I'll believe you, and I'll go get some sleep.*

"We think so," I nodded.

Her shoulders dropped and her face peeled into a smile too broad to be real. "Thank God. I thought I was going crazy."

I patted her shoulder. "Strap in and get some rest," I told her. She did.

Finally, I was doing something. As Loadmaster, I could put an end to this nonsense. So I did the work. I unstrapped the straps, climbed the other caskets, shoved the top one out of place, carried it, secured it, removed the next one, carried it, secured it, and again. The joy of easy repetition.

It wasn't until we got to the bottom one, the noisy one, that Hadley stopped. He stood there watching me as I pulled it out of place enough to examine it. His stance was level, but even so it spoke of revulsion, something that, among swaggering Air Force veterans and over beers, he could conceal. Not now, not to me.

I did a cursory examination of the deck where it had sat, of the caskets next to it, and saw no damage or obvious flaws.

A noise sounded—a moist "thunk." From inside. We flinched in unison. The engineer's cool loathing was impossible to conceal. I suppressed a tremble.

"We have to open it," I said.

The engineer didn't disagree, but like me, his body was slow to move. He squatted down and, with one hand firmly planted on the casket lid, unlatched the clasps on his end. I undid mine, finding my fingers slick on the cold metal, and shaking a little as I pulled them away and braced my hand on the lid. Our eyes met in one moment that held the last of our resolve. Together, we opened the casket.

\* \* \*

First, the smell: a mash of rotten fruit, antiseptic, and formaldehyde, wrapped in plastic with dung and sulfur. It stung our nostrils as it filled the hold. The overhead lights illuminated two shiny black body bags, slick with condensation and waste. I knew these would be the bodies of children, but it awed me, hurt me. One bag lay unevenly concealing the other, and I understood at once that there was more than one child in it. My eyes skimmed the juice-soaked plastic, picking out the contour of an arm, the trace of a profile. A shape coiled near the bottom seam, away from the rest. It was the size of a baby.

Then the plane shivered like a frightened pony and the top bag slid away to reveal a young girl, eight or nine at the most, half in and half out of the bag. Wedged like a mad contortionist into the corner, her swollen belly, showing stab wounds from bayonets, had bloated again, and her twisted limbs were now as thick as tree limbs. The pigment-bearing skin had peeled away everywhere but her face, which was as pure and as innocent as any cherub in heaven.

Her face was really what drove it home, what really hurt me. Her sweet face.

My hand fixed itself to the casket edge in painful whiteness, but I dared not remove it. Something caught in my throat and I forced it back down.

A lone fly, fat and glistening, crawled from inside the bag and flew lazily towards Hadley. He slowly rose to his feet and braced himself, as if against a body blow. He watched it rise and flit a clumsy path through the air. Then he broke the moment by stepping back, his hands flailing and hitting it—I heard the slap of his hand—and letting a nauseous sound escape his lips.

When I stood up, my temples throbbed and my legs weakened. I held onto a nearby casket, my throat filled with something rancid.

"Close it," he said like a man with his mouth full. "Close it."

My arms went rubbery. After bracing myself, I lifted one leg and kicked the lid. It rang out like an artillery shot. Pressure pounded into my ears like during a rapid descent.

Hadley put his hands on his haunches and lowered his head, taking deep breaths through his mouth. "Jesus," he croaked.

I saw movement. Pembry stood next to the line of coffins, her face pulled up in sour disgust. "What—is—that—smell?"

"It's okay." I found I could work one arm and tried what I hoped looked like an off-handed gesture. "Found the problem. Had to open it up though. Go sit down."

Pembry brought her hands up around herself and went back to her seat.

I found that with a few more deep breaths, the smell dissipated enough to act. "We have to secure it," I told Hadley.

He looked up from the floor and I saw his eyes as narrow slits. His hands were in fists and his broad torso stood fierce and straight. At the corner of his eyes, wetness glinted. He said nothing.

It became cargo again as I fastened the latches. We strained to fit it back into place. In a matter of minutes, the other caskets were stowed, the exterior straps were in place, the cargo netting draped and secure.

Hadley waited for me to finish up, then walked forwards with me. "I'm going to tell the AC you solved the problem," he said, "and to get us back to speed."

I nodded.

"One more thing," he said. "If you see that fly, kill it."

"Didn't you…"

"No."

I didn't know what else to say, so I said, "Yes, sir."

Pembry sat in her seat, nose wriggled up, feigning sleep. Hernandez sat upright, eyelids half open. He gestured for me to come closer, bend down.

"Did you let them out to play?" he asked.

I stood over him and said nothing. In my heart, I felt that same pang I did as a child, when summer was over.

When we landed in Dover, a funeral detail in full dress offloaded every coffin, affording full funeral rights to each person. I'm told as more bodies flew in, the formality was scrapped and only a solitary Air Force chaplain met the planes. By week's end I was back in Panama with a stomach full of turkey and cheap rum. Then it was off to the Marshall Islands, delivering supplies to the guided missile base there. In the Military Air Command, there is no shortage of cargo.

*E. Michael Lewis says:*
*"Of the nine hundred people who died in the Jonestown Massacre, nearly a third of them were under the age of eighteen. This story is dedicated to the families who lost loved ones at Jonestown, and to the servicemen and -women who brought them home."*

# IF ANGELS FIGHT

## RICHARD BOWES

### 1.

Outside the window, the blue water of the Atlantic danced in the sunlight of an early morning in October. They're short, quiet trains, the ones that roll through Connecticut just after dawn. I sipped bad tea, dozed off occasionally and awoke with a start.

Over the last forty years, I've ridden the northbound train from New York to Boston hundreds of times. I've done it alone, with friends and lovers, going home for the holidays, setting out on vacations, on my way to funerals.

That morning, I was with one who was once in some ways my best friend and certainly my oldest. Though we had rarely met in decades, it seemed that a connection endured. Our mission was vital and we rode the train by default: a terrorist threat had closed traffic at Logan Airport in Boston the night before.

I'd left messages canceling an appointment, letting the guy I was going out with know I'd be out of town briefly for a family crisis. No need to say it was another, more fascinating, family disrupting my life, not mine.

The old friend caught my discomfort at what we were doing and was amused.

A bit of Shakespeare occurred to me when I thought of him:

Not all the water in the rough rude sea
Can wash the balm off from an anointed king

He was quiet for a while after hearing those lines. It was getting toward twenty-four hours since I'd slept. I must have dozed because suddenly I was in a dark place with two tiny slits of light high above. I found hand- and foot-holds and crawled up the interior wall of a stone tower. As I got to the slits of light, a voice said, "New Haven. This stop New Haven."

2.

Carol Bannon had called me less than two weeks before. "I'm going to be down in New York the day after tomorrow," she said. "I wondered if we could get together." I took this to mean that she and her family wanted to get some kind of fix on the present location and current state of her eldest brother, my old friend Mark.

Over the years when this had happened it was Marie Bannon, Mark and Carol's mother, who contacted me. Those times I'd discovered channels through which she could reach her straying son. This time, I didn't make any inquiries before meeting Carol, but I did check to see if certain parties still had the same phone numbers and habits that I remembered.

Thinking about Marky Bannon, I too wondered where he was. He's always somewhere on my mind. When I see a photo of some great event, a reception, or celebrity trial, a concert or inauguration—I scan the faces wondering if he's present.

I'm retired these days, with time to spend. But over the years, keeping tabs on the Bannons was an easy minor hobby. The mother is still alive though not very active now. The father was a longtime Speaker of the Massachusetts House and a candidate for governor who died some years back. An intersection in Dorchester and an entrance to the Boston Harbor tunnel are still named for him.

Carol, the eldest daughter, got elected to the City Council at the age of twenty-eight. Fourteen years later she gave up a safe U.S. House seat to run the Commerce Department for Clinton. Later she served on the 9/11 commission and is a perennial cable TV talking head. She's married to Jerry Simone who has a stake in Google. Her brother Joe is a leading campaign consultant in D.C. Keeping up the idealistic end of things, her little sister Eileen is a member of Doctors Without Borders. My old friend Mark is the tragic secret without which no Irish family would be complete.

Carol asked me to meet her for tea uptown in the Astor Court of the St. Regis Hotel. I got there a moment after four. The Astor Court has a blinding array of starched white tablecloths and gold chandeliers under a ceiling mural of soft, floating clouds.

Maybe her choice of meeting places was intentionally campy. Or maybe because I don't drink anymore she had hit upon this as an amusing spot to bring me.

Carol and I always got along. Even aged ten and eleven I was different enough from the other boys that I was nice to my friends' little sisters.

Carol has kept her hair chestnut but allowed herself fine gray wings. Her skin and teeth are terrific. The Bannons were what was called dark Irish when we were growing up in Boston in the 1950s. That meant they weren't so white that they automatically burst into flames on their first afternoon at the beach.

They're a handsome family. The mother is still beautiful in her eighties. Marie Bannon had been on the stage a bit before she married. She had that light and charm, that ability to convince you that her smile was for you alone that led young men and old to drop everything and do her bidding.

Mike Bannon, the father, had been a union organizer before he went nights to law school, then got into politics. He had rugged good looks, blue eyes that would look right into you, and a fine smile that he could turn on and off and didn't often waste on kids.

"When the mood's upon him, he can charm a dog off a meat wagon," I remember a friend of my father's remarking. It was a time and place where politicians and race horses alike were scrutinized and handicapped.

The Bannon children had inherited the parents' looks and, in the way of politicians' kids, were socially poised. Except for Mark, who could look lost and confused one minute, oddly intense the next, with eyes suddenly just like his father's.

Carol rose to kiss me as I approached the table. It seemed kind of like a Philip Marlowe moment: I imagined myself as a private eye, tough and amused, called in by the rich dame for help in a personal matter.

When I first knew Carol Bannon, she wore pigtails and cried because her big brother wouldn't take her along when we went to the playground. Recently there's been speculation everywhere that a distinguished Massachusetts senator is about to retire before his term ends. Carol Bannon is the odds-on favorite to be appointed to succeed him.

Then, once she's in the Senate, given that it's the Democratic Party we're talking about, who's to say they won't go crazy again and run one more Bay State politician for President in the wild hope that they've got another JFK?

Carol said, "My mother asked me to remember her to you." I asked Carol to give her mother my compliments. Then we each said how good the other looked and made light talk about the choices of teas and the drop-dead faux Englishness of the place. We reminisced about Boston and the old neighborhood.

"Remember how everyone called that big overgrown vacant lot, 'Fitzie's'?" I asked. The nickname had come from its being the site where the Fitzgerald mansion, the home of "Honey Fitz," the old mayor of Boston, once stood. His daughter, Rose, was mother to the Kennedy brothers.

"There was a marble floor in the middle of the trash and weeds," I said, "and everybody was sure the place was haunted.

"The whole neighborhood was haunted," she said. "There was that little old couple who lived down Melville Avenue from us. They knew my parents. He was this gossipy elf. He had held office back in the old days and everyone called him, 'The Hon Hen,' short for 'the Honorable Henry.' She was a daughter of Honey Fitz. They were aunt and uncle of the Kennedys."

Melville Avenue was and is a street where the houses are set back on lawns and the garages are converted horse barns. When we were young, doctors and prosperous lawyers lived there along with prominent saloon owners and politicians like Michael Bannon and his family.

Suddenly at our table in the Astor Court, the pots and plates, the Lapsang and scones, the marmalade, the clotted cream and salmon finger sandwiches appeared. We were silent for a little while and I thought about how politics had seemed a common occupation for kids' parents in Irish Boston. Politicians' houses tended to be big and semi-public with much coming and going and loud talk.

Life at the Bannons' was much more exciting than at my house. Mark had his own room and didn't have to share with his little brother. He had a ten-year-old's luxuries: electronic football, enough soldiers to fight Gettysburg if you didn't mind that the Confederates were mostly Indians, and not one but two electric train engines, which made wrecks a positive pleasure. Mark's eyes would come alive when the cars flew off the tracks in a rainbow of sparks.

"What are you smiling at?" Carol asked.

And I cut to the chase and said, "Your brother. I remember the way he liked to leave his room. That tree branch right outside his window: he could reach out, grab hold of it, scramble hand over hand to the trunk."

I remembered how the branches swayed and sighed and how scared I was every time I had to follow him.

"In high school," Carol said, "at night he'd sneak out when he was supposed to be in bed and scramble back inside much later. I knew and our mother, but no one else. One night the bough broke as he tried to get back in the window. He fell all the way to the ground, smashing through more branches on the way.

"My father was down in the study plotting malfeasance with Governor Furcolo. They and everyone else came out to see what had happened. We found Mark lying on the ground laughing like a lunatic. He had a fractured arm and a few scratches. Even I wondered if he'd fallen on his head."

For a moment I watched for some sign that she knew I'd been right behind her brother when he fell. I'd gotten down the tree fast and faded into the night when I saw lights come on inside the house. It had been a long, scary night and before he laughed, Mark had started to sob.

Now that we were talking about her brother, Carol was able to say, almost casually, "My mother has her good days and her bad days. But for thirty years she's hinted to me that she had a kind of contact with him. I didn't tell her that wasn't possible because it obviously meant a lot to her."

She was maintaining a safe zone, preserving her need not to know. I frowned and fiddled with a sliver of cucumber on buttered brown bread.

Carol put on a full court press, "Mom wants to see Mark again and she thinks it needs to be soon. She told me you knew people and could arrange things. It would make her so happy if you could do whatever that was again."

I too kept my distance. "I ran some errands for your mother a couple of times that seemed to satisfy her. The last time was fourteen years ago and at my age I'm not sure I can even remember what I did."

Carol gave a rueful little smile, "You were my favorite of all my brother's friends. You'd talk to me about my dollhouse. It took me years to figure out why that was. When I was nine and ten years old I used to imagine you taking me out on dates."

She reached across the table and touched my wrist. "If there's any truth to any of what Mom says, I could use Mark's help too. You follow the news.

"I'm not going to tell you the current administration wrecked the world all by themselves or that if we get back in, it will be the second coming of Franklin Roosevelt and Abe Lincoln all rolled into one.

"I am telling you I think this is end game. We either pull ourselves together in the next couple of years or we become Disney World."

I didn't tell her I thought we had already pretty much reached the stage of the U.S. as theme park.

"It's not possible that Mark's alive," she said evenly. "But his family needs him. None of us inherited our father's gut instincts, his political animal side. It may be a mother's fantasy, but ours says Mark did."

I didn't wonder aloud if the one who had been Marky Bannon still existed in any manifestation we'd recognize.

Then Carol handed me a very beautiful check from a consulting firm her husband owned. I told her I'd do whatever I could. Someone had said about Carol, "She's very smart and she knows all the rules of the game. But I'm not sure the game these days has anything to do with the rules."

3.

After our little tea, I thought about the old Irish-American city of my childhood and how ridiculous it was for Carol Bannon to claim no knowledge of Mark Bannon. It reminded me of the famous Bolger brothers of South Boston.

You remember them: William Bolger was first the President of the State Senate and then the President of the University of Massachusetts. Whitey Bolger was head of the Irish mob, a murderer and an FBI informant gone bad. Whitey was on the lam for years. Bill always claimed, even under oath, that he never had any contact with his brother.

That had always seemed preposterous to me. The Bolgers' mother was alive. And a proper Irish mother will always know what each of her children is doing no matter how they hide. And she'll bombard the others with that information no matter how much they don't want to know. I couldn't imagine Mrs. Bannon not doing that.

What kept the media away from the story was that Mark had—in all the normal uses of the terms—died, been waked and memorialized some thirty-five years ago.

I remembered how in the Bannon family the father adored Carol and her sister Eileen. He was even a tiny bit in awe of little Joe who at the age of six already knew the name and political party of the governor of each state in the union. But Michael Bannon could look very tired when his eyes fell on Mark.

The ways of Irish fathers with their sons were mysterious and often distant. Mark was his mother's favorite. But he was, I heard it whispered, dull normal, a step above retarded.

I remembered the way the Bannons' big house could be full of people I didn't know and how all the phones—the Bannons were the only family I knew with more than one phone in their house—could be ringing at once.

Mike Bannon had a study on the first floor. One time when Mark and I went past, I heard him in there saying, "We got the quorum. Now who's handling the seconding speech?" We went up to Mark's room and found two guys there. One sat on the bed with a portable typewriter on his lap, pecking away. The other stood by the window and said, "...real estate tax that's fair for all."

"For everybody," said the guy with the typewriter. "Sounds better." Then they noticed we were there and gave us a couple of bucks to go away.

Another time, Mark and I came back from the playground to find his father out on the front porch talking to the press who stood on the front lawn. This, I think, was when he was elected Speaker of the Lower House of the Great and General Court of the Commonwealth of Massachusetts, as the state legislature was called.

It was for moments like these that Speaker Bannon had been created. He smiled and photographers' flashes went off. Then he glanced in his son's direction, the penetrating eyes dimmed, the smile faded. Remembering this, I wondered what he saw.

After it was over, when his father and the press had departed, Mark went right on staring intently at the spot where it had happened. I remember thinking that he looked kind of like his father at that moment.

One afternoon around then the two of us sat on the rug in the TV room and watched a movie about mountain climbers scaling the Himalayas. Tiny black and white figures clung to ropes, made their way single file across glaciers, huddled in shallow crevices as high winds blew past.

It wasn't long afterward that Mark, suddenly intense, led me and a couple of other kids along a six-inch ledge that ran around the courthouse in Codman Square.

The ledge was a couple of feet off the ground at the front of the building. We sidled along, stumbling once in a while, looking in the windows at the courtroom where a trial was in session. We turned the corner and edged our way along the side of the building. Here we faced the judge behind his raised desk. At first he didn't notice. Then Mark smiled and waved.

The judge summoned a bailiff, pointed to us. Mark sidled faster and we followed him around to the back of the building. At the rear of the courthouse was a sunken driveway that led to a garage. The ledge was a good sixteen feet above the cement. My hands began to sweat but I was smart enough not to look down.

The bailiff appeared, told us to halt and go back. The last kid in line, eight years old where the rest of us were ten, froze where he was and started to cry.

Suddenly the summer sunshine went gray and I was inching my way along an icy ledge hundreds of feet up a sheer cliff.

After a moment that vision was gone. Cops showed up, parked their car right under us to cut the distance we might fall. A crowd, mostly kids, gathered to watch the fire department bring us down a ladder. When we were down, I turned to Mark and saw that his concentration had faded.

"My guardian angel brought us out here," he whispered.

The consequences were not severe. Mark was a privileged character and that extended to his confederates. When the cops drove us up to his house, Mrs. Bannon came out and invited us all inside. Soon the kitchen was full of cops drinking spiked coffee like it was St. Patrick's Day and our mothers all came by to pick us up and laugh about the incident with Mrs. Bannon.

Late that same summer, I think, an afternoon almost at the end of vacation, the two of us turned onto Melville Avenue and saw Cadillacs double-parked in front of the Hon Hen's house. A movie camera was set up on the lawn. A photographer stood on the porch. We hurried down the street.

As we got there, the front door flew open and several guys came out laughing. The cameraman started to film, the photographer snapped pictures. Young Senator Kennedy was on the porch. He turned back to kiss his aunt and shake hands with his uncle.

He was thin with reddish brown hair and didn't seem entirely adult. He winked as he walked past us and the cameras clicked away. A man in a suit got out of a car and opened the door, the young senator said, "Okay, that's done."

As they drove off, the Hon Hen waved us up onto the porch, brought out dishes of ice cream. It was his wife's birthday and their nephew had paid his respects.

A couple of weeks later, after school started, a story with plenty of pictures appeared in the magazine section of the *Globe*: a day in the life of Senator Kennedy. Mark and I were in the one of him leaving his aunt's birthday. Our nun, Sister Mary Claire, put the picture up on the bulletin board.

The rest of the nuns came by to see. The other kids resented us for a few days. The Cullen brothers, a mean and sullen pair, motherless and raised by a drunken father, hated us for ever after.

I saw the picture again a few years ago. Kennedy's wearing a full campaign smile, I'm looking at the great man, open mouthed. Mark stares at the camera so intently that he seems ready to jump right off the page.

4.

The first stop on my search for Mark Bannon's current whereabouts was right in my neighborhood. It's been said about Greenwich Village that here time is all twisted out of shape like an abstract metal sculpture: past, present, and future intertwine.

Looking for that mix, the first place I went was Fiddler's Green way east on Bleecker Street. Springsteen sang at Fiddler's and Madonna waited tables before she became Madonna. By night it's a tourist landmark and a student magnet but during the day it's a little dive for office workers playing hooky and old village types in search of somewhere dark and quiet.

As I'd hoped, "Daddy Frank" Parnelli, with eyes like a drunken hawk's and sparse white hair cropped like a drill sergeant's, sipped a beer in his usual spot at the end of the bar. Once the legend was that he was where you went when you wanted yesterday's mistake erased or needed more than just a hunch about tomorrow's market.

Whether any of that was ever true, now none of it is. The only thing he knows these days is his own story and parts of that he can't tell to most people. I was an exception.

We hadn't talked in a couple of years but when he saw me he grimaced and asked, "Now what?" like I pestered him every day.

"Seemed like you might be here and I thought I'd stop by and say hello."

"Real kind of you to remember an old sadist."

I'm not that much younger than he is but over the years, I've learned a thing or two about topping from Daddy Frank. Like never giving a bottom an even break. I ordered a club soda and pointed for the bartender to fill Daddy Frank's empty shot glass with whatever rye he'd been drinking.

Daddy stared at it like he was disgusted then took a sip and another. He looked out the window. Across the street, a taxi let out an enormously fat woman with a tiny dog. Right in front of Fiddler's a crowd of smiling Japanese tourists snapped pictures of each other.

A bearded computer student sat about halfway down the bar from us with a gin and tonic and read what looked like a thousand-page book. A middle-aged man and his wife studied the signed photos on the walls while quietly singing scraps of songs to each other.

Turning back to me with what might once have been an enigmatic smile, Daddy Frank said, "You're looking for Mark Bannon."

"Yes."

"I have no fucking idea where he is," he said. "Never knew him before he appeared in my life. Never saw him again when he was through with me."

I waited, knowing this was going to take a while. When he started talking, the story wasn't one that I knew.

"Years ago, in sixty-nine, maybe seventy, it's like, two in the afternoon on Saturday, a few weeks before Christmas. I'm in a bar way west on Fourteenth Street near the meat-packing district. McNally's maybe or the Emerald Gardens, one of them they used to have over there that all looked alike. They had this bartender with one arm, I remember. He'd lost the other one on the docks."

"Making mixed drinks must have been tough," I said.

"Anyone asked for one, he came at them with a baseball bat. Anyway, the time I'm telling you about, I'd earned some money that morning bringing discipline to someone who hadn't been brought up right. I was living with a bitch in Murray Hill. But she had money and I saw no reason to share.

"I'm sitting there and this guy comes in wearing an overcoat with the collar pulled up. He's younger than me but he looks all washed out like he's been on a long complicated bender. No one I recognized, but people there kind of knew him."

I understood what was being described and memory supplied a face for the stranger.

"He sits down next to me. Has this piece he wants to unload, a cheap thirty-two. It has three bullets in it. He wants ten bucks. Needs the money to get home to his family. I look down and see I still have five bucks left."

I said, "A less stand-up guy might have wondered what happened to the other three bullets."

"I saw it as an opportunity. As I look back I see, maybe, it was a test. I offer the five and the stranger sells me the piece. So now I have a gun and no money. All of a sudden the stranger comes alive, smiles at me, and I feel a lot different. With a purpose, you know?

"With the buzz I had, I didn't even wonder why this was. All I knew was I needed to put the piece to use. That was when I thought of Klein's. The place I was staying was over on the East Side and it was on my way home. You remember Klein's Department Store?"

"Sure, on Union Square. 'Klein's on the Square' was the motto and they had a big neon sign of a right-angle ruler out front."

"Great fucking bargains. Back when I was six and my mother wanted to dress me like a little asshole, that's where she could do it cheap. As a kid I worked there as a stock boy. I knew they kept all the receipts, whatever they took in, up on the top floor and that they closed at six on Saturdays."

As he talked, I remembered the blowsy old Union Square, saw the tacky Christmas lights, the crowds of women toting shopping bags and young Frank Parnelli cutting his way through them on his way to Klein's.

"It's so simple I do it without thinking. I go up to the top floor like I have some kind of business. It's an old-fashioned store way back when people used cash. Security is one old guy wearing glasses. I go in the refund line and when I get up to the counter, I pull out the gun. The refunds ladies all soil their panties

"I clean the place out. Thousands of bucks in a shopping bag and I didn't even have to go out of my way. I run down the stairs and nobody stops me. It's dark outside and I blend in with the crowd. As I walk down Fourteenth, the guy from the bar who sold me the gun is walking beside me.

"Before he looked beat. Now it's like the life has been sucked out of him and he's the living dead. But you know what? I have a locker at Gramercy Gym near Third Ave. I go in there so I can change from my leathers into a warm-up jacket and a baseball cap. Like it's the most natural thing, I give the guy a bunch of bills. He goes off to his family. I don't ever see him again.

"I'm still drunk and amazed. That night I'm on a plane. Next day I'm in L.A. Both of those things for the first time. After that I'm not in this world half the time. Not this world like I thought it was anyway. And somewhere in those first days, I realized I wasn't alone inside my own head. A certain Mark Bannon was in there too."

I looked down the bar. The student was drinking his gin, turning his pages. The couple had stopped singing and were sitting near the window. The bartender was on his cell phone. I signaled and he refilled Frank's glass.

"It was a wild ride for a few years," Daddy Frank said, "We hitched up with Red Ruth who ran us both ragged. She got us into politics in the Caribbean: Honduras, Nicaragua, stuff I still can't talk about, Ruth and me and Bannon.

"Then she got tired of us, I got tired of having Mark Bannon on the brain and he got tired of me being me. It happens."

He leaned his elbow on the bar and had one hand over his eyes. "What is it? His mother looking for him again? I met her that first time when she had you find him. She's a great lady."

"Something like that," I said. "Anyone else ask you about Mark Bannon recently?"

"A couple of weeks ago someone came around asking questions. He said he has like a news show on the computer. Paul Revere is his name? Something like that. He came on like he knew something. But a lot smarter guys than him have tried to mix it up with me."

"No one else has asked?"

He shook his head.

"Anything you want me to tell Marky if I should see him?"

Without taking his hand away from his eyes, Daddy Frank raised the other, brought the glass to his lips, and drained it. "Tell him it's been thirty years and more and I was glad when he left but I've been nothing but a bag of muscles and bones ever since."

## 5.

As evening falls in the South Village, the barkers come out. On opposite corners of the cross streets they stand with their spiels and handbills.

"Come hear the brightest song writers in New York," said an angry young man, handing me a flyer.

A woman with snakes and flowers running up and down her arms and legs insisted, "You have just hit the tattoo jackpot!"

"Sir, you look as if you could use a good…laugh," said a small African-American queen outside a comedy club.

I noticed people giving the little sidelong glances that New Yorkers use when they spot a celebrity. But when I looked, the person was no one I recognized. That happens to me a lot these days.

Thinking about Mark Bannon and Frank Parnelli, I wondered if he just saw Frank as a vehicle with a tougher body and a better set of reflexes than his own? Did he look back with fondness when they parted company? Was it the kind of nostalgia you might have for a favorite horse or your first great car?

It was my luck to have known Mark when he was younger and his "guardian angel" was less skilled than it became. One Saturday when we were fourteen or so, going to different high schools and drifting apart, he and I were in a hockey free-for-all down on the Neponset River.

It was one of those silver and black winter Saturday afternoons when nothing was planned. A pack of kids from our neighborhood was looking for ice to play on. Nobody was ever supposed to swim or skate on that water so that's where a dozen of us headed.

We grabbed a stretch of open ice a mile or so from where the Neponset opens onto the Nantasket Roads, the stretch of water that connects Boston Harbor to the Atlantic Ocean. Our game involved shoving a battered puck around and plenty of body checks. Mark was on my team but seemed disconnected like he was most of the time.

The ice was thick out in the middle of the river but old and scarred and rutted by skates and tides. Along the shore where it was thin, the ice had been broken up at some points.

Once I looked around and saw that some kids eight or nine years old were out on the ice in their shoes jumping up and down, smashing through it and jumping away laughing when they did. There was a whir of skates behind me and I got knocked flat.

I was the smallest guy my age in the game. Ice chips went up the legs of my jeans and burned my skin. When I got my feet under me again, the little kids were yelling. One of them was in deep water holding onto the ice which kept breaking as he grabbed it.

Our game stopped and everyone stood staring. Then Mark came alive. He started forward and beckoned me, one of the few times he'd noticed me that afternoon. As I followed him, I thought I heard the words "Chain-of-Life." It was a rescue maneuver that, maybe, boy scouts practiced but I'd never seen done.

Without willing it, I suddenly threw myself flat and was on my stomach on the ice. Mark was down on the ice behind me and had hold of my ankles. He yelled at the other guys for two of them to grab his ankles and four guys to grab theirs. I was the point of a pyramid.

Somehow I grabbed a hockey stick in my gloved hands. My body slithered forward on the ice and my arms held the stick out toward the little kid. Someone else was moving my body.

The ice here was thin. There was water on top of it. The kid grabbed the stick. I felt the ice moving under me, hands pulled my legs.

I gripped the stick. At first the kid split the ice as I pulled him along. I wanted to let go and get away before the splitting ice engulfed me too.

But I couldn't. I had no control over my hands. Then the little kid reached firm ice. Mark pulled my legs and I pulled the kid. His stomach bounced up onto the ice and then his legs. Other guys grabbed my end of the stick, pulled the kid past me.

I stood and Mark was standing also. The little boy was being led away, soaked and crying, water sloshing in his boots. Suddenly I felt the cold—the ice inside my pants and up the sleeves of my sweater—and realized what I'd done.

Mark Bannon held me up, pounded my back. "We did it! You and me!" he said. His eyes were alive and he looked like he was possessed. "I felt how scared you were when the ice started to break." And I knew this was Mark's angel talking.

The other guys clustered around us yelling about what we'd done. I looked up at the gray sky, at a freighter in the distance sailing up the Roads toward Boston Harbor. It was all black and white like television and my legs buckled under me.

Shortly afterward as evening closed in, the cops appeared and ordered everybody off the ice. That night, a little feverish, I dreamed and cried out in my sleep about ice and TV.

No adult knew what had happened but every kid did. Monday at school, ones who never spoke to me asked about it. I told them even though it felt like it had happened to someone else. And that feeling, I think, was what the memory of his years with Mark Bannon must have been like for Daddy Frank.

6.

As soon as Frank Parnelli started talking about Paul Revere, I knew who he meant and wasn't surprised. I called Desmond Eliot and he wasn't surprised to hear from me either. Back when I first knew Des Eliot he and Carol Bannon went to Amherst and were dating each other. Now he operates the political blog, *Midnight Ride: Spreading the Alarm.*

A few days later, I sat facing Eliot in his home office in suburban Maryland. I guess he could work in his pajamas if he wanted to. But, in fact, he was dressed and shaved and ready to ride.

He was listening to someone on the phone and typing on a keyboard in his lap. Behind him were a computer and a TV with the sound turned off. The screen showed a runway in Jordan where the smoking ruins of a passenger plane were still being hosed down with chemicals. Then a Republican senator with presidential ambitions looked very serious as he spoke to reporters in Washington.

A brisk Asian woman, who had introduced herself as June, came into the office, collected the outgoing mail, and departed. A fax hummed in the corner. Outside, it was a sunny day and the trees had just begun to turn.

"Yes, I saw the dustup at the press conference this morning," he said into the phone. "The White House, basically, is claiming the Democrats planted a spy in the Republican National Committee. If I thought anyone on the DNC had the brains and chutzpah to do that I'd be cheering."

At that moment Des was a relatively happy man. *Midnight Ride* is, as he puts it, "A tool of the disloyal opposition," and right now things are going relatively badly for the administration.

He hung up and told me, "Lately every day is a feast. This must be how the right wing felt when Clinton was up to his ass in blue dresses and cigars." As he spoke he typed on a keyboard, probably the very words he was uttering.

He stopped typing, put his feet up on a coffee table, and looked out over his half-frame glasses. His contacts with the Bannons go way back. It bothers him that mine go back further.

"You come all the way down here to ask me about Mark Bannon," he said. "My guess is it's not for some personal memoir like you're telling me. I think the family is looking for him and thinks I may have spotted him like I did with Svetlanov."

I shook my head like I didn't understand.

"Surely you remember. It was twenty years ago. No, a bit more. Deep in the Reagan years. Glasnost and Perestroika weren't even rumors. The Soviet Union was the Evil Empire. I was in Washington, writing for *The Nation,* consulting at a couple of think tanks, going out with Lucia, an Italian sculptress. Later on I was married to her for about six months.

"There was a Goya show at the Corcoran that Lucia wanted to see. We'd just come out of one of the galleries and there was this guy I was sure I'd never seen before, tall, prematurely gray.

"There was something very familiar about him. Not his looks, but something. When he'd talk to the woman he was with, whatever I thought I'd recognized didn't show. Then he looked my way and it was there again. As I tried to place him, he seemed like he was trying to remember me.

"Then I realized it was his eyes. At moments they had the same uncanny look that Mark Bannon's could get when I first knew him. Of course by then Mark had been dead for about thirteen years.

"Lucia knew who this was: a Russian art dealer named Georgi Svetlanov, the subject of rumors and legends. Each person I asked about him had a different story: he was a smuggler, a Soviet agent, a forger, a freedom fighter."

Eliot said, "It stuck with me enough that I mentioned it the next time I talked to Carol. She was planning a run for congress and I was helping. Carol didn't seem that interested.

"She must have written the name down, though. I kept watch on Svetlanov. Even aside from the Bannon connection he was interesting. Mrs. Bannon must have thought so too. He visited her a few times that I know of."

Marie Bannon had gotten in touch with me and mentioned this Russian man someone had told her about. She had the name and I did some research, found out his itinerary. At a major opening at the Shafrazi Gallery in SoHo, I walked up to a big steely-haired man who seemingly had nothing familiar about him at all.

"Mark Bannon," I said quietly but distinctly.

At first the only reaction was Svetlanov looking at me like I was a bug. He sneered and began to turn away. Then he turned back and the angel moved behind his eyes. He looked at me hard, trying to place me.

I handed him my card. "Mark Bannon, your mother's looking for you," I said.

"That's her number on the back." Suddenly eyes that were very familiar looked right into mine.

Des told me, "I saw Svetlanov after that in the flesh and on TV. He was in the background at Riga with Reagan and Gorbachev. I did quite a bit of research and discovered Frank Parnelli among other things. My guess is that Mark Bannon's…spirit or subconscious or whatever it is—was elsewhere by nineteen-ninety-two when Svetlanov died in an auto accident. Was I right?"

In some ways I sympathized with Eliot. I'd wondered about that too. And lying is bad. You get tripped by a lie more often than by the truth.

But I looked him in the face and said, "Mark wasn't signaling anybody from deep inside the skull of some Russian, my friend. You were at the wake, the funeral, the burial. Only those without a drop of Celtic blood believe there's any magic in the Irish."

He said, "The first time I noticed you was at that memorial service. Everyone else stood up and tiptoed around the mystery and disaster that had been his life. Then it was your turn and you quoted Shakespeare. Said he was a ruined king. You knew he wasn't really dead."

"Des, it was 1971. Joplin, Hendrix. Everyone was dying young. I was stoned, I was an aspiring theater person and very full of myself. I'd intended to recite Dylan Thomas's 'Do Not Go Gentle' but another drunken Mick beat me to that.

"So I reared back and gave them *Richard the Second*, which I'd had to learn in college. Great stuff:
'Not all the water in the rough rude sea
Can wash the balm off from an anointed king;
The breath of worldly men cannot depose
The deputy elected by the Lord'

"As I remember," I said, "the contingent of nuns who taught Mark and me in school was seated down front. When I reached the lines:
"…if angels fight,
Weak men must fall…"

"They looked very pleased about the angels fighting. Booze and bravura is all it was," I said.

Partly that was true. I'd always loved the speech, maybe because King Richard and I share a name. But also it seemed so right for Mark. In the play, a king about to lose his life and all he owns on Earth invokes royal myth as his last hope.

"When I was dating Carol I heard the legends," Des told me. "She and her sister talked about how the family had gotten him into some country club school in New Jersey. He was expelled in his third week for turning the whole place on and staging an orgy that got the college president fired.

"They said how he'd disappear for weeks and Carol swore that once when he came stumbling home, he'd mumbled to her months before it happened that King and Bobby Kennedy were going to be shot.

"Finally, I was at the Bannons with Carol when the prodigal returned and it was a disappointment. He seemed mildly retarded, a burnout at age twenty-five. I didn't even think he was aware I existed.

"I was wrong about that. Mark didn't have a license or a car anymore. The second or third day he was back, Carol was busy. I was sitting on the sun porch, reading. He came out, smiled this sudden, magnetic smile just like his old man's and asked if that was my Ford two-door at the end of the driveway.

"Without his even asking I found myself giving him a lift. A few days later I woke up at a commune in the Green Mountains in New Hampshire with no clear idea of how I'd gotten there. Mark was gone and all the communards could tell me was, 'He enters and leaves as he wishes.'

"When I got back to Boston, Carol was pissed. We made up but in a lot of ways it was never the same. Not even a year or two later when Mike Bannon ran for governor and I worked my ass off on the campaign.

"Mark was back home all the time then, drinking, taking drugs, distracting the family, especially his father, at a critical time. His eyes were empty and no matter how long everyone waited, they stayed that way. After the election he died, maybe as a suicide. But over the years I've come to think that didn't end the story."

It crossed my mind that Eliot knew too much. I said, "You saw them lower him into the ground."

"It's Carol who's looking this time, isn't it?" he asked. "She's almost there as a national candidate. Just a little too straight and narrow. Something extra needs to go in the mix. Please tell me that's going to happen."

A guy in his fifties looking for a miracle is a sad sight. One also sporting a college kid's crush is sadder still.

"Just to humor you, I'll say you're right," I told him. "What would you tell me my next step should be?"

The smile came off his face. "I have no leads," he said. "No source who would talk to me knows anything."

"But some wouldn't talk to you," I said.

"The only one who matters won't. She refuses to acknowledge my existence. It's time you went to see Ruth Vega."

## 7.

I was present on the night the angel really flew. It was in the summer of '59 when they bulldozed the big overgrown lot where the Fitzgerald mansion had once stood. Honey Fitz's place had burned down just twenty years before. But to kids my age, "Fitzie's" was legendary ground, a piece of untamed wilderness that had existed since time out of mind.

I was finishing my sophomore year in high school when they cleared the land. The big old trees that must have stood on the front lawn, the overgrown apple orchard in the back were chopped down and their stumps dug up.

The scraggly new trees, the bushes where we hid smeared in war paint on endless summer afternoons waiting for hapless smaller kids to pass by and get massacred, the half flight of stone stairs that ended in midair, the marble floor with moss growing through the cracks, all disappeared.

In their place a half-dozen cellars were dug and houses were built. We lost the wild playground but we'd already outgrown it. For that one summer we had half-finished houses to hide out in.

Marky and I got sent to different high schools outside the neighborhood and had drifted apart. Neither of us did well academically and we both ended up in the same summer school. So we did hang out one more time. Nights especially we sat with a few guys our age on unfinished wood floors with stolen beer and cigarettes and talked very large about what we'd seen and done out in the wide world.

That's what four of us were up to in a raw wood living room by the light of the moon and distant street lamps. Suddenly a flashlight shone in our faces and someone yelled, "Hands over your heads. Up against the wall."

For a moment, I thought it was the cops and knew they'd back off once they found out Marky was among us. In fact it was much worse: the Cullen brothers and a couple of their friends were there. In the dim light I saw a switchblade.

We were foul-mouthed little twerps with delusions of delinquency. These were the real thing: psycho boys raised by psycho parents. A kid named Johnny Kilty was the one of us nearest the door. Teddy—the younger, bigger, more rabid Cullen brother—pulled Johnny's T-shirt over his head, punched him twice in the stomach, and emptied his pockets.

Larry, the older, smarter, scarier Cullen, had the knife and was staring right at Marky. "Hey, look who we got!" he said in his toneless voice. "Hands on your head, faggot. This will be fucking hilarious."

Time paused as Mark Bannon stared back slack-jawed. Then his eyes lit up and he smiled like he saw something amazing.

As that happened, my shirt got pulled over my head. My watch was taken off my wrist. Then I heard Larry Cullen say without inflection, "This is no good. Give them their stuff back. We're leaving."

The ones who held me let go; I pulled my T-shirt back on.

"What the fuck are you talking about?" Teddy asked.

"I gotta hurt you before you hear me?" Larry asked in dead tones. "Move before I kick your ass."

They were gone as suddenly as they appeared, though I could hear Teddy protesting as they went through the construction site and down the street. "Have you gone bird shit, stupid?" he asked. I didn't hear Larry's reply.

We gathered our possessions. The other guys suddenly wanted very badly to be home with their parents. Only I understood that Mark had saved us. When I looked, he was staring vacantly. He followed us out of the house and onto the sidewalk.

"I need to go home," he whispered to me like a little kid who's lost. "My angel's gone," he said.

It was short of midnight though well past my curfew when I walked Marky home. Outside of noise and light from the bars in Codman Square, the streets were quiet and traffic was sparse. I tried to talk but Marky shook his head. His shoes seemed to drag on the pavement. He was a lot bigger than me but I was leading him.

Lights were on at his place when we got there and cars were parked in the driveway. "I need to go in the window," he mumbled and we went around back. He slipped as he started to climb the tree and it seemed like a bad idea. But up he went and I was right behind him.

When the bough broke with a crack, he fell, smashing through other branches, and I scrambled back down the trunk. The lights came on but I got away before his family and the governor of the Commonwealth came out to find him on the ground laughing hysterically.

The next day, I was in big trouble at home. But I managed to go visit Mark. On the way, I passed Larry Cullen walking away from the Bannons' house. He crossed the street to avoid me.

Mark was in bed with a broken arm and a bandage on his leg. The light was on in his eyes and he wore the same wild smile he'd had when he saw Larry Cullen. We both knew what had happened but neither had words to describe it. After that Mark and I tended to avoid each other.

Then my family moved away from the neighborhood and I forgot about the Bannons pretty much on purpose. So it was a surprise years later when I came home for Christmas that my mother said Mark Bannon wanted to speak to me.

"His mother called and asked about you," she said. "You know I've heard that Mark is in an awful way. They say Mike Bannon's taken that harder than losing the governorship.

My father looked up from the paper and said, "Something took it out of Bannon. He sleepwalked through the campaign. And when it started he was the favorite."

Curiosity, if nothing else, led me to visit Mark. My parents now lived in the suburbs and I lived in New York. But the Bannons were still on Melville Avenue.

Mrs. Bannon was so sad when she smiled and greeted me that I would have done anything she asked.

When I saw Mark, one of the things he said was, "My angel's gone and he's not coming back." I thought of the lost, scared kid I'd led home from Fitzie's that night. I realized I was the only one, except maybe his mother, who he could tell any of this to.

I visited him a few times when I'd be up seeing my family. Mostly he was stoned on pills and booze and without the angel he seemed lobotomized. Sometimes we just watched television like we had as kids.

He told me about being dragged through strange and scary places in the world. "I guess he wasn't an angel. Or not a good one." Doctors had him on tranquilizers. Sometimes he slurred so badly I couldn't understand him.

Mike Bannon, out of office, was on committees and commissions and was a partner in a law firm. But he was home in his study a lot and the house was very quiet. Once as I was leaving, he called me in, asked me to sit down, offered me a drink.

He wondered how his son was doing. I said he seemed okay. We both knew this wasn't so. Bannon's face appeared loose, sagging.

He looked at me and his eyes flashed for a moment. "Most of us God gives certain…skills. They're so much a part of us we use them by instinct. We make the right move at the right moment and it's so smooth it's like someone else doing it.

"Marky had troubles but he also had moments like that. Someone told me the other day you and he saved a life down on the river when you were boys because he acted so fast. He's lost it now, that instinct. It's gone out like a light." It seemed he was trying to explain something to himself and I didn't know how to help him.

Mark died of an overdose, maybe an intentional one, and they asked me to speak at the memorial service. A few years later, Big Mike Bannon died. Someone in tribute said, "A superb political animal. Watching him in his prime rounding up a majority in the lower chamber was like seeing a cheetah run, an eagle soar…"

"…a rattlesnake strike," my father added.

## 8.

A couple of days after my meeting with Des Eliot, I flew to Quebec. A minor border security kerfuffle between the U.S. and Canada produced delays at both Newark International and Jean Lesage International.

It gave me a chance to think about the first time I'd gone on one of these quests. Shortly after her husband's death Mrs. Bannon had asked me to find Mark's angel.

A few things he'd told me when I'd visited, a hint or two his mother had picked up, allowed me to track one Frank Parnelli to the third floor of a walk-up in Washington Heights.

I knocked on the door, the eyehole opened and a woman inside asked, "Who is it?"

"I'm looking for Ruth Vega."

"She's not here."

"I'm looking for Mark Bannon."

"Who?"

"Or for Frank Parnelli."

The eyehole opened again. I heard whispers inside. "This will be the man we had known would come," someone said and the door opened.

Inside were statues and pictures and books everywhere: a black and white photo of Leon Trotsky, a woman's bowling trophy, and what looked like a complete set of Anna Freud's *The Psychoanalytic Study of the Child.*

A tiny old woman with bright red hair and a hint of amusement in her expression stood in the middle of the room looking at me. "McCluskey, where have you been?"

"That's not McCluskey, Mother," said a much larger middle-aged woman in a tired voice.

"McCluskey from the Central Workers Council! Where's your cigar?" Suddenly she looked wise. "You're not smoking because of my big sister Sally, here. She hates them. I like a man who smokes a cigar. You were the one told me Woodrow Wilson was going to be president when I was a little kid. When it happened I thought you could foretell the future. Like I do."

"Why don't you sit down," the other woman said to me. "My niece is the one you're looking for. My mother's a little confused about past and present. Among other things."

"So McCluskey," said the old woman. "Who's it going to be next election? Roosevelt again, that old fascist?" I wondered whether she meant Teddy or FDR.

"I know who the Republicans are putting up," she said. It was 1975 and Gerald Ford was still drawing laughs by falling down stairs. I tried to look interested.

"That actor," she said. "Don Ameche. He'll beat the pants off President Carter." At that moment I'd never heard of Carter. "No not Ameche, the other one."

"Reagan?" I asked. I knew about him. Some years before he'd become governor of California, much to everyone's amusement.

"Yes, that's the one. See. Just the same way you told me about Wilson, you've told me about Reagan getting elected president."

"Would you like some tea while you wait?" asked the daughter, looking both bored and irritated.

We talked about a lot of things that afternoon. What I remembered some years later, of course, was the prediction about Reagan. With the Vega family there were always hints of the paranormal along with a healthy dose of doubletalk.

At that moment the door of the walk-up opened and a striking couple came in. He was a thug who had obviously done some boxing, with a nicely broken nose and a good suit. She was tall and in her late twenties with long legs in tight black pants, long red hair drawn back, a lot of cool distance in her green eyes.

At first glance the pair looked like a celebrity and her bodyguard. But the way Ruth Vega watched Frank Parnelli told me that somehow she was looking after him.

Parnelli stared at me. And a few years after I'd seen Marky Bannon's body lowered into the ground, I caught a glimpse of him in a stranger's eyes.

That was what I remembered when I was east of Quebec walking uphill from the Vibeau Island Ferry dock.

Des knew where Ruth was, though he'd never actually dared to approach her. I believed if she wanted to stop me from seeing her, she would already have done it.

At a guess, Vibeau Island looked like an old fishing village that had become a summer vacation spot at some point in the mid-twentieth century and was now an exurb. Up here it was chilly even in the early afternoon.

I saw the woman with red hair standing at the end of a fishing pier. From a distance I thought Ruth Vega was feeding the ducks. Then I saw what she threw blow out onto the Saint Lawrence and realized she was tearing up papers and tossing them into the wind. On first glance, I would have said she looked remarkably as she had thirty years before.

I waited until I was close to ask, "What's wrong, Ms. Vega, your shredder broken?"

"McCluskey from the Central Workers Council," she said, and when she did, I saw her grandmother's face in hers. "I remember that first time we met, thinking that Mark's mother had chosen her operative well. You found her son and were very discreet about it."

We walked back to her house. It was a cottage with good sight lines in all directions and two large black schnauzers snarling in a pen.

"That first time was easy." I replied. "He remembered his family and wanted to be found. The second time was a few years later and that was much harder."

Ruth nodded. We sat in her living room. She had a little wine, I had some tea. The décor had a stark beauty, nothing unnecessary: a gun case, a computer, a Cy Twombly over the fireplace.

"The next time Mrs. Bannon sent me out to find her son, it was because she and he had lost touch. Frank Parnelli when I found him was a minor Village character. Mark no longer looked out from behind his eyes. He had no idea where you were. Your grandmother was a confused old woman wandering around her apartment in a nightgown.

"I had to go back to Mrs. Bannon and tell her I'd failed. It wasn't until a couple of years later that Svetlanov turned up."

"Mark and I were in love for a time," Ruth said. "He suggested jokingly once or twice that he leave Parnelli and come to me. I didn't want that and in truth he was afraid of someone he wouldn't be able to control.

"Finally being around Parnelli grew thin and I stopped seeing them. Not long afterward Mark abandoned Parnelli and we both left New York for different destinations. A few years later, I was living in the Yucatan and he showed up again. This time with an old acquaintance of mine.

"When I lived with Grandmother as a kid," Ruth said, "she was in her prime and all kinds of people were around. Political operatives, prophetesses, you name it. One was called Decker, this young guy with dark eyes and long dark hair like classical violinists wore. For a while he came around with some project on which he wanted my grandmother's advice. I thought he was very sexy. I was ten.

"Then he wasn't around the apartment. But I saw him: coming out of a bank, on the street walking past me with some woman. Once on a school trip to the

United Nations Building, I saw him on the subway in a naval cadet's uniform.

"I got home that evening and my grandmother said, 'Have you seen that man Decker recently?' When I said yes, she told me to go do my homework and made a single very short phone call. Decker stopped appearing in my life.

"Until one night in Mexico a knock came on my door and there he stood looking not a day older than when I'd seen him last. For a brief moment, there was a flicker in his eyes and I knew Mark was there but not in control.

"Decker could touch and twist another's mind with his. My grandmother, though, had taught me the chant against intrusive thoughts. Uncle Dano had taught me how to draw, aim, and fire without even thinking about it.

"Killing is a stupid way to solve problems. But sometimes it's the only one. After Decker died I played host to Mark for about an hour before I found someone else for him to ride. He was like a spark, pure instinct unfettered by a soul. That's changed somewhat."

When it was time for my ferry back to the city, Ruth rose and walked down to the dock with me.

"I saw his sister on TV the other night when they announced she would be appointed to the Senate. I take it she's the one who's looking for him?"

I nodded and she said, "Before too long idiot senators will be trying to lodge civil liberty complaints after martial law has been declared and the security squads are on their way to the capital to throw them in jail. Without Mark she'll be one of them."

Before I went up the gangplank, she hugged me and said, "You think you're looking for him but he's actually waiting for you."

After a few days back in New York memories of Vibeau Island began to seem preposterous. Then I walked down my block late one night. It was crowded with tourists and college kids, barkers and bouncers. I saw people give the averted celebrity glance.

Then I spotted a black man with a round face and a shaven head. I did recognize him: an overnight hip-hop millionaire. He sat in the back of a stretch limo with the door open. Our eyes met. His widened then dulled and he sank back in his seat.

At that moment, I saw gray winter sky and felt the damp cold of the ice-covered Neponset. *On old familiar ground,* said a voice inside me and I knew Mark was back.

## 9.

Some hours later passengers found seats as our train pulled out of New Haven.

"Ruth said you were waiting for me," I told Mark silently.

*And Red Ruth is never wrong.*

"She told me about Decker."

*I thought I had selected him. But he had selected me. Once inside him I was trapped. He was a spider. I couldn't control him. Couldn't escape. I led him to Ruth as I was told.*

He showed me an image of Ruth pointing an automatic pistol, firing at close range.

*I leaped to her as he died. She was more relentless than Decker in some ways. I had to promise to make my existence worthwhile. To make the world better.*

"If angels fight, weak men must fall."

*Not exactly an angel. Ego? Id? Fragment? Parasite?*

I thought of how his father had something like an angel himself.

*His body, soul, and mind were a single entity. Mine weren't.*

I saw his memory of Mike Bannon smiling and waving in the curved front windows of his house at well-wishers on the snowy front lawn. Bannon senior never questioned his own skills or wondered what would have happened if they'd been trapped in a brain that was mildly damaged. Then he saw it happen to his son.

Once I understood that, he showed me the dark tower again with two tiny slits of light high above. I found hand- and foot-holds and crawled up the interior stone walls. This time I looked through the slits of light and saw they were the eyeholes of a mask. In front of me were Mike and Marie Bannon looking very young and startled by the sudden light in the eyes of their troublingly quiet little boy.

When the train approached Boston, the one inside me said, *Let's see the old neighborhood.*

We took a taxi from Back Bay and drove out to Dorchester. We saw the school we'd gone to and the courthouse and place where I'd lived and the houses that stood where Fitzie's had once been.

*My first great escape.*

That night so long ago came back. Larry Cullen, seen through the eyeholes of a mask, stood with his thin psycho smile. In a flash I saw Mark Bannon slack-jawed and felt Cullen's cold fear as the angel took hold of his mind and looked out through his eyes.

*Cullen's life was all horror and hate. His father was a monster. It should have taught me something. Instead I felt like I'd broken out of jail. After each time away from my own body it was harder to go back.*

Melville Avenue looked pretty much the way it always did. Mrs. Bannon still lived in the family house. We got out of the car and the one inside me said, *When all this is over, it won't be forgotten that you brought me back to my family.*

In the days since then, as politics has become more dangerous, Carol Bannon has grown bolder and wilier. And I wonder what form the remembering will take.

Mrs. Bannon's caregiver opened the door. We were expected. Carol stood at the top of the stairs very much in command. I thought of her father.

"My mother's waiting to see you," she said. I understood that I would spend a few minutes with Mrs. Bannon and then depart. Carol looked right into my eyes and kissed me. Her eyes flashed and she smiled.

In that instant the one inside my head departed. The wonderful sharpness went out of the morning and I felt a touch of the desolation that Mark Bannon and all the others must have felt when the angel deserted them.

# THE CLAY PARTY

## STEVE DUFFY

**From the Sacramento *Citizen-Journal*, November 27, 1846**

Disquieting news reaches the offices of the *Citizen-Journal* from our correspondent at Sutter's Fort, where the arrival of a party of settlers embarked on an untried and hazardous new crossing has been anxiously expected since the beginning of the month. November having very nearly elapsed with no word of these prospective Californians as yet received, it is feared by all that their party is become stranded in the high passes with the onset of winter. There is a general agreement among mountain men and seasoned wagoneers alike that the route believed travelled by these unfortunate pilgrims is both unorthodox and perilous in the extreme, it being the handiwork of a Mr Jefferson Clay of New Hampshire, a stranger to these parts with no reputation as a pioneer or a capable navigator. We hear anxious talk of a rescue party being recruited, once the worst of the snow has passed...

\* \* \*

**From the *Diary of John Buell*, 1846**

*May 17ᵗʰ, Independence, Missouri:* Embarkation day. At last! Set out at nine sharp with our fellow Californians—for so we shall be entitled to call ourselves, in but a little while. A great clamour of oxen and horses along Main Street, and the most uproarious cheering from all the townsfolk as they bid us farewell. It is sad to reflect that among these friendly multitudes there should be faces—dear faces, friends and relatives among them—that we shall never see again; and yet the prospect of that providential land in the West recalls us to our higher purpose, and strengthens us in our resolve. We carry the torch of Progress, as our mentor Mr Clay has written, and it is most fitting that he should be at the head of our party as we depart. We are forty-eight in number: seven families, a dozen single men, our great wagons pulled by sturdy oxen. Surely nothing can stop us.

Elizabeth concerned at the possible effects of the crossing on little Mary-Kate; also, that the general health of her mother is not all it might be. Again I remind her that the balmy air of California can only strengthen the old lady's general constitution, and that no other place on God's earth affords such opportunities for our daughter and ourselves. This she accepts, and we are fairly bound on our way. So it's "three cheers for Jeff Clay, boys," as the wagoneers sang out at our departure—and onwards into the West. Lord, guide us in this great undertaking!

*May 26th:* The plains. An infinite expanse of grassy prairie, profoundly still and empty. Surely God created no more unfrequented space among all His mighty works. Thunder in the nights, and storms away off on the horizon. Mud along the trail, thick and treacherous, so that we must double-team the oxen on the inclines. The rate of our advance is measured, yet perfectly steady. If only there were some sign by which we could mark our progress! I long for mountains, such as we knew back home in Vermont. Elizabeth's mother no better; she eats but little, and is silent as these endless brooding plains. Mary-Kate in excellent health, thank God.

*May 31st:* The Big Blue, and our first real reverse. River swollen with much rain: unfordable. We are obliged to construct a temporary ferry. It will take time.

*June 3rd:* On our way again. It was the Lord's own struggle crossing the Big Blue, and we were fortunate not to lose more than a couple of our oxen, but now at least we have an opportunity to make up for lost time. Mrs Stocklasa now very weak, though generally quiet and uncomplaining. Elizabeth says little, except to cheer me up with her words of tender encouragement, but I know her every waking hour is filled with anxiety for her ailing mama. Perhaps at Fort Laramie we shall find a doctor.

*June 16th:* Laborious progress up the Platte; mud still obliging us to double-team on the slightest incline. Found Elizabeth outside the wagon this evening after settling Mary-Kate for the night, weeping freely and most bitterly. She fears her mother's mortal crisis is approaching. God grant it may not be so. Throughout the night she watches over her, soothing her when she wakes, speaking to her in that strange language of her homeland. It gives the old lady much comfort—which may be all that we have left to give her.

*June 18th:* With a heavy heart I must record the most sorrowful of all tidings: Elizabeth's mother died around sunset yesterday. The entire party much distressed and brought low by this melancholy event. We dug her grave at a pretty spot on a little knoll overlooking the valley, with up ahead the still-distant prospect of mountains. Would that she had been destined to stand on their peaks with us, and gain a Pisgah view of the promised land! The Lord giveth and the Lord taketh away. One of the wagoneers has inscribed with hot-iron a simple wooden marker for her grave: *JULIA STOCKLASA—Born 1774, Wallachia, Died 1846, Missouri Territory, bound for California—Tarrying here awhile.* It is a curious thing to come across in such a lonely place, the humble marker atop its little cairn of rocks; and a sad enough sight for we who mourn, to be sure. But may it not be the case that for those Westerners yet to pass along this trail, it will speak, however haltingly, of home and God and goodness, and may even serve as a first, albeit melancholy sign of civilisation in this great American wilderness? It is hard to envisage this now, as the wolves cry out in the night-time, and Elizabeth starts into wakefulness once more, her features drawn and thin, her eyes reddened with much sorrow. But it may be so.

*June 30th:* Fort Laramie, at the foothills of the mountains. Revictualling and recuperating after our grim passage across the plains, for which we paid with much hardship and great sorrow.

*July 4th:* Celebrations in the evening, sky-rockets and dancing to fiddle music; all marred somewhat by an altercation between our leader Jefferson Clay and certain of the mountain men. These rough-hewn, barbarous individuals are much in evidence at the fort, paying homage to the independence of our fair Republic by drinking strong whiskey till they can barely stand. Some of these fine fellows engaged Mr Clay in conversation, in the course of which he showed them the maps laid out in his booklet *California, Fair Garden of the West.* Herein lay the roots of the discord. The mountain men would not concede that his route—a bold and imaginative navigation of the Great Salt Desert and the mountain passes beyond—represents the future of our nation's westward migration. Harsh words were exchanged, till Mr Clay suffered himself to be led away from the scene of the quarrel. I was among those who helped remove him, and I recall in particular his strong patrician countenance flushed with rage, as he shouted at the top of his voice—"It's the nigher way, I tell you! The nigher way!"

*July 5th:* On our way again. We were happy enough to arrive at Fort Laramie, but I guess we shall not miss it overmuch.

*July 12th:* Another black day for our party: Mrs Hiderick dead of a fit in the night. Hiderick, a silent black-browed German-Pennsylvanian, buried her himself before sunup.

*July 20th:* Hard going. Storms bedevil us still, and we are pretty well accustomed now to our night-time serenades of rolling thunder and the howling of far-off coyotes and wolves. Even Mary-Kate does not stir from her childish slumbers. On nights when the storms are at their worst, the oxen stampede, half-mad from the thunder and the lightning. Regrouped only with much labour. And then the endless sage, and the all-enveloping solitude of the plains. The passage through to California must indeed be a great prize, to be gained at such a cost.

*July 25th:* The Continental Divide, or so we reckon. From here on in, Oregon country. A thousand miles out, a thousand still to go, says Mr Clay. It is comforting to know that the greater part of our endeavours are now over. I say this to Elizabeth, who I know is grieving still for her beloved mama, and she agrees with me.

*July 27th:* A curious conversation with Elizabeth, late last night. She asked me if there was anything I would not do to protect our family. Of course I said there was nothing—that her safety, and the safety of our beloved daughter, must always be foremost in my mind, and if any action of mine could guarantee such an outcome, then I would not hold back from it for an instant. She said she knew it, and rallied a little from her gloom; or tried to. What can all this mean? She pines for her mother, of course; and fears what lies ahead. I must seek to reassure her.

*July 28th:* The Little Sandy river. Here we arrive at the great parting of the ways; while the other wagon trains follow the deep ruts of the regular Oregon trail to our right, heading North, we shall strike out south along Mr Clay's cut-off. A general air of excitement throughout the company. Even Elizabeth rallies somewhat from her melancholy reveries.

*July 31st:* Fort Jim Bridger. Supplies and rest. Elizabeth and Mary-Kate the subject of some wonderment among the bachelor gentlemen of the fort, when taking the air outside the wagon this morning. It is quite comical to see such grizzled individuals turn as silent and bashful as a stripling lad at his first dance. Such is the effect of my schoolteacher lady, and our little angel!

*August 2nd:* Bad feeling again in the fort. Cagie Bowden came to our wagon this morning, with news that Mr Clay was once more in dispute with the mountain men last night. Bowden says that together with Mr Doerr & Mr Shorstein he was obliged to remove Mr Clay from the proceedings; also, that in their opinion he was every bit as drunk as the mountain men. Let us not tarry overlong in this place.

*August 3rd:* On our way once more, along the cut-off. Thus we reckon to save upwards of three-hundred and fifty miles, and should reach Sutter's Fort within six or seven weeks.

*August 9th:* Ten, fifteen miles a day, when we had reckoned on twenty. Reasonable progress, still we must not fall behind our schedule. Difficult terrain ahead.

*August 17th:* A wilderness of canyons. Impassable except by much labour. Entire days wasted in backing out of dead-ends and searching for another route. We are falling behind, and the seasons will not wait. Mr Clay delivered the harshest of rebukes to Cagie Bowden for suggesting we turn back to Fort Jim Bridger and the northern trail. (And yet it is only what some of the others are saying.) Too late now in any case.

*August 23rd:* Lost for the last six days. Only this morning, when Mr Doerr climbed a tall peak and scouted out a surer way, were we freed at last from the hell of the canyons. Much time lost here. Mr Clay is now generally unapproachable except by a very few. He will not suffer the Bowdens to come nigh him. It is regrettable.

*August 27th:* Into the trackless wastes along the Wasatch. Two and three miles progress in a day. Aspen and cottonwoods choking up the canyons; cleared only with superhuman effort. Weary to my very bones. Elizabeth tells me not to over-exert myself, but there is no choice. I brought my wife & baby daughter into this place, and now they must always be at the forefront of my thoughts. We *must not* be caught here in the wilderness when winter comes.

*August 29th:* Some of the other families have proposed that we abandon the larger wagons, which they believe cannot be driven through this mountainous territory. They called a meeting tonight, at which Mr Clay overruled them, assuring the party that we have passed through the worst of the broken land, and speaking passionately of the ease and speed with which our passage shall be completed once we leave behind the canyon country. Cagie Bowden pressed him on the details, upon which he became much agitated, and attempted to expel the Bowdon wagon from the party. On this he was overruled, by a clear majority of the settlers. He retired with much bitterness to his wagon, as did we all. A general air of foreboding over all the party.

*August 30th:* Seven of the single men missing this morning; gone with their horses. The party is fractured clean down the middle. No-one looks up from his labours save with a grave and troubled face. Double-teaming all day. Elizabeth urges me to rest tonight, and cease from writing. God grant we shall one day read these words, settled safe in California, and wonder at the tribulations of the passage across.

*September 1st:* Out of the canyons at last! and on to the low hilly land above the salt flats. Six hundred miles from our destination. A chance to recoup lost time, and fresh springs in abundance. Charley and Josephus, the Indian guides we engaged at Fort Bridger, went from wagon to wagon warning us to take on board all the water we might carry, and to hoard it well—no good springs, they said, for many days' march ahead. On hearing of this Mr Clay had the men brought to him, and cursed them for a pair of craven panic-mongers and Godless savages. Hiderick was for lashing them to a wagon-wheel and whipping them—restrained with some difficulty by the rest of us men. Heaven help us all.

*September 2nd:* A note found stuck to the prickerbushes by the side of the trail, by the Indian Charley scouting ahead. He brought it to me at the head of the wagon train, and with some difficulty Bowden and I pieced it together. We believe it to be the work of several of the single men who cleared out last week—it tells of hard going up ahead, and warns us to turn back and make for Fort Bridger while we have the chance. I was for keeping it from Jefferson Clay till we had spoken to the other families, but nothing would do for Bowden but to force the issue. Once more Clay and Bowden wound up at each other's throats, and were separated only by the combined exertions of all present. An ill omen hangs over this party. Ahead lies the desert. Into His hands we commend our spirits, who brought His chosen ones through forty years of wandering to the promised land.

*September 3rd:* Slow passage across the face of the great salt desert. Hard baked crust over limitless salty mud, bubbling up to the surface through the ruts left by our wagon wheels. The wagons sink through to above the wheel-hubs, and the going is most laborious. Again we fall behind, and the season grows late.

*September 4th:* Endless desolation—no safe land—no fresh water. This is a hellish place.

*September 5th:* Disaster in the night. The oxen, mad with thirst, stampeded in the night; all but a handful lost out on the salt pans. Four of the wagons have been abandoned, and the families must carry what they can. All have taken on board as much as they can carry, and the overloaded wagons sink axle-deep into the mud. Surely God has not set his face against us?

*September 7th:* Passage still devilish slow; no sign of an end to the desert. Bitter cold in the night time—we huddle with the dogs for warmth, like beasts in the wilderness. Little Mary-Kate screams in disgust at the bitter salt taste that fills her pretty rosebud mouth. Vainly she tries to spit it out, as her mother comforts her. Would that I could rid my own mouth of the bitter taste of defeat. ~~I have led them into this hell~~ (*remainder of sentence erased—Ed.*)

*September 9th:* Off the salt pans at last. Oxen lost, wagons abandoned, and no prospect of a safe retreat to Fort Bridger. To go back now would surely finish us off. In any case, the provisions would not last—Bowden says they will barely serve for the passage through the mountains. He is for confronting Clay, once and for all, and holding a popular vote to determine who should lead the party from here on in to California. I counsel him to wait till our strength is somewhat recouped. None of us have the belly for such a confrontation at present.

*September 13th:* Ahead in the distance, the foothills of the Sierras. White snow on the hilltops. Dear God, that it should come to this.

*September 20th:* No slackening in our progress, no rest for any man; but we are slow, we are devilish slow. Without the oxen and the wagons we lost out on the salt pans our progress is impeded mightily, and much effort is expended in the securing of provisions. Clay now wholly removed from the rest of the party; like a general he rides alone at the head of the column, seeing nothing but the far horizon while all around him his troops suffer, close to mutiny. Around our wagons each night, the howling of wolves.

*September 23rd:* Desperation in the camp, which can no longer be hidden. The remaining single men have volunteered to ride on ahead, that they might alert the Californian authorities to our plight; they set out this morning. All our chances of success in this forlorn undertaking ride with them.

*October 2nd:* The Humboldt river. According to Charley the Indian guide, we are now rejoined with the main trail, and done at last with Clay's damned cut-off. No sign of any other parties along the banks of the river. It is late in the season—they will be safe across the mountains and in California now. A note from the men riding on ahead was discovered on the side of the trail, and brought straight to Clay. He will not disclose its contents. I am persuaded at last that the time has come to follow Bowden's counsel, and force a reckoning.

*October 3rd:* A catastrophe. The thing I most feared has come to pass. Last night Cagie Bowden led a deputation of the men to Clay's wagon and demanded he produce the note. Clay refused, and upon Bowden pressing him, drew a pistol and shot him through the chest. Instantly Clay was seized by the men, while aid was summoned for the stricken Bowden; alas, too late. Within a very little time he expired.

I was for burying him, then abandoning Clay in the wilderness and pressing on. Hiderick would have none of it, calling instead for frontier justice and a summary settling of accounts. His hotter temper won the day. Hiderick caused Clay's wagon to be tipped over on its side, and then hanged him from the shafts. It was a barbarous thing to watch as he strangled to death at the end of a short rope. Are we no better than beasts now? Have our hardships brought us to such an extremity of animal passion? Back in the wagon, I threw myself to the floor in a perfect storm of emotion; Elizabeth tried to comfort me, but I could take no solace even from her sweet voice. I have failed her—we have all failed, all of us men who stood by and let vanity and stupidity lead us into this hell on earth. Now on top of it all we are murderers. The mark of Cain lies upon us.

*October 4th:* In all my anguish of last night I forgot to set down that the note was found on Clay's body after all, tucked inside his pocket-book. It read—"Make haste. Indians in the foothills. Snow already on the peaks. Waste no time."

*October 11th:* Forging on down the valley of the Humboldt. Such oxen as remain alive are much weakened through great exertion and lack of fodder, and to save their strength we walk where we can. No man talks to his neighbour; our gazes are bent to the trail ahead, and our heads hang low. Why should we look up? Snow-caps clearly visible atop the mountains in the West.

*October 23rd:* In the night, a great alarm: Indians, howling down from the hills, attacking our wagons. Four wagons lost before we knew it—nine men dead in the onslaught. They have slaughtered half of the oxen too, the brutes. As they vanished back into the hills, we heard them laughing—a terrible and callous sound. I hear it now as I write, and it may be that it shall follow me to my grave: the mocking of savages in this savage land. Savages, I say? At least they do not kill their own as we have done.

*October 31st:* Our progress is so slow as to be hardly worth recording. Oxen dying between the wagon-shafts; if we are to make the crossing into California, I believe we shall have to rely on the mules and upon our own feet. Thunder atop the peaks, and the laughter of the Paiutes, echoing through these lonely canyons. They do not bother us much now, though; even the wolves leave us alone. We are not worth the bothering.

*November 4th:* Very nigh to the mountains now—can it be that the Lord will grant us safe passage before the winter comes? Dark clouds over all the white-capped peaks. One more week, Lord; one more week. At night on our knees by the bunks we pray, Elizabeth & I—God grant us another week.

*November 8th:* In the high passes. So close! Lord, can it be?

*November 9th:* Snow in the night, great flakes whirling out of a black sky. We pressed on without stopping, but in the morning it commenced again, and mounted to a wild flurry by midday. The oxen are slipping, and the wagons wholly ungovernable. We made camp by the side of a lake nigh to the tree-line, where some party long since departed fashioned four or five rough cabins out of logs.

For tonight we must bide here by the lakeside, and pray for no more snow.

*November 10th:* Snow all through the night. Trail impassable—neither man nor beast can battle through the drifts. Exhausted, hope gone. Wind mounting to a howling frenzy, mercury falling, sky as black as lead. We have failed. The winter is upon us and we are lost in the high passes. God help us.

\* \* \*

**From the Sacramento *Citizen-Journal*, February 2, 1847**

Our readers, anxious for fresh news of the wagon-train of settlers trapped in the mountains, will doubtless remember our interview with Mr Henry Garroway, one of the outriders sent on ahead of the party who arrived in California last November, with the first of winter's storms at his heels. Mr Garroway, it will be recalled, announced it as his intention to lead a rescue company at the earliest opportunity, made up of brave souls from the vicinity of Sutter's Fort, kitted out and victualled by the magnanimous Mr John Augustus Sutter himself. Alas, grave news reaches us from the fort: the ferocity of the January storms has rendered even the lowest of the Western passes wholly impenetrable. Drifts higher than a man on horseback have been reported as the norm, and even the most sanguine estimate cannot anticipate the departure of any rescue party until March at the earliest…

\* \* \*

**Addendum to the *Diary of John Buell* (undated, made by his wife, Elizabeth)**

I had not thought to take up my dear husband's pen and bring the story of our family's tribulations to its conclusion; however, should this diary be all that remains of us, then it may serve as a testament—to much bravery, and also to wickedness beyond measure.

We have been snowed in at the lakeside for nigh on three months now. Things have gone hard with us since the beginning: our provisions were scanty on arrival, and dwindled soon enough to nothing. I have seen people trying to eat shoe-leather and the binding of books; bark and grass and dirt they have eaten, twigs and handfuls of leaves. We were thirty-five on our arrival, thirty-two adults and three nursing children including my angel Mary-Kate. Now we are reduced to three.

The hunger swallows all things. Whole days will pass, and we think of nothing save food, how it would be to fill our bellies to repletion. There is a narcotic in it; it lulls one into a dangerous inactivity, a dull vacant torpor. I have seen this look settle upon a score of people; in each case the end came very nigh after. Daily I look for it in myself. I must be strong, for my angel's sake.

The provisions ran out before the end of November: the last of the oxen were slaughtered and eaten by then, and the mules too. One of the children was the first to die, Sarah Doerr's little Emily; soon after her, Missy Shorstein, and her father the next day. Our sorrow was great—we had no way of knowing that all too soon death would become a familiar thing with us. It is hard to mourn, when horror is piled upon horror and the bodies are beyond counting or remembrance; but it is necessary. It is the most human of emotions, and we must remain human, even in this uttermost remove of hell.

From the start it was clear that some would not last the year out. A great depression settled over our camp like a funeral pall, and many succumbed to its all-embracing pressure. It was most prevalent among the men—not least in my dear husband John. From the first he reproached himself, and for many days after our arrival, half-crazy with remorse, he would not stir from his bed of leaves and moss in our cabin. Many times I spoke with him, and sought to assure him he was not to blame for our predicament; but he would not be consoled, and turned his head away to the wall. Greatly I feared for his life; that he would give up the will to live, and fade away like so many of the others.

But my husband John Buell was a strong man, and a brave one, and soon enough he arose from his bed and was about the general business. He managed to trap some small animals for the pot; hares and crows and the like. He helped weather-proof our cabin, and the cabins of our neighbours. And around the middle of December, when folks were dying and all hope seemed forlorn, he set forth a plan.

Together with three of the other man—Bill Doerr, Martin Farrow and young Kent Shorstein—he purposed to cross the mountains on foot and fetch help. The Indians, Charley and Josephus, would accompany them, guiding them safe through to California. It was a desperate plan, fraught with much peril and offering but little chance of success, but it was voted the last best hope of our pitiful assembly, for all were in agreement when the plan was presented for approval. Here I must be honest, and record that in private I counselled against the expedition—I wept and pleaded with John, that he should stay with us and not throw his life away on such a rash and impetuous undertaking. He would not listen, though: it was as if he saw in this reckless plan a last chance, not just for our beleaguered party, but for himself—as if he might thus redeem himself in my eyes, when all along he was my hero and my one true love.

They set out in the second week of December; and soon afterwards Hiderick presented his awful proposition to the remainder of the party.

Now I must be brave, and record the facts of the matter without flinching. Hiderick said that the rescue party were doomed to failure, and would undoubtedly die in the mountain passes; we should not rely on them for assistance. I could have struck him—that he could thus impugn my husband, and his brave allies, when he had not the courage to do aught save cower in his cabin! But I must tell it aright, and not let myself be sidetracked.

Hiderick said that we were doomed, and should not make it through to the spring, save for one chance. He said that we were surrounded by fresh meat, if we had only the brains to see it, and the nerve to do something about it; he said he was a butcher by trade, and would show us what he meant. If I live another fifty years I shall not forget what he did next.

He went to the door of the big cabin and flung it wide open. The snow rose up in drifts all around, parted only where a path had been cleared between the cabins. All around were the graves of those who had already succumbed to the hunger and the cold; maybe nine or ten by that time. We could not dig them in the ground, for that lay ten feet beneath the snowdrifts, and was frozen hard as iron. Instead we lay them wrapped in blankets in the snow, where the cold would preserve them till the spring.

Hiderick pointed to the nearest of the graves—little Missy Shorstein's. "There's your meat," he said, in his thick guttural voice. "Like it or not, it's the only vittles you'll get this side of the thaw."

There was an uproar. Old man Shorstein struck Hiderick full in the face, and swore he would take a pistol and spill Hiderick's brains on the snow before he ever disturbed the grave of his daughter. Hiderick wiped the blood from his cheek, licking his hand clean in a way that made me sick to watch, and merely said, "You'll see. None need eat his own kin, if we handle it right."

But Mr Shorstein himself was in his grave before Christmas-day, and two others with him. Two more the next day, and three the next—and soon after that the first of the families took to eating the dead.

Hiderick dressed the bodies, and distributed the parcels of meat. Like a terrible black-bearded devil he passed from cabin to cabin; always he would knock upon our door, and always I would refuse to answer. Sometimes the ghoul would show his grinning face at the window; I would hold little Mary-Kate close to my bosom, and pray for our deliverance. Five of the seven families partook; let the record show that the Buells and the Shorsteins never ate human flesh. It is not my place to judge them—Mama told me more than once that survival runs close to the bone, closer than anything save the blood. But the flesh of our friends and fellow-Christians! Dear Lord, no.

I trapped what I could, enough for Mary-Kate at least: back in Vermont when I was but a little child, Mama had showed me many ways to catch the small creatures of hills and woodland. Still the hunger was always with us, and Mary-Kate grew awful thin and pale; yet no unholy flesh passed our lips. As for the rest of them: they ate or fasted according to their consciences, and yet even for those who chose to partake there was scarce enough meat to grow fat on, so little was there left on the bones of the dead. They cheated death for but a little while, but at what cost, Lord? At what cost?

Even this grisly feasting was all but through by the January, and folk were dying again almost daily, when out of the mountains staggered Kent Shorstein and the Indian Josephus, carrying between them the body of my dear brave husband John Buell.

We buried John in the snowdrifts out back of the cabin. Kent Shorstein told me of the great hardships endured by the five of them up in the mountains; he said that they lost their way searching for a pass that was not entirely blocked, and so within a week they were starving and nigh to death themselves. Doerr and Farrow were for killing the Indians, and eating their flesh; on this Charley rose up and ran Martin Farrow through with a knife, and Bill Doerr shot Charley dead on the spot. Josephus would have killed him for it, but John and young Kent restrained him. Best if they had not, maybe, for next morning when they awoke they found Doerr eating Charley's liver by the campfire. Kent and my dear John refused to join him in the gruesome repast, and instead they entreated Josephus to lead them away, back to our camp by the lake. The last they saw of Bill Doerr was him raving and singing to himself among the pine trees, waving a gobbet of meat on a stick.

Poor Kent Shorstein told me all this from his sick-bed; he shivered like a man with the ague, and I was not surprised when two days later, his body was taken for burial by his grieving sisters. Soon they too had joined him at rest; and then began the grimmest passage of my travails.

With John dead and the last of the Shorsteins gone also, there now remained of the party only Mary-Kate and I who refused to eat the flesh of the deceased. Hiderick was now pre-eminent among us; he roamed from cabin to cabin like a robber baron, adorned—I can scarce bring myself to speak of it!—adorned with a gruesome sort of necklace, fashioned from small knuckle-bones and vertebrae strung on a leather strip. He said they were from the mules and the oxen, though everybody knew this to be a lie. Who though could reproach him? He fed them, and they depended on him. On his shoulders he wore a cape of wolfskin—the wolves surrounded the camp but would not come close, for I had set up snares all around as Mama showed me how to do, and we still had ammunition enough to shoot them.

It was the practice of the families to place over the bodies of their loved ones a marker made of wood, together with a small tag hung round the neck, lest anyone should eat his own kin. In the cases of the Shorsteins and us Buells, this marker served to warn away the ghoul Hiderick entirely. Imagine then the distress and the horror with which I found, when going to pray awhile at John's graveside, that the bodies of Adolph and Bella Shorstein had been dragged from their sacred resting-place around to Hiderick's cabin, whither I dared not go. What to do?

In the presence of all those remaining in the party—few enough, Lord, few enough! and yet sufficient to deal with Hiderick, had they but dared—I confronted him with the foul deed. He merely laughed and said, "Hain't I got to put meat on the table? They ain't so particular about their food now, I reckon." No-one would take my part in it; they slunk away like so many starving jackals, licking the bloody hand that feeds them. I took Mary-Kate back to our cabin, and wept throughout the night. I vowed to myself: she is my angel, and I will do what I must to protect her. Let the others throw in their lots with the ghoul,

I said, and see what comes of it.

Death came of it, I believe as much of shame as hunger in the end. People could scarce bear to look at one another, and took to their beds, and come morning they were dead; only Hiderick seemed to thrive on his grisly diet. He ruled over all, and grew fat on the bodies of his erstwhile subjects.

Josephus would have taken my part, for he too—let his name be recorded among the virtuous!—never ate of the cursed meat; but he was gone. After bringing John back to the camp he spent a night resting, then another day crouching out in the snow beneath the mightiest of the trees around the camp, muttering to himself some words of heathen prayer. The wolves came right up to him, but did not touch him; for his part, he hardly seemed to heed their presence. At dusk he came down from the treeline to knock on my cabin door and tell me he was departing. Would I come with him, he asked?  I said I could not, and showed him Mary-Kate asleep in her rough cot. He nodded, and said a curious thing: "You are best fitted of all of them to look after her, maybe. I will see you again." Then he looked at me for the longest time, so long that I felt uncomfortable and averted my eyes from his keen and curious gaze—upon which he turned on his heel and departed. That night—I am sure it was him—he left the dressed-out carcass of a deer at our door. We never saw him again.

Now we are through February and into March, and still no sign of a thaw, nor any hope of rescue. Instead the snow redoubles, and my traps are empty come the morning. There were upward of a dozen souls remaining in our party when John's companions dragged him back into camp. Today, there are but three remaining, Mary-Kate and me—and Hiderick.

Oh, unutterable horror!  That such things could exist under the sun!  The deserted camp is like some awful frozen abattoir. Long streaks of blood disfigure the white snowdrifts. Here and there lie the horrible remains of some devil's feast—a long bone picked clean, a shattered skull—and barricaded inside our cabin we hear, Mary-Kate and I, the ravings of the maniac outside.

This afternoon—I can scarce bear to set the words down. I must be strong. This afternoon, he came to the cabin door and hammered it till I opened. He was stripped to the waist, I thought at first; then I realised I could not see his mop of greasy black hair and bristling beard, and thought he wore some sort of leathern cap over all. What it was—

What he wore was the skin of my dear husband John Buell, stretched over his head and shoulders like an awful mask. He was laughing like a madman, and bawling at the top of his cracked and shrieking voice: "You like me?  You like me now, huh?  I fitten enough for you now, maybe?"

I raised John's pistol level with my eyes, and said, I know not how I managed it but I said: "Get out." He scarcely heard me, so filled with the spirit of devilishness and insanity was he. I did not hesitate. I fired the pistol. The load flew so close by his head—closer than I had intended it to, I think—that it served to rouse him from his madness. He stared at me, but all I could see were the features, blackened and distorted, of my dear sweet John. The horror of it—the horror—

"Get out now," I said.

"I'll come fer you," he said, and I swear there was nothing in his voice that was halfway human any more. "I'm your husband, now, don't you see, and I'll come fer you. You'll want me by and by, I reckon. I got meat—got good meat—" and he raised his hand to show me some hideous gobbet of flesh—please God let it not have been *his*, oh merciful Lord please!  He brandished it before him like a dreadful prize.

I fired again, and this time the bullet took the greater part of his ear off. He dropped the stinking piece of carrion and screamed; with the incredible clarity of great stress and panic, I saw his traitor's blood spilling out on the white and blameless snow. Like the basest coward in creation he scuttled back to his shack, shrieking and cursing all the while. For the time being he is quiet; but I doubt not that he will come for us, maybe tonight when the moon is up. My bullet only wounded him, he will survive. But shall we, Mary-Kate and I?

Alone; abandoned; forsaken. How shall I protect my darling babe from this madman, from this wolf at the door?  All that drives me on is the remembrance of Mama, those nights she lay nigh death in the wagon, how she clasped my hand in hers and gripped it and told me that I would survive, though she might not. I said mama, mama, no, it shan't be, you're strong, you're so strong, and I am weak, but she said I would change. When the time came I would change. I do not know whether she was right, but I feel at the end of myself.

The moon is up. Its broad full face smiles down on this stained defiled earth. The howling of the wolves echoes out across the frozen lake and through the deserted cabins, up into the snow-choked trees. Four bullets left. Not near enough, I fear, but one each for me and Mary-Kate at need. Grant me the strength to do what I must, to survive this night!

* * *

**From the Sacramento *Citizen-Journal*, April 27, 1847**

### THE MIRACLE OF THE MOUNTAINS
#### A CHILD FOUND IN THE WILDERNESS
#### *GUARDED BY WOLVES—HORRORS STREWN ALL ABOUT*
*Full particulars*

The most shocking and incredible news from Mr Henry Garroway's rescue party, who rode to the assistance of the wagon train forced to winter in the high mountains, is setting all California ablaze. Wild rumors have been bruited on all sides, and it is incumbent upon the *Citizen-Journal* to set down the facts as we have learned them, *directly from Mr Garroway himself.*

The party set out from Sutter's Fort in the last week of March, and battled through mighty snow-drifts to the far side of the peaks, where lay the encampment of the unfortunate settlers stranded by the winter storms. The first of the outriders drew up short on reaching the outskirts of the camp, so appalling was the scene which lay before their eyes. Together the would-be rescuers prayed for strength and marshalled their forces, before entering into a scene of horror no pen can describe, fit only for some grim courageous Dante of the New World.

Five cabins of rough construction lay before them, their roofs alone visible above the snow. No sign of chimney-smoke, or indeed of any human activity, could be seen; instead, between the cabins, there were bloodied trails, as of the aftermath of a great slaughter. One veteran member of the party, Mr Frederick Marchmont of Sacramento, swears that the carnage wreaked upon that place surpassed in horror anything seen by the most hardened of frontier campaigners; not even the savage Apache, he avers, could have left in his wake so much bloodshed and butchery.

Great was the dismay with which the rescuing party gazed upon this devastation; heavy were the hearts of all as the search from cabin to cabin began. Horrible to relate, all about the cabins were portions of human flesh and bone, torn as if by wild animals; so atrocious was the general aspect of the place that several of the rescuers were all but unmanned, falling to their knees and praying to the Lord that this bitter cup should pass them by.

Imagine, then, the wonderment with which the assembled men of the rescue party heard, in all that great stillness of desolation, the crying of a little child!

\* \* \*

**From a private letter of Elizabeth Buell to her daughter Mary-Kate, held within the Garroway family**

My darling, I believe they are coming soon. Last night I heard them, ever so far off, up in the peaks—I smell them now, their scent travels on the thin spring wind. Tomorrow they will arrive, and they will find you.

It will be the cruellest and most bitter thing to leave you, crueller even than the burying of my own dear husband, your loving father John Buell. I saw his body once Hiderick had done with it: oh, my child, pray you never have to look on such a sight! Hard it was to look upon; till now, the hardest thing in that long season of sadness and hardship that began with the death of your grandmother, Julia Stocklasa, at the commencement of all our wanderings.

Your father, as he lay raving in his cabin by the lakeside, called this a godless place; and then cursed himself for a blasphemer. God has abandoned us, he screamed into the night; better say that God was never here, my darling. Better say that we rode beyond His grace into some strange and ancient land, where the old gods still hold sway, where blood and death and the animal passions yet contend for mastery of the earth. Your grandmother knew it, Mary-Kate; as she lay on her deathbed she whispered it in my ear. Remember, she said, you will change at need. You will change, she said, and I did not know what she meant at first. Then she told me of the shapeshifter women of her homeland, those that go out into the woods on nights when the moon is full, and the change comes upon them. She told me what to do if I wished to survive the peril she foresaw, and to protect you. I did not believe her at first, but perhaps only in the uttermost desperation can such things ring true. I did what she told me, and everything changed, my darling—everything, save my love for you.

I thought I could come back, after it was done. For it was only to protect you, my darling, that I did what I did that night of the full moon when Hiderick came for us; little did I care for my own life, only for yours, since to stay alive would be to keep you safe from harm, and that was all that mattered to me. How could I know that what is done, is done, once and for all; that *there can be no changing back*? How could I live among men again, after such a fearful alteration? Now I have other family, and must leave you to your own kind.

They wait for me among the trees, my new kin, tongues lolling from their strong jaws as they grin and pant, coats wet from the melting snow. How it feels to run with them, to fling myself into snowbanks and roll and play and lie together—this you can never know, my darling. Josephus, who helped save you, knew: straight away I recognized him, after the deed was done and the rest of the wolves came down to the camp to look upon the slaughter. I looked into his eyes as I lay there full changed, streaked and clotted still with Hiderick's reeking blood, and he looked back into mine. This time I did not turn away.

Did I do wrong? I did what I had to do. Did I betray my dear husband? At least I did not fail our beautiful and most perfect daughter, first in both our affections and ever dearest to us. So how bitter, my darling, to leave you for these men to find. They will take you across the mountains, whither your father and I cannot follow: we shall remain here as you ride away. At least you shall find your home in the new Eden: east of Eden is fit enough for such as we, who have the stain of blood on us.

Perhaps this land, that has so much escaped God's grace, may still be subject to His justice; perhaps I will be punished for what I have done. As if there could be a worse punishment than knowing you to be alive and well in that promised land beyond the mountains, and I not able to see you, or hold you in my arms and hear your pretty laugh.

Hark! They are coming down from the mountain. I must go, and leave you now. All my love goes with you. Be good, my darling; be kind, be honest, be faithful, and know that your Mama will love you always. Listen for me, nights when you lie abed and the moon is up. The pack are waiting for me. I must go—

# PENGUINS OF THE APOCALYPSE

## WILLIAM BROWNING SPENCER

I was watching a nature documentary on the small television I'd taken into exile with me. Several thousand hapless Emperor penguins huddled together on a vast plain of snow while blasts of ice-laden air furrowed their feathers. Tough little birds, sleek little stoics that made my flimsy misfortunes (unemployed, divorced, alcoholic) seem like the hothouse complaints of a pampered child. But wait… perhaps these birds weren't even roughing it. If I could zero in on a single bird amid this huddled mass, if I could read its mind, I might find it thinking: "This is great, the lot of us here, comrades, all for one and one for all. Would you look at the way the sun blazes on the ice! Beautiful! What a magnificent day to huddle together. And there's a nice breeze, too!"

I live over a bar, and when my own thoughts get too much for me, I go down to the bar and Evil Ed, the bartender, draws me a free beer from the tap. This should not be mistaken for generosity. Later, he runs my tab up extravagantly, claiming I've bought beers for people I don't remember and who, I suspect, are the imaginary spawn of Evil Ed's accounting practices.

Evil Ed and I both have apartments above the bar. I rented my apartment through Evil Ed, who was representing our landlord, Quality Rentals, Inc. QR resides, as do we, in Newark, New Jersey, or, at least, that's where QR's post office box is located.

Evil Ed is an ex-con, his muscled arms covered with primitive tattoos, the strangest of which is a heart among many knives with the initials A.B. in the heart's center and a little banner over that with the single word WHITE printed on it. Why a black man would wish to have an Aryan Brotherhood tattoo is beyond me, but I don't know him well enough to ask. Evil Ed keeps to himself, and he doesn't feel compelled to engage in the sort of small talk that passes for social interaction between strangers. I appreciate his self-containment. Surely the virtue of silence, of allowing others their space, should be taught in kindergarten.

Such schooling shouldn't have to wait until prison.

Anyway. It was a Saturday, which might suggest a crowd, but this wasn't a Saturday-night kind of bar. This was more the sort of bar you went to because you had gone to it the day before.

The place could get a little rowdy sometimes, and Evil Ed had nailed a holster up under the counter near the cash register. Lodged inside that holster was a Walther P38 that looked old enough to have been pried from a Nazi's cold dead fingers. As far as I knew, no one had ever tried to rob the place. Evil Ed's demeanor did not suggest a man willing to hand over cash without a fight.

This Saturday night, the bar (which, by the way, has no name, being identified only by the vertical neon letters B-A-R) was sparsely populated with regulars (Rat Lady, Freddie Famous-Long-Ago, Bullshit George, and The Nameless Perv). There were a couple of Goth kids, happy to be miserable, and three bulky guys wearing dresses, transvestite empowerment night, I guess, and, somewhere in the shadows, Derrick Thorn, waiting to meet me, waiting to befriend me.

The television over the bar had the same penguin show on, and now a seal was chasing a penguin through the water. The seal, its mouth wide and bristling with pointy teeth, shot through the ocean, shedding iridescent bubbles, its eyes black, demonic, the eyes of some angry ghost-child from a Japanese horror flick. I had never seen seals from this perspective. Scary stuff!

A voice that was not mine seemed to pluck the thought from my head: "It does not seem right, a seal animal to eat a penguins, the both of them slippery, swimmy things that should be happy brothers together in the oceans."

I turned to behold a large pear-shaped man, smooth-faced, hairless as a cave salamander. His face was oddly blurred, and he may have tried to remedy this lack of definition by the application of eyeliner to his forehead, but the eyebrows created in this manner only seemed to emphasize the absence of any assertive facial features. He wore a black sweatshirt with the hood thrown back and pleated black pants. The contours of his sweatshirt suggested lumpy pudding flesh beneath; pale hands, small as a child's, sprouted from black sleeves. I assumed that this much strangeness had to be calculated, that he was some sort of artist.

"Let us make of each other the acquaintance," he said. I'm not the least bit fastidious when it comes to drinking companions, so we moved to a corner booth, and we drank a lot of beer, which he must have paid for, because my bar tab didn't grow at all that night.

It's not clear what Derrick Thorn revealed of himself. I came away with the knowledge that English was not—surprise!—his native language ("It fall down on my tongue, these English"), but if he told me the country he called home, my brain failed to log it. He was in some sort of business requiring a lot of travel, and he lived alone. He must have volunteered this info; I know I didn't ask. A maudlin, drunken state had overtaken me, and at such times a drinking companion is merely an opportunity for a monologue. I told him I was divorced, unemployed, and paying child support to a woman so mean that her death would cause a thousand of Hell's toughest demons to opt for early retirement. I was exaggerating, out of bitterness and an alcohol-induced love of hyperbole.

Derrick nodded as I spoke. At some point during the evening, he took out a handkerchief and mopped the sweat from his brow, eradicating one eyebrow and smearing the other.

I was flickering in and out of a blackout, that alcoholic state in which the mind visits the moment, departs, and returns sporadically, illuminating scenes as might the world's slowest strobe. A moment that my mind chose to save consisted of Derrick, solemn and slick-faced, leaning toward me and saying, "At end times, the penguins will remember those who friended them." I recall this (now) because, in the context of whatever I was saying (and I can't remember what that was), it seemed profound.

It was very late when I found myself back in my room. I turned the television on while waiting for the floor to settle. Another nature documentary was in progress. Monkeys were eating mud.

When I woke in the morning, the television was taking it easy, some people slumped in sofas, talking about social ills with the calm resignation of people who only expect things to get worse.

I can't always tell when I'm ill, because I drink a lot, and the aftermath of drinking has many flu-like symptoms. But I was sneezing in the morning, and my forehead felt as hot as heated asphalt. My thoughts were trying to devour each other, a sign, I've found, of fever.

I thought of calling Victoria and telling her I couldn't make it, but she'd accuse me of being a selfish drunken bastard who cared nothing for anyone other than himself. I hate defending myself against accusations that are fundamentally true, so I made some coffee and drank it and rallied as best I could.

At night, I empty the contents of my pants pockets on the floor, and I was reassigning these items (car keys, lighter, artfully wadded-up bills, sundry coins, pens, et cetera) to the pockets of a clean pair of jeans when I found a business card of the inexpensive thermal-printed sort you might purchase from an Internet site for a pittance. It read:

**Derrick Thorn**
businesses • helping persons • solving problems
good deals by mutual bargain
*friendship and opportunity guaranteed*
please be calling at ➜

A telephone number was hand-printed on the other side of the card. *Well,* I thought, *not a misspelled word in the lot.* Not that it made any sense. I tossed the card in the nightstand's drawer, where it would lie with other business cards, many of unknown provenance.

I got dressed, regarded myself in the bathroom mirror, said, "If no one has told you they love you today, there's a good reason for that," and left my apartment. Evil Ed was in the hall, a garbage bag on his shoulder, heading to the stairs that led to the dumpster out back. He nodded to me and I nodded back, neither of us compelled to smile or speak.

It was snowing, slow dizzy wet flakes that turned black in the gutters. Aside from a couple of homeless people hunkered in doorways and a skeletal dog that was tearing apart a black plastic trash bag, spilling empty beer cans into the street, it was quiet the way Sunday mornings are in my neighborhood. The God of Church has either got you, swept you up and dragged you into some storefront salvation shop, or you are lying low, hardly breathing, feeling the oppressive holiness of the day coming for you like a hearse.

We were in the holiday season, almost Thanksgiving, and I could already feel Christmas bearing down on me, a black cloud of obligations and money-draining events. My bank account was no longer being fed by a salary—BC Graphics had fired me three weeks ago for excellent reasons that have no part in this narrative—and I hadn't informed Victoria of this reversal in my fortunes. I couldn't imagine her saying anything helpful.

Victoria, my ex, has never entirely approved of me. She married me, I suspect, because her father *despised* me. In marrying me against his wishes, she was getting back at him for being a distant, aloof parent during her formative years. As time went by, the old man warmed to me. I turned out to be his ally in a sea of women—*five daughters, no sons, a harridan of a wife!*—and Victoria felt betrayed.

I married Victoria because I loved her, and, in the fullness of time, that love disappeared as though a magician had snapped his fingers. *Behold this shiny love. Keep your eyes on it, ladies and gentlemen. Are you watching? Voila!* Gone in a flash of smoke, vanished in a whoop, and before I could catch my breath, there it was again, transformed, love sauntering in from offstage, grinning, the magician's misdirection flawless, as good as a miracle, there: Danny Boy Silvers, our son.

He was five now, and I was on my way into the heart of the suburbs to pick him up and take him to the zoo in West Orange.

"Can we stop at MacDonald's?" he asked, looking out the car's passenger window at the falling snow.

"If you don't tell your mother," I said. This was a Sunday tradition, covert MacDonald's, a small father-son conspiracy against a powerful regime that could crush us without raising a sweat.

"I won't tell," Danny said. He waited. Waited and grew impatient. "Why shouldn't I tell?"

"Because she'd slap us so hard our spines would fly out our butts!" I said.

Danny giggled.

"She'd stomp us so hard we'd pop like bugs on a griddle."

My son laughed, leaning forward.

"She'd knock us all the way into next year. She'd whack us till our tongues jumped out of our heads. And once a tongue gets away, it burrows down into the earth, quick as a snake, and you have to get a spade and dig like crazy, and by the time you catch it and put it back in your mouth… well, it doesn't taste very good, I can tell you that."

A stand-up comic is only as good as his audience. My audience was small but enthusiastic, giggling and hooting, his knees bouncing, his nose running, spittle flying.

"She'd shake us until we were so dizzy we couldn't tell up from down, and we would fall right into the sky and keep on falling until our asses hit the moon!"

In the MacDonald's we both ordered Egg McMuffins, hash browns, and chocolate shakes, the major food groups.

"When we go to the zoo, can we see the snakes?" Danny asked.

"This isn't a really big zoo or anything. I don't know if they have snakes."

"They do! Mom went on the Internet and showed me a picture. They have a Reptile House."

"Okay," I said. "Sure." Secretly, I was a little miffed. What was Victoria doing, prematurely unwrapping my gift to Danny, *my* zoo? Oh, how petty are the skirmishes of the heart.

From the parking lot, the zoo didn't look very imposing. There were two round towers from which flags fluttered, suggesting one of those Renaissance fair events in which one is harried by costumed jugglers, street musicians, and mimes. Once we got our tickets and got through the gate, jostled by a group of elderly women wearing identical bowling league jackets (*Queen of the Lanes* emblazoned on the backs), we consulted the signs and settled on a plan: monkeys to big cats to otters to hippos and rhinos to giraffes to birds and, saving the most anticipated for last, to reptiles. The Reptile House was near the gate and a logical last stop before leaving the zoo.

These things never go as planned.

"Dad! What are those monkeys doing?" Danny was wide-eyed, open-mouthed.

"Fornicating," I said.

"What's that?"

"It's like fighting," I said.

A tall guy next to me, obviously another divorced, weekend-dad with two small, identical girls, each clinging to a hand, nodded his head. "You can say that again."

There were lots of small, fidgety monkeys that seemed completely baffled by their cages, as though they had been caught earlier that day and were still thinking, "What the hell? I'm trapped! I'm getting the hell out of… what's this? I can't get out this way either! *What's going on here?"*

In a large cage with black bars, a reddish-brown orangutan slumped in the crook of a tree. His boredom was palpable and made me ashamed of my scrutiny. Forget spying on people having sex or practicing some special perversion. What is sadder, more dismal, than witnessing another person's boredom, the slow, dim-witted crotch-scratching lethargy that is often the existential lot of a person alone? You might note that orangutans are apes, not people, but that didn't keep me from hurrying Danny on to the Lion House, which, if possible, smelled worse than the Monkey House.

And on we went: to the zany otters, the bloated hippos, the absent rhinos (on vacation? escaped? indisposed? deceased?), the really tall giraffes, and into the raucous bird house. As a father and font-of-all-knowledge, I read out-loud the various plaques that described the animals, their habits, their character, their troubles, and Danny listened politely. Other weekend fathers were also reading these plaques to their kids, and I felt a certain disdain for their efforts. As if they knew anything beyond what they were reciting! Pathetic.

We came to a great, curving arc of glass, a vista which promised a view of—yes!—penguins. I had much to say about these amazing birds, the saga of their days fresh in my mind, and was dismayed to find myself gazing at brown concrete curves, blackened and desolate, an emptiness as unwelcoming as some demolished urban block. A sign announced that the penguin habitat was closed for renovation, and my mood worsened, which, I confess, caused a bit of bad behavior. A guard caught me trying to teach an intellectually overrated grey parrot (said to have a vocabulary of over two hundred words) to say, "Kiss my ass"—and Danny and I were escorted out of the building.

That left the Reptile House, and Danny loved it, loved the brightly colored poisonous frogs (not reptiles at all, but always welcome in reptile houses), the lethal, arrow-headed vipers, the boas and the immense anaconda. And the penguins! I couldn't believe it when we came upon them. But it made sense. They had to stay somewhere, and here's where they were, slumming with the reptiles. Since birds evolved from dinosaurs, it even made some taxonomic sense, I guess.

I was glad to see them, shuffling around in a glass-fronted cage that might, at one time, have housed alligators or crocodiles.

They weren't Emperor penguins. According to the plaque, these were Fiordland Crested penguins, an endangered species, with long, pale-yellow slashes over their eyes, like an old man's eyebrows.

"Danny, did you know—"

"They have captured these penguins! What crime the penguins perform to make them prisoners, I do not know. The snakes! Hah, that is easy, they bite the peoples, and they are, anyway, Satan's spawn, as is said long ago in your Bibles."

I jumped, I think. I turned, and there he was.

He was dressed exactly as he had been last night. The lights in the Reptile House were muted, and his pale flesh seemed to glow with a faint blue sheen. He had restored his eyebrows since I'd last seen him, and he appeared to have added purple lipstick to his cosmetic effects.

"It is good to meet you again, Mr. Sam Silvers. I hope you remember me. I am Derrick Thorn."

"What are you doing here?"

He nodded vigorously, as though I were a good student who had asked a clever question.

"I am enjoying the seeing of the animals that are here for their offenses." He spread his arms and turned slowly to the left and right to demonstrate how his enthusiasm included all the creatures in the room.

Odd didn't begin to describe this guy.

"Did you follow me here?" I asked.

"I am coming after you did. Would that be to follow? You told me you were to come to this zoos with the child person of your support."

"I did?"

"Yes, and I am pleased to be here and to witness the progeny of your troubles."

"Well, fine. Look, I've got to be going. Derrick, you have a nice day."

I grabbed Danny's hand and headed for the entrance. Derrick shouted after me, but I didn't turn around.

"I will be pleased to be having the nice day, Sam Silvers," he shouted. "I will make for you the nice day also. I have not forgotten our bargains."

The temperature had dropped, and the snow was falling with new purpose, frosting the parking lot, glazing car roofs and fenders. I dug through the glove compartment's summer detritus (daytrip maps, sunglasses, suntan lotion, an amusement park brochure) until I found the ice scraper.

I got out of the car and went around to the front windshield where I began scraping a gritty mix of snow and ice from the glass. From within, Danny waved at me, grinning.

Back in the car, I had to sit for a minute, catching my breath, as though I'd been engaged in heavy labor.

"Dad, who were you talking to?"

"Just some guy I met recently," I said. I looked at my son. Danny was frowning, puzzled.

I leaned over and ruffled his hair. "Your mom says you've got a girlfriend."

Danny grinned. "Her name's June. She's got a snake for a pet."

"All right!" I turned the key in the ignition. "My kind of woman," I said, as the car moved slowly forward.

I returned Danny to his mother, the usual sense of loss already rising in my chest like black water.

"I tried to call you on your cell," she said. She knelt down in the doorway and brushed snow from her son's hair and shoulders. She looked up at me. "It's out-of-service. Why's that?"

I shrugged. "I decided I didn't need a cell phone."

She stood up for a better, unimpeded glare. "If this arrangement is going to work, I need to be able to get ahold of you. The roads are bad. I was worried."

"Nothing to worry about," I said, squeezing Danny's shoulder. "We had fun at the zoo, didn't we?"

"It was great!" Danny said, and began to catalog its many wonders. Feeling hollow in a superfluous-dad sort of way, I waved a goodbye and headed for the car.

I stopped at the bar on the way to my apartment. If I was going to quit drinking, it might make sense to move to other lodgings, but I wasn't going to, was I? I dispatched two beers and went on up to my apartment, pleased with my restraint. There were two six packs in the fridge, and I drank them, unintentionally. As I remember it, I drank a single beer and didn't wish to leave an odd number of beers, so I drank another one. After that, my reasoning grew convoluted until it occurred to me that drinking *all* the beer in the fridge, thus leaving none to tempt me in the morning, would be a good start on a new, beer-free life.

My phone rang in the chill of the morning, and I burrowed under the covers, a rabbit fleeing the hounds, and I heard my answering machine click on—"This is Sam Silvers. I'm not here"—and Victoria's voice: "Sam."

I leapt from the bed and snatched up the receiver, hearing the fear in her voice, and knowing, instantly, the precise sound of *this* fear, its only possible subject, our only shared and immutable bond. "Danny's gone," she said.

We sat on the sofa while the detectives interviewed us. "On a school day," Victoria said, "Danny gets up at seven. He sets his alarm at bedtime, and sometimes, when it wakes him in the morning, he turns it off and goes back to sleep—not very often, but sometimes—and I have to go in and get him up. This morning the alarm just kept ringing, and when I went in, the bed was empty, and I thought he might be in the bathroom, but he wasn't. He wasn't anywhere in the house."

To someone who didn't know her, my ex-wife might have appeared calm, purposeful, in control, the slight tremor in her folded hands understandable enough. But I could see the care with which she answered every question, as though each word, the order of each word and its cautious articulation, might restore the world to sanity, might, by its intense rationality, restore our son. She would not break down; she would not show emotion. To do such a thing would be to collaborate in Danny's disappearance. She would not, by hysteria, acknowledge its reality.

This I knew of Victoria, and my heart ached for her, as it ached for myself. And

Danny? Does a five-year-old get up in the middle of the night and walk out into a snow storm, leaving his winter coat in the closet? Or does someone come for him, silently, in the middle of a ghostly storm, enter the locked house without any signs of forced entry, and walk away with the boy without awakening his mother, just down the hall and a light sleeper, always restless. How often, in our marriage, in the years we lay beside each other, had Victoria come awake at the sound of midnight rain, tree branches shaken by a wind, a car passing on the street at three in the morning? I'd wake, oblivious to the noises that had roused her but attuned to Victoria and called awake by *her* wakefulness. That seemed a long time ago, in a distant, implausible past.

When I left Victoria, it was to accompany the detectives back to my apartment. I was aware that I was a suspect—or at least an obligatory part of the investigation—and I wasn't surprised or offended by this. How often had an ex-husband, frustrated by circumstances that kept him from seeing his child, simply grabbed the kid and run? They weren't going to find Danny in my apartment, but I guess, if I had spirited him away in the dead of night, I could have stashed him with a friend.

I answered all their questions. Most of the questions were asked by the shorter cop, a black man with high cheekbones and a formal way of speaking, the word "sir" punctuating his sentences with sibilant force. The other officer was taller, older, white and balding, and I noticed he would occasionally interrupt to ask a question his partner had already asked. I guess he was interested in what my answers would sound like the second time I gave them.

After they had been gone a couple of hours, I glanced out the window and saw three uniformed cops out back. A female officer, dark, Hispanic, held the taut leash of a German Shepard as it nosed around the back of the dumpster and then moved out across the vacant lot that separated the bar from the rest of the strip mall. Only then did I realize that I might be suspected of something worse than kidnapping my own son. They might be looking for his body.

And why not? You read the papers; these things happen. Some enraged psycho wants to make his ex-wife regret leaving him, and he knows the way to her heart, he knows how to do real damage.

I made it to the bathroom in time to vomit in the toilet, retching up Victoria's coffee, something in my skull rumbling. Something big, monstrous, had broken free and was lurching around on the deck of a world so fucked-up that the worst stuff, the unthinkable, had a hundred, a thousand, precedents.

I lay on the bed for a while, and then I got up and went down to the bar. Evil Ed saw me and brought me a beer.

"You need to lawyer up," he said. I was impressed: advice from Evil Ed!

"Thanks," I said. "But I didn't *do* anything. I don't have anything to hide. And Danny—" I stopped. Water rushed into my eyes, violently, as though I'd been shoved under a river and was being held there, breathless. I marshaled my paltry resources, gulped the beer.

Evil Ed shrugged and mopped the counter with a grey cloth. "You notice I don't ever take a drink? Might be you are bringing yourself bad luck, swallowing it right down your throat."

"What are you talking about?"

"They got this old Chinese saying goes like this: 'First the man takes a drink. Then the drink takes a drink. Then the drink takes the man.'"

"I still don't know what you're talking about."

"I guess you don't." Evil Ed slapped his palm down on the counter. Beneath it was a white envelope. He took his hand away, revealing my name on the front of the envelope, printed crudely with what looked like black crayon. "This was here on the counter when I opened this morning. I don't know what's inside it, and I don't want to know, and I should have handed it on to the cops when they were talking to me earlier today, but I didn't. It's yours. You do what you like with it."

I took the envelope and turned it over. It was sealed, and too light to contain anything more than a sheet or two of paper. I looked at the front again. All caps: SAM SILVERS.

I turned away from my unfinished beer and went back up to my room. I lay on the bed, my heart beating fiercely. I was afraid to open the envelope. Should I call the police? Perhaps it was a ransom note, and in opening it I'd destroy evidence. Forensics could do wonders, right?

Should I call Victoria? But that would be the same as calling the police; Victoria trusted authority. And I did not. I was raised on media tales of law enforcement agencies that bungled kidnappings, hostage situations, terrorist confrontations. Too often the innocent died with the guilty.

Hands trembling, I tore open the envelope and pulled the single sheet of paper free. A ball-point pen with blue ink had printed words whose letters jumped above and below the baseline, investing the sentences with a childish energy.

This is what I read:

> I have solved your child support! If there is no child there can
> be no support of a child and no need for these moneys of which
> your wife makes you pay and pay! Ha! I am very clever you
> must agree. This is bragging, but it is so. All your worries are
> overboard! I hope to talk to you sooner. —D.T.

I walked around the room, sneezing. My body ached, an aggressive pain, as though I'd been injected with poison. My throat was on fire. I was not feeling well. But that wasn't the problem, except to the extent that this flu-thing might keep me from thinking clearly. Why, for instance, hadn't I said anything to the police about Derrick Thorn? Did I really think it was a coincidence that he had shown up at the zoo? Did I think he was harmless? Did his crooked diction make him somehow childlike, did an innocence of English syntax indicate moral innocence? Hardly.

I sat down on the edge of the bed and tried to recall what I'd thought and said to the detectives. I shook my head to clear it, which made the room waver like an undulating funhouse mirror. At Victoria's... the thought of Derrick Thorn had not *once* entered my mind. It was as though I'd completely forgotten the man's existence. Surely he was too strange to forget. I tried to picture him now, to bring him into focus by an act of will, but all I could see was his stout, pear-shaped body, a silhouette in the Reptile House, his face in shadow, his words... something about Danny... about child support.

How would I describe him to the police? A fat man in black who might, or might not, be sporting purple lipstick and false eyebrows? Wait, Evil Ed must have seen him. Sure. He brought us drinks. He came to the booth with the drinks.

I ran downstairs, too fast, slipping, saving myself from a sudden dive forward by snagging the wooden railing just in time. I stumbled into the bar. Evil Ed was at the opposite end of the bar listening to Rat Lady, who appeared to be wearing a bathrobe.

"Hey!" I shouted, and Evil Ed looked my way, saw me, and nodded, no doubt pleased to be moving out of the range of one of Rat Lady's monologues.

He drew a beer from the keg as he made his way toward me, but I shook my head.

"I don't want a beer. I've got a question."

Evil Ed raised his eyebrows, set the beer down, folded his arms, and leaned back some.

"You saw him. Could you describe him?"

"Describe who?"

"The guy I was talking to the night before last. Fat guy, really pale skin?"

He shook his head. "Wasn't but you. Sitting in that booth, drinking yourself into a coma, talking to yourself, coming out with a laugh every now and then, nothing happy about it, that laugh."

I kept on: "His name was Derrick Thorn. He was some kind of foreigner, spoke funny." *But no accent,* I thought, for the first time. "He paid for the beers."

Ed frowned. "You paid for your beers your ownself."

I had him there. "Then how come I didn't have a tab run up?"

"You did. You paid it at the end of the evening."

"I never do that," I said.

Evil Ed laughed. "That's right. Took me by surprise. You was drunker than usual, which is saying something."

Reflexively, I reached for the beer. This was to be a medicinal beer, a beer for clarity. If I could slow my thoughts down, I could sort them out.

It took more than one beer. A lot more. When Evil Ed came by, he would glower at me, maybe thinking I had more important things to do then sit and drink beer. But I was working, thinking, and finally it came to me: I remembered what I needed, staggered to my feet, and headed back toward the stairs.

Back in my room, I headed straight for the nightstand, grabbed the drawer, yanked it—*too hard*—and it flew out, and all the cards and pens and antacid tablets jumped up in the air and scattered over the floor. *Shit.*

There were a lot of business cards. And, of course, amid this ridiculous surfeit of self-advertising, there wasn't, *of course, of course,* any card bearing the name Derrick Thorn and promising "good deals by mutual bargain" a phrase goofy enough to lodge in my mind even if the creator of that inanity was as elusive as truth at the White House, even if—

I let out a whoop of triumph and pounced on the card. I turned it over, saw the number, and without consulting my fever-riddled and almost worthless mind, I ran to the phone, snatched up the receiver, and made the call.

The phone rang and rang. Having no alternate plan, I was willing to sit there with it ringing. Maybe it rang for thirty seconds, maybe thirty minutes, I don't know. Then the ringing stopped and static rushed in, like an ocean wave over the sand.

I thought I heard a voice. I shouted, "Hello! Hello, Derrick Thorn!"

The tide of static ebbed. "Yes," the voice said.

I couldn't speak. *Who was this?* But then: "Hello Mr. Sam Silvers. You are calling with the congratulations! Yes. Ha, Ha! No more the child support, no more the, how did you say, blood from the turnip!"

"You son of a bitch!" I screamed. "Where's Danny? Where's my son?"

"Do not be worried. I will take the care of it. Trust me, like money in the bank!"

I was squeezing the receiver as though it were Thorn's throat. "I need to see you," I said. That was better, much better than saying I intended to kill him. *Oh, I am clever in a clinch.* There was a long silence, in which I thought the phone might go dead. But some urgent certainty told me I couldn't speak again; I had to wait.

"Yes. Sure. We make the bargains," he said. "Now you help me, one hand scratching the other. I will meet you tonight. Look at your watch and I will look at mine. Just us to meet, no body elses. At ten of the watch tonight. At the zoo."

"What?"

"At the zoo. To bring justice to the penguins."

"What?"

"The penguins, they do nothing wrong. They are good birds. But they have the enemies just the same, the seals and others. I think they are political. I am sure they are prisoners of the government."

I wasn't following this. "I will be there at ten tonight. Is Danny there? Let me talk to him," I said.

He hung up.

The zoo's parking lot hadn't been cleared. The unseasonably nasty weather had closed the zoo for the day; temperatures were supposed to rise tomorrow, and, despite the desultory falling snow, I could see stars sprinkled between the clouds.

The parking lot was a white expanse, blue in the shadow of a bare-branched tree, gold under the single street lamp. I looked at my watch. It was ten minutes to ten. The tracks of my boots were all that marred the lot's smooth surface, which meant that Derrick Thorn hadn't arrived yet.

I waited, shivering with fever and the chill air, my breath coming out in white clouds. Ten came, and 10:05, and 10:10. I could feel the gun in my coat pocket, its weight both threat and reassurance. When Evil Ed's back had been turned, I'd leaned across the counter and retrieved it. I had to hope that Evil Ed wouldn't notice its absence. And if he did? He wouldn't report a missing gun to the cops. But he might figure out who took it, and Evil Ed could be scarier than any cop I'd ever met.

In my room, I'd confirmed that the clip was full, and on my way to this rendezvous, I'd stopped the car along the highway and walked off into a patch of evergreens and indulged in some target practice, sending a bullet into the trunk of a dead pine tree. It worked, and the seven remaining bullets were seven more than I'd need, unless he'd harmed Danny, in which case all seven slugs would be residing in Derrick Thorn's flesh.

I am not a fan of guns, but I know something about them. My father had been a collector, and, when I was young and under his spell, we would bond at the shooting range. I lost interest when he left my mother to run off with his secretary, an ancient, dishonorable tradition (my father's dad had, incredibly, done the same thing). I was fifteen when Dad left.

So here was my legacy: I knew how to shoot a handgun.

At 10:15, I was getting restless, panicky. I walked up to the gate, gripped the bars and peered in at the animal statues and kiosks. The gate swung open, taking me by surprise, and I slipped, falling forward, banging my head against the gate. My knees skidded on the snow-covered ground, but I managed to get my hands in front of me in time to prevent my face from colliding with the icy bricks. I knelt there on all fours, dazed, and then I saw the small blue-shadowed footprints that marched between my hands: the bare footprints of a child. The snow was wet and preserved the imprint of each toe. Were these my son's footprints?

I followed the footprints, moving as fast as I could but not running for fear I'd fall and break something. I looked up, and the Reptile House loomed in front of me, more imposing than I remembered it, its crenellated towers given authority by the night. The footprints were farther apart as they neared the steps leading to the door; Danny had been running—and, yes, I was certain it was Danny now, for no reason except that I knew it to be so.

The footprints climbed the steps and ended at the door. I gripped the door's handle and pushed. *Locked.* No, it moved, but there was resistance. I leaned into the door with my shoulder, and it moved reluctantly. There was light from within, gleaming on the blue marble floor, and black, no red... There was a great smear of blood—another thing I knew with a certainty beyond logic; *blood!*—curving away, under the door, behind the door. I entered the room and closed the door, and the body lay revealed, up against the wall, where I had shoved it with my shoulder against the door.

The security guard had been a small man, but bigger than my son, much bigger than Danny, and he lay curled on his side, oddly crumpled as though thrown there by some vast malevolent force, and in my horror and fear I felt a rush of relief because that's the way our hearts are made and this was not my son.

I turned away from the body and saw Derrick Thorn across the room in front of the glass cage where the penguins resided. Danny stood on his right, and Thorn had his right hand resting on my son's shoulder, a companionable pose. Danny was wearing his Harry Potter Order of the Phoenix t-shirt and bunny pajama bottoms. His feet were bare.

"Hello Mr. Sam Silvers!" Derrick shouted, raising his left hand as though hailing a taxi, his voice reverberating in the high-ceilinged room. "I have been worrying of your coming, thinking you did not keep your bargains."

"Move away from my son," I said, walking toward him. I had my hand in my pocket, my fingers already around the pistol grip, my forefinger on the trigger. Waves of dark power rushed up my arm, filling my heart with rage.

Thorn lifted his hand from Danny's shoulder and waved an admonitory finger at me. "You are angry because the child of your support is still here and you think, 'We had a bargains but it is broken because, before my eyes, the boy is still here.' Do not be full of the worry, Mr. Silvers. I, Derrick Thorn, have always the keeping of my word through time longer than you know."

"What do you want?" I asked.

"I have been thinking of the penguins and our agreeable conversations," he said. "We like the penguins. But they must do something wrong these penguins to be in jail, I think." He lifted his right hand this time and waved it toward the penguin cage.

"Danny," I said. "Come here."

Danny looked up, but his eyes failed to focus. There was no glint of recognition within them. Was he drugged?

"I think," Derrick continued, "that the government does not like the penguins, and I ask myself why this is so, because the penguins are good birds who have only, for enemies, the seals who are hungry to eat them, which is sad but is Nature's Law. 'Why,' I say to myself, 'is the government hating of the penguins?'"

"Danny," I said. "Come to me."

And Danny's eyes widened, and he took a faltering step forward, then stopped again, as Derrick continued, "And then I think of the canaries, the little yellow birdies, and how, in a coal mine, the canary dies and everyone says, 'Oh, the canary has died and we must run away,' and so they all run away and the bosses say, 'The canary is bad. She dies and no one will work. Stop looking at the canary,' but peoples look at the canary and say, 'I quit!' and run away and business is bad."

Danny began to walk again. He raised his arms and walked toward me, arms out, and I walked to meet him. I took my hand out of my pocket, and I lifted him in my arms and hugged him. He pushed his face against my neck and made a small, muffled noise, a child's displeasure at being jostled in his sleep. "It's okay," I said.

"The penguins," Derrick said, engrossed in his rant, "they are birdies like the canaries. They die and people say, 'This is of the global warmings! Stop the global warmings of the factories and the cars and the coal that is burning! The penguins are dying!' And the government says, 'Pay not the attention to these stupid penguins! Don't look at them! They are trouble makers!' And so the governments are putting the penguins in the prisons, you see?"

"Derrick," I said. "I don't know who you are or *what* you are"—I could admit this, to myself, at least—"but I am taking my son and leaving. If you attempt to follow me, I will kill you."

"But we have the bargains," Derrick said. "We must set the penguins free, and I will save you the child support."

"No," I said. "We have no bargain."

I expected some reaction, but my words seemed to deflate him somehow. His hands dropped to his sides and he stared at the floor.

I turned away and walked back toward the door of the Reptile House. When I reached the door, I looked back. He was gone.

The security guard's ravaged body no longer lay in the shadow of the door.

I carried my son out of the building and past the statue of a smiling hippopotamus and out the gate. I unlocked the car door and put him in the passenger seat. I pulled the seatbelt across his chest and snapped it into its latch. I got the scraper out of the glove compartment and scraped ice from the windshield. I noticed that the sky was full of cold light, but finding myself in what appeared to be the afternoon of a different day did not strike me as remarkable.

Danny was waking up when I climbed into the driver's seat. One of his shoelaces was untied, and so I tied it. Something seemed wrong with those shoes—and his winter coat, which, I noticed, was buttoned wrong. I re-buttoned the coat. For whatever reason, the image of Harry Potter, famous boy wizard, flashed through my mind.

"Dad, who were you talking to?" Danny asked, still woozy.

Victoria was angry. She'd tried to call me on my cell, and when I told her I'd discontinued the service, she said, "If this arrangement is going to work, I need to get ahold of you. The roads are bad. I was worried."

And for a time, I remembered none of this. And why should I remember a thing that never happened? Had it happened, had my son actually disappeared, Victoria and Evil Ed would certainly have refreshed my memory.

I drank more, every day, sometimes passing out in the afternoon, and then getting drunk all over again in the evening.

Evil Ed told me about a drink taking a drink, and it sounded familiar. One time, I woke to find the television on, not unusual in itself, but this time cartoon penguins were tap dancing, and I was filled with improbable terror, caught in the sheets, falling out of bed. Unable to find the remote, I crawled to the television and slapped the power button, saving myself from… from what? Not for the first time, I thought, "Maybe I need to stop drinking."

In the newspaper, a photo of someone named Calvin Oster surprised me with another frisson of déjà vu. He had been a security guard at the Hillary Memorial Zoo in West Orange and, it appeared, a victim of gang violence. That explained it: I had, no doubt, seen him at the zoo and—what an amazing magpie, the mind—recorded his image without knowing it. That did not, however, account for my certainty that no inner-city gang had killed him.

Then, one day, somewhere between Thanksgiving and Christmas, somewhere in a stew of bad weather and strangers and a mugging (my own) that I tried to prevent, being too drunk for discretion's better part, I woke in a hospital ward with a bandaged arm and an I.V.

"How am I doing?" I asked a large, truculent nurse wearing green scrubs.

"Depends," she said. "That cut on your arm ain't nothing. But you got bad alcoholism. You been thrashing around considerable, plain out of your mind, and there's an orderly here name of Joshua, real big boy, six feet ten inches. He don't want to come round you. He says you got a demon, need to be exercised."

"What do you think?" I asked.

"I think I should have learned computers, stayed clear of all the misery and blood of this here nursing profession. An alcoholic ain't nothing but a sorry tale unfolding, lessen he gets sober. There's a fellow came in asking about you. I see him sometimes at the meetings they bring here on Tuesdays and Thursdays. He says he'll be back. Hope you don't owe him money."

"Why's that?"

"I wouldn't want to be crosswise of him is all. He got an evil eye on him."

Sure enough, Evil Ed visited me. We went down in an elevator to the second floor and listened to some guy tell his story, how drink had ruined him but then he had embraced the twelve steps of Alcoholics Anonymous, sobered up, and was now the president of a bank.

"What did you think about that?" Evil Ed asked.

"I don't know," I said.

"You could do a lot worse than that answer," he said. He said he'd come around some more.

When the hospital discharged me, I started going around to AA meetings with Evil Ed. I drove. Evil Ed said he didn't want to take his car; it might get stolen, whereas no one would covet my ratty Escort, which was true I guess but hurt my feelings.

We went to a lot of AA meetings, traveling around to church basements and storefront clubs. Some of the neighborhoods were rough, and the AA meetings reflected that, with drunks sleeping it off on ratty sofas and old winos trying to steal a couple of bucks from the coffee-money can. One time a furious fight erupted between two members over which of the AA founders was wiser, Dr. Bob or Bill W. Sometimes I was the only white guy in the room, which didn't bother me particularly since I often thought I was the only guy on the planet. There are levels of alienation, and mine was way beyond racial.

I wanted to drink, but I didn't. Evil Ed couldn't always make it to a meeting, and I started going to meetings by myself. I went to a meeting every day, sometimes two, sometimes three. There was a club called "The Into Action Group" that was within walking distance of my apartment, so I went there a lot.

And if I got restless, I could always go down to the bar and talk to Evil Ed. He was almost chatty on the subject of alcoholism.

"Drinking has got consequences," he said. "You get a tattoo when you're drunk, it's still there in the damned morning. I been sober nine years, and people say, 'You should get that tattoo removed or inked up so it's different,' but I say it's a reminder of the consequences of drinking, and anything that reminds me why I don't want to go drinking again is a good thing."

One day I saw a help-wanted sign on the door of a print shop, and I walked in, talked to the manager, and got a job on the graphics side, not quite the art director position I'd left at BC Graphics, but it paid the rent and required me to get up in the morning.

A couple of days before Christmas, Evil Ed's sponsor was celebrating at a big speaker's meeting, and we went and listened to him tell how he'd wound up in AA and how come he hadn't had a drink in thirty-two years. He was a small, India-ink-colored old man with white hair, and he wore a three-piece suit. After the meeting, Evil Ed and I went to a party someone was throwing for him.

I was feeling my usual alienated, awkward self, so I found a place on the sofa, out of the way of all the hilarity. The television was on, and the station was showing an old Jimmy Stewart movie called *Harvey*. It was about this sweet-tempered alcoholic who is befriended by a giant rabbit that only he can see. I watched the movie with more interest and trepidation than it warranted. It was a harmless, mildly amusing piece, but I was so caught in its spell that I jumped when Evil Ed's sponsor sat down next to me.

"Still a little jumpy!" he said. He squeezed the back of my neck and laughed.

He leaned forward and peered at the television set. "Well no wonder you're jumpy. You're watching a movie about a *pooka!* That's what they call that invisible bunny in the movie, say it's a mischievous spirit. They got that right! But mischief isn't a strong enough word. A pooka can do a world of harm. They are entities that attach themselves to alcoholics, and they can do more harm than a rabid dog. I've seen them destroy a man. They have great power to shift time and space. They can bend reality like a pretzel. It's not uncommon for a drunk to have acquired a pooka or two. Used to be, when I'd go see an alcoholic in detox, I'd get old Sally LaBon to come along with me, and she'd pray and work her potions, and once—you don't have to credit this—I saw a dog-like creature come howling out of a poor fellow's mouth and fly right through the ceiling. No one holds with praying out demons anymore. And I guess the program itself can rid a man of his demons, but I've seen times when some of Sally's righteous magic would do a world of good."

A pretty young woman came up and hugged the old man; such women have the power to dominate an elder's mind, and he forgot I was there. They got up and went off, to dance, I think, and I finished watching the movie. Despite its happy ending, I felt a sense of deep disquiet.

Christmas day didn't go well. I'd bought Danny some stuff that I knew he'd wanted, and he'd been really excited and happy with his presents, but I thought Victoria was acting odd, and when her friend Julie arrived with her husband, I figured it out. Julie and her man had brought another of Victoria's office mates with them, a big-smiling, handsome-and-he-knew-it guy with carefully tousled, jet-black hair.

His name was Gunther, and when he walked in the door, Danny looked up and grinned and said, "Hey, Gun!" and my mood deteriorated. I decided not to stay for the meal, and Victoria accompanied me out the door to tell me that I needed to reflect on my selfishness and think of my son for a change, and Gunther came out, asking if he could be of any help. By throwing the first punch, I may have managed to break his nose, but I didn't win the fight. When I came to, I was lying in the snow on the front yard, a couple of yards away from my car in the driveway. The car's driver-side door was open, suggestively, and I got up, collected myself—no large bones broken—and drove away.

"What happened to you?" Evil Ed wanted to know.

"Christmas dinner with the ex," I said.

"Looks like the turkey got the stuffings knocked out of him," he said.

It took a week of stewing, of feeling ill-used and done-wrong, of wallowing in self-pity, but, finally, I picked up a drink. There was this little well-lit delicatessen with a liquor license, right next door to the print shop. It wasn't some dive filled with comatose barflies. It was clean and bright, you might even say wholesome. I drank a couple of beers there before going home one evening. It didn't seem like such a big deal.

But it's the first drink that gets you drunk, even if that first drink takes a few days to really kick in.

So I was drunk in my room in my underwear. I hadn't gone to the print shop for a week or so. After the second day, my boss had stopped leaving messages on the answering machine. My guess was I didn't have that job anymore.

The television was on, as it often was, babbling away in its news voice, a serious Iraq-Darfur voice over a blighted greyscape, muddy video-people moving around, digital zombies. I wasn't watching closely, but the voice droned on, the non-stop monologue of a demented relative. Then the voice turned hearty, and I looked up for the good-news segment, some cheery thing about toddlers helping the homeless or octogenarians climbing a mountain, human *interest* as opposed to the tedium of human death.

A reporter was standing in front of the zoo in West Orange (I recognized the crenellated towers and little flags). I tapped the remote's volume control, raising the volume in time to hear her say, "….going home. That's right, these penguins, extremely rare, are on their way back to New Zealand where they will be re-introduced to their native habitat. The Fiordland Crested penguin's numbers have been reduced by…"

I stared at the full-screen close-up of this endangered penguin as it tilted its head back and forth, flashing those familiar eyebrows. I reached for the remote and punched the power button.

Where did this penguin dread come from? Penguins were not, generally, considered creatures capable of inspiring much in the way of horror and loathing. Was I losing my mind?

That was a question I rarely asked myself. I knew where my mind was. All right, in the years I'd had this mind, I hadn't always used it carefully, hadn't checked off every single 5,000-mile oil change, hadn't even done a crossword puzzle or read a challenging novel in the last ten years, but was there anything fundamentally wrong with my mind?

There *was* this penguin glitch. But I could work around that. How hard was it to avoid penguins? And the zoo was sending *those* penguins back to New Zealand, in any event, so I could even go to the zoo with Danny… go again, that is.

I was starting to panic. My heart shivered, like some small bird in an ice storm. I heard a sudden loud, thumping sound, and I looked to the door, but the sound was behind me, coming from the kitchen. I got up from the bed; my legs felt boneless but, by an effort of will, I was able to walk.

I reached the doorway to the kitchen and leaned against the frame. The sound was coming from within the refrigerator, a muffled, booming sound. The fridge rocked from side to side, and half a dozen cockroaches skittered out from under it and shot across the dirty linoleum.

The refrigerator's door banged open releasing billowing clouds of grey mist that blew over me, soaking me, plastering my hair to my forehead. I closed my eyes, and when I opened them, he was there. He was wearing a tuxedo, and his eyebrows were now complete circles around his eyes. He'd drawn a small purple patch of mustache above his purple lips. These embellishments still failed to define him. He was a sort of manic blur, a creature my mind refused to bring into focus.

"Derrick Thorn," I said.

He clapped his white-gloved hands. "Yes. I think sometimes you forget me, but then I come back because you remember me, you remember me and you keep your bargains!"

I did remember him. It wasn't like remembering, though. It was like entering a room that held stuff you'd lost, stuff you'd completely forgotten about, and now, here it was. You recognized it immediately, and that was the word, really, *recognized.*

I recognized the bloodstains on his white dress shirt and on his gloves.

"What did you do?" I asked.

"We have the bargains, you remember? You say, 'Forget the bargains. I take my son of the child support and I leave, and no more bargains.'"

He shook his head ruefully, studying the floor. "That is the rule. Is up to you. No bargains? Very well, no bargains, and I go away."

"And now? Why are you here now?"

"Ha, ha! I am always around, but you cannot see me, and so you must drink the alcohol and then—ha! ha!—I am clear as sunshine."

"You came because I started drinking?" I was talking to a supernatural creature, a *pooka.* Or maybe I was talking to my hallucinatory self. Did it matter?

Derrick shook his head. "No, I come because you of the slyness are. You say, 'No bargains!' but then you be the clever one and go through the channels! Yes, the channels! The penguins at the apocalypse they will be of rejoicing and singing your name 'Silvers! Silvers! Silvers!' They will say, 'We be always holding for you gratitude and love!'"

"I don't understand," I said.

"You be joking all the way through, I see. Okay! But the penguins, you give them the freedom! You get them out of the prison and to going home! Hooray!"

I remembered. "No bargain," I had said, and this creature, this pooka, had let Danny go. And now this creature thought that I had set the penguins free and—

"So I keep the bargains!" Derrick shouted. "We make the deals! Is done! Done deal! I see you at the Christmases with the ex-wives of your anger. I confess, I be the spy on the wall. I see your *true* wishes, and I obey them. And no troubles for you, be so assured of this."

"What have you done to Danny!" I screamed, and I lunged forward. Maybe

I expected my hands to slide through him; I don't know what I expected, but my hands found his neck, and his flesh was cold and boneless, and I squeezed, and his neck, like some balloon thing, no, like paste in a tube, his neck collapsed beneath my fingers, and his head swelled, seemed to leap at me like a child's toy, his head round and smooth and big as a basketball and growing bigger, tongue out—*bright blue!*—and teeth every which way like a ragged shark's mouth and, from this mouth, a high, keening sound that was, I'm sure, laughter.

Derrick's head exploded with a bang, so loud that my eardrums seemed to have burst in sympathy. I fell back and watched as Derrick, headless, ran in circles, making a *huh, huh, huh,* sound, flapping his arms like some big water bird slowly building for take-off, before he came to rest with his back to the wall, and slid down the wall, legs straight out in front of him, convulsing briefly, and finally growing utterly still, above him a great swatch of bright red like a thick exclamation point ending in his body.

I went back into the bedroom. I didn't have any plan, exactly, but I didn't need one because the phone rang. I answered it. It was Danny asking if I still planned on taking him to the ice skating rink next Sunday, and I said sure. He wanted to know if I could pick up June too; she lived close by, and it was okay with her parents. "Sure," I said.

Danny said goodbye, and I put the phone down, got up and went back into the kitchen. Derrick Thorn was gone, it seemed, leaving nothing but a lot of blood. On closer inspection, I found a tiny, balloon-like skin. I was able to make out the bowtie, even the tiny, polished shoes. I carried this deflated cast-off to the sink, turned the garbage disposal on, and dropped it down. The disposal made a stuttering, chugging noise, as though gagging.

I walked to the refrigerator and opened the door. The fridge was empty except for a six pack of beer and Gunther's head. I poured the six pack out in the sink, and went back and regarded Gunther's head again.

I don't feel good about this. I mean, I'm not a complete asshole, and I realize that my problems with Gunther weren't Gunther's fault. I could have explained that to that stupid pooka if he'd taken the time to ask.

I do have to say that even in death Gunther had managed to hold on to his deeply refined, disapproving air. He wasn't wearing a horrified grimace; he seemed sort of serene. I guess I'm saying that he didn't appear to have suffered. I double-bagged him in black plastic trash bags and took him down to my car.

They never did find Gunther's body. They won't find his head, either.

I know I had a part in Gunther's demise, but it would be hard to explain the nature of my involvement to the police, and I'm not going to try. You're my sponsor, and I trust you. This is fifth step stuff, and I know it won't go any further.

I know one thing: I'm done with drinking. I'm back to a meeting a day, two-a-day on weekends. I know I'm powerless over alcohol. And I know I don't want to ever see Derrick Thorn again, and I'm pretty sure I won't. Oh, I don't think he is dead. In fact, I'm certain his departure was just another one of his jokes.

Remember that hospital meeting you took me to last week? There was this guy sitting across the room in a hospital gown. He stared at me throughout the meeting, and he headed straight for me when it ended. He looked bad, the left side of his face scraped raw and something seriously wrong with one of his legs so that he moved up and down and left and right like some busted wind-up toy. The worst thing, when he got up close—and he got *close*, his face six inches from mine—was the death in his eyes, the cold-water craziness at the bottom of those muddy, red-rimmed pupils. Or maybe the phlegmy sound of his voice was worse, I don't know. Maybe it was the sum of his infirmities, the weight of ruined days, the dank reek of his breath. No, probably the worst was what he said: "I know you. We got a friend in common. He says, 'Don't be a stranger.' He says maybe he'll see you around, and you can share a few beers and have good times." He shambled off, just another wretched, booze-ruined derelict. But I had to sit back down in a chair and ride out the vertigo, because I didn't think it was a case of mistaken identity.

If I take a drink, he'll be waiting. I'll walk into a bar somewhere. I'll sit down on one of the bar stools. I'll look up at the television, and I'll see a lot of penguins tobogganing on their bellies down an ice slope, and behind me, I'll hear his voice. "Oh, the happy penguins!" he will shout.

Pookas are called up by alcohol, by the darkness that blooms in an alcoholic's soul after that first drink, and with AA and these steps I think I can avoid that drink.

Maybe I'm arrogant, but I'm honestly not that worried about my sobriety. I am, I guess, still a little worried about global warming, and I still wonder what we'll say to the penguins when the end times are upon us.

# ESMERALDA

## THE FIRST BOOK DEPOSITORY STORY

## GLEN HIRSHBERG

"I care not how humble your bookshelf may be, nor how lowly the room which it adorns. Close the door of that room behind you, shut off with it all the cares of the outer world, plunge back into the soothing company of the great dead…"

— Arthur Conan Doyle, *Through the Magic Door*

PROLOGUE

We first heard about them the way one hears about everything these days: on the web. Some self-styled "urban explorer," wired on whatever and driven by transgressive urges most people claim they get over in high school, snuck into his 532$^{nd}$ abandoned building in the Detroit metropolitan area. Fortunately, he brought his digital camera and an extra memory card.

Within hours, the first Flickr page went up. Within weeks, the first wiki/blogspot/Facebook groups appeared. The histories of that initial depository were always stitched together out of tall tales and myths. Someone could have found some Roosevelt School District official and asked, but no one did. Soon, the first Crawlers—no one seems to know where that name came from—began braving the empty streets to start exploring and mapping the place. Not long after that came the first trespassing arrests, and the first disappearances. Before too long, the various strands of lore surrounding the Roosevelt Book Depository had coalesced into a story composed of enough truth to become the truth, as far as anyone who studies such things in centuries to come—and publishes them in whatever digital or ethereal or cerebral format one publishes in those times—will ever be able to tell:

*A public school district, emptying of students as the last desperate families flee the neighborhoods, its buildings collapsing and its funding gutted, quietly takes over an abandoned tire warehouse on one of those Detroit streets that hasn't seen a*

109

*functioning streetlamp since the Riots. There, school functionaries—or, more likely, the gang thugs and drunken ex-Teamsters they pay with the last of the district's cash—begin delivering truckloads of used or never used textbooks, supplies, notepads, posters, maps, writing implements, and whole libraries full of outdated, donated boys' and girls' novels and biographies of presidents and sports stars to what they have already christened the Depository. The plan, originally, is to sell it all, in the hopes of renovating the last functioning elementary school in the area.*

*Then the elementary school closes. The funding is zeroed. The officials disperse back to their homes, which have never been nearby. The ex-Teamsters return to their barstools, the thugs to their gangs.*

*And in their warehouse with its smashed-in windows and gaping doorframes and ruthlessly tagged cement walls, the books and notebooks and maps and visual aides of the former Roosevelt District Schools lie where they've been tossed, in tottering dunes or great lakes of paper. They huddle like penguins in the Michigan winter snows. They curl and molt in the sucking humidity of mid-summer. They are shredded for nests to house raccoons, rats, pigeons, the homeless. They begin to decompose. To sprout weeds and toadstools. To change.*

*By the time that first unnamed explorer finds them, they have lain in that space for more than thirty years.*

After that, less than six months passed before the discovery—or creation—of the second depository, in the mildew-ravaged, fogbound port hangars near Fisherman's Wharf. That one drew an entirely different breed of explorer. There were boho college kids drifting up the coast through the Youth Hostels. Then a team of college professors from Berkeley who wrote the first academic papers and held the first symposium on the subject, which they dubbed The End. If they were aware of any irony in naming a brand new phenomenon that, they kept it to themselves.

By the end of 2010, there were depositories in Chicago, St. Louis, Ft. Lauderdale. They were always urban at first, their foundations usually the refuse from bankrupt school systems. But then the owners of the last used bookstore in Dallas—a giant conglomerate formed by the desperate owners of the twenty-five largest remaining open shops in Texas—announced that they were closing. And instead of holding a final sale, or throwing everything up for auction on eBay or listing it on ABE, they rented twenty-five U-Haul trailers, filled them at random, and dispersed across the country to seed the depositories.

Other shop owners followed suit. It became an ethical stance, a point of pride, a last great act of self-defeating defiance. They would not scrape the last, dreadful pennies from the bottom of the book well. Instead, they would spread their wares like spores, bury them like acorns in the rich, loamy mulch of decomposing language in the depositories, in the hopes that they would sprout there. Grow a new generation, not of readers—people still read, despite what the academicians tell us—but bibliophiles. A healthier, younger subculture.

Then individuals began following the shop owners' lead. Readers who'd spent their whole lives building and tending their personal libraries formulated wills directing their children to wheel whatever they didn't want to the nearest depots and bury them there. Without open shops, and with the online outlets flooded with merchandise that few sought, selling books became a chore, and a fruitless one at that. Easier by far to find a depository and leave everything there, for whoever might want it.

Of course, the depositories didn't mostly attract bibliophiles. They drew squatters, first. Pushers and junkies. Cultists. Fetishists. When the rate of reported disappearances began to climb, the police took to discouraging, then forbidding visiting the depositories. But they never cleaned them out, rarely patrolled them. And people—whatever their reasons—kept coming, though less often and usually after dark.

Meanwhile, the books lay atop each other like bodies in ditches. In breezes, or in a beam of sudden flashlight, they stirred, seeming not so much to have come to life but retained it, somehow. Occasionally, a page even lifted like a waving hand, extending itself toward whatever had disturbed it, or else waving goodbye.

\* \* \*

## ESMERALDA

I'm already in bed when the knock comes. Sitting up, shivering as the twist of sheet and heavy blanket slides from me, I stare at the misshapen shadows stretched over the hardwood floor. It's the snow outside that has given them their head-like humps, their ice-claws. They look like illustrations in a book of fairy tales. Ezzie would have loved them.

I'm musing on that, wondering whether the bottle of rye on the bedside table is as empty as it looks and also whether I've stored another in the bathroom medicine chest five steps from my cot, when the knock comes again. So there really is someone out there, and that means one of two things: the police have finally found something, or Ezzie's relentless sister Sarah has finally found me.

"Just a…" I start, but my voice comes out even thicker than its current usual, and I suck rye-residue and sleep-fur off my teeth and try again. "Hold on."

My feather-robe and fuzzy slippers were both gifts from Ezzie, of course. For the feather-robe and fuzzy slipper birthday party she threw me during our first year in the downtown Detroit loft. Not so long ago, really. Christ, barely three years.

It's my lucky night, turns out; there is indeed a fresh rye in the medicine cabinet, right between the ibuprofen and Ezzie's razor case, which is my only keepsake. She would have approved, if she'd approved of anything I do anymore. The thing she'd held most dear, after all. Unlike most cutters, from what I gather, for Ezzie it was less about the wounds than the weapon.

Uncorking the rye, I take a swig, then replace the bottle and slide the razor case under my robe into my pajama shirt pocket. I turn toward the door, pull the robe as closed as it will go against the constant chill, and as an afterthought decide to take the rye along. In eight steps, I've crossed my lake-rot, one-room efficiency to the front door so I can peer through the fish-eye.

"Knock knock," I say.

The guy out there is big, maybe six-five, in a black coat that looks warmer than all the clothes I own combined, plus black gloves and a black Derby, even. Not a cop. Also not Sarah, unless she's grown a foot and a half and cut off all her hair. Sarah and Ezzie and their dark waterfalls of black curls…

"What?" the guy asks.

"Knock knock."

He stares at the door, and the Lake Superior wind whips up and blows snow on him. It's kind of great, really. A strapping young Oedipus befuddled by the Sphynx. Me. Finally, he takes the plunge.

"Who's there?"

"Exactly," I say.

Pause. Befuddlement.

"Exactly who?"

"Exactly my question."

Poor Oedipus. Big wind. I gulp rye from the bottle I have every intention of sharing with my caller, providing he convinces me to let him in.

"Please," he says, and he sounds nothing like a cop or a vengeful relative or anyone else I know anymore. I open the door. He hurries past me and stands shivering in the center of my all but empty room. Then he starts to unbutton his coat.

"I wouldn't suggest it," I tell him. "It's not much better in here."

Experimentally, he loosens another button. His head almost brushes the bulbous, bug-filled light-fixture that provides the efficiency's only illumination when I bother to switch it on, which isn't often. He removes his hat, and I can't help but smile at the hair, which is black and flat as road tar, with little flattened spikes jagging down his forehead. Little-kid-after-sledding hair.

He takes in my cot, the nightstand, the remaining 365 or so square feet of empty space.

"No…no books," he says, and I understand, abruptly. I consider showing him my iRead, which is the only thing I use now, just to see his face. There's nothing quite like confronting a Crawler with an iRead.

Except I can't quite bring myself to do it. Every time my heart beats, it bangs against the razor case in my pocket. Cold and plastic and empty of Ezzie.

"How'd you find me?" I ask.

"Will," he says. "I'm Will."

"That's nice."

"Can I sit?"

The question cracks me up. I gesture around the couchless, chairless, rugless, room. "Pick a wall."

Instead, he sits where he is, folding his long legs under him and his arms across his chest. Then he looks expectantly at me with wide, shiny eyes. I hold out the rye bottle.

"You're going to need it," I say.

"Not as much as you do," says Will, without guile.

I laugh again, glancing down at myself. Feather-robe with the feathers molting. Slippers with the toes poking through. I can't see my hair, of course, but I can feel it trying to flap off my head in a thousand different directions every time the draft pours through the windows.

I take a gulp, extend the bottle again, and he says, "Look. I'm sorry. I don't mean to intrude. I just…I have to know what you saw."

The laughter evaporates in my throat, and the rye on my tongue.

"Please. I have to know."

"I'm not sure I know what you mean," I lie. My hands start to shake, and I slip the one not holding the bottle into my pocket.

But he's all too eager to explain. "Oh. I see. You probably…I mean, since you don't…since I'm guessing you don't go to the depots anymore, you probably aren't keeping up with what's happening."

"Probably not." Ezzie's lens case beats, and I sit down opposite my guest.

"I just need to ask you one thing, okay? Then I'll leave you alone. At the moment your wife—"

"She wasn't my wife."

"Sorry. Lover—"

I start to squelch that, too, but how to explain? The simple truth was that we'd almost never been physical with each other, and even if we'd wanted to be, the overgrown bramble-hedge of scabs and scarring up both of Ezzie's thighs would have been a serious turn-off for me. I hate pain. The funny thing about Ezzie—it took years of our friendship for me to learn this—was that she did, too.

My visitor hesitates a moment longer. Then he tries again. "At the moment she…vanished…"

Again, he waits for me to chime in. I can't, and don't.

"I just need to know," says Will. "Did you see anyone?"

Careful, now. Careful. How is this supposed to work? How does the story they all tell themselves go? "How do you mean?" I say eventually. "Are you asking were there others with us in the Depository that night? There were." That was true enough, although they'd all been on the ground floor. None of them had even heard Ezzie scream.

My visitor stares at me, and I realize I've played too dumb. And this is no journalist, no private investigator. He's a fellow Crawler. Maybe even fellow ex-Crawler. And he's paid for the privilege, same as me.

Or, not quite the same.

"Sorry," I say. "Habit."

"So," says Will. "Did you?"

I blow out a long breath. My heart bangs, and my skin prickles in the cold.

Ghost-touch of Ezzie's hair across my forearms. "The thing is, I don't really know when it happened. I mean, not the exact moment. Do you?"

Abruptly, Will begins to weep. He wipes the tears away once with the heel of one huge hand, but otherwise he remains motionless. His voice comes out hoarse, as though ice has lodged in it. "Now I do."

In spite of myself—in spite of everything—I lean forward, clutching the rye bottle. "How?"

He tells me.

\* \* \*

"It was going to be our last one, at least for a long time. The St. Paul. Have you heard about that one? It's massive. It's in six abandoned warehouses right on the Mississippi. It stinks. Some local told us the river itself catches fire a couple times a year near there. And there aren't any windows, so the wind blows all the filth from the barges and all the snow and ice in the winter right into the depot. So the books are in awful shape, even by depot standards.

"But God, there are so many. So, so many.

"And they're not even textbooks, mostly. Not shit stuff. This one started just like Dallas. The last used shop owners in the Twin Cities all closed on the same date, in the middle of a snowstorm in the middle of January in the middle of the night. They brought everything they had left to the warehouses. I've heard Crawlers say that for that first year or so, there were even sections. *Local History. True Crime. Classics.*

"Sections. Can you imagine?

"Anyway. This was our honeymoon. It was Bri's idea, even though I'm the Crawler. I don't even think she'd been to a depot before she met me. But she loved the adventure. Dressing up in black, going to those neighborhoods, getting dirty. Hiking between twenty-foot mounds of books with our flashlight beams on each other's faces and all that moldy paper whispering all over the place. Bri used to say it was like sneaking into an old-age home and finding all the residents sitting up in their beds gossiping all night.

"You know how it is, I guess. I don't know why I'm telling you.

"This was summer before last. Our St. Paul night. It was so humid. The river wasn't on fire, but it smelled oily. There's a park on the Minneapolis side where I guess people with no sense of smell can picnic and watch barges, but on the St. Paul side, there's just warehouses and landfills and five hundred million mosquitoes. That whining never leaves your ears. I swear, it's like the world has sprung a leak, and everything is just spilling out of it somewhere.

"For our honeymoon, we'd hit five depots in four cities in four days. St. Louis, Topeka, Lincoln, Wall. You been to Wall? South Dakota? It's right on the prairie, maybe a hundred yards from that famous drug store. It's just a big barn. There's almost nothing in it but maps and dried-out pens and thousands of copies of some old biology textbook about evolution. But we saw a buffalo. It strolled right past the doors while we were inside. One buffalo. Bri loved it."

He stops, and I think he's going to weep again. He seems to think so, too, and keeps one hand hovering near his eyes. But then he drops the hand and goes on.

"At the first four depots—every night until the last night—Bri covered herself completely before we went. Black tights, long black skirt, black sweater, black wool hat. She said it was for germs, and I teased her so hard. My little suburban rich girl. Hardly held a book in her life. Not a real one, and definitely not one anyone else had read first. She always said she'd be sure to send the ambulance when I got diphtheria and collapsed, and I told her I wasn't planning on drinking the books, just touching them, maybe taking a few, and she'd say, 'Diphtheria. Don't say I never told you so.' She had this way of saying things like that. And this laugh. She could make 'Hello' into a running joke. She had so many fucking friends…"

Will is weeping again, and this time he takes the bottle when I offer it. If he sees my hand shaking, he's polite enough not to say so or smart enough not to ask.

Diphtheria. Bri might have had many friends, but Ezzie wouldn't have been one of them. *Diphtheria—virulent and fatal disease causing permanent and irreversible dippiness. No known cure.* That's what Ezzie would have said.

But Will's story has brought it all back. Our first depot night, at the very first depot. The Roosevelt, Michigan warehouse, where the books sprout mushrooms from their ruined pages and the hills of still-shrinkwrapped texts and composition notebooks rise shoulder high and higher, a mountain range of waste paper complete with alpine meadows of pink and green binders and waterfalls of paperclips and liquid paper bottles. Miles and miles of them. There's even weather; the rot and damp create a haze that rises from the ground on warmer nights and drifts about the giant, echoing space, as though the words themselves have lifted right off the pages like little Loraxes and floated toward the window sockets to dissipate over the abandoned thoroughfares of the Motor City.

We were there for hours, sifting things, picking toadstools, staring at the giant graffiti phoenix on the second story wall, massive and orange and angry, rising out of the mural of a broken hardback. I didn't find anything worth having, and Ezzie brought home just one book. *The Scott Michelin 4th Grade Guide to Native America, Eighth Edition.*

That very night, though we got back to our loft after four in the morning, Ezzie began to work. For weeks, night after night, all night long, she kept at it, barely speaking, rarely even retreating into the bathroom for her razor blades. Finally, I came home from work one evening to find the table bedecked with roses, a plate of the Hungarian goulash she never made anymore steaming on the table, and Ezzie's first real masterpiece laid beside the vase for my perusal.

What she'd done was so simple, really. So quiet. At first, I wasn't even sure she'd done anything. Then, as I flipped the pages, past sketches of Sacajawea and photographs of wigwams, I began to notice little smudges that might have been accidental fingerprints from tiny nine-year-old hands, except there were too many, and sometimes they were strewn across the page in unlikely or impossible patterns: half a forefinger here, a thumb all the way down next to the number, a red pen splash in the middle of a chart. As though a spider had stepped in an inkwell and then danced over the text. Then I started noticing the words missing. Some whited away, some stitched closed. Then there were the blotches, bug-shaped, pressed between lines. Some of them, I think, really were bugs. And then the little razor cuts. Thousands of them. If I removed the binding, I half-suspected, and unfolded the whole, I'd find a snowflake pattern in the pages. Or something else entirely.

There was more. I can't explain the effect. It wasn't any one thing, but the cumulative impact. An invented history of a history book no one had read, or would ever read.

That night, while I was asleep, Ezzie went back to the Roosevelt Depot without me. I couldn't believe it when I woke, told her how crazy that had been and how dangerous that place was, as if she needed me to tell her. But she was already back at her work table, hunched over her next project.

I close my eyes, and just like every time I close my eyes, now, I see her there. Crouched in her chair in the middle of the night, cross-hatched thighs drawn up under her nightshirt, unbound hair hooding her, blocking the light of her face from my sight like a blackout shade.

\* \* \*

"I don't know why Bri didn't take her gloves to St. Paul," Will says. "Other than that it was crazy hot. Just putting on my hat felt like dumping a bucket of sweat on my head. We caught a bus across the river. There weren't any stops near the depot, and the guy didn't want to let us off, but Bri chatted him up and got him whistling Janet Jackson songs, and finally he agreed to drop us. He even said he'd come back in three hours, and that we'd better be there, for our own sakes.

"We walked the warehouses, and the sun went down. At first, we were trying everything we could think of to fend off mosquitoes, but eventually we gave up and let the little fuckers feast. We watched the trash barges floating in the middle of the big, brown river. They weren't even moving. They could have been swim rafts, except no one in their right mind would stick a toe in that water, let alone swim it. In that park I told you about—the one on the Minneapolis side?—there was some kind of military band. We could barely hear it. Not the tune or anything, just that there was one.

"The St. Paul side was completely empty, though. There were a couple abandoned cars, one working streetlight, some pigeons hopping around, and that's about it. But there wasn't anything threatening. Not like St. Louis or Detroit or anything. It was just empty.

"We weren't even the only ones at the depot. Not even close. We came around the corner of this huge ship-container building, and there was this old woman sitting in what I guess must have been the parking lot on a little pile of tires. She had a parasol over her head and everything, and a thermos full of lemonade. She gave us some. She had this whole stack of tatty Dickens novels with her. I have no idea whether she brought them or found them. They were just crappy school editions, nothing valuable, but intact. Totally readable. Nice.

"'It's like summer camp in there tonight,' she told us.

"It was more like a library, though. Isn't it weird how books do that? I mean, who established the whispering rule for depots?

"There were certainly plenty of other Crawlers in the warehouse. Probably fifteen, maybe even twenty. It seemed like most of them knew each other. We figured they came in a group, maybe some community college urban archaeology class or something. We kept seeing them in little bunches, picking apart a book pile or kneeling near some torn-up notepads or just standing in one of the makeshift rows, taking it all in. It almost felt like we were wandering in a downtown Japanese garden, not a depot, with all those flashlights everywhere and the moonlight outside and the snatches of music from over the river.

"For the first hour or so, Bri stayed by me. I think the place had been a canning factory, once; there were these little curls of rusty metal all over the place. I picked Bri a bouquet of toadstools, and she slid one through the top buttonhole of her sweater. That's when I noticed she wasn't wearing her gloves, and I almost said something. For a while afterwards, I thought maybe that's what had happened, or why it had happened then. Until I started hearing about all the others.

"Do you think there's some reason it's mostly happening to women?"

He stops again, as though he actually thinks I can enlighten him. As though he and I have anything whatsoever in common, except loss. As if anyone does. There's a bleak joke here, somewhere. Something about there always having been more women readers. Instead of making it, I jam the rye bottle in my mouth. In the draft, in the Lake Superior wind, I hear Ezzie's laughter.

"Well," he says. "What happened is, I found a book. *Adventures for the Young and Adventurous.* I only picked it up because it was still sealed in a wrinkly plastic baggy. The spine almost fell apart when I eased the covers open. But the first story was "The Man with the Cream Tarts." You know it? I didn't. I didn't even know it was Stevenson until…until months later. When everything was over. The title page had so much mold, even I wished I had Bri's gloves. I used my sleeve to turn it. But the inside pages were relatively clean. And right off, I hit one of those sentences: '*He was a remarkable man even by what was known of him; and that was but a small part of what he actually did.*' God."

Will makes a whistling sound. Then he shudders.

"There was a little window way up the wall behind where we were, and I just sat down right there. I started to read aloud to Bri, but it was too echoey. Every 's' sounded like a rattlesnake.

"Bri finally grinned and pointed at the mold on my book. She mouthed, 'Diphtheria' at me. Then she wandered off around a mound of staplers with their tops pried up. As soon as she was out of sight, I went back to reading.

"I read the whole story. By then, the moon had risen past the window, and most of the light was gone. But my eyes had adjusted. At some point, I realized it had been a long time since I'd heard any music from across the river or muffled conversations from our companions in the depot. I closed the book, and the cover came away in my hands like an old scab.

"As soon as I stood up, I finally started to understand how vast this place was. It might be the biggest one of all. When we came in, there'd been shadows, at least, and most of them were moving. But now nothing was distinct, everything was just dark, and I couldn't hear a thing. I felt like I'd fallen asleep in school and gotten locked in overnight. I opened my mouth to call for Bri, then thought better of it and moved off in the direction she'd gone.

"I wasn't going to shout. Not in there. Not yet. But looking for someone in a depot is kind of like looking for land in the middle of the ocean, you know? There aren't any aisles. There's no reason for anybody to have gone one way or another. There's no food court. There's only deeper into the depot, or out the doors.

"My first thought was that Bri had gone out. That old woman with the lemonade would have drawn her. She liked people the same way you and I like books.

"So I went what I thought was back the way we'd come. Only there weren't flashlight beams around anymore, and it's not as though we'd dropped a bread-crumb trail or paid any attention to where we were or anything. I walked what felt like a quarter mile in as straight a line as I could judge, and all I saw were huge piles of paperbacks and towers of old cardboard boxes. I didn't hear anything except my own feet. There was a little light, and it didn't seem far away, just indirect. I couldn't get a fix on the source. Twice, I thought I heard the river to my right and turned down the first passage I came to, only to find another endless depot row.

"By now, I was calling Bri's name. Not too loud. But I was definitely making myself heard. Even to myself, I sounded strange, like some croaking bird in the eaves. I had a flashlight, but I wasn't using it. I kept hoping I'd spot hers. Or anyone's.

"In my mind—I know this can't be true, but I swear I remember every step I took—I walked for an hour. Either it had gotten darker or I'd gone deeper into the depot or my eyes had stopped adjusting, because I could barely even see my hands. A couple times, I put my foot down on a shifting pile of papers and slipped. The first time, I cut my hand bad on a little semi-circular metal scrap. The next, the paper I fell into was all wet, and it stank. It was like lying on lilies in a dead pond. I'd had enough. I opened my mouth to start yelling Bri's name, and then...

"Then..."

For a second, I think Will has stopped because my face has given me away. Of course it must have. I can't seem to get my mouth to close, and the goddamn draft has cemented me where I am, crystallized me like an icicle. He probably thinks it's because I'm anticipating what comes next. Really, I'm just fixating on the scrap of metal, the cut it must have opened in his hand. Little razor cut.

All at once, he's on his feet, looming. I still can't make myself move, but the survival instincts that got me out of Detroit three years ago, that have kept me moving to new places ever since, that launch me out of bed and to the grocery store for rye but also carrots and cereal and winter gloves, has awoken at last. I'm trying to remember where I left the snow-shovel, just in case I need to murder my way out of this room.

But Will, it seems, just wants to weep some more. And why not? What's happened to him has nothing to do with me. Even less than he thinks.

"Look, dude. The woman I saw…This is why I'm here. This is what I'm telling you, the thing I've learned. It's a breakthrough. Maybe the first one. It might help you, too; if you go find some of the others, I can even give you some addresses and—"

"You're babbling," I snap. Now I'm on my feet, too, waving my feathered arms and squawking in my ridiculous voice, hoarse from disuse. "What do you want here? Why are you bothering me? What could I possibly tell you about what happ—"

"I learned her name," he says.

My jaw smacks shut. My arms are still out, as though I'm going to take flight. But I'm frozen again.

"The one I saw. Her name was Anna." He wipes his tears with his long, bony hand. Despite his size, he looks even younger, now. The tiny bit of me that doesn't want to hurl him through my window wants to make him hot chocolate.

"Her name was Anna."

"Tell me," I hear myself say.

"Like I said. There was nothing. Just blackness, and I was bleeding all over myself. I couldn't even find the doors, let alone Bri. I started to get up, and for some reason, I looked to my left. And there she was.

"She was just standing there. Dark hair, kind of bushy, pulled back in a ponytail. Glasses. Pale cheeks, penny loafers, flashlight. Clutching a composition notebook against her chest, as though she'd stepped right off the cover of a Nancy Drew novel. She looked at me for about three seconds, maybe even less. This is the strangest part, except it won't sound strange to you; everyone who's experienced it says the same thing. It was the most peaceful three seconds of my life.

"'Hey,' I started to say, and that was it. Poof. No penny loafer girl. No light. Nothing but depot junk. '*Hey!*' I shouted, and once I'd started shouting, I couldn't stop.

"I have no idea how long I was in there. Not much longer, I don't think. Suddenly, I was at the doors, different doors than the ones we'd entered through, maybe half a block farther down the street. I ran back to the lot where we'd seen the old woman, but she was gone, too. I ran to the first set of doors, and I screamed Bri's name over and over and over, but I couldn't make myself go back in there, and my voice didn't even seem to penetrate. It was like screaming into a mattress.

"Finally, I ran back to where the bus driver had let us off, and the bus came, and the driver radioed for the cops. They got there pretty fast, too, for all the good it did. For all the good they ever do.

"For weeks afterward—months—I kept waking up every night thinking I'd heard the key in the lock. Even now, I sometimes think I smell her. Hear her whispering 'diphtheria' in my ear. I went to a grief counselor, and he said losing a loved one like that, when you don't completely *know*, is like losing a limb. There's a part of you that won't ever accept that she's not there.

"I don't know what made me go back to the depot forum websites. I didn't ever want to go to a depot again. But one night I surfed by, and I started clicking around, and I kept following links, and somehow I wound up in a discussion thread marked 'HAVE YOU SEEN…' which I assumed was about book-hunting. The first post read:

"*Jamie. Twenty-four. Straight blonde hair, beach sandals, pink button-up shirt, gypsum pendant necklace, plastic cereal-box rings on fingers. Vanished Long Beach Depot, 7/22/10.* At the end was a photo of her.

"There were 488 follow-up posts. The 432nd read:

"*Laughing, dark-haired Anna. Twenty-eight. Penny loafers. Glasses. Always looks at you sideways. Vanished San Antonio Depot, 2/14/11.* There wasn't any picture. But I knew.

"Now, you see, right? Now you understand why I'm here. I just want to know she's…somewhere. I just want to know someone's seen her. So please. I'm begging."

He's begging, alright. Weeping again.

But I'm panicking. Trying to dredge up some face from my high school yearbook, someone I can pretend I glimpsed, so he can say *Gee, no, that's not Bri*, and get out of my apartment and let me start throwing my things in a duffel so I can disappear again. He thinks this is news to me, that so many Crawlers have had the same experience. And it is, in a way. The fact that they're seeing each other's ghosts, that the lost ones are somehow finding their way back, but to the wrong places, or else they've become pressed permanently into some new universe of fictional characters who live (or don't live) like dried butterflies in the pages of discarded books, forever who they were at the last moment they were anyone, still accessible to us but at random, a collective cultural memory instead of a personal one…

I'd be fascinated, really. If it had anything whatsoever to do with me.

"Dude," says Will, and now, finally, he's grabbed me. I knew he would. I have that effect, these days, on people like Will. "Please. I don't mean to dredge up bad memories. Maybe there's even hope, have you thought of that? If we're all seeing them, maybe we can get them back? Or at least see our own again. Wouldn't you like to? Wouldn't it be worth anything—*anything*—just to see her one more time?"

I almost break, then. I almost give him exactly what he wants. The whole, pathetic story. Me getting mugged and beaten bloody by some cranked-up street thug who'd been using the Roosevelt Depot as a warm, dark place to freebase. The laughing Crawlers who found me an hour or so later and shoved cigarettes in my mouth and fed me beer and got me on my feet again. Going up that rotted, collapsing staircase in the dark to find Ezzie and show her my new bruises and bring her down to meet my new friends.

Finding her.

How much of it did she intend? That's the only thing that haunts me. Most of it, clearly. Almost all of it. It was the logical extension, after all, of everything she'd done as an artist, but also as a person. That desperate, driving hunger to get inside other people's stories. To leave traces. To cut deep enough below the surface of absolutely everything to determine, once and for all, whether there was anything in there. Or to prove that there wasn't.

It must have taken her hours.

All around her, arrayed in a perfect square just longer and wider than her body, she'd laid paper. Some of it blank and white, some of it torn from whatever texts were near, or maybe she'd picked them specifically. Probably, she did. I'll never know. Even if I saw, I wouldn't remember.

The only thing I will ever remember about that moment is Ezzie lying atop the paper, stark naked in the icy February dark, head tilted almost onto her right shoulder, the spray of her blood fanning onto all that whiteness like great, red wings she'd finally unfolded. Her arms and legs a relief map of tiny and less tiny cuts, each of them flowing into the next, pouring like long, red tributaries toward the great, spurting geyser on her right thigh, where she'd pressed too hard—or exactly hard enough—and severed the femoral artery.

For too long, maybe the critical few seconds, I couldn't move. I couldn't do anything but stare. I thought she was already dead, which was so stupid, I mean, I could see the blood still pumping. That new, red ocean bubbling out of the crack Ezzie had opened in herself and spreading across the paper continents she'd created. But she wasn't moving, didn't seem to be breathing. The color had gone completely out of her; she was whiter than the paper. And she looked…not happy, not even at rest, just…still. I'd never known Ezzie still.

Then she woke up, for the last time. That's when she screamed. She even got out a sentence as I lunged forward. "*Stop it!*"

Did she mean staunch the wound? Or get away from her? I didn't care. Slipping and sticking, I dropped onto my knees and plunged my hands onto the open spot, but they went straight through, her skin was like spring ice stretched too thin. It wasn't even warm inside her, just sticky-wet. I could feel the severed strands of artery, or I felt artery, anyway, gristly bits, but trying to grab anything and hold it closed was like trying to tie silly string. I ripped off my coat and started sliding it under her to make a tourniquet, but that just made her scream louder.

I'm pretty sure I was screaming, too, and then—God knows how, maybe it was reflex—one of her hands shot up and grabbed my arm.

"Lawrence," she snarled. "It hurts."

And I understood. I still think I really did. It was already too late to save her. If I was going to do anything for her, I had to do it then. I grabbed the first thing handy, and it was as though it had been laid there for me. *The World Book Encyclopedia, 1978*. Heavy and frozen hard as a stone.

Lifting it, I looked once more into Ezzie's eyes. I saw the defiance there. The ruthless, obsessive imagination. The unimaginable pain, and—more surprisingly—the panic. Because she thought I wouldn't do it? Because she suddenly knew I would?

I didn't ask. I slammed the book down and smashed in her skull with one blow.

I don't know how long I stayed there. I remember noticing that the blood against my legs wasn't pumping anymore, and stirred only with my own movements. I remember getting cold.

I have no memory of going downstairs. But the people who'd helped me were still there. What a sight I must have been. Beaten purple from my own encounter an hour or so earlier, shirt and pants saturated with Ezzie's blood, fingertips dripping with her brains. Somehow, I must have communicated that they should go upstairs, because some of them did. When they came down, one of them lifted me out of my crouch and said, "Man, you need a hospital."

Then they took me to one. The next morning, the police were by my bed to take my report. It was a long time before I realized they were asking only about the mugging. That they didn't know about Ezzie. I told them they needed to go back to the depot, check the second floor under the phoenix mural.

They found blood there, gouts of it. But no Ezzie. "You're lucky to be alive," they told me the last time they came. I gave them my address, promised I'd let them know where I was, though they didn't ask me to. Then they left me alone.

How did Sarah even find me in the hospital? How did she hear about what had happened? I have no idea. But she's as relentless as her sister was. Also less creative, and less fun. An hour before the doctors discharged me, she called my bedside from her Connecticut home.

"Where's Ezzie?" she said as soon as she heard my voice.

I hung up on her, unplugged the phone, and waited to be released. When I got back to our loft, there were seventeen messages from Sarah. The last one said, "I'm coming."

I packed my duffel. Just clothes and bathroom stuff and a rye bottle. No notebooks, and definitely no books. Ezzie's empty razor case, but none of the artifacts she'd made. I moved to Battle Creek. When I arrived, I let the Detroit police know my new address. The next time I moved, I did the same. If they ever find anything, or they want to do anything about me, I want them to be able to.

But not Sarah. I can't face Sarah.

I look up at Will, who is still staring at me out of his childlike, teary eyes. Child-like, because he still really believes there's more to his story. Maybe there is.

"I'm sorry," I tell him, and I mean it, in my way. "I didn't see anyone."

He just puts on his hat, then. His shoulders have slumped. Shrugging back into his coat, he turns for the door. He's got it open when I grab him, abruptly.

"You didn't answer *my* question," I say.

Now he just looks stupid. Blind, befuddled Oedipus again. Or is that me?

"How did you find me, Will?"

"I…don't remember," he says. "Wait, yes I do. There was an e-mail."

"An e-mail." From a cop, maybe? Someone working the chat rooms and message boards in the hopes of solving something?

"It mentioned you and gave me your address."

"From whom?"

"Didn't say. They rarely do." He takes a step outside in the Marquette wind, turns abruptly back. "I think it came from Arizona, though."

Now it's my turn to stare. "Arizona?"

"I'm just guessing. From the e-mail addy. Phoenixgirl. At gmail, I think."

In my hands, the empty rye bottle seems to throb. Pump. Against my chest, the razor case beats.

"Jesus," Will says, "I'm sorry. I almost forgot. She asked me to give you a message if I saw you."

"A message." Are these tears in my eyes? Is this fear? Am I scared of what Ezzie will do when she finds me? Or heartbroken that her last great effort was a failure, that she couldn't, finally, cut her way in. Or out. Or wherever it was she always wanted so desperately to go.

Am I even sure phoenixgirl is Ezzie? If it's Sarah, then Sarah finally knows.

I'm grabbing the frozen doorframe. It's so cold that it burns my bare fingers. I hang on anyway.

"It wasn't much of a message," Will tells me. "I think it was just…it just said, '*Tell him I'll see him soon.*'"

# THE HODAG

## TRENT HERGENRADER

I still remember that cold October afternoon in 1936 when Whitey McFarland's old coonhound Maggie dragged herself out of the forest, whimpering and yowling. Her skin hung off her sides in red flaps and her eyes rolled wildly. She collapsed on the ground and howled.

All us kids loved Maggie, but not one of us dared go near her, not while she was baring her teeth and snarling. Benny Carper dropped the bat and ran off; Ira Schmidt just stood there staring at the half-dead animal as it pawed the frozen dirt. I tugged on Whitey's sleeve and told him to stay with Maggie while I got my dad—Whitey's dad was a drunk and never easy to find. When he finally nodded in understanding, I took off running.

Tears streamed down my cheeks as I ran past the loggers walking home for the evening. Oswego was a tiny lumber town in northern Wisconsin and our neighbors were almost like family, but even when the men called after me, I kept running. I found my dad in the mill yard picking up tools, and he caught me up in those tree-trunk arms of his. Between panting and sobbing, I told him that something had hurt Maggie real bad and she looked like she might die. He tucked his lips into his beard and his eyes hardened in his usual look of concern. He slung my legs around his waist and had me hold around his neck as he ran home. The wind bit my cheeks. Even now I can almost smell that musky flannel.

Dad banged open the patio door and my mom must have jumped a foot off the kitchen floor. Before she could scold him, he told her to draw up a warm bath as it sounded like the McFarland dog had a run in with a wolf or a cougar, or maybe Mr. McFarland. Without another word, he went to the closet and grabbed an old blanket and headed out again, pausing only to hold the storm door open for me to follow.

It was dark by the time we got back to Whitey's yard. Whitey was lying next to Maggie, stroking her head and speaking in a low voice. I felt a lump in my throat thinking we were too late, but when we got closer I heard whimpering and I could see her flayed side rising and falling. I noticed her fur was streaked with black, greasy marks. Then the smell hit us and I immediately felt sick. I didn't know how Whitey could stand it.

I asked my dad if it was a skunk but he didn't respond. He cast the blanket over Maggie and the wild look came back to her eyes. She yipped when my dad scooped her up and she snapped weakly at his face. He gently shushed her and held her close to his chest as we trotted home.

Maggie screeched when dad lowered her into the tub while Whitey, my mother, and I looked on. Maggie thrashed and sloshed water everywhere, but my father held her in place and she soon gave up. We watched in silence as he picked twigs and bits of dirt from Maggie's wounds. She hardly made a sound. My mother clasped and unclasped her hands beneath her chin and her lower lip trembled but she never said a word. The bath water turned a pinkish hue and then it got so dark you couldn't see to the bottom. Dad peeled the tar-like junk off Maggie's fur and that made the water stink something fierce. He told my mother to heat up more water and then he drained the tub and repeated the process.

When he'd gotten her reasonably cleaned up, he patted Maggie dry and let Whitey and me help wrap bandages around her middle and legs. We covered her with a blanket on my parents' bedroom floor and she fell asleep immediately. Mom said Whitey could stay the night and, after a quick dinner, we piled a mountain of blankets next to my parents' bed and nestled the dog between us, listening to her shallow breathing.

Whitey drifted off right away but I kept my eyes on the dark hump that was Maggie. She whimpered and kicked her back legs as she dreamed, but she never woke. I never remembered falling asleep.

In the bed above me, I could hear my father turning throughout the night.

* * *

"Wasn't a dog or cougar that did that," my father said, and my mother told him to lower his voice.

Morning sunlight spilled through the frost-wreathed window. Whitey snored quietly beside me. Maggie's face peeked out from the blankets. My father paced in the kitchen and, between his thumping footfalls, I caught snatches of conversation.

"Whatever got at her was mean. Real mean. It didn't want to kill her or she'd be dead. It just toyed with her. I'm amazed she survived."

My mother said something I couldn't hear.

"Keep him closer to the house, that's all. Make sure he doesn't go wandering over creation." His clomping boot heels blocked out the rest.

"What do you think it was, Jack?" my mother asked.

There was a long pause before my father answered. "I don't know," and even without seeing his face I could tell he was lying. I'm sure my mother knew it too.

The bedroom door creaked and I snapped my eyes shut. I waited an eternity before opening them again and when I did, I saw my father leaning on the door-frame, staring at me, his face creased, his lips buried in the depths of his beard.

\* \* \*

It took Maggie a few days before she could walk comfortably and Whitey stayed with us the whole time. At age nine, I hardly noticed that my parents took smaller portions to help the food go around four ways instead of three. Dad never mentioned it and neither did mom.

Whitey's dad finally came around looking for him. Whenever he realized he hadn't seen his boy for a few days, he'd stagger the streets shouting Whitey's name and expecting the boy to appear. My father stepped onto our porch and waved Mr. McFarland over. Mom kept us from the door but we still heard dad telling him that "he'd whip his ass" if he so much as laid a hand on either the dog or the boy.

My mother and I watched through the kitchen window as Whitey followed his dad across the yard with Maggie hobbling after them, wrapped in a fresh set of bandages. My dad closed the door, then knelt and gripped my shoulders.

"Did you hear me and your mother talking the other morning?"

"No sir."

His eyes smiled but his lips did not. "Well, if you had been listening, you'd have heard me telling her that I don't know what did that to Maggie. Could be a wolf or some kind of nasty cat but whatever it was, it's dangerous. I can't find any tracks or any other sign, so who knows where the dog found that trouble. Some other fathers and I are going to look around again tomorrow, but I'm telling you Jacob, you stay close to home, you understand?"

"Yes sir," I said.

The humor in his eyes had completely disappeared.

\* \* \*

Oswego was never a big town, not even in its heyday when the lumber industry was booming. The population had been halved after the First World War and dropped by another half during the Depression. Oswego wasn't unique. The same thing was happening all over the country, but us kids didn't know we were poor and the adults never talked about times being hard. It's amazing what you don't think about until you're older.

Telling a nine-year-old boy to stay close to home in a small town defines im-possibility. To this day, I can't honestly say whether Whitey and I deliberately went looking for trouble or whether it somehow found us. We went for our usual Friday after school ramble with Maggie, and we roamed a little further than usual—both of us noticing that we'd wandered more than we should have, both of us understanding that we ought to turn back, but neither of us saying a word. Nine-year-old boys can communicate in such ways.

We were on the winding path near the woods when Maggie stopped and raised her nose.

"What is it, girl?" Whitey said as she growled at the air. She stared across a grass field that separated us from Pochman's Pond. Maggie barked once, then again, then whimpered and looked at Whitey with frightened eyes.

"What do you think it is?" I asked.

In my mind, I can still see Whitey's profile against the steel-gray sky as he stared across the field. The trees on the horizon had lost their leaves and looked like black, spiny fingers reaching for the sky. Whitey's face was set in a frown, his forehead wrinkled beneath his crew cut. His right eye was bruised and his cheek below it shiny, his lip slightly split at the corner. Whitey had told me he'd been hit by a baseball playing catch with his dad and I believed him, or told myself I did. We never talked about Whitey's dad.

Whitey took a step into the long grass. Maggie barked and ran a few yards in the opposite direction. She barked again and then took off towards home.

"Come on," Whitey said, taking a step forward. "She knows the way back."

I swallowed and followed him. The yellow grass rolled like waves in wind. We didn't have to go very far, only a few dozen yards of high stepping through the tall grass before we found it.

It was a dead deer, but unlike any carcass we'd ever seen. Hunting season hadn't opened yet but it wasn't uncommon to find deer parts in a field. Still, we knew no hunter was responsible for what we saw.

The deer had been ripped from the throat down and its insides had been strung out in a wide, rusty red circle around the body. Its skin had puncture wounds as though it had been jabbed with a serrated knife. Three of its legs had been broken, the bones jutting from the flesh like pieces of splintered wood, and the fourth leg had been ripped off completely. Strings of intestine were draped from its antlers, hanging across its face as it stared into the sky with black, vacant eyes. Both the carcass and the circle of matted grass were smeared with greasy, charcoal-black streaks.

We stood gaping at the mutilated carcass as our eyes flitted from detail to gruesome detail. Then the wind dropped and that familiar rotting smell overwhelmed us. I nearly threw up right there but I made it back to the path before I puked up my lunch. I heard Whitey retching next to me.

We ran all the way back to town.

When we reached the McFarlands' tumbledown shack, Whitey's dad was waiting for us, swaying in the yard. "Where the hell you been? Your goddamn dog been wanderin' all over the place," he slurred.

"Dad," Whitey said and tried to catch his breath. "We saw something. Out in the field. A dead deer."

"Get home," he said to me without sparing a look. He grabbed Whitey's jacket collar with one hand and tugged off his belt with the other. "The dog's been howlin', gettin' on people's property. Makes me look bad."

Whitey looked at me with the same terrified expression Maggie had when she caught a whiff of the deer. I looked back, helpless.

Whitey's dad jerked his son towards the house. He fixed a hard, glassy gaze on me and said a single word: "Get." It was every inch a threat as a command.

I sprinted home, my lungs burning from swallowing the chill air and choking on my tears.

My dad's mouth drew into that thin, straight line when I told him what happened. I didn't know what bothered him more, the dead deer or Mr. McFarland. He knew Whitey's dad from when they both worked at the mill. Once I asked my dad what was wrong with Mr. McFarland, and he told me that Whitey's mother had run off with some traveling snake oil salesman and his father had been living in a bottle ever since. The mill was always looking for excuses to trim payroll and it wasn't long before they gave Mr. McFarland his walking papers. Then things got worse.

That's no excuse and I still hate him for how he treated Whitey, but that doesn't make what happened next any easier to talk about.

\* \* \*

That next morning, my dad formed a posse armed with rifles, hatchets, hoes and they headed out towards the woods. They trudged back at dusk, weapons slung over their shoulders, heads bowed. I remember my mother waiting on the porch working her hands and my dad giving her a slow, apologetic shake of the head when he got home.

Weeks passed, and the temperature plummeted, too cold to even snow. Eventually, the fervor died down and parents slowly loosed the reins on their children. The escorts to and from the schoolhouse ended, but not before my parents sat me down at the kitchen table and told me, in no uncertain terms, that I was to stay within earshot of home at all times. Under no circumstances was I to wander outside of town. Not in the woods, not down by the stream, and nowhere near the pond. My dad shook one calloused palm and said he'd give me the hiding of my life if I disobeyed and, even though he'd never as much as spanked me, I believed him. I'd wager the same conversation transpired in every kitchen in Oswego.

Yet sometimes trouble comes out of nothing. We weren't doing anything wrong, just playing baseball with Ira, Benny, and Whitey in his yard like always. We had a diamond worn into the grass and Whitey's dad didn't care if we tore up the yard sliding into the bases. He was never around anyway to yell if the ball hit the house and we could be as loud as we liked, so we played there most often.

Ira Schmidt was two years older than Whitey and me and could really knock the cover off the ball. He used to say he could hit it even further in the cold air. At his turn at bat, he cracked the ball into the weeds behind Whitey's house where they grew thick and deep before tapering off at the edge of the forest. We spread out looking for it but it was Whitey who made the big find, and I don't mean the baseball. I wish to God it had been me or one of the other boys, but it was Whitey.

I was parting handfuls of frozen grass when I heard Whitey say in a flat voice, "A boot." He lifted a brown workman's boot from the grass. I glanced over and went back to searching when I heard his strangled gasp. I looked up and saw that the boot still had a foot in it; it terminated at the ankle in a maroon stump with a circle of white bone, sheared cleanly like one of the fancy steaks in the butcher's shop.

Whitey's girlish scream sounded comical and for a second I thought it was a gag, but then his eyes fluttered back and the boot slipped from his fingers as he collapsed. I tried to move but I couldn't, transfixed by the boot resting on its side on the bloodstained grass.

"What is it?" Benny asked, but my mouth wouldn't work. I looked around and in a moment of stark clarity, I couldn't believe we hadn't seen the clues. They were faint but patently obvious now. The ruffled swaths of grass. The rust-colored ring. The scratch marks in the dirt where something had been dragged into the forest. My shocked brain wasn't fully registering what I was seeing, but I suppose I knew even then that what had been dragged was Whitey's dad.

My memory gets foggy after that. I remember some women shouting, hands grabbing me by the shoulders, and Benny's mom's face in mine asking me what happened. I just pointed to the boot in the grass. Then I remember being dragged back towards town while two other women struggled to lift Whitey to his feet.

Then my mother was there, and she had me under the arm. She led me and Whitey, now conscious and stumbling under his own power, back to our house. She had just seated us at the kitchen table when the porch door flew open and my father barged through. He grabbed his padded flannel and the rusty spade we used to feed the stove. My mother asked what was happening. "We're going after it. Stay put," he said and disappeared out the door.

My mother paced the kitchen. None of us spoke. She put her arms around our heads and drew us to her while she murmured something about things being okay. "Whitey, your ears are freezing," she said and placed a hand on his face. "Your cheeks, too. Let me grab a blanket." She disappeared into the bedroom.

I looked at Whitey who was staring past me. He leaned so far to one side I thought he might fall off his chair. "Whitey," I said in a small voice. "You okay?"

He focused on me as if just realizing I was there, then shook his head. We sat in silence for another moment and I heard my mother quietly curse as she rummaged through the linen closet for the heavy blankets we only broke out in the deepest winter.

Whitey's eyes met mine again, then he bolted from his chair like a frightened deer. The porch door hadn't even had a chance to slam shut before I was after him, my mom's shouts drowned out by the wind in my ears.

"Whitey, stop!" I yelled as I ran but I knew he wouldn't, and honestly, I didn't want him to. Chasing him would be my excuse to follow the hunting party, and I knew it.

Whitey raced past his house and the field and I was on his heels as he headed into the trees. As we reached the far end of the forest where it opened to the pond, we heard men shouting and the crash of a shotgun.

Whitey stopped dead at the frozen edge of Pochman's Pond and put his hands on his knees to catch his breath. I skidded to a halt behind him and together, silent except for our panting, we watched the events unfold.

A dozen men stood in a wide semicircle twenty yards away out on the ice. All of them wielded some type of make-shift weapons—hatchets, hoes, Benny Carper's dad and two others carried shotguns—and they surrounded a broad, four-legged creature. At first, I thought it was a black alligator, but I knew alligators weren't that big and didn't have long snaking tails with a spade at the end. Plate-sized ridges ran the length of the creature's back.

The winter air exploded with a confusion of sounds: the men shouting over each other, the creature's low growl like an engine that won't catch, and the deep groan of the ice under their weight. The tips of the men's weapons glanced off the thing's hide with metallic clanks. Its tail whipped high and low to fend off the attackers; it swept out the feet of one man. The creature scrabbled to attack him but thankfully its claws couldn't find purchase on the ice. Mr. Carper fired the shotgun into the creature's side and it jerked its head around, seemingly more at the sound than in reaction to being shot. And that's when we saw its face.

The face looked hauntingly human despite its oblong shape, the mouth crowded with sharp teeth, and its black leathery skin. The eyes burned like embers and there was an unmistakable intelligence behind them, perhaps even cunning. Worse, the face was grinning in pure malice. The creature's eyes locked on us across the pond and I swear it licked its lips. My stomach fell into my shoes and I felt sick.

Mr. Carper shot the thing point-blank in the face and it just flapped its head, like a dog getting water out of its ears. It whipped its tail over its head at Mr. Carper, who fell onto the ice. The spade came down and crushed the ice between his legs instead of his skull.

We heard a rumble we thought was thunder, then dark cracks spider webbed across the ice . The men bolted for shore but they couldn't get more than a few yards before the whole ice sheet collapsed with a sharp crack and groan, dumping them all into the water in a cacophony of shouts and splashes. The thing sprayed a plume of water like a whale then sank out of sight.

"C'mon Whitey," I screamed, barely noticing he hadn't followed. I found a downed branch and extended it into the open water where the men half-swam, half-pulled themselves towards shore. The ice broke beneath me and I plunged into the pond up to my waist. Air burst from my lungs with the shocking cold, but I managed to hang on as the men used the branch to pull themselves to shore.

"W-what are you d-doing here?" my father stuttered as he stood shivering, his beard already frozen. He turned to look at the hole in the ice. No bubbles broke the surface, no signs of movement in the water. "C'mon," he said and grabbed my collar with a wet and freezing hand.

We stumbled back, each man's family collecting him at the edge of the forest. "Come with us, Whitey," dad said in a tone that brooked no argument. Whitey paused to look at the shack where he lived, then to the long grass where he'd found his father's foot. My dad caught Whitey under his arm and held him close.

Even though my dad was a block of ice by then, Whitey didn't pull away.

\* \* \*

Us kids were under complete lock-down for the next week. No school, no leaving the house, no nothing. My dad said they never found any sign of Mr. McFarland, but parents sometimes forget kids are neither stupid nor blind. They couldn't hide the black tendrils of smoke rising from the field bordering the forest and we all knew it wasn't dried leaves they were burning.

Oswego hunkered down for the winter like northern towns do and the months passed, cold and harsh. Whitey spent time with a number of different families, ours the most, until one clear, freezing February morning the county sheriff arrived with a wiry man who said he was Whitey's uncle, come to bring Whitey to live with him in Wausau. You could tell Whitey didn't want to go but those were lean times for everyone and getting leaner, and no one wanted to interfere with what boiled down to a family matter.

My dad wore a pinched expression but, in the end, said nothing. He had his hands on my shoulders as I waved to Whitey who looked back out the police car's rear windshield. Unfortunately, it wouldn't be the last time he saw the world from that perspective.

The mill closed that March and we moved to Marquette, Michigan before the thaw. Just a few years later, my dad would be called up for World War Two and killed in combat. I never got the chance to ask him about that afternoon at Pochman's Pond.

As a teenager, I wrote Whitey McFarland a letter to see what he remembered from that November afternoon. Six months later, Whitey's uncle responded with a curt note informing me Whitey had been sent to the juvenile home in Rhinelander and wasn't accepting letters. The note was accompanied by my envelope, still unopened.

\* \* \*

The years rolled by, many of them hard, but Mom and I survived. I went to college, met a lovely girl, and we had a son. He's grown now with a family of his own. I've been blessed with a life with far more ups than downs. Through all those years, I tried not to think about that afternoon at the pond but it haunted me across those years. I always felt that faded memory lurking deep in my mind, waiting to surface.

And it finally did.

For my eightieth birthday, my granddaughter gave me an encyclopedia of Wisconsin folklore. Quite a tome, it became a nightly ritual of mine to sit in my favorite reading chair under a halo of light, browsing deep into the night about Bigfoot, the haunting of Science Hall on the UW campus, and the ghoulish history of mass murderers Ed Gein and Jeffrey Dahmer.

Late one night, unsuspecting, I turned a page and I felt my heart seize. Staring up at me was the likeness of the thing from Pochman's Pond—those same evil eyes sizing me up, the fang-filled mouth, the twisted grin.

My pajamas clung to my sweaty skin and I couldn't catch my breath. I forced myself to calm down, to take deep breaths and relax before I gave myself a heart attack. I had told myself that I wasn't in danger, that the house was still dark and quiet, that my wife was still upstairs peacefully asleep; that we were safe. The damn thing hadn't gotten me then, and it sure as hell wouldn't get me now.

I composed myself enough to read the page. The thing was a hodag, a mythical creature of the Wisconsin northwoods. Legends say the beast rose from the ashes of a lumberjack's ox whose body had been burned for seven years to cleanse it of the profanity the loggers had hurled at it. The depiction of the creature wasn't quite right, a little too cartoony, but it was damn close. They got the eyes and the grinning mouth perfect though, and that was enough.

I read and reread that page for God knows how long before I set the book down with a trembling hand and, without knowing exactly why, I wept. Unbidden, memories rushed back. Memories of Whitey, his father and mine, and how you can't always catch the curveballs life throws at you. We all knew the thing hadn't been killed that day—it just sank into Pochman's Pond and crawled back into the dark.

I dried my eyes, turned off the light, and went upstairs, wincing with each creak of the steps. I crept into my own bed and slid a hand on my wife's warm stomach. She murmured something and I kissed her silver hair. I drifted off telling myself my family was warm, happy, and safe.

\* \* \*

That night I dreamt of the northwoods in the splendor of autumn. I was skipping stones on Pochman's Pond with my grandkids beneath a canopy of colored leaves. I keep telling them to get away from the water's edge but they don't listen.

Whitey McFarland's there too. He's still only nine years old and he's wearing his swimsuit. He dares no one in particular to race him out and back, and wades into the pond up to his knees.

I shout for Whitey to stop but it's a perfectly warm, sunny day and the pond is dark and cool. Suddenly, I feel very small and I start to panic. I shout again.

Whitey doesn't say anything. He doesn't even turn to look at me. He just watches the breeze rippling the water's surface.

# VERY LOW-FLYING AIRCRAFT

## NICHOLAS ROYLE

From a distance of thirty yards, Ray saw immediately what was happening. There was Flynn, in his new full uniform, which the two older men, in engineer's overalls, would have insisted he wear. Ray stepped back behind the trunk of a palm tree, observing.

Several ginger-cream chickens pecked in the sand, looking for seed that the two engineers, whom Ray recognised as Henshaw and Royal, would have scattered there. Ray could see Henshaw talking to Flynn, explaining what he needed to do, Flynn looking unsure in spite of the new recruit's desire to please. Henshaw was a big man with red hair cut severely short at the back and sides of his skull. Royal—the shorter of the two engineers, with a greased quiff—who had been bending down watching the chickens, stood up and took something from the pocket of his overalls, which he handed to Flynn.

Ray caught the flash of sunlight on the blade.

Henshaw mimed the action Flynn would need to copy.

Ray considered stepping in, stopping the ritual, for it *was* a ritual. He hadn't had to suffer it on his arrival on the island, but only because he had been a little older than Flynn on joining up. Henshaw and Royal were younger than Ray, which would have been enough to dissuade them.

But for the time being, he remained where he was.

Flynn, his golden hair falling in front of his face, took the knife in his left hand. With his right, he loosened his collar. He would have been very warm in his blue airman's uniform, and he clearly wasn't looking forward to using the knife. His shoulders drooping, he made a last, half-hearted appeal to the two engineers. Henshaw made a dismissive gesture with his hands as if to say it wasn't such a big deal. It was just something that had to be done. The squadron had to eat.

Flynn tried to catch one of the wary chickens, but found it difficult to do so and hang on to the knife at the same time. Henshaw swooped down, surprisingly quickly for such a big man, and grabbed a chicken. Flynn bent over beside him and switched the knife to his right hand, looking set to do the job while the bird was held still, but Henshaw indicated that Flynn needed to hold the chicken himself. He passed it over and swiftly withdrew. Royal took several steps back as well.

Flynn secured the chicken between his legs and encircled its neck with his left hand, then glanced over his shoulder for encouragement. Royal gave a vigorous nod, and as Flynn turned back to the chicken the two older men exchanged broad smiles.

Ray knew this was the moment at which he ought to step in, but still he made no move from behind the tree.

To his credit, Flynn got through the neck of the struggling chicken with a single slice and leapt back as a jet of red spurted. Liberated, the chicken's body spun, spraying the airman with arterial blood until his uniform was soaked. The recruit dropped the severed head as if it were an obscene object, which of course suddenly it was.

The butchered bird ran round in ever decreasing circles still pumping out blood. At a safe distance the two engineers laughed. Ray glared at them as he approached. He put a protective arm around the shoulders of Flynn and muttered comforting words, but the young airman, not yet out of his teens, seemed traumatised.

"Come on," said Ray. "They were just having a bit of fun." Though he didn't know why he should excuse their behaviour.

Flynn wouldn't move. The chicken's body had given up and had slumped to the sand. But it was the bird's head that transfixed Flynn. It twitched. The eye moved in its socket. A translucent film closed over the eyeball and then retracted again.

"It can still see," Flynn whispered.

"It's just a nervous spasm," Ray said.

"No, it's still conscious," said the teenager. "Look."

As they watched, the bird blinked one more time, then the eye glazed over and it finally took on the appearance of death.

Ray looked over his shoulder and saw that Henshaw and Royal were now a long way down the beach, their dark overalls shimmering in the heat haze, which caused their bodies to elongate and become thinner, while their heads became distended, like rugby balls hovering above their shoulders.

Insulated from the pain that had cut him off from England for ever, Raymond Cross prospered in the Royal Air Force, which had a small presence on Zanzibar. Prospered insofar as he seemed to find satisfying the narrow range of tasks assigned to him. He ticked boxes on checklists, got his hands dirty in the engines of the few planes that were maintained daily. They were taken up only once or twice a week, to overfly the island and to hop across to Mombasa to pick up supplies. Ray was allowed to accompany the tiny flight crew if he wasn't busy:

he could be made useful loading and unloading.

In his spare time in the barracks, Ray listened to jazz records on an old gramophone the base commander had picked up on a trip to the mainland. Milt Jackson and Thelonious Monk riffed until the needle was practically worn away. No one could say where the records had come from. Some nights he got out of his head on Kulmbacher lager they had flown over from Germany. It was dropped at night, illegally, in wooden crates that burst open on the beach, scattering the ghost crabs that rattled about on the foreshore. He drank steadily—sometimes with the other men, usually on his own—and spoke to none of his comrades about his reasons for joining the RAF.

When the conditions were right—and they usually were between June and March, outside the rainy season—and Squadron Leader William Dunstan was piloting the mission, they would take a small detour before heading for the airstrip. On returning from Mombasa or a tour of the island, Billy Dunstan would take the Hercules north to Uroa where he would swoop down over the beach and buzz the aircraftmen and flight lieutenants stationed there. Ray was soon organising his time around Dunstan's schedule, so that when the flamboyant squadron leader was in charge, Ray was invariably waiting at the airstrip to go up with the crew. Dunstan ran a pretty relaxed ship.

The men at Uroa station would hear the Hercules's grumbling approach rise above the constant susurration of the wind in the palms and run out on to the beach waving their arms. Dunstan would take the plane down as low as possible; on occasion he even lowered the landing gear and brushed the surface of the beach a few hundred yards before or after the line of men, raising huge ballooning clouds of fine white sand.

After his pass, the line of men on the beach applauding as they turned to watch, Dunstan would tilt to starboard over the ocean and climb to a few hundred feet before doubling back and flying down the coast to the base at Bwejuu. Every time, Ray would be standing hunched up in the cockpit behind Dunstan for the best view. The squadron leader enjoyed showing off; Ray's enjoyment lay in watching Dunstan's reaction as he risked going lower and lower each time, but there was more to it than that. There was another element to it for which Ray had yet to find expression.

The next day, during a break from duties, Ray saw a lone figure standing by the shoreline. He wandered over, clearing his throat once he was within earshot, and came to a halt only when he had drawn alongside. The two men looked out at the horizon. Some three hundred yards out, the reef attracted a flurry of seabirds. They hung in the air as if on elastic, a short distance above the water.

"I'm sorry I didn't get there sooner," Ray said. "In time to stop them, I mean."

Flynn shrugged. "They'd have got me another time," he said.

"Probably. No harm done, eh?"

"I was scrubbing away at my uniform for at least an hour this morning," the younger man said.

Ray felt the breeze loosen his clothes and dry the sweat on his body.

"I've heard stories," Flynn continued, "about beheadings in the Mau Mau Uprising. They used machetes. They'd cut someone's head off and the eyes would still be blinking, still watching them. What must that be like? Still being able to see."

They watched the horizon without speaking for a few moments. Ray broke the silence.

"I'm not sure you should be left alone with your thoughts."

They watched the rise and fall of the seabirds, at this distance like a cloud of midges.

"Do you leave the base much?" Ray asked.

"I go to Stone Town…"

Ray turned to look at the young airman. He was wearing fatigues and a white vest. His eyes, which didn't deviate from the view in front of him, were a startling blue. He didn't seem to want to elaborate on what he got up to in Stone Town. Ray bent down and picked up a shell. He turned it over and ran his thumb over the ridges and grooves.

"There you go," he said, handing it to Flynn. "Don't say I never give you anything."

Ray had joined the RAF as a way of getting out of Britain in the early 1960s. His wife had died giving birth to their only child and it would have broken him if he hadn't got out. Some say it did break him anyway. Others that it just changed him. The pinched-faced moralisers among his family said it had no effect on him: he'd always only ever been in it for himself. These are the people you might have expected to have got their heads together to decide who was best placed to offer the infant a home, until such time as his father tired of the tropics. But they didn't exactly fight among themselves for that right.

Ray himself had been born into a community so tightly knit it cut off the circulation. His own domineering mother and subjugated father, all his uncles and aunts, were regular church-goers. Some gritty, northern, unforgiving denomination, it would have been, where prayer cushions would have been considered a luxury.

It wouldn't have mattered who Ray brought back to the house in Hyde as his intended, they weren't going to like her. They'd have looked down on her whatever she was, princess or pauper. Not that they had any money of their own to speak of, they didn't. But pride they had.

Perhaps Ray bore all of this in mind when he took the Levenshulme bingo caller to the Kardomah in St Anne's Square. *Victoria*. Vic, Ray called her—his queen. She may have been only a bingo caller to the family, but Ray worshipped her. She turned up in the Cross household one blustery night in a new mini-skirt.

"Legs eleven," he blurted out, ill-advisedly. "Your father and I will be in here," his mother said, frowning in disapproval and pointing to the front room; Ray's father shuffled obediently. "You can sit in 't morning room," she said to Ray.

The morning room, an antechamber to the kitchen, was dim and soulless in the morning and didn't get any lighter or warmer as the day wore on. Somehow it failed to benefit from its proximity to the kitchen. No one used it, not even his mother, despite her being temperamentally suited to its ambience.

Ray and Victoria's options were few, if they had any at all, and sticking around wasn't one of them. Ray got a job with the Post Office in Glossop, so they packed what little they had and moved out along the A57. He worked hard and earned more than enough for two, so that when the first signs of pregnancy appeared, they didn't think twice. It didn't matter that the baby hadn't been planned; it was welcome.

After the birth, Ray held the tiny baby once, for no more than a few seconds. Victoria lost so much blood, the hospital ran out of supplies. She suffered terribly for the next twelve hours, during which time Ray stayed by her side. Twice the nurses asked him if they'd thought of a name for the baby. Each time he waved them away.

When the RAF asked Ray his reasons for wanting to join up, he said he liked the uniform and had no objection to travelling, the latter being an understatement. They sent him to the island of Zanzibar, thirty miles or so off the coast of Tanganyika in East Africa. A greater contrast with east Manchester must have been hard to imagine. The family declared him heartless and cruel, swanning off to a tropical island when he should have been mourning his wife and looking after his kid. Their hypocrisy galvanised him, and he brought his departure date forward. He needed to put some distance between himself and his family in order to mourn. Five thousand miles wasn't bad going.

Ray wasn't surprised when Billy Dunstan invited the two girls to join them on a flight around the island. Joan and Frankie were English nurses working in a clinic in Zanzibar Town. Dunstan and one of his fellow officers, Flight Lieutenant Campbell, had met the pair one evening on the terrace of the Africa House Hotel where all the island's expats went to enjoy a drink and to watch the sun go down in the Indian Ocean.

On the agreed afternoon, the nurses were brought to the base at Bwejuu by an RAF auxiliary. Ray looked up from polishing his boots and saw all the men stop what they were doing as the women entered the compound. Henshaw stepped forward with a confident smirk, wiping his hands on an oily rag. The other men watched, with the exception of Flynn, whose uniform still bore one or two of the more obstinate traces of the engineers' ritual humiliation of him on the beach. The airman coloured up and looked away.

Dunstan appeared and made a swift assessment of the situation.

"Henshaw," he said, "shouldn't you be driving the supply truck up to Uroa?

You'll have it dark, lad. Take Flynn with you."

Flight Lieutenant Campbell had been called away to deal with a discipline problem on Pemba Island, Dunstan explained to the two women. Because of the nurses' schedule, there wouldn't be another opportunity for a fortnight and Dunstan didn't want them to go away disappointed. Ray watched him stride out across the landing strip to the Hercules, his white silk scarf, an affectation only he had the dashing glamour to carry off, and then possibly only in Ray's opinion, flapping in the constant onshore breeze. Joan trotted behind him. Frankie stopped to fiddle with her heel and while doing so looked back at the men watching from the paved area outside the low huts. Ray, who was among those men, was struck for the first time by her resemblance to Victoria. When she smiled, it seemed directed straight at him. A nudge in the ribs from Henshaw confirmed this.

"Didn't you receive an order?" muttered Ray.

"Yes, Corporal," Henshaw replied sarcastically.

Ray looked away from Henshaw towards Flynn, who had also been watching the exchange of looks between Ray and Frankie with, it seemed to Ray, a look of hurt in his blue eyes.

"Corporal Cross," came a cry from the airstrip. "Get your flying jacket."

"Now it's your turn to be ordered about," said Henshaw. "Lucky bastard."

As Ray left to join Dunstan and the two girls, he passed close to Flynn.

"You'll get your chance, son," he said quietly.

As they taxied to the beginning of the landing strip, Ray looked out of the cockpit to see the fair head of Flynn bobbing into the supply truck alongside Henshaw.

"Hold tight, ladies," shouted Dunstan over the noise of the four engines as the plane started to rumble down the runway.

They flew across the island to Zanzibar Town. Dunstan pointed out the Arab Fort and the Anglican cathedral. Frankie spotted the clinic where she and Joan worked on the edge of the Stone Town. Dunstan turned the plane gently over the harbour and flew back over the so-called New City in a south-easterly direction so that he was soon flying parallel with the irregular south-west coastline.

"Uzi Island," shouted Dunstan as he pointed to the right. The two girls leaned over the back of his seat to get the best view. Ray watched the way their hips and bellies pressed into Dunstan's shoulders. The squadron leader seemed to sit up straighter, flexing the muscles at the top of his back, as if maximising the contact between them, his hands maintaining a firm grip on the controls.

"Where's that?" asked Joan, pointing to a tiny settlement in the distance.

"Kizimkazi. Not much there. Hang on." So saying, he banked sharply to the left, unbalancing both girls, who toppled over then picked themselves up, giggling. Ray watched a twitch of pleasure in Dunstan's cheek. Frankie smiled hopefully in Ray's direction. He smiled back instinctively, but looked away somewhat awkwardly at the same time.

They crossed the southern end of the island, then kept going out to sea before turning left again and gradually describing an arc that would eventually bring the plane back over land north of Chwaka Bay. The horizon—an indistinct line between two blocks of blue—had become a tensile bow, twisted this way and that in the hands of a skilled archer: the plane itself was Dunstan's arrow. Ray watched the squadron leader's hands on the controls, a shaft of sunlight edging through the left-side window and setting the furze of reddish hairs on his forearm ablaze.

The RAF station at Uroa came into view: a couple of low-lying buildings in a small compound, a handful of motorbikes, a Jeep and one truck that Ray surmised would be the supply vehicle driven there by Henshaw and Flynn. As they overflew the station, several men appeared from inside one of the huts, running out on to the beach waving their arms. Ray looked back as Dunstan took the Hercules into a steep left-hander and headed away from the island once more.

"They're moving the truck," Ray said. "They're driving it on to the beach."

"They must want to play," said Dunstan with a grin as he maintained the angle of turn.

The nurses grabbed on to the back of the pilot's seat.

"This is like going round that roundabout," said Frankie to Joan, "on the back of your Arthur's motorbike."

Dunstan looked around.

"My ex," Joan elucidated.

"What we're about to do," Dunstan yelled, "you can't do on a motorbike, no matter who's driving it. Hold on tight and don't look away."

Dunstan took the plane lower and lower. The beach was a mile away, the altitude dropping rapidly.

"Five hundred feet," Dunstan shouted. "At five hundred feet you can make out cows' legs."

"There aren't any cows," Frankie shouted back.

"That's why I'm using this," said Dunstan, tapping the altimeter with his finger nail.

Ray watched the needle drop to four hundred, three hundred and fifty, three hundred.

"Two hundred and fifty!" Dunstan roared. "Sheep's legs at two hundred and fifty. Not that there's any sheep either. We are now officially low flying, and below two hundred and fifty," he shouted as he took the rattling hull down even lower, "is classified as *very* low flying."

The ground looked a lot closer than two hundred and fifty feet to Ray, who knew that the palm trees on this side of the island grew to a height of more than thirty feet. He watched their fronds shudder in the plane's wake, then turned to face forward as the station appeared beneath them once more. The truck had been parked in the middle of the beach, the men standing in a ragged line either side of it, raising their hands, waving at the plane. From this distance—by now, free of the palm trees, no more than fifty feet—it was easy to recognise Henshaw, and Flynn, who was jumping up and down in boyish enthusiasm. The girls whooped as the Hercules buzzed the truck, leaving clearance of no more than thirty feet. Ray turned to watch the men raise their hands to cover their faces in the resulting sandstorm.

"Fifty feet, ladies," Dunstan boasted, enjoying showing off. "We're allowed to fly this low to make free drops."

"What are free drops when they're at home?" asked Joan.

"When we want to drop stuff without parachutes. Boxes of supplies. Equipment. Whatever."

Frankie had fallen silent and was looking back at the line of men.

"What is it?" Joan asked her.

"That young one, the blond one, I'm sure I've seen him before."

"He's been in the clinic, Frankie. I saw him in the waiting room. He must have been your patient, because he wasn't mine. I'd have remembered him, if you know what I mean."

Frankie put her hand up to her mouth as she did remember.

"Oh God, yes," she said. "Such a nice boy. He was so embarrassed. I felt terribly sorry for him."

Dunstan had already started to go around again. The blue out of the left-hand side of the plane was now exclusively that of the ocean, the sky having disappeared. Ray waited to see if Frankie would say more about Flynn. She saw him watching her and fell silent.

She was similar to Victoria, but when Ray looked at her he felt nothing. Victoria was gone and the feelings he had had for her were gone also. It didn't mean they hadn't existed. But they could not be reawakened. Something in Ray had changed, even if he didn't understand the full nature of the change. He didn't doubt that he was still grieving for Victoria, but living on the island, in the company of Dunstan and the other men, was changing him. He couldn't have said what he did feel, only what he didn't.

"Can you take it any lower this time?" Joan was asking Dunstan as she leaned over the back of his seat and the line of men grew bigger in the pilot's windshield.

"What's that boy doing?" Ray muttered, as Flynn clambered on top of the cab of the supply truck that was still parked on the beach.

"Sometimes we fly as low as fifteen feet," Dunstan shouted, sweat standing out on his forehead as he clung to the controls and fought to keep the plane steady. He knew that one mistake would be fatal. If the right-hand wing tip caught the trunk of a palm tree, if the wake of the aircraft created an updraught that interfered with the rudder, control would be wrested from him in an instant, setting in motion a chain of events that would be as swift as it would be inevitable. Ray knew this and he knew that Dunstan knew it. He could sense that the two girls were beginning to realise it, as they watched, wide-eyed and white-knuckled.

The line of men was no more than a hundred yards away, the plane travelling at 140 knots.

"Be careful, sir," Ray murmured. "Watch Flynn."

The youngster was standing on the roof of the cab, stretching his arms in the air, his face ecstatic, hair swept back.

As the plane passed over him, they felt a bump. It would have felt harmless to the nurses, but Ray knew nothing is harmless in a plane of that size flying at that kind of altitude. He twisted around and looked back through the side window. He saw a figure in a blue uniform falling from the roof of the truck and something the size of a football rolling down the beach towards the sea.

"Christ!" said Ray.

One of the girls started screaming.

The golden sand, the turquoise sea. Rolling and rolling. A line of palm trees, the outermost buildings of the station. Henshaw, eyes wide, mouth hanging open. Another engineer bent double. Over and over. The golden sand, darker now, black, the sea, fringe of white foam, the vast blue sky. The black cross of the Hercules climbing steeply, banking sharply, heading out to sea. The golden sand. A body, damaged, somehow not right, lying on the sand by the supply truck. A quickly spreading pool of blood. The golden sand, line of trees, the vast empty sky, the distant plane, a line of men, men running, a body on the sand. The golden sand. Ghost crabs. A shell. Shells. The vast blue sky, line of trees. The supply truck. The golden sand. Palm trees swaying, blown by the wind. Henshaw. The golden sand again, darker, wetter. White foam, tinged pink. The blue of the sky. The body by the truck. Line of men, line of trees. The golden sand.

# WHEN THE GENTLEMEN GO BY

## MARGARET RONALD

It wasn't a sound that woke her this time, nor the soft slow lights that came dancing through the curtains. She thought in that first wakening haze that it might be a scent, like the "bad air" her mother had talked about, creeping in to announce their presence. Then full wakefulness and knowledge struck her, and her only thought was *Not yet*.

Laura rolled out of bed, making sure not to disturb Jenny, who'd crawled in about an hour after bedtime. Toby, in the crib, slept like a swaddled stone. The nightlight cast a weak gold glow over them, but the first hints of blue had begun to creep in, cool and unfriendly. She glanced back once at the sound of Jenny's whimper, then turned her back on her sleeping children.

At least their father wasn't here.

It was an old bargain, old as the Hollow at least. With bargains you had to uphold your side; she'd learned that early, probably before she even knew about the Gentlemen.

Her bedroom in her parents' house had faced the street, and when she was five the changing shapes of headlights across the far wall had fascinated her. One night she woke to see a block of light against the far wall, flickering in all the colors of frost. When the light stayed put, as if the car that cast it had parked outside, she sat up in bed, then turned to the window.

The light was just outside, on the strip of green that her father liked to call the lawn. She crawled out of bed, dropping the last couple of inches to the floor, and reached for the curtain.

"Don't look."

Laura turned to see her mother standing in the doorway. "Mumma?"

Her mother crossed the room in two strides and took Laura into her arms, cradling her head against her shoulder. "Don't look, baby, don't look."

145

Obediently, Laura laid her head against her mother's shoulder and listened as something huge or a hundred smaller somethings passed by with a thunderous *shussh*. Her mother's eyes were closed tight, and she rocked Laura as if she were an infant again, even though Laura had two little brothers and hadn't been rocked since the first one was born. The sleeve of her mother's bathrobe was damp with a thousand tiny droplets.

In the morning, she tried to talk about it. "I had a dream last night—" she said at the breakfast table.

"I expect we all had dreams," her mother said, pouring milk over her Cheerios. "What with all that pizza last night. Bet you had them worst of all, right, Kyle?"

Her brother Kyle, six years old and indeed the one who'd eaten the most, shook his head and began to cough.

The light was stronger in the living room. Soon it would be strong enough for her to read by, if she'd ever had the urge to do so. Laura closed the bedroom door behind her, making sure it latched, and picked her way through the maze of toys that covered the carpet. She watched the blue-edged shadows rise over the edge of the couch and drew a deep breath. *I wonder what they'll bring,* she made herself think over the rising dread in the back of her mind. *And to whom they'll bring it.*

*They bring gifts. I have to remember that. They bring gifts too.*

It wasn't till she reached second grade, just after Kyle's funeral, that she found a name for them. It was in a book of children's poems, the old kind that usually read as if they'd been dipped in Karo Syrup. But this one, "The Smuggler's Song," wasn't like that at all. It made the room seem darker when she read it, and darker still when she thought about it. Even after she learned that the poet hadn't ever set foot in Brooks' Hollow, she still secretly called them the Gentlemen, after the poem.

*Five and twenty ponies / trotting through the dark…*

She waited until her father took her remaining brother out to play baseball before talking to her mother about it. "Mumma," she asked as they washed dishes together, "why did Kyle get sick?"

Her mother's hands paused, wrist-deep in sudsy water. "Well," she said after a moment, in that careful voice adults used when they didn't know how to say something, "people in the Hollow get sick sometimes. It's just something in the air."

"Oh."

"You don't need to worry, sweetie. I won't let anything—" She stopped, her lips pressed together, and went on in a different tone. "You know what the pioneers used to say about our land? Good land, bad air. They might have been right about the air, but we had the best farms for miles. Still do. The Hollow's a good place, Laura. I want you to remember that."

Later that evening, after the boys had settled in to watch football, her mother took her by the hand and led her upstairs, where she rummaged in the back of the closet until she found an old cardboard box. "I thought you might want to try this on," she said, and took out a fragile crown, woven out of hair-thin wire and stones like gleaming ice, so delicate it chimed in her hands. She set it on Laura's head and held up a mirror. "Don't you look just like a princess, now."

Laura caught her breath. "I do! Mumma, I do!"

"I thought you might." Her mother smiled.

Laura shivered to remember that crown. It was here somewhere, in the boxes she'd packed up after her mother's death, but she hadn't ever gone looking for it. She sometimes dreamed of wearing it, and woke up with bile in her throat.

She reached up and took down the little blue notebook from its place above the television. It had pages of notes about the sound the Gentlemen made: pines in the wind, highway traffic very far away, heavy rain, but none of them quite caught it. She'd been keeping the notes ever since she could write, first on what it looked like when the Gentlemen went by, then—later, as she grew up and began to understand—the annotations.

And the more she watched the indistinct shapes through the curtain, the more she felt as if her whole life became only watching. Her second brother's death, her graduation, the strikes at the cabinet factory—all images apart from her. Even now, she was at a distance, watching herself sitting huddled wrong-way-round on the couch, a patch of drying formula stiff and sticky under her left forearm.

Sometimes they brought things, she told herself again. A crown, a song, a whisper in someone's ear. And their trail was thick with flowers, even when they passed by late in October.

And the Hollow was a friendly place, after all. It seemed there was always a family to bring a casserole; it seemed there was always a service "for those taken from us" at the little church that was the only official marker of Brooks' Hollow, and the pews were always full.

But you didn't talk about it. You shrugged, and blamed bad air, and made sure your child's last months were comfortable, treating them like a stranger the whole time, and then you buried them in the good rich earth of the Hollow.

The light grew, shimmering like opals, and with it came a faint scent: greenery, growing things. But there was an edge to it as well, something like grass clippings left in the rain and then rotting in the sun. Something green gone wrong. Laura held the book tight against her chest, as if it might hide her, her and her children. "The Smuggler's Song" was inked in blue on the inside flap, an addition she'd made just after her wedding.

*Them that asks no questions isn't told a lie. / Watch the wall, my darling, when the Gentlemen go by!*

In her senior year at the county high she met Rich. Rich came from the north of the county, and he played guitar, and when he smiled at her Laura felt her heart come unstuck. For the first time in ages she felt as if she could be part of the world again.

She was worried at first what her parents would say. Some of her girlfriends had had to move out of the Hollow because their parents had kicked them out for any number of reasons—going out with boys, going out with only one boy, getting pregnant, not staying pregnant. Her parents turned out to like Rich, though, and they even helped them find a place to live.

They got married on the hottest day of the year. But the sky was clear, the beer was cold, and Rich looked at her like she was the sun come to earth. At the reception, she tore her hem dancing and had to go looking for her mother. She finally thought to look for her in the bathroom, only to find her talking to an old friend. "Rich tells me they've bought a trailer down in the Hollow," said Laura's old babysitter.

"It's a nice little place," Laura's mother said. Laura shrank back against the door.

"That ain't right, Missy. Bringing someone new into the Hollow ain't right, especially not a good sort like Rich. Why didn't you send her away?"

Laura held her breath. "She's all I got," her mother said after a moment. "I can't send her away."

"Oh, Missy. That's no way to treat a good girl. You know what the Hollow's like—that's why we've been sending our girls out. I know. You get sent or you get taken, and that's it."

"Or maybe you spend a good long life in the Hollow, like me and Bobby." Laura's mother sniffed. "Maybe that's what I want for my girl. You think of that? Besides, the way you keep sending your girls out, there won't be hardly any families left, and it'll be harder for anyone who stays. You think you're doing it for the whole Hollow, but it's just for yourself."

"That's not it," Laura's babysitter insisted. "That's not why. There's things a girl should know, if she's going to be a mother in the Hollow. You think she can handle that? *I* can't handle that, and I'm twice her age. It's not worth it."

". . . she's all I got."

The other woman sighed. "Well, God keep you both."

Laura hesitated a moment longer, then thumped the door as if she'd just opened it. "Mumma?" she called. "I need some help with my dress."

"Be there in a moment," her mother said.

Not worth it. She formed the words, but couldn't make herself push the breath behind them. It was easy to forget, sometimes, amid the gifts tangible and intangible. No woman in the Hollow ever miscarried. No plants died in the ground, no house ever caught fire, no one ever quite starved. When you looked at the uncertain world, you could be forgiven for thinking that maybe Kyle's life had been a good trade.

At least Laura hoped you could be forgiven.

What was it the union man had said, just before she'd had to leave for Toby's birth? "The contracts need to be renegotiated," he'd said, and there was more. Most of it she hadn't paid attention to, being nine months pregnant and having what her friend Charlene called "baby brain." She'd thought it was dumb at the time—you make a bargain, you stick with it—but that had been before Rich came back.

Maybe bargains went bad, sometimes. Maybe they went bad and there wasn't anything you could do but stick with it and hope for the best.

The closest anyone ever came to saying anything out loud was just after her mother's death (no Gentlemen, just three packs of Marlboros every day for twenty years). A lawyer in a rumpled blue suit had arranged for a big town meeting, and he'd gotten nearly the whole Hollow to attend on the promise of free barbecue. He had charts, and maps, and he talked excitedly about disease clusters and the factory up the road. And after half an hour of silence from the good folks of the Hollow, he'd asked them to join in a class action suit.

The minister of First Church, acting for all of them, had smiled and nodded and escorted him to the door. "A lawsuit can't help us," he'd said, "even if you knew who to sue."

It was right after he closed the door that someone could have spoken, could have broken that throat-tightening silence and actually said who was to blame. But the lawyer drove off, the silence won out, and the minister shrugged and sighed.

Rich went to the war. Rich came back. Laura had written him about Toby's birth, and it made her heart fly free again to see him smile. But the look he turned out the windows was haunted, and with more than just wartime ghosts. He couldn't drive any more, not without pulling over and putting his head down every few miles. So he spent more time in the Hollow, and the Hollow clotted around him.

In April, after the Gentlemen's spring visit (which would later be annotated with Ashley Irvine, 6, 4 mos. after G.), they had a fight. It wasn't even a real fight; she'd dropped a glass, and he'd charged into the kitchen so fast he almost knocked over Toby. He yelled at her, she yelled back, both scared and angry at each other for being scared, and Laura didn't even see the slap coming until her cheek was already burning with it. She raised a hand to her face, disbelieving. Rich stared at her as if she'd grown horns, then turned and ran out the door, heedless of Toby's yowls.

Laura didn't go after him, even when dinner and sunset passed without his return. She took extra time putting the kids to bed, and didn't get up when she heard the front door open.

When she came out from the bedroom, she found him sitting at the kitchen table, staring at his hands. She sat down across from him, and after a while, he began to talk.

"They told me I might have trouble, coming back," he said, and this time he didn't move away when Laura took his hands in hers. "And I think I was okay, for a little while… But something about here, it's like, like I keep seeing things I oughtn't, and it just keeps getting worse. Like something keeps poking at my head." He glanced out the window, as if something was watching him.

Laura said nothing, only thought of how smart Rich had been in high school, how quickly he saw things that it took her ages to notice, and how she should have known that wouldn't change.

"Let's get out of here," he said, and kissed her fingers. "I don't know where just yet, but we can live with my folks a while."

Laura unknotted her hands from his and went to stand by the window. "This is my home," she said.

Rich's eyes went wide and broken. "I know, babe, but it's not a good place. We need to get out."

*I do. But you get sent or you get taken, and that's it.* "So," she said, "either I go with you, or you go alone."

"What? No, that's not—"

"I know." She turned and smiled at him, blinking back tears. "I'm sending you away, Rich. I'm sending you out of my life." *And out of the Hollow.*

The divorce hadn't been pretty—it couldn't have been, with the two of them still in love. Rich called her and left messages, angry or maudlin or pleading, and she'd listened to them all, hugging herself so tight there would be white marks in her arms when the message ended. Toby began to fuss more, and Jenny started to crawl into bed with her at night.

But Rich was free. Rich was out of it, and she could never, ever hand him over to them. Even if she sometimes woke and cried over the cold side of the bed. Even if she was back watching her life again.

The lights hadn't changed, and the whispering had stilled. And now Laura had to admit it, had to see that the Gentlemen had come to her house. *Oh, I tried, I tried,* she thought. *I could have sent the kids away, I could…*

But would it have done anything? The old women, like Laura's babysitter, had sent their kids away. And some had then died alone and unnoticed, so successful at cutting the ties between their loved ones and the Hollow that they'd cut their own lifelines. Even that wouldn't have been enough.

She'd gotten as far as the border of the Hollow, car packed to the gills and kids in the backseat, before the strength left her limbs and she found herself unable to leave. She'd even thought about ringing the house with iron and salt, the way one woman had back in '09, but that woman's family had all died in a gas explosion two months after. The Gentlemen took their claim. You had to carry out a life to them, and you had to let them carry that life away.

It was an old bargain, old as the Hollow at least. And you had to keep bargains.

A soft trill shook the window panes, traveling from them down to the tips of her fingers through some malign conduction. Her first instinct was to categorize it, and she thought of flutes, screech owls, mourning doves, before she quite heard it, and hearing it was lost.

This was right, the cry said. Children die, and if one of them had to, who better to choose than their mother? She sat up—looking, had she known it, very like her mother—then got to her feet.

She ghosted into the bedroom and gazed at her children. *Toby,* she thought, *he's too young to really understand about being sick. No, Jenny, because she's had at least some time. No…*

Something burred against her consciousness, a wrong note in the Gentlemen's music.

*Decide. You have time. Just decide.*

But the burr remained, coming through in bursts like—*like a phone,* she realized, and glanced over her shoulder in time to see the harsh red light of the answering machine flick on.

"Uh. Hi. It's me," Rich's voice said, crackling over the tape. "Look, I know you're not awake—Jesus, I hope I didn't wake the kids, I'm sorry—but I had to talk to you." He went on, but Laura was no longer paying attention. His voice was harsh and ragged and so unlike the Rich she'd known, but it was enough to drown out the Gentlemen's echoes.

Laura looked back at her children. She could let herself walk into the room, as she was doing now, let herself pick up a child and go outside. And she could tell herself later, when her child died, that she hadn't really done it, that she'd just watched herself do it.

She thought of the crown, and of Kyle.

Jenny shifted, putting out a hand to the empty space where Laura had slept, and sat up. "Mumma?"

"Stay inside, sweetie," Laura said. She crossed her arms, denying herself a last hug in case her resolve failed. "Stay inside and under the covers. I'll be back—" She caught the lie between her teeth and shook her head. "Sleep tight, sweetie. Love you."

She turned her back, ignoring Jenny's scared squeak, and closed the door. The last moments of Rich's message cut off, cut short by the tape, and Laura touched the answering machine as she passed. "Love you too."

Finally she closed her eyes, opened the front door, and stepped out into light. The trill sounded again, closer, all around her, and she opened her eyes with a gasp. Two dozen sets of eyes regarded her, wide and unblinking.

They didn't ride horses, of course; at the back of her mind she was proud of herself for having figured that out. They rode owls, giant white faces staring at her without curiosity. That was the only thing recognizable about them; it was as if the owls, strange and gigantic as they were, were a concession to reality.

They were made of light, and they shone, oh they shone. For a second she thought they could be angels, but the memory of the little blue notebook tainted that thought. One of the riders—white and blue, and human only in shape—leaned over his reins toward her and gestured toward the house.

"No," she said aloud. "You didn't get Rich. You don't get them. You get me."

The rider slashed one hand across his chest: rejection. Others agreed, some agitating their mounts so that the huge birds hopped from one foot to the other.

She shook her head. "I don't care what you want. You don't get to choose. And I choose this. I choose me." She leaned forward, and was rewarded by the sight of the head rider leaning away from her.

*You think you're doing it for the Hollow, but it's just for yourself.* The words were her mother's, but the head of one of the Gentlemen moved, as if speaking her thoughts.

Laura shook her head. "No. For the Hollow. For the dead of the Hollow." All the services, all the casseroles, all the dead then and now.

There came a familiar prickling on the back of her neck. If she turned now, she knew, she'd be able to see Jenny at the window, nose mashed up against the glass, mouth open in the beginning of a sob.

She didn't turn, not even to say goodbye. *Watch, darling. Watch.* "This bargain is ended," she said. "We will not be renegotiating."

The head rider motioned to the others, and they advanced on her, cruel hooked beaks clashing. Laura held her ground. It always hurt to break a bargain; there was always something that got lost. But it was worth it, if the contract was no good.

The owls took her by hand and foot and hair, and their beaks were sharp. The first cut came, and with it a rending deeper than her skin, deeper than her heart: the Hollow breaking, breaking so that it could never be repaired, and her blood turning the rich soil to useless swamp.

*Watch. Oh, watch.*

# THE LAGERSTÄTTE

## LAIRD BARRON

*October 2004*

Virgil acquired the cute little blue-and-white-pinstriped Cessna at an auction; this over Danni's strenuous objections. There were financial issues; Virgil's salary as department head at his software development company wasn't scheduled to increase for another eighteen months and they'd recently enrolled their son Keith in an exclusive grammar school. Thirty grand a year was a serious hit on their rainy-day fund. Also, Danni didn't like planes, especially small ones, which she asserted were scarcely more than tin, plastic, and balsawood. She even avoided traveling by commercial airliner if it was possible to drive or take a train. But she couldn't compete with love at first sight. Virgil took one look at the four-seater and practically swooned, and Danni knew she'd had it before the argument even started. Keith begged to fly and Virgil promised to teach him, teased that he might be the only kid to get his pilot's license before he learned to drive.

Because Danni detested flying so much, when their assiduously planned weeklong vacation rolled around, she decided to boycott the flight and meet her husband and son at the in-laws place on Cape Cod a day late, after wrapping up business in the city. The drive was only a couple of hours—she'd be at the house in time for Friday supper. She saw them off from a small airport in the suburbs, and returned home to pack and go over last minute adjustments to her evening lecture at the museum.

How many times did the plane crash between waking and sleeping? There was no way to measure that; during the first weeks the accident cycled through a continuous playback loop, cheap and grainy and soundless like a closed circuit security feed. They'd recovered pieces of fuselage from the water, bobbing like cork—she caught a few moments of news footage before someone, probably Dad, killed the television.

They threw the most beautiful double funeral courtesy of Virgil's parents, followed by a reception in his family's summer home. She recalled wavering shadowbox lights and the muted hum of voices, men in black hats clasping cocktails to the breasts of their black suits, and severe women gathered near the sharper, astral glow of the kitchen, faces gaunt and cold as porcelain, their dresses black, their children underfoot and dressed as adults in miniature; and afterward, a smooth descent into darkness like a bullet reversing its trajectory and dropping into the barrel of a gun.

Later, in the hospital, she chuckled when she read the police report. It claimed she'd eaten a bottle of pills she'd found in her mother-in-law's dresser and curled up to die in her husband's closet among his little league uniforms and boxes of trophies. That was simply hilarious because anyone who knew her would know the notion was just too goddamned melodramatic for words.

*March 2005*

About four months after she lost her husband and son, Danni transplanted to the West Coast, taken in by a childhood friend named Merrill Thurman, and cut all ties with extended family, peers, and associates from before the accident. She eventually lost interest in grieving just as she lost interest in her former career as an entomologist; both were exercises of excruciating tediousness and ultimately pointless in the face of her brand new, freewheeling course. All those years of college and marriage were abruptly and irrevocably reduced to the fond memories of another life, a chapter in a closed book.

Danni was satisfied with the status quo of patchwork memory and aching numbness. At her best, there were no highs, no lows, just a seamless thrum as one day rolled into the next. She took to perusing self-help pamphlets and treatises on Eastern philosophy, and trendy art magazines; she piled them in her room until they wedged the door open. She studied Tai Chi during an eight week course in the decrepit gym of the crosstown YMCA. She toyed with an easel and paints, attended a class at the community college. She'd taken some drafting as an undergrad. This was helpful for the technical aspects, the geometry of line and space; the actual artistic part proved more difficult. Maybe she needed to steep herself in the bohemian culture—a coldwater flat in Paris, or an artist commune, or a sea shanty on the coast of Barbados.

Oh, but she'd never live alone, would she?

Amidst this reevaluation and reordering, came the fugue, a lunatic element that found genesis in the void between melancholy and nightmare. The fugue made familiar places strange; it wiped away friendly faces and replaced them with beekeeper masks and reduced English to the low growl of the swarm. It was a disorder of trauma and shock, a hybrid of temporary dementia and selective amnesia. It battened to her with the mindless tenacity of a leech.

She tried not to think about its origins, because when she did she was carried back to the twilight land of her subconscious; to Keith's fifth birthday party; her wedding day with the thousand-dollar cake, and the honeymoon in Niagara Falls;

the Cessna spinning against the sun, streaking downward to slam into the Atlantic; and the lush corruption of a green-black jungle and its hidden cairns—the bones of giants slowly sinking into the always hungry earth.

*The palace of cries where the doors are opened with blood and sorrow. The secret graveyard of the elephants. The bones of elephants made a forest of ribcages and tusks, dry riverbeds of skulls. Red ants crawled in trains along the petrified spines of behemoths and trailed into the black caverns of empty sockets. Oh, what the lost expeditions might've told the world!*

She'd dreamt of the Elephants' Graveyard off and on since the funeral and wasn't certain why she had grown so morbidly preoccupied with the legend. Bleak mythology had interested her when she was young and vital and untouched by the twin melanomas of wisdom and grief. Now, such morose contemplation invoked a primordial dread and answered nothing. The central mystery of her was impenetrable to casual methods. Delving beneath the surface smacked of finality, of doom.

Danni chose to endure the fugue, to welcome it as a reliable adversary. The state seldom lasted more than a few minutes, and admittedly it was frightening, certainly dangerous; nonetheless, she was never one to live in a cage. In many ways the dementia and its umbra of pure terror, its visceral chaos, provided the masochistic rush she craved these days—a badge of courage, the martyr's brand. The fugue hid her in its shadow, like a sheltering wing.

*May 6, 2006*
(D. L. Session 33)

Danni stared at the table while Dr. Green pressed a button and the wheels of the recorder began to turn. His chair creaked as he leaned back. He stated his name, Danni's name, the date and location.

—How are things this week? He said.

Danni set a slim metal tin on the table and flicked it open with her left hand. She removed a cigarette and lighted it. She used matches because she'd lost the fancy lighter Merrill got her as a birthday gift. She exhaled, shook the match dead.

—For a while, I thought I was getting better, she said in a raw voice.

—You don't think you're improving? Dr. Green said.

—Sometimes I wake up and nothing seems real; it's all a movie set, a humdrum version of *This Is Your Life*! I stare at the ceiling and can't shake this sense I'm an imposter.

—Everybody feels that way, Dr. Green said. His dark hands rested on a clipboard. His hands were creased and notched with the onset of middle age; the cuffs of his starched lab coat had gone yellow at the seams. He was married; he wore a simple ring and he never stared at her breasts. Happily married, or a consummate professional, or she was nothing special. A frosted window rose high and narrow over his shoulder like the painted window of a monastery. Pallid light shone at the corners of his angular glasses, the shiny edges of the clipboard, a piece of the bare plastic table, the sunken tiles of the floor. The tiles were dented and scratched and bumpy. Fine cracks spread like tendrils. Against the far walls were cabinets and shelves and several rickety beds with thin rails and large, black wheels.

The hospital was an ancient place and smelled of mold and sickness beneath the buckets of bleach she knew the custodians poured forth every evening. This had been a sanitarium. People with tuberculosis had gathered here to die in the long, shabby wards. Workers loaded the bodies into furnaces and burned them. There were chutes for the corpses on all of the upper floors. The doors of the chutes were made of dull, gray metal with big handles that reminded her of the handles on the flour and sugar bins in her mother's pantry.

Danni smoked and stared at the ceramic ashtray centered exactly between them, inches from a box of tissues. The ashtray was black. Cinders smoldered in its belly. The hospital was "no smoking," but that never came up during their weekly conversations. After the first session of him watching her drop the ashes into her coat pocket, the ashtray had appeared. Occasionally she tapped her cigarette against the rim of the ashtray and watched the smoke coil tighter and tighter until it imploded the way a demolished building collapses into itself after the charges go off.

Dr. Green said, —Did you take the bus or did you walk?

—Today? I walked.

Dr. Green wrote something on the clipboard with a heavy golden pen. —Good. You stopped to visit your friend at the market, I see.

Danni glanced at her cigarette where it fumed between her second and third fingers.

—Did I mention that? My Friday rounds?

—Yes. When we first met. He tapped a thick, manila folder bound in a heavy-duty rubber band. The folder contained Danni's records and transfer papers from the original admitting institute on the East Coast. Additionally, there was a collection of nearly unrecognizable photos of her in hospital gowns and bathrobes. In several shots an anonymous attendant pushed her in a wheelchair against a blurry backdrop of trees and concrete walls.

—Oh.

—You mentioned going back to work. Any progress?

—No. Merrill wants me to. She thinks I need to reintegrate professionally, that it might fix my problem, Danni said, smiling slightly as she pictured her friend's well-meaning harangues. Merrill spoke quickly, in the cadence of a native Bostonian who would always be a Bostonian no matter where she might find herself. A lit major, she'd also gone through an art-junkie phase during grad school which had wrecked her first marriage and introduced her to many a disreputable character as could be found haunting the finer galleries and museums. One of said characters became ex-husband the second and engendered a profound and abiding disillusionment with the fine-arts scene entirely. Currently, she made an exemplary copy editor at a rather important monthly journal.

—What do you think?

—I liked being a scientist. I liked to study insects, liked tracking their brief, frenetic little lives. I know how important they are, how integral, essential to the ecosystem. Hell, they outnumber humans trillions to one. But, oh my, it's so damned easy to feel like a god when you've got an ant twitching in your forceps. You think that's how God feels when He's got one of us under His thumb?

—I couldn't say.

—Me neither. Danni dragged heavily and squinted. —Maybe I'll sell Bibles door to door. My uncle sold encyclopedias when I was a little girl.

Dr. Green picked up the clipboard. —Well. Any episodes—fainting, dizziness, disorientation? Anything of that nature?

She smoked in silence for nearly half a minute. —I got confused about where I was the other day. She closed her eyes. The recollection of those bad moments threatened her equilibrium. —I was walking to Yang's grocery. It's about three blocks from the apartments. I got lost for a few minutes.

—A few minutes.

—Yeah. I wasn't timing it, sorry.

—No, that's fine. Go on.

—It was like before. I didn't recognize any of the buildings. I was in a foreign city and couldn't remember what I was doing there. Someone tried to talk to me, to help me—an old lady. But, I ran from her instead. Danni swallowed the faint bitterness, the dumb memory of nausea and terror.

—Why? Why did you run?

—Because when the fugue comes, when I get confused and forget where I am, people frighten me. Their faces don't seem real. Their faces are rubbery and inhuman. I thought the old lady was wearing a mask, that she was hiding something. So I ran. By the time I regained my senses, I was near the park. Kids were staring at me.

—Then?

—Then what? I yelled at them for staring. They took off.

—What did you want at Yang's?

—What?

—You said you were shopping. For what?

—I don't recall. Beets. Grapes. A giant zucchini. I don't know.

—You've been taking your medication, I presume. Drugs, alcohol?

—No drugs. Okay, a joint occasionally. A few shots here and there. Merrill wants to unwind on the weekends. She drinks me under the table—Johnny Walkers and Manhattans. Tequila if she's seducing one of the rugged types. Depends where we are. She'd known Merrill since forever. Historically, Danni was the strong one, the one who saw Merrill through two bad marriages, a career collapse and bouts of deep clinical depression. Funny how life tended to put the shoe on the other foot when one least expected.

—Do you visit many different places?

Danni shrugged. —I don't—oh, the Candy Apple. Harpo's. That hole-in-the-wall on Decker and Gedding, the Red Jack. All sorts of places. Merrill picks; says it's therapy.

—Sex?

Danni shook her head. —That doesn't mean I'm loyal.

—Loyal to whom?

—I've been noticing men and... I feel like I'm betraying Virgil. Soiling our memories. It's stupid, sure. Merrill thinks I'm crazy.

—What do you think?

—I try not to, Doc.

—Yet, the past is with you. You carry it everywhere. Like a millstone, if you'll pardon the cliché.

Danni frowned. —I'm not sure what you mean—

—Yes, you are.

She smoked and looked away from his eyes. She'd arranged a mini gallery of snapshots of Virgil and Keith on the bureau in her bedroom, stuffed more photos in her wallet and fixed one of Keith as a baby on a keychain. She'd built a modest shrine of baseball ticket stubs, Virgil's moldy fishing hat, his car keys, though the car was long gone, business cards, cancelled checks, and torn up Christmas wrapping. It was sick.

—Memories have their place, of course, Dr. Green said. —But you've got to be careful. Live in the past too long and it consumes you. You can't use fidelity as a crutch. Not forever.

—I'm not planning on forever, Danni said.

*August 2, 2006*

Color and symmetry were among Danni's current preoccupations. Yellow squash, orange baby carrots, an axis of green peas on a china plate; the alignment of complementary elements surgically precise upon the starched white table-cloth—cloth white and neat as the hard white fabric of a hospital sheet.

Their apartment was a narrow box stacked high in a cylinder of similar boxes. The window sashes were blue. All of them a filmy, ephemeral blue like the dust on the wings of a blue emperor butterfly; blue over every window in every cramped room. Blue as dead salmon, blue as ice. Blue shadows darkened the edge of the table, rippled over Danni's untouched meal, its meticulously arrayed components. The vegetables glowed with subdued radioactivity. Her fingers curled around the fork; the veins in her hand ran like blue-black tributaries to her fingertips, ran like cold iron wires. Balanced on a windowsill was her ant farm, its inhabitants scurrying about the business of industry in microcosm of the looming cityscape. Merrill hated the ants and Danni expected her friend to poison them in a fit of revulsion and pique. Merrill wasn't naturally maternal and her scant reservoir of kindly nurture was readily exhausted on her housemate.

Danni set the fork upon a napkin, red gone black as sackcloth in the beautiful gloom, and moved to the terrace door, reaching automatically for her cigarettes as she went. She kept them in the left breast pocket of her jacket alongside a pack of matches from the Candy Apple.

The light that came through the glass and blue gauze was muted and heavy even at midday. Outside the sliding door was a terrace and a rail; beyond the rail, a gulf. Damp breaths of air were coarse with smog, tar, and pigeon shit. Eight stories yawned below the wobbly terrace to the dark brick square. Ninety-six feet to the fountain, the flagpole, two rusty benches, and Piccolo Street where winos with homemade drums, harmonicas, and flutes composed their symphonies and dirges.

Danni smoked on the terrace to keep the peace with Merrill, straight-edge Merrill, whose poison of choice was Zinfandel and fast men in nice suits, rather than tobacco. Danni smoked Turkish cigarettes that came in a tin she bought at the wharf market from a Nepalese expat named Mahan. Mahan sold coffee too, in shiny black packages; and decorative knives with tassels depending from brass handles.

Danni leaned on the swaying rail and lighted the next to the last cigarette in her tin and smoked as the sky clotted between the gaps of rooftops, the copses of wires and antennas, the static snarl of uprooted birds like black bits of paper ash turning in the Pacific breeze. A man stopped in the middle of the crosswalk. He craned his neck to seek her out from amidst the jigsaw of fire escapes and balconies. He waved and then turned away and crossed the street with an unmistakably familiar stride, and was gone.

When her cigarette was done, she flicked the butt into the empty planter, one of several terra cotta pots piled around the corroding barbeque. She lighted her remaining cigarette and smoked it slowly, made it last until the sky went opaque and the city lights began to float here and there in the murk, bubbles of iridescent gas rising against the leaden tide of night. Then she went inside and sat very still while her colony of ants scrabbled in the dark.

*May 6, 2006*
(D. L. Session 33)

Danni's cigarette was out; the tin empty. She began to fidget. —Do you believe in ghosts, Doctor?

—Absolutely. Dr. Green knocked his ring on the table and gestured at the hoary walls. —Look around. Haunted, I'd say.

—Really?

Dr. Green seemed quite serious. He set aside the clipboard, distancing himself from the record. —Why not. My grandfather was a missionary. He lived in the Congo for several years, set up a clinic out there. Everybody believed in ghosts—including my grandfather. There was no choice.

Danni laughed. —Well, it's settled. I'm a faithless bitch. And I'm being haunted as just desserts.

—Why do you say that?

—I went home with this guy a few weeks ago. Nice guy, a graphic designer. I was pretty drunk and he was pretty persuasive.

Dr. Green plucked a pack of cigarettes from the inside pocket of his white coat, shook one loose and handed it to her. They leaned toward one another, across the table, and he lighted her cigarette with a silvery Zippo.

—Nothing happened, she said. —It was very innocent, actually.

But that was a lie by omission, was it not? What would the good doctor think of her if she confessed her impulses to grasp a man, any man, as a point of fact, and throw him down and fuck him senseless, and refrained only because she was too frightened of the possibilities? Her cheeks stung and she exhaled fiercely to conceal her shame.

—We had some drinks and called it a night. I still felt bad, dirty, somehow. Riding the bus home, I saw Virgil. It wasn't him; he had Virgil's build and kind of slouched, holding onto one of those straps. Didn't even come close once I got a decent look at him. But for a second, my heart froze. Danni lifted her gaze from the ashtray. —Time for more pills, huh?

—Well, a case of mistaken identity doesn't qualify as a delusion.

Danni smiled darkly.

—You didn't get on the plane and you lived. Simple. Dr. Green spoke with supreme confidence.

—Is it? Simple, I mean.

—Have you experienced more of these episodes—mistaking strangers for Virgil? Or your son?

—Yeah. The man on the bus, that tepid phantom of her husband, had been the fifth incident of mistaken identity during the previous three weeks. The incidents were growing frequent; each apparition more convincing than the last. Then there were the items she'd occasionally found around the apartment—Virgil's lost wedding ring gleaming at the bottom of a pitcher of water; a trail of dried rose petals leading from the bathroom to her bed; one of Keith's crayon masterpieces fixed by magnet on the refrigerator; each of these artifacts ephemeral as dew, transitory as drifting spider thread; they dissolved and left no traces of their existence. That very morning she'd glimpsed Virgil's bomber jacket slung over the back of a chair. A sunbeam illuminated it momentarily, dispersed it amongst the moving shadows of clouds and undulating curtains.

—Why didn't you mention this sooner?

—It didn't scare me before.

—There are many possibilities. I hazard what we're dealing with is survivor's guilt, Dr. Green said. —This guilt is a perfectly normal aspect of the grieving process.

Dr. Green had never brought up the guilt association before, but she always knew it lurked in the wings, waiting to be sprung in the third act. The books all talked about it. Danni made a noise of disgust and rolled her eyes to hide the sudden urge to cry.

—Go on, Dr. Green said.

Danni pretended to rub smoke from her eye. —There isn't any more.

—Certainly there is. There's always another rock to look beneath. Why don't you tell me about the vineyards. Does this have anything to do with the *Lagerstätte?*

She opened her mouth and closed it. She stared, her fear and anger tightening screws within the pit of her stomach. —You've spoken to Merrill? Goddamn her.

—She hoped you'd get around to it, eventually. But you haven't and it seems important. Don't worry—she volunteered the information. Of course I would never reveal the nature of our conversations. Trust in that.

—It's not a good thing to talk about, Danni said. —I stopped thinking about it.

—Why?

She regarded her cigarette. Norma, poor departed Norma whispered in her ear, *Do you want to press your eye against the keyhole of a secret room? Do you want to see where the elephants have gone to die?*

—Because there are some things you can't take back. Shake hands with an ineffable enigma and it knows you. It has you, if it wants.

Dr. Green waited, his hand poised over a brown folder she hadn't noticed before. The folder was stamped in red block letters she couldn't quite read, although she suspected ASYLUM was at least a portion.

—I wish to understand, he said. —We're not going anywhere.

—Fuck it, she said. A sense of terrible satisfaction and relief caused her to smile again. —Confession is good for the soul, right?

*August 9, 2006*

In the middle of dressing to meet Merrill at the market by the wharf when she got off work, Danni opened the closet and inhaled a whiff of damp, moldering air and then screamed into her fist. Several withered corpses hung from the rack amid her cheery blouses and conservative suit jackets. They were scarcely more than yellowed sacks of skin. None of the desiccated, sagging faces were recognizable; the shade and texture of cured squash, each was further distorted by warps and wrinkles of dry-cleaning bags. She recoiled and sat on the bed and chewed her fingers until a passing cloud blocked the sun and the closet went dark.

Eventually she washed her hands and face in the bathroom sink, staring into the mirror at her pale, maniacal simulacrum. She skipped makeup and stumbled from the apartment to the cramped, dingy lift that dropped her into a shabby foyer with its rows of tarnished mailbox slots checkering the walls, its low, grubby light fixtures, a stained carpet, and the sweet-and-sour odor of sweat and stagnant air. She stumbled through the security doors into the brighter world.

And the fugue descended.

Danni was walking from somewhere to somewhere else; she'd closed her eyes against the glare and her insides turned upside down. Her eyes flew open and she reeled, utterly lost. Shadow people moved around her, bumped her with their hard elbows and swinging hips; an angry man in brown tweed lectured his daughter and the girl protested. They buzzed like flies. Their miserable faces blurred together, lit by some internal phosphorous. Danni swallowed, crushed into herself with a force akin to claustrophobia, and focused on her watch, a cheap windup model that glowed in the dark. Its numerals meant nothing, but she tracked the needle as it swept a perfect circle while the world spun around her. The passage, an indoor-outdoor avenue of sorts. Market stalls flanked the causeway, shelves and timber beams twined with streamers and beads, hemp rope and tie-dye shirts and pennants. Light fell through cracks in the overhead pavilion. The enclosure reeked of fresh salmon, salt water, sawdust, and the compacted scent of perfumed flesh.

—*Danni.* Here was an intelligible voice amid the squeal and squelch. Danni lifted her head and tried to focus.

—*We miss you,* Virgil said. He stood several feet away, gleaming like polished ivory.

—What? Danni said, thinking his face was the only face not changing shape like the flowery crystals in a kaleidoscope. —What did you say?

—*Come home.* It was apparent that this man wasn't Virgil, although in this particular light the eyes were similar, and he drawled. Virgil grew up in South Carolina, spent his adult life trying to bury that drawl and eventually it only emerged when he was exhausted or angry. The stranger winked at her and continued along the boardwalk. Beneath an Egyptian cotton shirt, his back was almost as muscular as Virgil's. But, no.

Danni turned away into the bright, jostling throng. Someone took her elbow. She yelped and wrenched away and nearly fell.

—Honey, you okay? The jumble of insectoid eyes, lips, and bouffant hair coalesced into Merrill's stern face. Merrill wore white-rimmed sunglasses that complemented her vanilla dress with its wide shoulders and brass buttons, and her elegant vanilla gloves. Her thin nose peeled with sunburn. —Danni, are you all right?

—Yeah. Danni wiped her mouth.

—The hell you are. C'mon. Merrill led her away from the moving press to a small open square and seated her in a wooden chair in the shadow of a parasol. The square hosted a half-dozen vendors and several tables of squawking children, overheated parents with flushed cheeks, and senior citizens in pastel running suits. Merrill bought soft ice cream in tiny plastic dishes and they sat in the shade and ate the ice cream while the sun dipped below the rooflines. The vendors began taking down the signs and packing it in for the day.

—Okay, okay. I feel better. Danni's hands had stopped shaking.

—You do look a little better. Know where you are?

—The market. Danni wanted a cigarette. —Oh, damn it, she said.

—Here, sweetie. Merrill drew two containers of Mahan's foreign cigarettes from her purse and slid them across the table, mimicking a spy in one of those '70s thrillers.

—Thanks, Danni said as she got a cigarette burning. She dragged frantically, left hand cupped to her mouth so the escaping smoke boiled and foamed between her fingers like dry ice vapors. Nobody said anything despite the NO SMOKING signs posted on the gate.

—Hey, what kind of bug is that? Merrill intently regarded a beetle hugging the warmth of a wooden plank near their feet.

—It's a beetle.

—How observant. But what kind?

—I don't know.

—What? You don't know?

—I don't know. I don't really care, either.

—Oh, please.

—Fine. Danni leaned forward until her eyeballs were scant inches above the motionless insect. —Hmm. I'd say a *Spurious exoticus minor*, closely related to, but not to be confused with, the *Spurious eroticus major*. Yep.

Merrill stared at the beetle, then Danni. She took Danni's hand and gently squeezed. —You fucking fraud. Let's go get liquored up, hey?

—Hey-hey.


*May 6, 2006*
(D. L. Session 33)

Dr. Green's glasses were opaque as quartz.

—The *Lagerstätte*. Elucidate, if you will.

—A naturalist's wet dream. Ask Norma Fitzwater and Leslie Runyon, Danni said and chuckled wryly. —When Merrill originally brought me here to Cali, she made me join a support group. That was about, what? A year ago, give or take. Kind of a twelve-step program for wannabe suicides. I quit after a few visits. Group therapy isn't my style and the counselor was a royal prick. Before I left, I became friends with Norma, a drug addict and perennial house guest of the state penitentiary before she snagged a wealthy husband. Marrying rich wasn't a cure for everything, though. She claimed to have tried to off herself five or six times, made it sound like an extreme sport.

—A fascinating woman. She was pals with Leslie, a widow like me. Leslie's husband and brother fell off a glacier in Alaska. I didn't like her much. Too creepy for polite company. Unfortunately, Norma had a mother-hen complex, so there was no getting rid of her. Anyway, it wasn't much to write home about. We went to lunch once a week, watched a couple of films, commiserated about our shitty luck. Summer camp stuff.

—You speak of Norma in the past tense. I gather she eventually ended her life, Dr. Green said.

—Oh, yes. She made good on that. Jumped off a hotel roof in the Tenderloin. Left a note to the effect that she and Leslie couldn't face the music anymore. The cops, brilliant as they are, concluded Norma made a suicide pact with Leslie. Leslie's corpse hasn't surfaced yet. The cops figure she's at the bottom of the bay, or moldering in a wooded gully. I doubt that's what happened though.

—You suspect she's alive.

—No, Leslie's dead under mysterious and messy circumstances. It got leaked to the press that the cops found evidence of foul play at her home. There was blood or something on her sheets. They say it dried in the shape of a person curled in the fetal position. They compared it to the flash shadows of victims in Hiroshima. This was deeper, as if the body had been pressed hard into the mattress. The only remains were her watch, her diaphragm, her *fillings*, for Christ's sake, stuck to the coagulate that got left behind like afterbirth. Sure, it's bullshit, urban legend fodder. There were some photos in the *Gazette*, some speculation amongst our sorry little circle of neurotics and manic depressives.

—Very unpleasant, but, fortunately, equally improbable.

Danni shrugged. —Here's the thing, though. Norma predicted everything. A month before she killed herself, she let me in on a secret. Her friend Leslie, the creepy lady, had been seeing Bobby. He visited her nightly, begged her to come away with him. And Leslie planned to.

—Her husband, Dr. Green said. —The one who died in Alaska.

—The same. Trust me, I laughed, a little nervously, at this news. I wasn't sure whether to humor Norma or get the hell away from her. We were sitting in a classy restaurant, surrounded by execs in silk ties and Armani suits. Like I said, Norma was loaded. She married into a nice Sicilian family; her husband was in the import-export business, if you get my drift. Beat the hell out of her, though; definitely contributed to her low self-esteem. Right in the middle of our luncheon, between the lobster tails and the éclairs, she leaned over and confided this thing with Leslie and her deceased husband. The ghostly lover.

Dr. Green passed Danni another cigarette. He lighted one of his own and studied her through the blue exhaust. Danni wondered if he wanted a drink as badly as she did.

—How did you react to this information? Dr. Green said.

—I stayed cool, feigned indifference. It wasn't difficult; I was doped to the eyeballs most of the time. Norma claimed there exists a certain quality of grief, so utterly profound, so tragically pure, that it resounds and resonates above and below. A living, bleeding echo. It's the key to a kind of limbo.

—The *Lagerstätte*. Dr. Green licked his thumb and sorted through the papers in the brown folder. —As in the Burgess Shale, the La Brea Tar Pits. Were your friends amateur paleontologists?

—*Lagerstätten* are "resting places" in the Deutsch, and I think that's what the women meant.

—Fascinating choice of mythos.

—People do whatever it takes to cope. Drugs, kamikaze sex, religion, anything. In naming, we seek to order the incomprehensible, yes?

—True.

—Norma pulled this weird piece of jagged, gray rock from her purse. Not rock—a petrified bone shard. A fang or a long, wicked rib splinter. Supposedly human. I could tell it was *old*; it reminded me of all those fossils of trilobites I used to play with. It radiated an aura of antiquity, like it had survived a shift of deep geological time. Norma got it from Leslie and Leslie had gotten it from someone else; Norma claimed to have no idea who, although I suspect she was lying; there was definitely a certain slyness in her eyes. For all I know, it's osmosis. She pricked her finger on the shard and gestured at the blood that oozed on her plate. Danni shivered and clenched her left hand. —The scene was surreal. Norma said: *Grief is blood, Danni. Blood is the living path to everywhere. Blood opens the way*. She said if I offered myself to the *Lagerstätte*, Virgil would come to me and take me into the house of dreams. But I wanted to know whether it would really be him and not… an imitation. She said, *Does it matter?* My skin crawled as if I were waking from a long sleep to something awful, something my primal self recognized and feared. Like fire.

—You believe the bone was human.

—I don't know. Norma insisted I accept it as a gift from her and Leslie. I really didn't want to, but the look on her face, it was intense.

—Where did it come from? The bone.

—The *Lagerstätte*.

—Of course. What did you do?

Danni looked down at her hands, the left with its jagged white scar in the meat and muscle of her palm, and deeper into the darkness of the earth. —The same as Leslie. I called them.

—You called them. Virgil and Keith.

—Yes. I didn't plan to go through with it. I got drunk, and when I'm like that, my thoughts get kind of screwy. I don't act in character.

—Oh. Dr. Green thought that over. —When you say called, what exactly do you mean?

She shrugged and flicked ashes into the ashtray. Even though Dr. Green had been there the morning they stitched the wound, she guarded the secret of its origin with a zeal bordering on pathological.

Danni had brought the weird bone to the apartment. Once alone, she drank the better half of a bottle of Maker's Mark and then sliced her palm with the sharp edge of the bone and made a doorway in blood. She slathered a vertical seam, a demarcation between her existence and the abyss, in the plaster wall at the foot of her bed. She smeared Virgil and Keith's initials and sent a little prayer into the night. In a small clay pot she'd bought at a market, she shredded her identification, her (mostly defunct) credit cards, her social security card, a lock of her hair, and burned the works with the tallow of a lamb. Then, in the smoke and shadows, she finished getting drunk off her ass and promptly blacked out.

Merrill wasn't happy; Danni had bled like the proverbial stuck pig, soaked through the sheets into the mattress. Merrill decided her friend had horribly botched another run for the Pearly Gates. She had brought Danni to the hospital for a bunch of stitches and introduced her to Dr. Green. Of course Danni didn't admit another suicide attempt. She doubted her conducting a black-magic ritual would help matters either. She said nothing, simply agreed to return for sessions with the good doctor. He was blandly pleasant, eminently nonthreatening. She didn't think he could help, but that wasn't the point. The point was to please Merrill and Merrill insisted on the visits.

Back home, Merrill confiscated the bone, the ritual fetish, and threw it in the trash. Later, she tried like hell to scrub the stain. In the end she gave up and painted the whole room blue.

A couple days after that particular bit of excitement, Danni found the bone at the bottom of her sock drawer. It glistened with a cruel, lusterless intensity. Like the monkey's paw, it had returned and that didn't surprise her. She folded it into a kerchief and locked it in a jewelry box she'd kept since first grade.

All these months gone by, Danni remained silent on the subject.

Finally, Dr. Green sighed.—Is that when you began seeing Virgil in the faces of strangers? These doppelgängers? He smoked his cigarette with the joyless concentration of a prisoner facing a firing squad. It was obvious from his expression that the meter had rolled back to zero.

—No, not right away. Nothing happened, Danni said. —Nothing ever does, at first.

—No, I suppose not. Tell me about the vineyard. What happened there?

—I… I got lost.

—That's where all this really begins, isn't it? The fugue, perhaps other things.

Danni gritted her teeth. She thought of elephants and graveyards. Dr. Green was right, in his own smug way. Six weeks after Danni sliced her hand, Merrill took her for a daytrip to the beach. Merrill rented a convertible and made a picnic. It was nice; possibly the first time Danni felt human since the accident; the first time she'd wanted to do anything besides mope in the apartment and play depressing music.

After some discussion, they chose Bolton Park, a lovely stretch of coastline way out past Kingwood. The area was foreign to Danni, so she bought a road map pamphlet at a gas station. The brochure listed a bunch of touristy places. Windsurfers and birdwatchers favored the area, but the guide warned of dangerous riptides. The women had no intention of swimming; they stayed near a cluster of great big rocks at the north end of the beach—below the cliff with the steps that led up to the posh houses; the summer homes of movie stars and advertising executives; the beautiful people.

On the way home, Danni asked if they might stop at Kirkston Vineyards. It was a hole-in-the-wall, only briefly listed in the guidebook. There were no pictures. They drove in circles for an hour tracking the place down—Kirkston was off the beaten path; a village of sorts. There was a gift shop and an inn, and a few antique houses. The winery was fairly large and charming in a rustic fashion, and that essentially summed up the entire place.

Danni thought it was a cute setup; Merrill was bored stiff and did what she always did when she'd grown weary of a situation—she flirted like mad with one of the tour guides. Pretty soon, she disappeared with the guy on a private tour.

There were twenty or thirty people in the tour group—a bunch of elderly folks who'd arrived on a bus and a few couples pretending they were in Europe. After Danni lost Merrill in the crowd, she went outside to explore until her friend surfaced again.

Perhaps fifty yards from the winery steps, Virgil waited in the lengthening shadows of a cedar grove. That was the first of the phantoms. Too far away for positive identification, his face was a white smudge. He hesitated and regarded her over his shoulder before he ducked into the undergrowth. She knew it was impossible, knew that it was madness, or worse, and went after him, anyway.

Deeper into the grounds she encountered crumbled walls of a ruined garden hidden under a bower of willow trees and honeysuckle vines. She passed through a massive marble archway, so thick with sap it had blackened like a smoke stack. Inside was a sunken area and a clogged fountain decorated with cherubs and gargoyles. There were scattered benches made of stone slabs, and piles of rubble overrun by creepers and moss. Water pooled throughout the garden, mostly covered by algae and scum; mosquito larvae squirmed beneath drowned leaves. Ridges of broken stone and mortar petrified in the slop and slime of that boggy soil and made waist-high calculi amongst the freestanding masonry.

Her hand throbbed with a sudden, magnificent stab of pain. She hissed through her teeth. The freshly knitted, pink slash, her Freudian scar, had split and blood seeped so copiously her head swam. She ripped the sleeve off her blouse and made a hasty tourniquet. A grim, sullen quiet drifted in; a blizzard of silence. The bees weren't buzzing and the shadows in the trees waxed red and gold as the light decayed.

Virgil stepped from behind stalagmites of fallen stone, maybe thirty feet away. She knew with every fiber of her being that this was a fake, a body double, and yet she wanted nothing more than to hurl herself into his arms. Up until that moment, she didn't realize how much she'd missed him, how achingly final her loneliness had become.

Her glance fell upon a gleaming wedge of stone where it thrust from the water like a dinosaur's tooth, and as shapes within shapes became apparent, she understood this wasn't a garden. It was a graveyard.

Virgil opened his arms—

—I'm not comfortable talking about this, Danni said. —Let's move on.

*August 9, 2006*

Friday was karaoke night at the Candy Apple.

In the golden days of her previous life, Danni had a battalion of friends and colleagues with whom to attend the various academic functions and cocktail socials as required by her professional affiliation with a famous East Coast university. Barhopping had seldom been the excursion of choice.

Tonight, a continent and several light-years removed from such circumstances, she nursed an overly strong margarita, while up on the stage a couple of drunken women with big hair and smeared makeup stumbled through that old Kenny Rogers standby, "Ruby, Don't Take Your Love to Town." The fake redhead was a receptionist named Sheila, and her blonde partner, Delores, a vice president of human resources. Both of them worked at Merrill's literary magazine and they were partying off their second and third divorces respectively.

Danni wasn't drunk, although mixing her medication with alcohol wasn't helping matters; her nose had begun to tingle and her sensibilities were definitely sliding toward the nihilistic side. Also, she seemed to be hallucinating again. She'd spotted two Virgil look-alikes between walking through the door and her third margarita; that was a record, so far. She hadn't noticed either of the men enter the lounge, they simply appeared.

One of the mystery men sat amongst a group of happily chattering yuppie kids; he'd worn a sweater and parted his hair exactly like her husband used to before an important interview or presentation. The brow was wrong though, and the smile way off. He established eye contact and his gaze made her prickle all over because this simulacrum was so very authentic; if not for the plastic sheen and the unwholesome smile, he was the man she'd looked at across the breakfast table for a dozen years. Eventually he stood and wandered away from his friends and disappeared through the front door into the night. None of the kids seemed to miss him.

The second guy sat alone at the far end of the bar; he was much closer to the authentic thing; he had the nose, the jaw, even the loose way of draping his hands over his knees. However, this one was a bit too raw boned to pass as *her* Virgil; his teeth too large, his arms too long. He stared across the room, too-dark eyes fastened on her face and she looked away and by the time she glanced up again he was gone.

She checked to see if Merrill noticed the Virgil impersonators. Merrill blithely sipped her Corona and flirted with a couple lawyer types at the adjoining table. The suits kept company with a voluptuous woman who was growing long in the tooth and had piled on enough compensatory eye shadow and lipstick to host her own talk show. The woman sulked and shot dangerous glares at Merrill. Merrill smirked coyly and touched the closest suit on the arm.

Danni lighted a cigarette and tried to keep her expression neutral while her pulse fluttered and she scanned the room with the corners of her eyes like a trapped bird. Should she call Dr. Green in the morning? Was he even in the office on weekends? What color would the new pills be?

Presently, the late dinner and theater crowd arrived en masse and the lounge became packed. The temperature immediately shot up ten degrees and the resultant din of several dozen competing conversations drowned all but shouts. Merrill had recruited the lawyers (who turned out to be an insurance claims investigator and a CPA) Ned and Thomas, and their miffed associate Glenna (a court clerk), to join the group and migrate to another, hopefully more peaceful watering hole.

They shambled through neon-washed night, a noisy, truncated herd of quasi-strangers, arms locked for purchase against the mist-slick sidewalks. Danni found herself squashed between Glenna and Ned the Investigator. Ned grasped her waist in a slack, yet vaguely proprietary fashion; his hand was soft with sweat, his paunchy face made more uncomely with livid blotches and the avaricious expression of a drowsy predator. His shirt reeked so powerfully of whiskey it might've been doused in the stuff.

Merrill pulled them to a succession of bars and nightclubs and all-night bistros. Somebody handed Danni a beer as they milled in the vaulted entrance of an Irish pub and she drank it like tap water, not really tasting it, and her ears hurt and the evening rapidly devolved into a tangle of raucous music and smoke that reflected the fluorescent lights like coke-blacked miners lamps, and at last a cool, humid darkness shattered by headlights and the sulfurous orange glow of angry clouds.

By her haphazard count, she glimpsed in excess of fifty incarnations of Virgil. Several at the tavern, solitary men mostly submerged in the recessed booths, observing her with stony diffidence through beer steins and shot glasses; a dozen more scattered along the boulevard, listless nomads whose eyes slid around, not quite touching anything. When a city bus grumbled past, every passenger's head swiveled in unison beneath the repeating flare of dome lights. Every face pressed against the dirty windows belonged to him. Their lifelike masks bulged and contorted with inconsolable longing.

Ned escorted her to his place, a warehouse apartment in a row of identical warehouses between the harbor and the railroad tracks. The building had been converted to a munitions factory during the Second World War, then housing in the latter '60s. It stood black and gritty; its greasy windows sucked in the feeble illumination of the lonely beacons of passing boats and the occasional car.

They took a clanking cargo elevator to the top, the penthouse as Ned laughingly referred to his apartment. The elevator was a box encased in grates that exposed the inner organs of the shaft and the dark tunnels of passing floors. It could've easily hoisted a baby grand piano. Danni pressed her cheek to vibrating metal and shut her eyes tight against vertigo and the canteen-like slosh of too many beers in her stomach.

Ned's apartment was sparsely furnished and remained mostly in gloom even after he turned on the floor lamp and went to fix nightcaps. Danni collapsed onto the corner of a couch abridging the shallow nimbus of light and stared raptly at her bone-white hand curled into the black leather. Neil Diamond crooned from velvet speakers. Ned said something about his record collection and, faintly, ice cracked from its tray and clinked in glass with the resonance of a tuning fork.

Danni's hand shivered as if it might double and divide. She was cold now, in the sticky hot apartment, and her thighs trembled. Ned slipped a drink into her hand and placed his own hand on her shoulder, splayed his soft fingers on her collar, traced her collar bone with his moist fingertip. Danni flinched and poured gin down her throat until Ned took the glass and began to nuzzle her ear, his teeth clicking against the pearl stud, his overheated breath like smoldering creosote and kerosene, and as he tugged at her blouse strap, she began to cry. Ned lurched above her and his hands were busy with his belt and pants, and these fell around his ankles and his loafers. He made a fist in a mass of her hair and yanked her face against his groin; his linen shirttails fell across Danni's shoulders and he bulled himself into her gasping mouth. She gagged, overwhelmed by the ripeness of sweat and whiskey and urine, the rank humidity, the bruising insistence of him, and she convulsed, arms flailing in epileptic spasms, and vomited. Ned's hips pumped for several seconds and then his brain caught up with current events and he cried out in dismay and disgust and nearly capsized the couch as he scrambled away from her and a caramel gush of half-digested cocktail shrimp and alcohol.

Danni dragged herself from the couch and groped for the door. The door was locked with a bolt and chain and she battered at these, sobbing and choking. Ned's curses were muffled by a thin partition and the low thunder of water sluicing through corroded pipes. She flung open the door and was instantly lost in a cavernous hall that telescoped madly. The door behind her was a cave mouth, the windows were holes, were burrows. She toppled down a flight of stairs.

Danni lay crumpled, damp concrete wedged against the small of her back and pinching the back of her legs. Ghostly radiance cast shadows upon the piebald walls of the narrow staircase and rendered the scrawls of graffiti into fragmented hieroglyphics. Copper and salt filled her mouth. Her head was thick and spongy and when she moved it, little comets shot through her vision. A moth jerked in zigzags near her face, jittering upward at frantic angles toward a naked bulb. The bulb was brown and black with dust and cigarette smoke. A solid shadow detached from the gloom of the landing; a slight, pitchy silhouette that wavered at the edges like gasoline fumes.

*Mommy?* A small voice echoed, familiar and strange, the voice of a child or a castrato and it plucked at her insides, sent tremors through her.

—Oh, God, she said and vomited again, spilling herself against the rough surface of the wall. The figure became two, then four and a pack of childlike shapes assembled on the landing. The pallid corona of the brown bulb dimmed.

She rolled away, onto her belly, and began to crawl…

*August 10, 2006*

The police located Danni semiconscious in the alley behind the warehouse apartments. She didn't understand much of what they said and she couldn't muster the resolve to volunteer the details of her evening's escapades. Merrill rode with her in the ambulance to the emergency room where, following a two-hour wait, a haggard surgeon determined Danni suffered from a number of nasty contusions, minor lacerations, and a punctured tongue. No concussion, however. He punched ten staples into her scalp, handed over a prescription for painkillers, and sent her home with an admonishment to return in twelve hours for observation.

After they'd settled safe and sound at the apartment, Merrill wrapped Danni in a blanket and boiled a pot of green tea. Lately, Merrill was into feng shui and Chinese herbal remedies. It wasn't quite dawn and so they sat in the shadows in the living room. There were no recriminations, although Merrill lapsed into a palpable funk; hers was the grim expression of guilt and helplessness attendant to her perceived breach of guardianship. Danni patted her hand and drifted off to sleep.

When Danni came to again, it was early afternoon and Merrill was in the kitchen banging pots. Over bowls of hot noodle soup Merrill explained she'd called in sick for a couple days. She thought they should get Danni's skull checked for dents and rent some movies and lie around with a bowl of popcorn and do essentially nothing. Tomorrow might be a good day to go window shopping for an Asian print to mount in their pitifully barren entryway.

Merrill summoned a cab. The rain came in sheets against the windows of the moving car and Danni dozed to the thud of the wipers, trying to ignore the driver's eyes upon her from the rearview. He looked unlike the fuzzy headshot on his license fixed to the visor. In the photo his features were burnt teak and warped by the deformation of aging plastic.

They arrived at the hospital and signed in and went into the bowels of the grand old beast to radiology. A woman in a white jacket injected dye into Danni's leg and loaded her into a shiny, cold machine the girth of a bread truck and ordered her to keep her head still. The technician's voice buzzed through a hidden transmitter, repulsively intimate as if a fly had crawled into her ear canal. When the rubber jackhammers started in on the steel shell, she closed her eyes and saw Virgil and Keith waving to her from the convex windows of the plane. The propeller spun so slowly she could track its revolutions.

—The doctor says they're negative. The technician held photographic plates of Danni's brain against a softly flickering pane of light. —See? No problems at all.

*The crimson seam dried black on the bedroom wall. The band of black acid eating plaster until the wall swung open on smooth, silent hinges. Red darkness pulsed in the rift. White leaves crumbled and sank, each one a lost face. A shadow slowly shaped itself into human form. The shadow man regarded her, his hand extended, approaching her without moving his shadow legs.*

Merrill thanked the woman in the clipped manner she reserved for those who provoked her distaste, and put a protective arm over Danni's shoulders. Danni had taken an extra dose of tranquilizers to sand the rough edges. Reality was a taffy pull.

*Pour out your blood and they'll come back to you, Norma said, and stuck her bleeding finger into her mouth. Her eyes were cold and dark as the eyes of a carrion bird. Bobby and Leslie coupled on a squeaking bed. Their frantic rhythm gradually slowed and they began to melt and merge until their flesh rendered to a sticky puddle of oil and fat and patches of hair. The forensics photographers came, clicking and whirring, eyes deader than the lenses of their cameras. They smoked cigarettes in the hallway and chatted with the plainclothes about baseball and who was getting pussy and who wasn't; everybody had sashimi for lunch, noodles for supper, and took work home and drank too much. Leslie curdled in the sheets and her parents were long gone, so she was already most of the way to being reduced to a serial number and forgotten in a cardboard box in a storeroom. Except, Leslie stood in a doorway in the grimy bulk of a nameless building. She stood, hip-shot and half-silhouetted, naked and lovely as a Botticelli nude. Disembodied arms circled her from behind, and large, muscular hands cupped her breasts. She nodded, expressionless as a wax death masque, and stepped back into the black. The iron door closed.*

Danni's brain was fine. No problems at all.

Merrill took her home and made her supper. Fried chicken; Danni's favorite from a research stint studying the migration habits of three species of arachnids at a southern institute where grits did double duty as breakfast and lunch.

Danni dozed intermittently, lulled by the staccato flashes of the television. She stirred and wiped drool from her lips, thankfully too dopey to suffer much embarrassment. Merrill helped her to bed and tucked her in and kissed her goodnight on the mouth. Danni was surprised by the warmth of her breath, her tenderness; then she was heavily asleep, floating facedown in the red darkness, the amniotic wastes of a secret world.

*August 11, 2006*

Merrill cooked waffles for breakfast; she claimed to have been a "champeen" hash-slinger as an undergrad, albeit Danni couldn't recall that particular detail of their shared history. Although food crumbled like cardboard on her tongue, Danni smiled gamely and cleared her plate. The fresh orange juice in the frosted glass was a mouthful of lye. Merrill had apparently jogged over to Yang's and picked up a carton the exact instant the poor fellow rolled back the metal curtains from his shop front, and Danni swallowed it and hoped she didn't drop the glass because her hand was shaking so much. The pleasant euphoria of painkillers and sedatives had drained away, usurped by a gnawing, allusive dread, a swell of self-disgust and revulsion.

The night terrors tittered and scuffled in the cracks and crannies of the tiny kitchen, whistled at her in a pitch only she and dogs could hear. Any second now, the broom closet would creak open and a ghastly figure shamble forth, licking lips riven by worms. At any moment the building would shudder and topple in an avalanche of dust and glass and shearing girders. She slumped in her chair, fixated on the chipped vase, its cargo of wilted geraniums drooping over the rim. Merrill bustled around her, tidying up with what she dryly attributed as her latent German efficiency, although her mannerisms suggested a sense of profound anxiety. When the phone chirped and it was Sheila reporting some minor emergency at the office, her agitation multiplied as she scoured her little address book for someone to watch over Danni for a few hours.

Danni told her to go, she'd be okay—maybe watch a soap and take a nap. She promised to sit tight in the apartment, come what may. Appearing only slightly mollified, Merrill agreed to leave, vowing a speedy return.

Late afternoon slipped over the city, lackluster and overcast. Came the desultory honk and growl of traffic, the occasional shout, the off-tempo drumbeat from the square. Reflections of the skyline patterned a blank span of wall. Water gurgled, and the disjointed mumble of radio or television commentary came muffled from the neighboring apartments. Her eyes leaked and the shakes traveled from her hands into the large muscles of her shoulders. Her left hand ached.

A child murmured in the hallway, followed by scratching at the door. The bolt rattled. She stood and looked across the living area at the open door of the bedroom. The bedroom dilated. Piles of jagged rocks twined with coarse brown seaweed instead of the bed, the dresser, her unseemly stacks of magazines. A figure stirred amid the weird rocks and unfolded at the hips with the horrible alacrity of a tarantula. *You filthy whore.* She groaned and hooked the door with her ankle and kicked it shut.

Danni went to the kitchen and slid a carving knife from its wooden block. She walked to the bathroom and turned on the shower. Everything seemed too shiny, except the knife. The knife hung loosely in her fingers; its blade was dark and pitted. She stripped her robe and stepped into the shower and drew the curtain. Steam began to fill the room. Hot water beat against the back of her neck, her spine and buttocks as she rested her forehead against the tiles.

*What have you done? You filthy bitch.* She couldn't discern whether that accusing whisper had bubbled from her brain, or trickled in with the swirling steam. *What have you done?* It hardly mattered now that nothing was of any substance, of any importance besides the knife. Her hand throbbed as the scar seperated along its seam. Blood and water swirled down the drain.

*Danni.* The floorboards settled and a tepid draft brushed her calves. She raised her head and a silhouette filled the narrow door, an incomprehensible blur through the shower curtain. Danni dropped the knife. She slid down the wall into a fetal position. Her teeth chattered, and her animal self took possession.

She remembered the ocean, acres of driftwood littering a beach, Virgil's grin as he paid out the tether of a dragonhead kite they'd bought in Chinatown. She remembered the corpses hanging in her closet, and whimpered.

A hand pressed against the translucent fabric, dimpled it inward, fingers spread. The hand squelched on the curtain. Blood ran from its palm and slithered in descending ladders.

—Oh, Danni said. Blearily, through a haze of tears and steam, she reached up and pressed her bloody left hand against the curtain, locked palms with the apparition, giddily cognizant this was a gruesome parody of the star-crossed lovers who kiss through glass. —Virgil, she said, chest hitching with sobs.

—You don't have to go, Merrill said and dragged the curtain aside. She too wept, and nearly fell into the tub as she embraced Danni and the water soaked her clothes, and quantities of blood spilled between them, and Danni saw her friend had found the fetish bone, because there it was, in a black slick on the floor, trailing a spray of droplets like a nosebleed. —You can stay with me. Please stay, Merrill said. She stroked Danni's hair, hugged her as if to keep her from floating away with the steam as it condensed on the mirror, the small window, and slowly evaporated.

*May 6, 2006*
(D. L. Session 33)
—Danni, do you read the newspapers? Watch the news? Dr. Green said this carefully, giving weight to the question.

—Sure, sometimes.

—The police recovered her body months ago. He removed a newspaper clipping from the folder and pushed it toward her.

—Who? Danni did not look at the clipping.

—Leslie Runyon. An anonymous tip led the police to a landfill. She'd been wrapped in a tarp and buried in a heap of trash. Death by suffocation, according to the coroner. You really don't remember.

Danni shook her head. —No. I haven't heard anything like that.

—Do you think I'm lying?

—Do you think I'm a paranoid delusional?

—Keep talking and I'll get back to you on that, he said, and smiled. —What happened at the vineyard, Danni? When they found you, you were quite a mess, according to the reports.

—Yeah. Quite a mess, Danni said. She closed her eyes and fell back into herself, fell down the black mineshaft into the memory of the garden, the *Lagerstätte*.

Virgil waited to embrace her.

Only a graveyard, an open charnel, contained so much death. The rubble and masonry were actually layers of bones; a reef of calcified skeletons locked in heaps; and mummified corpses; enough withered faces to fill the backs of a thousand milk cartons, frozen twigs of arms and legs wrapped about their eternal partners. These masses of ossified humanity were cloaked in skeins of moss and hair and rotted leaves.

*Norma beckoned from the territory of waking dreams. She stood upon the precipice of a rooftop. She said, Welcome to the* Lagerstätte. *Welcome to the secret graveyard of the despairing and the damned. She spread her arms and pitched backwards.*

Danni moaned and hugged her fist wrapped in its sopping rags. She had come unwitting, although utterly complicit in her devotion, and now stood before a terrible mystery of the world. Her knees trembled and folded.

Virgil shuttered rapidly and shifted within arm's reach. He smelled of aftershave and clove, the old, poignantly familiar scents. He also smelled of earthiness and mold, and his face began to destabilize, to buckle as packed dirt buckles under a deluge and becomes mud.

*Come and sleep,* he said in the rasp of leaves and dripping water. His hands bit into her shoulders and slowly, inexorably drew her against him. His chest was icy as the void, his hands and arms iron as they tightened around her and laid her down in the muck and the slime. His lips closed over hers. His tongue was pliant and fibrous and she thought of the stinking, brown rot that carpeted the deep forests. Other hands plucked at her clothes, her hair; other mouths suckled her neck, her breasts, and she thought of misshapen fungi and scurrying centipedes, the ever scrabbling ants, and how all things that squirmed in the sunless interstices crept and patiently fed.

Danni went blind, but images streamed through the snarling wires of her consciousness. *Virgil and Keith rocked in the swing on the porch of their New England home. They'd just finished playing catch in the backyard; Keith still wore his Red Sox jersey, and Virgil rolled a baseball in his fingers. The stars brightened in the lowering sky and the streetlights fizzed on, one by one. Her mother stood knee-deep in the surf, apron strings flapping in a rising wind. She held out her hands. Keith, pink and wrinkled, screamed in Danni's arms, his umbilical cord still wet. Virgil pressed his hand to a wall of glass. He mouthed, I love you, honey.*

*I love you, mommy, Keith said, his wizened infant's face tilted toward her own. Her father carefully laid out his clothes, his police uniform of twenty-six years, and climbed into the bathtub. We love you, girlie, Dad said, and stuck the barrel of his service revolver into his mouth. Oh, quitting had run in the family, was a genetic certainty given the proper set of circumstances. Mom had drowned herself in the sea, such was her grief. Her brother, he'd managed to kill himself in a police action in some foreign desert. This gravitation to self-destruction was ineluctable as her blood.*

Danni thrashed upright. Dank mud sucked at her, plastered her hair and drooled from her mouth and nose. She choked for breath, hands clawing at an assailant who had vanished into the mist creeping upon the surface of the marsh. Her fingernails raked and broke against the glaciated cheek of a vaguely female corpse; a stranger made wholly inhuman by the slow, steady vise of gravity and time. Danni groaned. Somewhere, a whippoorwill began to sing.

Voices called for her through the trees; shrill and hoarse. Their shouts echoed weakly, as if from the depths of a well. These were unmistakably the voices of the living. Danni's heart thudded, galvanized by the adrenal response to her near-death experience, and, more subtly, an inchoate sense of guilt, as if she'd done something unutterably foul. She scrambled to her feet and fled.

Oily night flooded the forest. A boy cried, *Mommy, mommy!* Amid the plain-tive notes of the whippoorwill. Danni floundered from the garden, scourged by terror and no small regret. By the time she found her way in the dark, came stumbling into the circle of rescue searchers and their flashlights, Danni had mostly forgotten where she'd come from or what she'd been doing there.

Danni opened her eyes to the hospital, the dour room, Dr. Green's implacable curiosity.

She said, —Can we leave it for now? Just for now. I'm tired. You have no idea.

Dr. Green removed his glasses. His eyes were bloodshot and hard, but human after all. —Danni, you're going to be fine, he said.

—Am I?

—Miles to go before we sleep, and all that jazz. But yes, I believe so. You want to open up, and that's very good. It's progress.

Danni smoked.

—Next week we can discuss further treatment options. There are several medicines we haven't looked at; maybe we can get you a dog. I know you live in an apartment, but service animals have been known to work miracles. Go home and get some rest. That's the best therapy I can recommend.

Danni inhaled the last of her cigarette and held the remnants of fire close to her heart. She ground the butt into the ashtray. She exhaled a stream of smoke and wondered if her soul, the souls of her beloved, looked anything like that. Un-certain of what to say, she said nothing. The wheels of the recorder stopped.

# HARRY AND THE MONKEY

## EUAN HARVEY

Urban legend: a modern story of obscure origin and with little or no supporting evidence that spreads spontaneously in varying forms and often has elements of humor, moralizing, or horror: *Are there alligators living in the New York City sewer system, or is that just an urban legend?*

Also called urban myth.
[Origin: 1970–75]

Based on the *Random House Unabridged Dictionary,*
© Random House, Inc. 2006.

\* \* \*

This is a true story.

I have three kids, all boys. Son number three is Harry. He's younger than the others by three years (he is three and a half when this story begins); he looks more like me, and he's a devious and unscrupulous manipulator—like all youngest children. He laughs a lot, cries a lot, breaks things a lot, and fights with his brothers a lot. He goes to kindergarten with all the other kids, plays football (well... runs after the ball flapping his arms and howling with glee, anyway), enjoys twisting the arms and heads off his collection of cheap plastic action figures, and gets cranky when he's tired.

The reason I'm telling you this is simple: Harry's a perfectly normal kid. Average and unremarkable.

If you think about it, that makes what happened even more unsettling.

What if it's not only him?

What if it's all kids?

* * *

You've heard of the crocodile in the sewers, right? Kid gets reptile for present, reptile grows (as they do), kid gets bored, flushes it down toilet. Only… the croc doesn't die. It stays down there, preying on rats and swimming around in the pungent dark. Getting bigger. And perhaps, as it grows, it tires of rats. Then one day, when it's down in the fetid gloom, just its evil little eyes above the surface of the water, it sees a splash of light: a man holding a flashlight. Next thing is a little v-shaped ripple, and the eyes draw closer to the puddle of light and the man wearing his bright yellow rubber boots. Closer, and closer…

A nasty little image. And one that's recognizable to anyone from the West. The story may not be true—but it resonates.

But in Thailand, where I live, that particular myth isn't part of the culture. No resonance. Mention it in conversation, and you'll get a WTF? look. No crocs in the sewers here. At least, no *stories* about crocs in the sewers—but we'll come to that later.

There are urban myths in Thailand, though—just not the ones we have in the West. And like all urban myths, they've got a very nasty little core to them, a little splinter of horror embedded in the story, something that festers in your mind so that you absolutely *must* tell someone else.

The nastiest one I've heard is the *rot jap dek*.

See, there's this van. A black van, with shiny windows so you can't see in. And this van cruises round the main roads, and into the sois, and through the moobahns, and it's looking for children. What happens is this: the van follows a kid, and if the van sees that the kid is alone, then it silently (because the engine in this van is specially made to be very quiet) pulls up next to the kid, and the doors to the van quietly slide open, and a pair of very long and very thin arms snatches up the kid, and pulls him (screaming, kicking) into the thick darkness inside the van. Then the doors close, the van purrs off, and no one ever sees the kid again.

Unpleasant, right?

The trimmings to this story vary. Some versions sound plausible—if horrific. There's one that says the van is driven by Chinese organleggers, and the kids have their hearts, lungs, kidneys, and all the rest chopped out and sold on the black market. Less believable versions say it's Cambodians, the Khmer Rouge stealing Thai kids to raise them as guerrillas, Janissary-style. I've even heard it's a *luk-chin* factory, which has found out that human flesh makes its meatballs more delicious.

But though the semiotic crud the story has accumulated varies, the central element remains the same: a black minivan that steals children.

This is the *rot jap dek*.

Remember this. It's important, and if you're very unlucky, there may be a test. Black van: *rot jap dek*.

* * *

The most famous monkey colony in Thailand is in Lopburi. There, as in Delhi, monkeys scamper through traffic, beg (or steal) food, execute primal snatch-and-grab raids on unwary tourists, swarm over the Angkor-period ruins in the town center, and generally make a bloody nuisance of themselves.

There are however numerous other monkey colonies in urban areas in Thailand, some surprisingly close to Bangkok. One of these is at Don Hoi Lod in Samut Songkhram, about two hours drive from my house. Don Hoi Lod is on the coast—but if you're getting an image of palm trees and white sand, bin it. Just south of Bangkok, the coast of Thailand is swamp and mangrove forest. The "beach" at Don Hoi Lod is mud. Lots of mud, with masses of mangroves. So why go?

Well, crabs like mangroves. A lot. And so, it turns out, do other edible sea creatures. Which in turns means that Don Hoi Lod is famous for cheap seafood: crabs, oysters, tiger prawns, and fish—they're all there in abundance.

And so, for some reason, are monkeys. Whether the monkeys lived there before and the restaurants at Don Hoi Lod just encroached on their habitat, or whether the monkeys moved in to scavenge off the seafood leftovers, I don't know. What I do know is that Don Hoi Lod is crawling (scampering?) with monkeys.

So there I was, driving down the narrow road that leads from the Thonburi-Paktho highway. It's a holiday—the Day of Vesak, if I remember right—so the traffic's fairly heavy and we're just bimbling slowly along, not quite in a traffic jam, but not moving very fast, either. Hunger is making the boys grumpy, the air-con is giving me a headache, and the sun keeps catching the back windscreen of the car in front, making me wince.

And then Robert (son number one) does something unpleasant to Harry. I can't remember what exactly; I think it had to do with sweets and the denying thereof. Harry starts squalling, and tugging on my shirt from behind demanding that I intervene. Fon (my wife) snarls at Harry (she's got a worse headache than me). In response to this, Harry starts yelling, and the other two boys in the back start squabbling loudly.

In short, we're right at that stage familiar to every parent, that point just before you crack and start doing all the things that parenting books tell you not to.

However, right at that very moment, a monkey jumped up onto the hood of the car. It knuckle-walked to the windshield, then sat scratching its bottom and peering at me with benign interest.

I seized the opportunity thus offered. "Look, Harry! A monkey!"

Harry's mouth shut with a click of teeth. His eyes widened, then he scrambled forward, pointing at the windshield. "Monkey! Monkey! Daddy, monkey!"

The monkey yawned, showing yellow and rather alarmingly long teeth, scratched its rump, then ambled up the windshield and onto the roof, leaving a trail of muddy little pawprints up the glass.

Harry watched it go, then stared at the roof intently, as if he could see through the metal. After a few moments, he looked at me, then pointed to the roof and said solemnly, "Monkey." Then, in case his mother didn't understand, he helpfully translated it into Thai for her, "*Ling.*"

For the rest of the day, Harry was easily distracted. Any sign of grumpiness, and I'd point at some random location and say, "Harry, look! The monkey! Can you see the monkey?"

Harry would spring to his feet, quivering with excitement and peer in the direction I'd pointed. If there did actually happen to be a monkey there, he'd stare at it, then shout, "Monkey! Monkey! Monkey! Daddy, monkey!" If there was no monkey there (as there most often wasn't), he'd look at me and ask where it had gone. So I said that he'd have to be quick, as monkeys were very shy and didn't like people staring at them.

But as it turned out, that last part only really applied to me, and not Harry.

\* \* \*

This really is a true story. What comes below is from the *Bangkok Post*, Saturday November 10, 2007:

> IN-DEPTH: MISSING CHILDREN
> *In 2006, more than 46,000 children were reported missing in Thailand, according to the two-year-old National Missing Person's Bureau. But as staggering as that number is, yet more alarming is the fact that this represents a year-on-year increase of 6% over 2005.*

46,000. Now you think about that for a moment.

\* \* \*

Monkeys creep me out. Really, they're just... horrible. First, monkeys have very large teeth relative to the size of their head. Imagine a human whose canines are as long as the distance from the nose to the chin—about one third of the length of the head. Now imagine what it looks like when this person yawns.

Yes. Exactly. Just like that.

Second, monkeys have that whole almost-human-but-not-quite thing going on. Like their hands. They're *almost* human, but... deformed. Yes, I know that they're not really deformed, but as a human, my frame of reference for non-deformed is human. Dog's paws? No, they're not deformed. They're not close enough to trigger the human interpretation. But monkey's paws, that's a different story. Close enough to human so that your mind goes *click*, and instead of looking at them as an animal, you're interpreting in terms of the human. And from that perspective, monkeys *are* deformed. Freaks. The thumb's all wrong, and the joints are off, and they've got that depressed forehead with dead little black eyes peering out from underneath. You look at their feet, and they're almost human.

Almost… but not quite.

* * *

*The Bangkok Post,* Tuesday July 10, 2007

> *Samut Sakhon—Police announced they were scaling back their search for a missing 5-year-old girl yesterday, saying they would focus instead on tips on the girl's location. Sirikul Siriyamongkol was last seen on Sunday morning playing in the soi in front of the house her parents live in near Om Noi. More than 100 police officers and neighbors searched for the girl on Monday, making house-to-house enquiries as well as posting signs asking for help in locating her.*

Like I said: it's all true. If they've found the little girl, there hasn't been a damn thing about it in the *Bangkok Post*. Of course, maybe the editor just decided the return of the kid wasn't newsworthy.

Maybe.

Om Noi is about five klicks from my house.

* * *

When I was young, my father had something called the "doolally." When he wanted to get rid of me and my brother, he'd go to the kitchen door, stare down the garden—sometimes shielding his eyes with his hand, as if staring off in the far distance—and he'd slowly say, "You know, I think that's a doolally down there." He'd pause, then he'd say to me and my brother, "Quick! Go and get him! The doolally's eating our apples! Quick! Run!" And off my brother and I would toddle, down the garden to the apple trees, there to search fruitlessly for the fabled doolally, which I always pictured as some variety of fat pink bird, rather like a dodo, only squawkier and with a silly-looking head.

My father fooled me for *years* with the doolally. To me, it was real, and it was my sacred duty to stop it from nibbling on our apples. I could see its foolish head, its watery eyes framed by long curling lashes, and I knew it had wobbly legs like a chicken. We tried everything, my brother and I: traps, sneaking down the garden rather than running, even building a hide and concealing ourselves in it as we waited for the doolally to arrive (I was unclear as to whether it flew—clumsily, of course, shedding feathers and veering wildly to and fro—or stalked along like a heron, high-stepping over the fence from the neighbor's garden).

And, as all men turn into their fathers, I ended up doing the same thing to Harry as my father had done to me. Only, instead of a rather silly looking bird, Harry went chasing after a monkey.

I want you to picture a scene: It's a warm Saturday afternoon in the suburbs of Bangkok, the mango trees are whispering to themselves in the lazy breeze blowing through their leaves, kids are riding past my yard on their bikes whooping and hollering, and I'm sitting on my porch drinking a cold beer. Harry bimbles out of the house behind me and starts poking me with a fat finger. I look up, peer into the garden, then say slowly, "You know, I think I see the monkey over there." Harry runs to the porch rail, grips two of the railings in chubby hands, and peers into the garden. "There he is!" I say, pointing at the mango. "Harry! Go and get the monkey! Quickly!" And Harry races off, little legs twinkling as he runs to find the monkey, which apparently hides behind the largest of the three mango trees in our yard.

This goes on for months before things start to change.

The first change was small. My wife—the long-suffering Fon—had bought a huge bag of live king prawns, and we were going to barbecue them. The prawns were sitting in a bowl of water about a foot away from me, and I was getting the barbecue ready. Right at that moment, Harry came up to the bowl, looked down, then squatted next to it with an expression of intense interest on his face.

Every parent knows that expression: It's the one that kids get just before they try and stick the fork in the electrical outlet. I tried saying "no," but Harry took no notice, and poked one of the prawns experimentally. I knew what was coming next, so I pulled out the big guns: "Harry! Look over there! The monkey! Go and get him!"

Harry glanced over his shoulder at the mango tree, then shook his head. "Monkey *mai mi*," he said. (The monkey's not there.)

"Yes he is!" I said. "Look! Oo! The bugger's eating our mangos! Go get him, Harry!"

"Monkey *mai mi*," Harry repeated. Then he pointed behind me. "Monkey *yu ni*." (The monkey is here.)

I turned round. Behind me was the *Caryota mitis*—the Clumping Fishtail palm—I'd planted near the house. The Clumping Fishtail isn't a neat palm tree like the ones you see lining roads in Beverly Hills. This palm is more like a messy explosion in a frond factory. It's got dark green leaves that sprout from numerous subtrunks, and although I kept this particular Clumping Fishtail trimmed, it still had a thick collection of foliage, and mostly obscured the low wall behind it.

If this was an M. R. James story, there'd be some kind of smooth monkey face poking out of the foliage, probably with its eyes tightly shut. After a moment it would withdraw, quite possibly with a sinister rustle. If it was a Stephen King story, then maybe the monkey would step out from behind the palm and BITE MY FACE OFF!

But this is a true story. There was no monkey. Or rather... I couldn't see a monkey.

From that point on, the routine was that I would point out the monkey, and Harry would tell me I was wrong and tell me where the monkey really was. This was amusing for a while, and then Harry changed it again.

So there I am, different afternoon, a couple of months later. I'm on the verandah. I hear the door slam and the lines of shells above it tinkle—this means

Harry is coming.

I wait for a moment, and soon enough I become aware of a solemn presence beside me. I look down, and there's Harry, blanket over one shoulder, half-drunk bottle of milk in one hand.

"What?" I ask, when Harry says nothing.

With immense dignity, Harry points to the Clumping Fishtail palm next to the verandah.

There is a short silence as I wait for Harry.

"Yes?" I say finally.

"Daddy, monkey," Harry says. "Monkey *yu ni.*"

I blink. "What?"

Harry suddenly laughs, points to the palm tree, and says, "Daddy! Monkey *yu ni!* Monkey! Daddy, run!"

When I realize the cheeky little bugger has stolen my lines, I can't stop smiling. I rush after Harry, arms outstretched to tickle, and he shrieks in delight and runs indoors, waving his half-drunk bottle of milk above his head.

As I recall, I didn't actually look at the palm tree.

The very last change—right before the fecal matter hit the fan—was the most important. Some time after Harry had started pointing out the monkey to me, and suggesting that I run after it (little blighter), he had a nightmare.

My fault—he'd been watching a ghost movie, a rather nasty one, and now he was convinced that the headless ghost was coming for him. In fact, according to Harry, it was hiding behind the curtains above his bed, just waiting for me to leave so it could creep down and eat him. As it was a headless ghost, I attempted to point out the problems it would encounter in this endeavor (lack of teeth or mouth seeming to be the primary ones), but alas, Harry wasn't persuaded by my faultless logic.

I took him into our room (my wife's and mine), put out the small spare mattress and made a nest for him. He wouldn't settle though. (The ghost had apparently followed him in, the nasty little sneaker.) After twenty minutes or so of bleary-eyed comforting, I hit on what I thought was a brilliant solution: I told Harry that the monkey would protect him. Harry went very round-eyed at this. I asked him where the monkey was (it being well-established by now that only Harry knew the location of the monkey), and without hesitation Harry pointed to the door of the bathroom.

"Monkey *yu non,*" he said. (The monkey's in there.)

I said I wouldn't go in the bathroom, as I knew the monkey was shy, and I didn't want to scare him away. Harry agreed that would be a good thing, and I said that the monkey could protect him from the ghost, couldn't it?

Harry nodded, then promptly went to sleep.

I lay awake for some time, listening for… something. I don't know what. I didn't go into the bathroom.

I sometimes wonder if things would have turned out differently (horribly) if

I hadn't told Harry that.

\* \* \*

*The Bangkok Post,* Saturday November 10, 2007

> *Samut Prakarn—Deputy Social Development and Human Security Minister Poldej Pinprateep called yesterday for a special task force to trace missing children by coordinating information from relevant agencies. He said that the authorities lack the resources to find missing children, many of whom are snatched by human traffickers and forced into working as beggars, laborers or sex workers.*
>
> *Ekarak Lumchomkhae, head of the Mirror Foundation's information center, said that more than 650 cases of missing children have been reported to the center this year. The missing children have ranged from newborn infants to toddlers to children aged 9-12.*
>
> *Mr. Poldej said a task force should be set up to supplement the activities of the National Missing Person's Bureau, which lacks sufficient staff to find missing people quickly. The task force must be able to find people quickly, he added, noting that the more time that passes, the slimmer the chances of finding missing people become. He was speaking during a visit to seven families of missing children in the Om Noi district of Samut Sakhon. Cholada Siriyamongkol is the mother of Sirikul, or Nong Yui, 5, who has been missing since July 8th. She says she has not lost hope, and believes her daughter is still safe.*

Four months, and she says she hasn't lost hope. Now imagine it was your kid.

How long would it take you to lose hope?

\* \* \*

My university shuts down from the first week in December until the first week in January. One week after my holiday started, Harry caught a cold. Fon and I talked about it, then decided to send him to school. It wasn't that bad a cold, just a sniffle.

A little after midday, when I was just settling down to my lunch (chopped papaya salad, minced catfish salad, steamed sticky rice, and a cold beer), I got a phone call from Fon. The school had phoned her saying that Harry was running a temperature and could she come pick him up? As Fon was having her hair done (again), I was volunteered to go and pick Harry up from the school. I pointed out that I was just sitting down to lunch. Alas, her hair proved to be of more importance than my lunch, and for the sake of continued domestic harmony, I ended up driving to the school.

I picked Harry up, drove back home, planted him in front of the TV with a bottle of milk and the DVD of *Monster House*, and went back to my lunch, which was now rather soggy and dispirited.

My house has an open-plan ground floor. Sitting at the dining table, you can see into the lounge where the TV is. You can't see it all—the stairs get in the way, but there's a clear view of the end of the couch and the sliding doors leading onto the verandah. The way I'd put Harry onto the couch meant I couldn't see him. I could hear the TV, but I couldn't see Harry at all.

I sat down and ate my lunch. I drank two bottles of beer—the large ones. A large bottle of Heineken contains 750ml of beer, with an alcohol content of 5.6%. This comes to 8.4 units of alcohol, about the same as four pints of lager in a pub. (Real pints here, not your midget U.S. pints.) I'm not going to deny I'd been drinking, because I had. You can judge for yourself how much difference it made.

So the TV's on. The sound is going (*It mocks us with its… house-ness!*), I'm reading war-porn from Baen, the mynah birds are squawking in the papaya tree outside the back door, and although I can see clouds building up over the roof of the house next door, all is generally good with the world. I have a distinct 8.4-units-of-alcohol-happy-buzz thing going on.

Except when I get up to go to the bathroom, Harry isn't on the couch.

I look on the verandah. No Harry. I step out onto the verandah and look in the front yard. No Harry. Feeling a little nervous now, I walk round the left side of the house, round the back yard with the washing machine and the sink, continue round the house and back to the front yard.

No Harry.

I go to the gate—which someone has slid open. Not very much, but wide enough for a small boy to slip through.

Now I look back on it, I'm almost certain I shut that gate. Normally, I slide it shut every time, because if I don't the soi dogs get in and mangle my lawn. And besides, keeping the gate shut means Harry stays in the garden.

Maybe he opened it. Maybe I left it open.

Stories like this need a sin, don't they? It's the moralizing part in the urban legend. Don't sleep with your boyfriend. Don't speak to strangers. Don't steal. So maybe leaving the gate open was my sin—or Harry's sin.

Or maybe it was opened by… someone else.

I go out on the soi, look left and right. The soi dogs are sleeping at the far end of the soi. A couple of cars are parked: my neighbor's dark blue Kia, and the lawyer's silver Corolla. Clouds are dark to the west, above the sleeping soi dogs. Thunder rumbles.

I can't see Harry.

You can probably imagine my state right at that moment. If you have kids, I know that you know *exactly* what I was feeling. All parents have horribly vivid nightmares about nasty things happening to their kids.

I ran to the end of the soi and looked down the large road that runs through my moobahn. I couldn't see Harry. I ran to the entrance to the moobahn, ignoring the dogs barking at me over fences, and the looks I got from my neighbors. When I reached the security guard on duty, I asked him if he'd seen a little boy going out of the moobahn. He said no, and for a moment I relaxed, thinking Harry had to be somewhere in the moobahn and all I had to do was find him.

And then, as I looked along the entrance road—around two hundred yards long, leading to the main road beyond—I saw a black minivan waiting to turn left: indicator flashing, sunlight gleaming off the solar film in the back windows, thin puffs of blue exhaust as the engine burbled.

I'll be honest with you: I can't be sure quite what happened next. Strong emotion has a way of warping memory around it. I know I ran along the entrance road—not shouting, just running.

The van turned off onto the main road before I got within a hundred yards of it.

I didn't stop, of course. The next clear memory I have is reaching the end of the road and looking left, with that kind of hollow feeling you get when adrenaline has drowned everything else in your head.

The van was pulled over to the side of the road about fifty yards away, engine idling. It had stopped next to a huge clump of bamboo by the edge of the rice paddy. The bamboo rustled as the wind shook it.

Harry was standing behind the van, holding a half-drunk bottle of milk and bawling.

I ran to the van, still incapable of coherent thought, snatched Harry up and hugged him hard enough so that he yelled and hit me with his bottle of milk on the side of my head.

Then I thought about who was in the van and I turned round, clutching Harry hard. The sun was bright, and I couldn't see anything of the inside of the van except a slice of the floor near the door—even though both the mid-section door and the passenger door were open.

I took a half-step toward the van. I know it doesn't make any sense, but that's what I did. And you know, I wasn't thinking about crazed Chinese organleggers, or cannibal *luk-chin* makers, or wild-eyed Khmer Rouge straight out of the jungle.

No, what I was thinking about was the fact that the handle of the sliding door in the middle of the van was bent round like half a pretzel, and that in front of the door was a large footprint, squished into the soft mud in the side of the road. I looked hard at that footprint. Believe me.

And then three things happened at the same time. The first was that I heard a *snap* from behind me, the sound of a length of bamboo cracking. One of those thick stems of bamboo. The second was that Harry said, "Monkey! Look, Daddy! Monkey! Monkey!" The third was that I saw a spot of bright red liquid just inside the van, glistening crimson against the steel floor where the sun caught it.

I didn't turn round. I was looking at the footprint, and thinking about big yellow teeth, and how I'd told Harry that monkeys didn't like to be stared at.

"Monkey!" Harry repeated. He bounced against me. "Monkey! Monkey! Monkey! Daddy, look!" Then he laughed in delight and hit me on the side of my head again.

The bamboo rustled. There was a sound like something dragging against the ground.

"Monkey, bye, bye!" Harry said. "Daddy, bye, bye, monkey!"

I waited, then turned round. One of the bamboo stems on the side of the road was broken, snapped in half and crushed—what you'd expect if something heavy had pressed on it. There was a pair of footprints in the mud nearby. Two more footprints led down the bank of the rice paddy, heading toward the bright green rice and muddy water. Between the footprints were lines in the mud, like you'd get if you dragged something behind you. On the far side of the paddy, the thick brush waved. The top of a wild banana tree quivered. It might have been something pushing through the brush. (Something *big*.) But then again, it might have just been the wind from the approaching storm.

Then it started raining.

* * *

The police never identified the van, or traced its owner. The plates came from a Toyota Camry that had been stolen a month before, and the serial number on the engine block apparently belonged to a van scrapped six months before. The blood traces didn't lead anywhere either. The lead cop told me afterward the spots in the back came from at least six different people. The gaffer tape could have been bought anywhere, and the same went for the child-size Ultraman t-shirt.

They kept asking me about the door handle. But after they'd checked my prints against the ones they found, I stopped getting suspicious looks. I didn't touch the handle—but someone did. And whoever it was, they gripped it so hard they bent the metal like it was hot plastic.

I didn't tell the police about the footprints, and as they didn't ask me anything about them, I assume the rain must have washed them away. I think I'm glad about that.

You see, those footprints weren't shoeprints, or bootprints. They were *foot*prints, and they looked almost exactly like the footprints of a very large, barefoot man with long toes.

Almost… but not quite.

* * *

Some years ago, I read a story in the *Bangkok Post*. It's dropped off their archive pages now, but if you contacted them directly, they could probably send you a copy. (I told you this was a true story.)

I can't remember the exact wording, but the story itself and the accompanying photo are still very clear in my mind. The photo showed a small crocodile in a pen at the Samut Prakarn Crocodile Farm and Zoo. The croc was basking in the sun, managing the difficult task of looking both lazy and vicious, and a local government official was standing close behind it—but not *too* close. The official was beaming, and pointing to the croc's head with a length of rattan.

They'd caught the croc in Ayutthaya—a city about thirty klicks north of Bangkok. It must have escaped from one of the crocodile farms around there, and rather than head for the Chao Phraya, it decided to swim into a storm drain under a large market in the center of the tourist area of Ayutthaya. And there it lived for several years, eating rats, monitor lizards, snakes, and all the garbage washed into the drain from the market. A word about Thai storm drains here: they're square concrete ditches about two/three feet on an edge, and the top is covered with concrete slabs. At my university, the monitor lizards use them for running around the campus. And this croc had been using one to crawl around under the marketplace. For *years.*

It's not a sewer. Not quite. But it's close as damnit.

Urban myth: *A modern story of obscure origin and with little or no supporting evidence…*

Only sometimes, you know, they're actually true.

* * *

So here we are at the end. Kind of inconclusive, you may be thinking. And that's understandable, but this is a true story, and like Margaret Atwood says in *Happy Endings*, the only authentic conclusion to true stories is *John and Mary die.*

But though Harry could have died (or worse, just vanished forever), he didn't (and hasn't). As I sit here in the bedroom typing, the door to the room open behind me, the sound of him fighting with his brothers drifts up the stairs, and that's conclusion enough for me.

* * *

One last word: when or if you have children, and you're playing a game with them in which an invisible creature (be it monkey, doolally, or something entirely less ordinary) is an essential component, just make sure the invisible creature is one that has teeth.

Preferably *large* teeth.

# DRESS CIRCLE

## MIRANDA SIEMIENOWICZ

The musty smell of old carpet filled the corridor, hot with the press of the crowd. In the half darkness, Laura fingered the pair of tickets in her bag. She felt defiant to be here alone. They had been a gift for Markus, for the two of them to use together. The line jostled forward.

Two ushers stood on either side of the corridor where it met and opened into the theatre. Through gaps in the crowd, Laura saw rows of plush seats cascading towards the darkened stage. She pulled a ticket from her bag and offered it to the usher.

The short, uniformed man bent his head, turning the ticket over in his thick fingers. Clumps of wiry hair stood out from under his peaked cap.

"The dress circle?" he asked without raising his head.

"I guess. Is that what it says?"

The usher looked up. "Why, yes, it is." He tore the ticket in half and handed back the stub.

Movement at his feet caught Laura's eye. A monkey the size of a cat, dressed in an identical uniform of brass-buttoned jacket and cap, was stretching its paw up towards the usher's hand. In response to her startled gasp, the man swept the animal behind him with one leg and fixed Laura with a reproving glare.

"The dress circle," he said in a low voice, "is this way."

He folded one arm behind his back and extended the other to indicate a narrow corridor that reached into darkness behind him. The crowd continued to spill slowly into the theatre. Laura hesitated.

"Madam, please. The show is about to begin."

She stepped out of the stream of patrons and proceeded down the corridor. Glancing back over her shoulder as the gloom engulfed her, she saw the monkey scrabble up the fabric of the man's trouser leg and pluck the ticket stub from his hand.

The same odour of carpets and drapery stifled the air. Black paint obscured the walls and sapped what little light there was. Laura strained to find a door to lead her into the theatre. No one else came looking for their seats, though once she heard a quiet scuffle approach and overtake her in the corridor. She had walked at least the distance from the entrance to the orchestra pit when she finally paused, peering, and moved to turn back.

A woman emerged from the shadows in a voluptuous white gown, silver hair piled on her head. Her lips were lost behind an ornate stamp of ruby lipstick that spread onto pale-powdered cheeks.

"Your ticket?" she asked. A beauty spot danced beside her mouth.

Laura opened her hand. For an instant, the stub lay glinting before it collapsed into a film of grey ash. She flinched and the ash puffed into the air, dissolving from view.

"My ticket!"

"Ah, the dress circle, then."

The powdered matron closed a scarlet-clawed hand around Laura's arm and lurched down the corridor. Linen gushed and rustled around the hidden forms of her legs as she dragged her deeper into the building. The walls slid past with gathering speed and Laura wrenched against the grip of the thin fingers.

"What are you doing!"

Her captor glanced back, eyes like dark stones set in her ivory skin. "Faster," she hissed.

Laura struggled to match the woman's pace. Gusts of linen tangled themselves between her feet, keeping her attention on the billows of white fabric and the severely laced bodice of the matron's dress. The woman's waist was the width of a doll's. Suddenly, in a tumble of white and pain, Laura's ankle gave way. She cried out, sliding to the carpet only to have her arm jerked up as she found herself staggering on, shouting to be released.

They turned a number of corners. Laura was hauled into a maze of corridors, each narrower and more bleak than the last. Finally, they slowed where the walls were so near to one another that the matron's full skirts filled the way. Laura felt the grip on her arm loosen as a door in the wall opened and she was dragged through.

A yellow bulb hung, bare, from the ceiling. It was swinging lazily and the shadows thrown by the racks of white costumes along the walls swept the floor in pulsing arcs. A short man with carven features stood with his back to the dresses. His dark trousers hung below a protruding belly, held aloft by wide bands of suspenders that strained across his expansive gut.

"Is that her, then?" he asked the woman in white, scratching the stubble bristling from his neck.

"Yes, Director."

"Shall we see what we have?"

Laura backed away as they advanced, fingers scrabbling blindly behind. She closed a hand around the doorknob.

"What do you want with me?" she demanded.

The pair ignored her. They murmured to one another, crowding her, trapping her against the door.

"She's almost tall," said the matron, red nails tracing the line of Laura's jaw.

"Almost, almost. But her waist is so thick." The Director's stale breath was hot on Laura's face.

"Hips too low."

"Arms not slender enough."

Without warning, they seized her shoulders and began to pull at her clothes. Laura yelled as her arms were pinned above her head and her shirt was dragged up. She kicked out, her foot sinking into a yielding mass of linen.

Her back hit the floor and breath tore from her lungs. The glare of the light-bulb dazzled her, silhouetting the painted face of the matron. Hands pinched and ripped at her skin and the fabric of her clothes. First shouting but finally whimpering, cowed, Laura lay on the dusty floorboards with grit and chalk like a rash over her sweaty nakedness.

The Director's arm reached down. She beat at it ineffectually, curling onto her side. His fingers clutched her breast and lifted the flesh away from her body.

"No good. Needs a lot of work," he called over his shoulder.

The matron brushed past him with linen brimming from her arms. "This one."

Shivering and exposed, Laura let herself be thrust into the heavy costume. When they had pulled the dress over her head and twisted her arms through the capped sleeves, she was pushed onto all fours. A knee dug into the small of her back as the bodice of the dress jerked tight against her ribs.

"Much more, much more," came the Director's voice above her. "You'll have to hold her down."

He continued to haul the bodice tighter and Laura felt the matron lie bodily across her shoulders. Pain speared through her chest. Linen smothered her and the sharp smell of the matron's sweat flooded her nostrils.

Her waist crushed in the vice of the dress, the Director pulled her upright by the cords of the bodice. He spun her around to face the closed door, where a long mirror hung. Her reflection gazed from the glass like a ghost, her heavily padded bust and hips flaring monstrously from a waist she could all but enclose with her hands. Her face and arms were powder-pale, coated with dust from the floor. She gagged.

"She's almost beautiful!" cried the matron, clapping her hands like a child. "What a touch of make-up would do!"

The Director grunted. "No time," he said. "I'll have to take her immediately, like this."

He took her arm and Laura stumbled back into the corridor. Her tortured lungs ached for air as passage after passage blurred across her eyes. Through one open door, the uniformed back of the usher bent over a figure in a white gown. He moved back and Laura saw blood running down the woman's chin. Her lips had been scored with a razor; thin, vertical slits marched across her mouth, filling the outline of a gaudy lipstick.

The Director slowed to a halt and Laura felt plush drapes stroke her shoulders. A shove to her back sent her staggering forward, feet unsteady in a chaos of fabric. Brightness bathed her and the thunder that roared in her ears gradually resolved into applause.

She was on the stage.

The faces, hands and pale shirts of the audience hovered in a darkness held back by a row of glaring footlights. Laura felt their expectant gaze on her like an unbearable, demanding weight. She stood frozen, the barren expanse of stage before her gleaming.

Some distance behind stood the cardboard facade of an ancient Greek temple. As music rose like a mist from the orchestra pit she noticed movement in the wings on the far side. The usher, peaked cap still perched on his head, was buttoning a ruffled shirt. He straightened, brushed the cap to the ground and strode onto the stage. Applause swelled. He positioned himself on the far side of the temple, turned to the audience and with a majestic sweep of his arm began to sing.

The usher's bass voice throbbed with melodrama and yearning. His Latin rose trembling above the music and floated out into the darkened tiers of the audience. Laura began to back away, her head light with pain and confusion. Before she was completely hidden by the wings, a pair of hands clapped onto her shoulders and she twisted around in a flurry of skirts. The Director hissed, furious, and made to push her back out.

"What are you doing?" she whispered.

She wanted to yell, to claw at his craggy face, but as panic fought in her chest, the oppressive weight of the watching audience slowed something inside her. She was pushed back onto the stage, staggering into the hot lights. The pain in her ribs soared.

The usher sang on. He punched the air in defiance, sending shivers of emotion through the ruffled fabric of his shirt. Laura gazed, overwhelmed, at the audience.

As her eyes came into focus on the sea of vague faces, a familiar form emerged—Markus sat in the stalls, a dozen rows from the stage. Laura squinted against the footlights. She could just make out his proud, puzzled features. He had recognised her. Time crawled, then stopped. A woman younger than Laura leaned towards him and crooned into his ear. He turned and Laura lost him in the crowd as his raven hair obscured his face.

Laura peered, frowning. The light in the theatre was so very poor, mere dregs spilling from the stage. Her heart leapt in its cage; she must have mistaken another man for her faithless lover because there he was, Markus, sitting two rows further forward. His eyes were fixed on the wildly gesturing usher but when they settled on Laura he brought a hand to his mouth in shocked recognition. The woman on his arm cocked her head inquiringly but Markus simply shook his head, agape.

As the woman leaned closer, the broad rim of her hat hid his face and Laura realised that Markus was, in fact, seated much further to the right. His elbows were propped on his knees and he was staring incredulously in her direction, ignoring the woman stroking his arm.

Laura blinked. Markus sat in every row. His high forehead and bold jaw encompassed myriad expressions of astonishment. All through the theatre, Markus pointed or gasped in surprise. The women accompanying him whispered and nuzzled, intent on his attention.

The usher drew a colossal breath and his voice mounted incredible intervals to glide into the climax of his aria. It was clear he had not noticed the Markuses. Laura threw a glance at the Director. The portly man was frowning, one hand raised to the wall near his head. As she met his gaze he wrenched a great lever downwards, stepping aside to slam it into place. Laura looked into the audience to see Markus bend forward and hair fall over his face. Frantically, she searched the theatre but he was gone. The women were gone. Beyond the footlights was nothing but a chasm of empty chairs.

Her ears rang as the usher's singing continued to reverberate from the stage.

"Theatre is everything, pretty one," said a quiet voice.

Laura spun. The usher stood beside her with his mouth twisted in a superior sneer. Blood had smeared from his hands onto the ruffles of his shirt. He reached out.

"Don't touch me," hissed Laura, backing towards the set. The final lines of the usher's performance formed themselves in the air, his voice building in volume and passion above them as he stood, mute, regarding her. She stumbled to the rear of the stage.

"Run," he called softly under the singing. "Run. You might get back to the beginning, but you won't get further than that."

"Don't touch me!"

He stood without even reaching a hand towards her.

The deadening mass of the audience had lifted. Laura heaved herself up the stairs to the temple's cardboard columns. She pounded her fists against the painted image of the temple interior. The paper tore, the thick smell of incense flooding through the rent in the backdrop. She collapsed to her knees and crawled through.

The ground felt like stone under her fingers as Laura dragged herself blindly forward. The disembodied song of the usher had been cut off, as if by the slam of a door, and nothing disturbed the new silence save her shallow panting. Sagging with exhaustion, she looked up.

The temple stretched on all sides as far as Laura could see—a vast array of stone pillars interspersed with statues clothed in similar gowns to her own. Behind her was an enormous painted landscape, torn where she had crawled from the stage. From the painting emanated a dazzling, midday light that flooded the temple floor. The ceiling was lost in a haze of fragrant smoke.

One of the statues detached itself from the collection and approached her. It was the matron. The monkey, which had shed its uniform elsewhere and now wore only its cap, clambered down from one of the pillars and leapt onto her shoulder. A finger of smoke reached down momentarily in its wake.

"What is this place?" asked Laura, her voice hoarse. She rolled over, wincing, to sit limply on the floor with the mass of skirts splayed before her.

The matron bent over, near enough for Laura to make out the fine wrinkles that clustered around her eyes and the lines of scab that made up her lipstick.

"This is where we belong," she said.

"I need to get out."

The matron straightened with a peal of laughter that sent the monkey pouncing from her shoulder, shrieking. It landed softly on the floor and bared its teeth at Laura before scampering away among the pillars with its tail stiff overhead.

"Get out? You've only just arrived," said the matron.

"I can hardly breathe," pleaded Laura. "Help me."

The matron's eyes frowned in her powdered face.

"Why do you want my help? I'm no better than you. Perhaps even a little worse." A flourish of her hand indicated her painted face and she bent forward again.

"Escape is no secret," she said, her cracked and scarred lips shaping the words in a low voice. "You need only take off your costume."

Laura reached around her drawn waist and fumbled for the ties of the bodice. She could feel the lines of cord that crossed her punished torso but where the redundant length should have been tied there was nothing. The cords reached their final eyelets and seemed to dive into the fabric of the dress. Her breath quickened, straining her lungs against the crushing pressure on her ribs and belly.

"Not so easy?" The matron's voice rang above her like a bell.

Still sitting, Laura leaned forward and pulled up the heavy linen of her skirt. A mound of silk petticoats rose from underneath. She dragged these back towards herself in desperate handfuls and uncovered the tulle ruffles of her underskirts. The stiffened gauze scratched at her arms as she gathered these up, reaching over a growing pile of fabric.

That was the tulle. And below that, more silk. A knot began to clench in Laura's gut. Under the silk was spread the back of her linen skirt. She drew that into the pile, now barely contained in her arms, and felt her nails scrape the stone floor of the temple.

Laura retched. She let go of the fabric, which sprang out of her arms to cover the impossible view of bare stone, an empty mountain of linen and silk and gauze.

Her head was light and the statues were stirring around her. She heard the rustle of their skirts and, in the distance, an agonising shriek that could have been the monkey.

# THE RISING RIVER

## DANIEL KAYSEN

The pressure started in August with a long-distance call.

"We'd all love to have you here, Amy. It would be great if you could come. Really great."

I didn't say anything, I never do. Not when my brother gets on to that topic. I just stay silent, when the pressure starts.

I listened to the hum of the phone line.

He didn't give up. He never does. "Sarah and me. And the girls. We'd all love to see you. I mean it."

I hung up the phone.

* * *

"Bad news?" said Tish, my flat-mate, from the couch.

"Christmas," I said.

"Christmas is bad news," she said. "When you're older than eight it always sucks."

She'd been my flat-mate for a whole two weeks and we still knew little about each other, but we both knew we were going to get on.

"Hey, want to do Christmas together?" she said. "Here? Just the two of us?"

"Tish, it's *August*. It's a bit early to be making plans."

"You think you're going to get a better offer? Think about it—Christmas here, no family, no forced smiles at crap presents, just drunkenness and back-to-back DVDs. What's not to like?"

"Who's going to cook?"

"The Indian down the road will be open. We'll get a takeaway. Curry for Christmas lunch, what could be better?"

It didn't take much thinking about.

It was a prior engagement. It was a ready-made cast-iron excuse.

"Done deal," I said.

"Good," she said. "Just don't buy me bloody candles."

\* \* \*

In September my brother called again.

For once I had an answer.

"Look, I'm really sorry, but I've got plans already."

"You sure?"

"Yeah. It's firm. I'm sorry, but—"

"It's just…"

"I know," I said.

We hung up awkwardly.

\* \* \*

When he rang in October he gave me bad news, and a different kind of pressure.

\* \* \*

I couldn't bear to go to the funeral. I hate funerals. I always have done, ever since I was a child.

My brother insisted I went to this one, but I pictured my favourite grandmother looking down from heaven and telling me: "You stick to your guns, girl. Don't take any rubbish from *him*." She said things like that. It's why she was my favourite grandmother.

That and the fact that she'd said in her will that she wasn't fussed about a funeral but she definitely wanted a wake. My brother hated the idea. That added to the appeal.

So I skipped the funeral and drove instead to the designated pub.

Inside it was cosy and warm and already well-filled with saddened friends of the deceased. They were all in their eighties and nineties and couldn't possibly have made the church service, given that they could barely walk unassisted. But the pub, well that was entirely different. They gained new life, when it came to the pub.

\* \* \*

I got a drink and found a table with two familiar faces. The old man's eyes lit up at the sight of me.

"It's the little'un!"

"Hello, Mr Nash," I said.

"Eva, she remembers my name! Come little'un, sit down, sit down."

"Is there room?" I said.

"Room? Sure there is, sure there is. Move yourself over, Eva, let the little'un sit down next to me. Not often I get to sit next to such a pretty young thing."

Eva, distant, moved over.

I hesitated, wondering how brave I was feeling, but I sat down between the two of them.

"Hello, Mrs Nash," I said to Eva.

Her hearing's not so good. Most times she doesn't hear you and stares into space, preoccupied.

She died five years ago, but she had gone through and beyond and retained her Eva-ness.

And she recognised me. "Oh my. The little'un! How lovely."

"See!" said Mr Nash, to me. "See!"

We smiled at each other, me and Mr Nash, like the living do in the presence of ghosts.

* * *

"But—" said Tish.

I knew I was gabbling, but I couldn't help it. I just wanted to get it out in the open.

After the funeral I had taken a risk and told her everything. The unabridged version.

Tish was under her duvet on the couch.

Looking scared.

"Amy," she said, "are you on anything?"

"No. This is real."

"You spoke to a *dead* woman."

"Lots of dead women. And men."

"But…"

There were further questions.

We talked some more.

* * *

Then another question.

"Is this like *The Sixth Sense*?" she said, brow furrowed. "Am I dead too?"

"No. You're not dead. I'm not dead. No one is. I mean, lots of people are, but none that you know."

"Right," she said. "Okay," she said. "So. You talk to dead people, that's all." She tried to look alright with the idea.

"It's just good manners," I said. "Like: speak when you're spoken to."

She nodded, slowly. Taking it in.

"And those pills in the bathroom cabinet?"

"Thyroid," I said. "Promise."

We talked some more.

* * *

Then another, worse, thought struck her and she pulled the duvet tight around her.

"What?" I asked her.

"Are they *here?* The dead?" She looked round, frantic. Thin air was suddenly a threat.

"No," I said. "No dead here. No ghosts. None."

"Promise?"

To be honest, a home always has the dead in, but they're usually very faint. Far too faint to see. Just a sense of a whisper, here and there. I didn't tell her that, though.

"No, there's no ghosts here, at least none that I've seen," I said, wording it carefully.

"Thank God," said Tish. "So who knows about your sight?"

"My family. A few very close friends. You."

Then she looked at me a long time, making up her mind. "Okay. You have spiritualist tendencies. I've heard of it before, and I sort of believe in it and I can live with it just about, but don't do it anywhere near me, ever. I'm serious. No ghosts here, promise?"

I nodded. Sober and trustworthy.

"And you promise me we're all alive?"

"Totally alive," I said.

"There's no twist at the end?"

"None," I said, "I swear."

* * *

We survived it, Tish and I.

Useful, that.

Because in November it was back to the pressure from my brother.

"Why does it get to you so much?" said Tish, holding me as I wept after the call.

"Long story," I said, when I could speak. "Long fucking story."

"One of those long fucking stories which has such a happy ending that it makes a girl cry for half an hour?"

"No," I said. "Not one of those."

"Thought not," she said, softly.

And I cried some more. Proper crying. Ugly snot and tears and despair crying.

You'll know it if you've done it.

"Hush," said Tish. "Hush."

I did my best to hush. My best wasn't very good.

"You want to tell me the story?" she asked, when I was quieter.

"You up for it?"

"Hey, I know everything else. I know that you're see-ghosts-girl. I know your target weight. I know what you shout when you come."

Our bedrooms were next to each other. I'd had some dubious one-night stands.

I wiped some snot from my upper lip. "No you don't. You know what I shout when I'm *faking* it."

"Just tell me the story," she said.

And she held me real close then. Real close.

So I told her.

* * *

Her name was Alice. Alice-Jane.

She was five when she died.

I was seven, my brother was nine.

She was my little sister, and she died.

It was murder.

* * *

The story got a lot of coverage. There was a picture of me crying at the funeral. It made one of the national papers.

*Farewell to an Angel*, said the headline.

* * *

But it wasn't farewell, not really.

The night after her murder, Alice-Jane came into my bedroom.

A few hours later they took me to hospital.

* * *

I stopped and blew my nose.

Tish carried on holding me.

I asked her where I'd got to in the story.

"They sent you to hospital."

"Yeah. And I was grateful. I didn't want to stay in the house, not after seeing her. I was sedated and when I woke up a shrink asked me some questions. He gave me a teddy bear."

I began to feel cold.

Tish turned up the heating.

"So what did you tell the shrink?"

"I told him my parents had killed Alice-Jane."

Tish put her hand to her mouth.

I carried on with the story.

I told her how the shrink's face went very still behind his smile and then he asked me some more questions. I asked him when my parents would come to visit me. He said that they loved me but he didn't think they'd be able to come visit for a while.

He was right. They didn't come.

Instead there were a lot of whispered conversations in the corridors, and a lot more questions. Detectives came. There were more teddy bears. One day a social worker carefully asked me who I'd like to live with, if I had a choice. I said I wanted to live with my grandparents. So I went to live with my grandpa and grandma Robinson, may she rest in peace.

"She's the one whose funeral you went to?" said Tish.

"Yeah. It's why I was the star turn at the wake. All my grandma's friends and neighbours remembered me. I was the little'un. Mr Nash and Mrs Nash lived next door to my grandparents, and Mrs Nash used to babysit for me when my grandparents were out."

I stopped.

Tish stroked my hair.

I looked at my empty glass.

She poured me some more vodka.

And then, suddenly, I'd had enough of ancient history. I went to bed.

All night I heard Tish in the next room, unable to settle.

\* \* \*

Early December was drab and flat. The shopping was hollow. The rooms at home were cold.

It is hard to be cheerful when I know what I know, and the other person knows it too. Or most of it.

Tish and I bought all the Keanu Reeves DVDs we could find.

We spent too much money on each other, and told each other, so the other person knew.

\* \* \*

Mid-December my brother rang.

\* \* \*

"Hey," said Tish, after the call. "Hey."

She couldn't say bland comforting things like: *it can't be that bad*, because she still didn't really know how bad it was. We hadn't talked since that last conversation.

"I just want to make it past Christmas," I said.

"Sure," she said. "Sure."

\* \* \*

On Christmas Day Tish and I watched back-to-back Keanu movies, one after the other.

His suit is nice in *Johnny Mnemonic*.

His everything is nice in *Point Break*.

But *Speed* was our favourite.

It's the t-shirt, and the body, and the way he rescues the heroine. It's nice to think there's someone out there who will always save the girl.

We ate curry on the couch, wrapped in duvets, wishing we were Sandra Bullock for a day.

\* \* \*

That night, when we pressed eject on the final DVD Tish poured us more mulled wine, and we toasted a Christmas survived.

"A good plan of yours," I said.

"I like to think so." She smiled, and then, just casually, said: "How's it going, kid?"

"It doesn't get more relaxed than this," I said. And it was true. Movies and drink and not cooking always do it for me.

"Good," said Tish.

She was right, it was good. Except for the sudden sense of a whisper I had, the sense of words in the air around me. I looked round, wondering if I could see the speaker.

"What is it?" said Tish.

An image in the room then. A body, a face. Clearer and stronger than I'd seen in years.

"Can you hear someone at the door?" she said.

"Not exactly," I said. "Look, Tish, you might want to go bed now. Or phone a friend, see if you can stay at their place."

"Why would I want to do that?"

"I need to have a conversation."

"Well, fire away, let's talk," she said, uneasily.

"The conversation isn't going to be with you," I said.

"Then who—"

I watched her face change as it hit her. "Oh God. Not here. Not with … You *promised*."

"Just go to your room, it'll be fine."

She ran.

Little Alice-Jane appeared as the door slammed shut.

She'd come to wish me Happy Christmas.

\* \* \*

After, I took Tish hot sweet tea. She was in shock and couldn't stop shaking, even though the heating was turned up high. I put a couple of blankets over the duvet. Still she shook.

I climbed in beside her and held her and said *hey, hey, hey*, as she cried. As you do.

It didn't make much difference.

Never does.

* * *

She slept till long past noon and when she woke she tried to pretend that every-thing was okay, but she wasn't even fooling herself.

I waited till she'd had a shower, and coffee, and something to eat, and then I asked her, just casually, "How's it going, kid?"

"You never finished the story," she said, not bothering to fake that she was alright. We have neighbouring bedrooms. She can't fake for shit, we both knew that. "You didn't say whether—"

She stopped.

"It's okay," I said. "Ask me anything."

"Did your parents *really* kill your sister?"

"No, they didn't," I said.

Tish shook her head, as if I were a sudden stranger.

"But you told the shrink at the hospital that they did."

"Yes. And the police. And the social workers. And they all believed me. In fact, there was enough evidence for a conviction. My parents went to prison, and they committed suicide there. Not because they'd done it, but because they hadn't."

Tish stared at me. I watched her calmly, waiting for the inevitable next ques-tion.

It came out in a whisper.

"Amy, did *you* kill your sister?"

I shook my head. "No. I didn't kill my sister."

Tish breathed with relief. But then another question. There's always more.

"Then why? Why tell everyone your *parents* did it?"

I imagined my parents' ghosts, there at my brother's Christmas dinner table, happy in the bosom of their family, even though the living could not see them. Would they be bitter at their lives cut short? No, they wouldn't, even though their deaths had been ugly.

"The dead are very forgiving," I said. "There is a peace in heaven. They let bygones be bygones there."

"So who killed her?"

I sighed.

I hate that question.

It makes the world go blurry, like a night of vodka suddenly taking hold.

"Amy, *who killed her?*"

The question was like another double vodka on top of all you've had before. It was like late night and just wanting to sleep.

"Who killed *who?*" I said, trying to keep up.

All this talk of people killing each other. It had been the longest night. All I wanted was bed and eyes-shut and silence.

"Amy, *look* at me."

No, I didn't think I wanted to do that.

"Amy, it's Tish."

Do you know how much effort it takes, to keep everything going?

Do you know how much hard work it takes?

And always, the pressure, the pressure.

From everywhere.

"I used to like you," I said. My voice sounded slurred, even to me.

"Do you need pills or something?" she said. "Amy, *focus*."

She was a long way away.

I was too far gone.

It's always the way.

As soon as the killing questions start, things begin to drift out of order, and I really can't be going round dragging them all back into place.

I let them just be whispers, mostly, the questions, the voices.

Somewhere someone was saying: "Amy, I'm calling an ambulance."

An ambulance?

Preposterous, I'm fine.

But the words no longer came out.

* * *

The police came, as they do on such occasions.

I felt sorry for Tish. I'd lied to her, long ago, when I had told her there wasn't a twist.

Of course, there was.

Of course there was a fucking twist.

With ghosts, there always is.

* * *

But some girls are stronger than others.

Tish was a strong one. She came to see me in hospital, as soon as my doctor declared I was fit enough for visitors.

She brought a teddy bear. That made me smile. Gifts are always better when they're furry.

She sat on the edge of my bed, took my hand, smiled.

"How are you?" she said.

"Oh, you know. Clowns to the left of me." I lowered my voice. "Doctors to the right."

She took a split-second to decide that I was joking, which I was, pretty much.

She kissed my forehead.

I readied myself for the undoing of it all.

"So," I asked her, "have you talked to them?"

"Who?"

"Who do you think?"

"I think you mean your parents."

"I do. Have you talked to my parents, and Alice-Jane?"

"Yeah, I met them. They came round to the flat."

"What do you think?"

"Your parents seem, you know, pretty private. And your sister's…"

She tried to think of a polite word.

"It's okay," I said, "you can say it. She's a bitch. She was nicer when she was five. That's why she's always five years old, to me."

"Makes sense," said Tish.

She smiled.

"I like this bear," I said, clutching him. "Thank you."

"You're welcome."

"Have you moved out yet?"

"Out of where?"

"The flat."

"No. Why? Do you want me out?"

"Of course not. I want you there. If you want to be there."

"I want to be there."

"That's good," I said. "That's very good. One thing, though. We buy an answering machine. My brother rings me when the leaves start changing. Before, sometimes. Next year, I don't want to speak to him. Not in the run-up to Christmas. He's always the same. It drives me nuts. The pressure's—"

"We'll get an answering machine," Tish said.

"That's good," I said. "That's good. I hate that he rings me."

I held on to the bear.

"I know," said Tish.

"That's good too," I said.

She smiled, kissed my forehead again. "I should go, I'll come back tomorrow. Oh, I tell you someone else I met. I went to the pub. Mrs Nash is—"

"Alive and well, I know," I said. "It's just this thing I have. I get mixed up. It's…"

"I know," she said. "I know."

She stood up to go.

"Wait," I said, "I have a present for you."

I opened the drawer in the bedside table.

"You do?" she said.

The drawer was empty.

"Well, no. Not at the moment. But when I get home, I'll buy you something. Lots of things. Not candles though."

"You don't have to buy anything," she said. "Just look after the bear for me."

"Yes," I said. She turned to go. "And Tish?"

"What?"

"I know it's strange, but if my brother rings, could you tell him what's happened to me?"

"He already has," said Tish. "I spoke to him and told him everything's fine. He sends his love. He says to tell you the fishing's great."

She smiled.

She left.

\* \* \*

I looked at the bear.

The bear looked back at me, not up to speed.

I did my best.

"See," I said to the bear, "my brother worries about me, especially at Christmas. So he phones. You understand?"

Silence. Bears are slow, sometimes. Perhaps they give him drugs.

I sympathised. Been there, done that.

I carried on with the story. Slowly.

"My brother fell in the river, while he was fishing, when he was nine, and he didn't get out again. Actually, when I say he *fell* it was more like he was *pushed*. And guess who pushed him?"

Bear didn't care to guess, so I put my lips to his ear, and whispered it.

"It was little Alice-Jane that pushed him. But she was only five and she's forgotten. I saw it and I didn't forget, but I never told. I was seven, and I saved her from knowing what she did. But because of what she did she died in my mind, and because I couldn't tell my parents, they died too. It got mixed up. But it doesn't matter. My brother's body is water under the bridge and everything's fine. Except, well, he phones sometimes. That's not so fine."

And then I fell quiet and thought about all the ghosts who weren't ghosts, not really, and I thought about the single ghost who was.

"My brother doesn't have the family I made for him. There's no Sarah or the girls, not really. It's just him."

I looked at the bear.

I'd never told anyone any of this stuff.

"When we go home again, you mustn't tell Tish about my brother. She wouldn't like that. She'd leave. Bad enough living with someone who talks to a dead person. She'd hate it if she knew that *she* talks to him as well."

The bear looked dubious.

"Believe me," I said, "she'd hate it. Let's spare her that. She'd only leave."

And then I fell silent again, and thought about home, and how nice it would be when I got back. This time I'd be good and stay on the pills. I'd flushed them in July, before Tish moved in, and just stayed on the thyroid ones. This time, I'd be good, and Tish would help me take them.

"Everything is going to be fine," I said to the bear, to see what the words sounded like.

But he stayed quiet and stared glass-eyed at the ceiling, a million miles away, and it reminded me of my brother.

I closed my eyes against the idea of our telephone ringing, and Tish answering again, and his voice coming all the way from his far and empty home, where there was no family, no company, no fishing, no anything, just confusion and worrying when the leaves began to change.

I thought of the lonely flat I would go home to, if my brother told Tish where he was, under the water.

And then it would be me and the telephone, forever, just me waiting for his voice and—

But no.

This was a time for getting well and positive thinking.

\* \* \*

"Everything is going to be fine," I whispered to the bear.

A phone rang, then. It made me jump, just for a second.

But then I realised it was the phone that rang far down the hospital corridor. It was not an omen or a sign.

People ring telephones all the time, in hospitals.

I opened my eyes again.

I shifted so I lay on my back.

The bear and I stared at the ceiling together.

"What do you see?" I said to the bear.

But the bear kept his counsel and we lay there in silence, waiting for tomorrow and for Tish to come again and everything to be fine, as it would be, surely.

\* \* \*

The phone rang down the corridor, many times.

And though I jumped each time, it was okay. Bears stay quiet and telephones ring and girls get jumpy.

It's just the nature of things.

It's fine, it really is.

And pressure sometimes builds until you break.

\* \* \*

We lay there, staring up at the white of the ceiling all afternoon, and we stared up at the grey as the room turned darker as evening approached.

As night fell we stared at the darkness, lying still, just thinking.

And when the phone rang again and footsteps came down the hall towards my room to give me a message, it wasn't from my brother.

Someone else entirely had sent the message. The nonsense one about fishing and leaves, and water under the bridge.

It wasn't my brother. Of course not.

But the nurse said it was, and left the message on my bedside table.

Bear and I stared at it for most of the night, wondering if the world had gone quite mad.

\* \* \*

My flat-mate came to visit the next day.

I found out the most amazing thing: it's catching.

*She*, it seemed, saw ghosts now too. My parents, my sister—she saw them all.

Oh, the long conversations she'd had with them, face to face.

I told my doctor he should write it up. The second sight is a communicable disease. It would make his name.

We'd be famous. All of us.

\* \* \*

She did her best, my flat-mate. But she smiled too much.

I offered her some vodka, she certainly looked like she needed it, but they must have taken my bottle away, because the drawer was empty.

Or, I'd drunk it all.

"I feel like I've downed a whole bottle," I said.

She smiled. Too much.

And then she said: "Your brother rang. He sends his love."

Whoever she was went away, then, and it was me and the bear and a nurse looking jolly and worried, and fuck them all, really, apart from the bear.

He just stays quiet, like people should.

None of this shit about messages. None of this sending of love, which really means: "You really *must* come and stay with us for Christmas."

But it sounds so cold and far away, where he lives.

So I'll try to hang on. I'll try not to go.

We'll try to hang on together, won't we, bear?

\* \* \*

But the furry brute's silent.

And the river is rising and Christmas is coming.

And I guess I really should go.

# SWEENEY AMONG THE STRAIGHT RAZORS

## JOSELLE VANDERHOOFT

(after T. S. Eliot)

Switchblade Sweeney sweeps his floors—
grey curls and stubbly foam, stray molars'
snaggle roots, their pitted tops decayed
down to the stringing pulp. He hums

balladeer; *Scarborough Fair*, *Greensleeves*,
lampblack hair bound back to scrub and scour,
lips summer-chapped, eyes sleepless-rubbed, but clear.
The nightingales are singing in the eaves

and from the shop below, the swirl of starch
the onion sting and clink of ale, the *chop
chop chop* of carrot, shell of peas.
The unmistakable waft of oregano.

On palm and knee he pigeon-picks each hair,
each fleck of flesh, each shred of cuticle,
a writhing leech replaced in her glass bowl.
So much work to be done with surgeon's care

he near forgets the bigger mess—the man
ash-cheeked, exsanguinate, distressed
upon the chair. His fingers cramped to claws
even in death. The blood spreads everywhere.

Straight-edged Sweeney sighs like bakehouse smoke
and dips his rag into the lavabo.
The water drizzles gristle—like the pulp
that Mrs. Lovett folds into her pies.

Hair, teeth and surgery; the little things
school one in patience and respect. The way
the razor pares the flesh, the fallow bones
blasted from age and bodily neglect;

musculature of thorax, thigh and back;
mucous-machinery of myelin;
gut avenues beneath the stomach trap;
ghost lungs that in their silence lie

like lovers in dread of discovery.
The steel-jawed barber wonders, what is man,
(steadily as he carves), but sallow skin
gilding all this gross anatomy

as truth is buttered up in flattery
and crust covers Mrs. Lovett's pies?
How easy, then, it is to slice the meat,
drop it down the shaft, fetch broom and sweep?

His work almost complete, serrated Sweeney
magpie-picks the leavings for the gruel.
The day is done, and cruel things still are cruel.
The day is done, and smoke churns from the chimney.

From bone to skin, men are monstrosities.
The nightingales sing in the laurel trees.

# LOUP-GAROU

## R. B. RUSSELL

I first saw the film, *Loup-garou*, in 1989, in a little arts cinema in the centre of Birmingham. I had driven there for a job interview and, as usual, I had allowed far more time for the journey than was required. I had reasoned that it should take me two hours to travel there, to park, and to find the offices of the firm of accountants where I desperately wanted a position. The interview was at two-thirty, so I intended to leave home at midday. I had worked it all out the night before, but then became concerned that the traffic might be against me, and I decided to allow another half-hour for the journey. That morning I checked my map, but no car parks were marked on it and so I added yet another half-hour to the time I would allow myself. Leaving at eleven o'clock seemed prudent, but I was ready by half-ten and, rather than sit around the house worrying, I decided to set out.

I know my nervousness about travelling is a failing, but I've always lived and worked in this small provincial town and it is not a day-to-day problem. On this occasion it was made very obvious to me just how irrational my fear of being late for appointments really was; the traffic was light and the roads clear and I was in the centre of Birmingham by a quarter to twelve. I found a car park with ease and was immediately passed a ticket by a motorist who was already leaving, despite paying to stay the whole day. I parked, and as I walked out on to the street I could see the very offices that I wanted directly opposite. I had two and a half hours to kill.

For no reason other than to pass the time I looked into the foyer of the cinema which was immediately adjacent to the car park. Pegged up on a board was the information that a film called *Loup-garou* was about to start, and that it would be finished by two o'clock. It seemed the perfect solution to my problem.

I doubt if there were more than five or six people in the cinema. It was small and modern and the seat into which I settled myself was not too uncomfortable. I was in time to watch the opening credits slowly unfold. The sun was rising over a pretty, flat countryside, and the names of the actors, all French, slowly faded in and out as the light came up over fields and trees. It was beautifully shot, and a simple, haunting piano piece repeated quietly as the small cast were introduced, and finally the writer and director, Alain Legrand. I noted the name carefully from the information in the foyer when I left the cinema two hours later.

The film was incredibly slow, but each scene was so wonderfully framed, and the colours so achingly vivid that it was almost too lovely to watch. The sunlight, a numinous amber, slanted horizontally across the landscape as we were introduced to the hero, a boy who was walking from his home in the village to a house only a half-mile distant. The camera was with him every step of the way. There was a quiet voice-over, in French, that was unhurried enough for me to understand it. The boy was kicking a stone and noting that he had a theory that four was a perfect number, as exemplified by a square. Therefore, if he kicked this stone, or tapped the rail of a fence, he had to do it three more times to make it perfect. If, by some unfortunate mischance, he should repeat the action so that it was done, say, five times, then he would have to make it up to sixteen—four times four. The penalty for getting that wrong was huge; the action would need to be repeated again and again to make it up to two hundred and fifty-six, or sixteen times sixteen.

It was a rambling dialogue, and a silly little notion such as any young lad might have, but I was immediately struck that it had been an affectation that I myself had had as a teenager. Predisposed toward our hero on the strength of this, I was rather looking forward, as he was, to seeing his sweetheart, if the director would ever allow him to arrive at her house. When he eventually knocked at the door, predictably we had to wait for the mother to answer it, and for him to be shown into the comfortable, dark kitchen. He had to wait, of course, for the girl who, he was told, was brushing her hair upstairs and would not be long. He talked to the mother, stroked a cat and looked out of the window. Finally the object of his affections descended the stairs.

At this point I sat forward in my seat. The young girl looked exactly as my wife, Yvonne, had looked at that age. She was pretty, with startlingly blue eyes, and long blond hair. I was delighted by the coincidence.

They took their time, of course, in going outside to where the sun was now higher in the sky. I felt a frisson as they sat close together on the bench outside the door, and, unseen by the mother, he tenderly kissed the nape of her neck as she bent down to look into a box of buttons. I marvelled at the film-maker's art. As the boy's lips brushed the girl's skin she slid her hand through the buttons in a way that was incredibly sensual. Then she picked out a heavy green one, shaped like an apple, and asked him if he knew that it had once belonged to the costume of a famous clown?

Up until this point I had enjoyed the coincidences I had found in the film, but this was stretching them too far. My mother had also had a very similar button in a sewing box, which was also said to have once belonged to a well-known clown. I did not know what to make of its appearance in the film.

The hero and heroine then decided to take a walk through the fields, talking of love and their future. And then, in the woods, there was the most delicately handled love-making scene, shown to us through carefully concealing trees. When he eventually walked home we had another voice-over where he declared his love for the girl whom he inevitably calls Yvonne.

After a few more meetings between the two of them, the only scenes involving several other actors are played out on a day of celebration; their last at school. Here another character is introduced, an older boy who clearly has an interest in the heroine. I immediately cast around for the equivalent character in my youth. There had been jealousies in my relationship with Yvonne when we were still at school, but I had finally married my childhood sweetheart. Completely lost to the apparent reality of the film I hated this potential suitor with a passion. Suddenly it is revealed, in a scene where Yvonne tentatively kisses this second boy, that we had been watching the earlier love-making scene at a distance through our hero's eyes!

The film then changed in style. In an instant the long, beautifully framed scenes from a single static position were replaced by abrupt, short images from what appeared to be a hand-held camera, and which were presumably meant to be from our hero's viewpoint. It conveyed the black rage within him. He was retracing the journey to Yvonne's house from the start of the film, but this time at a run. He was looking all about him in desperation. When he arrived at the farmhouse he hammered at the door, and when the mother answered it she told him that the girl had gone out. He rushes off across the fields and into the woods, and as the hurried camera-work shows his journey the viewpoint subtly moves down from the eye-level of a young man to that of an animal running, finally, over the floor of the woods. For only a few moments we see the love-making couple once again. The hero rushes upon them and there are terrible screams and the wild movement of the camera makes it impossible to see what is happening. The screen goes black, and just as the audience is getting restless and wonders whether the film has finished, or if the reel has not been replaced by the projectionist, the picture slowly comes up to show an incredibly languid sunset, and the hero, looking dirty and ragged, crying uncontrollably, walks slowly back to the village.

We are back to the earlier, slow direction. He slips unnoticed into a dark garage, and in the dim light we see him loop a length of rope around the rafters. The music has started by this time, a variation on the opening theme, and in front of one long, apparently unedited shot we watch him climb a chair, tie the rope around his neck, and kick the chair from under him. By now it is so dark that we can't make out the details of his horrible death, and the music has taken the place of the sounds in the garage, but the imagination makes up for what is not shown.

I was emotionally drained by the film. I emerged into a Birmingham afternoon light, deeply affected by the closing scene and not thinking particularly of the earlier coincidences. The rage that had been in the hero as he rushed to find the lovers had seemed to grow in my own breast and it was a while before the shock passed. Eventually I remembered and was able to reflect upon the uncanny similarities between the hero's circumstances and my own. I could not work out what was real, what was my imagination, and what had been the film-maker's art. I was standing on the pavement outside the cinema, angry at the injustice of the film. To this day I do not know how I managed to compose myself for an interview thirty minutes later, and how I made the shortlist.

When I arrived home that evening and related the events of my day, the film assumed more importance than the interview. Yvonne listened to my description patiently, amused, and said that she too would like to see it. I had written on a flier taken from the cinema *Loup-garou* and the director's name, "Alain Legrand." She pointed out that *loup-garou* meant werewolf, which I had not registered at the time. "You've been watching horror movies then," she asked, and I had to agree that it was horrific.

Having unburdened myself to my wife, and, I am embarrassed to admit this, having cried while re-telling the story, I felt remarkably better, and with a little distance was able to be amused by the coincidences of the film. Perhaps I had made too much of them. As I lay in bed that night I told myself that if there was anything supernatural about the apparent coincidences, anything at all, then it was there to show me how lucky I was to have made my childhood sweetheart my wife. I looked at her as she slept beside me, at her tangled blond hair and fine skin, the shape of her nose and at her soft, parted lips. For the first time that day I thought of the hero as an actor rather than as myself, and I slept soundly.

I did not get the job when I was called back for the second interview, and in retrospect I am glad that I didn't. At the time I was disappointed, but my life carried on comfortably and provincially, and city life has never since appealed to me. On my return to Birmingham for the ill-fated second interview I looked in at the cinema but the film they were showing was apparently a Norwegian "comedy of manners." It didn't appeal, and I did not have the time to watch it.

Almost immediately *Loup-garou* became something of a joke amongst our friends. I had explained what had happened one evening to another couple at a dinner party, and my wife saw a tear in my eye as I explained the plot, and a great deal of fun was had at my expense. I played up to it, and berated my wife for leaving me for another in her filmic existence, and letting me, presumably, attack her and her lover and then commit suicide. My wife was quite fascinated by the idea of the film, and between ourselves we resolved that we would try and see it. Obscure French art films don't often appear on the provincial film circuit, though, and it was some years before I saw any reference to it anywhere.

For a while I bought a few books about werewolves, fiction and non-fiction, but it struck me that the power of the film didn't derive from the legends, but the way in which the film had been put together, and my fascination for the subject quickly waned. My interest in foreign cinema grew, though, along with my video collection, and soon I was quite knowledgeable on the subject of art-house European cinema. In my researches I found a reference to *Loup-garou* in the biography of the director, Alain Legrand, which claimed that the film had never been distributed because it had fallen foul of the censors (because it appeared to condone under age sex). A few years later it appeared on the internet in a French language film database which claimed that not only had it never been distributed, but had never even been edited. These claims were repeated, word for word, on other databases, and although a large reference book on European cinema later corrected these errors, those entries remain unrevised on the internet. The reference book added that those critics that had seen *Loup-garou* reported that it contained some of the most beautiful, as well as some of the most amateurish camera-work they had seen. The only other reference that I discovered in the intervening years was on a "werewolf" website, where it was described as "disappointing," and "hardly to be described as a werewolf film at all." Nowhere could I find any reference to it being made available in any form. Without any hope of success I programmed the details into internet search-engines with no result, and left it as a permanent "want" on an auction site, which I refreshed every year without success.

And then only a couple of weeks ago I had an email notification that the film was being offered for auction. A private seller had a DVD to sell that he admitted was an unauthorised copy from an unreleased studio video. I didn't hesitate to put £50 on as my maximum bid, and despite there being no other apparent competition, with a day to go I raised it to £100. I watched the end of the auction on a Sunday evening, waiting for the flurry of last-minute bidding, but none came. I won the DVD for the minimum bid of £5.

It arrived in the post two days later, sent by a Frenchman living in London. There was no accompanying receipt and the DVD was blank, with no artwork. Yvonne and I had decided to make an occasion of watching it, and planned to wait until the children were in bed. We had opened a bottle of wine in readiness, but a nagging headache that Yvonne had earlier complained of became worse, threatening to develop into a migraine, and she decided to go to bed.

I watched the film anyway. I knew that I'd be happy to see it again in a few days time when Yvonne was feeling better, but after all this time I could not wait.

In the quiet house I sat down before the television, and pressed "Play" on the remote control. The credits came up as they had done in the little cinema over fifteen years before. The picture jumped a couple of times at the beginning but settled down after that and the quality was good. The sound was clear, and the music was just as haunting as I remembered it. A part of me was worried that it wouldn't be quite as before, but it still looked beautifully shot, and I waited to see the young boy walking out towards the farmhouse. He duly appeared, and explained in the voice-over about his obsession with the number four. A shiver ran through me.

When the camera panned slowly around Yvonne's family kitchen I noticed a number of things that I hadn't seen on my initial viewing; the first being that their dresser was similar to one that my wife's family had once owned. The mother, too, looked a lot like her own mother. I drew in a breath as the young Yvonne started to come down the stairs, but suddenly found myself completely bewildered.

The girl that appeared was certainly not the girl that I remembered. This actress had dark hair, and was slightly plump as opposed to the skinny little thing from before.

As though wilfully ignoring my confusion the actress assumed the role as though it had always been hers.

Outside the door they sat on the bench, and the whole scene with the buttons was repeated exactly as I had retold the story to over the years. As far as I could tell, the walk across the fields and into the woods was the same, scene for scene, and the love-making was carefully, and enigmatically, handled as before. I could understand now that there might be some who would protest that the actor and actress were under age, but almost everything was inferred by the viewer; suggested but not shown by the director.

Disillusioned at my apparent inability to remember the film correctly I watched the scenes with the alternative suitor without quite the same passion as before. I had retold the story of the film on so many occasions and nobody had ever said that I had changed any details, therefore I must have reported it wrongly from the very beginning—immediately after I had seen it!

I was too annoyed with myself to enjoy the rest of the film, and suddenly it seemed to drag interminably. I made myself watch it, wondering if I'd even bother showing it to Yvonne, when the final scenes eventually appeared. The attack on the love-making couple was as sudden and almost as unexpected as before. But again I had got the details wrong. It was not the hero but the other boy who made his way back to the village, and into the darkened garage. He climbed the chair and fixed the rope. Barely perceptible in the dark, and with the sound masked by the music, he hanged himself.

The credits came up and I turned it off. I put the DVD back in its blank case and decided to go and get myself ready for bed. I locked up the house and turned off all but the landing light, where I stopped to look in at Yvonne, who was sleeping.

I sensed that something wasn't quite right, though, and walked into the room.

There, in our bed, was a dark-haired woman. I stood quite still, not wanting on any account to wake her. I found myself trembling, though, and backed out of the door, not knowing what to do. There, at the top of the stairs was our wedding photo, and I had problems standing as I saw myself, in a picture from twenty years ago, beside a pretty, plump, dark-haired woman.

I must have fallen asleep on the sofa that night, and the next morning was the usual whirlwind of getting the children's breakfast and taking them to school before I myself carried on to work. I murmured something to the darkened bedroom before I had left the house, trying not to think who was lying under the blankets.

I am not sure how I got through the day. All that I could think of was that my wife had changed. This was a ludicrous proposition, especially as the wedding photograph showed that it was my error. I certainly didn't feel mad, but through the whole day I examined every possibility, and the only one that made any sense was that I had made an error of vast proportions. This did not convince me, of course, and it was with the greatest trepidation that I made my way home that evening. I parked in the garage and stood in the dark, not wanting to go indoors. Despite the turmoil that my mind was in, I realised that I was not thinking about the dark-haired woman in my house, but of my confusion between the heroines of the film I had seen. It was when I found myself thinking about the last scene of the film that I decided to go indoors.

My daughter greeted me in the hall as though nothing was at all amiss. Indeed, she announced brightly that "Mummy is feeling better and is up, out of bed."

I walked through to the kitchen where the dark-haired woman was preparing dinner. My other daughter walked out with a cheery "hallo" as I walked in, and the woman saw me with a smile. She walked over to me and took my hands in hers.

"You watched that film last night, didn't you?" she asked.

I agreed that I had.

"I understand," she said. "We were meant to watch it together, but after all these years you couldn't wait to see if it was the same as you'd remembered it. I hope you don't mind, but when I got out of bed this afternoon I wasn't up to anything other than sitting in front of the television. I decided that I might as well watch the film as well. And you were right; it's a wonderful film, but you didn't remember the end properly, did you?"

I shook my head.

"But you were right about Yvonne… she is just like me."

And she hugged me, and although I could not see her face I knew that she was crying. I should have felt love for her, but all that I could think of was the dark garage, and the rage that was growing within me…

# GIRL IN PIECES

## GRAHAM EDWARDS

I was changing the filter on the coffee machine when two tons of wet clay crashed through my office door. The clay was wearing a yellow municipal jacket and dragging a garbage can. The clay was eight feet tall and bright like a Satsuma. The clay was a golem.

"I thought you apes took the garbage out," I said, clipping the coffee filter back.

"You a private detective?" said the golem.

"That's what it says on the door."

"You gotta help me." The golem held up the hand that wasn't holding the garbage can. It was holding a blood-streaked axe.

Rain gusted in, driving flecks of orange clay off the golem's legs. The carpet round his feet went dark.

"Don't they give you waterproofs?" I said.

"There ain't enough to go round. You gotta fight for them. Little guys like me—we don't stand a chance."

I started backing up: I don't like golems. "I'll take your word for it. Now, say your piece and get out."

"But you gotta help me."

"No, I don't."

"But I got no place else to go."

I'd backed up to the filing cabinet. I reached round and pulled open the second drawer. Rummaging blind, I found what I was looking for. I yanked it out and aimed it at the golem.

"What's that?" said the golem. The clay of his brow sagged to make a frown.

"Water pistol," I said.

"You what?"

"Don't be fooled by the size. The cops use these for crowd control. The clip's

221

got a wormhole feed from the Styx. I pull this trigger, it unloads sixteen tons of river water in about three seconds."

"Won't that make a mess on your carpet?"

"That mess will be you, pal. Now get out of my office before I turn you in."

The golem stood there, still frowning. The rain poured through the door.

I heard police sirens.

The golem brought the axe handle down on the garbage can lid. The can rang like a gong. "They found me!"

I flipped the safety off the water pistol.

The golem's gigantic head swung from side to side as he searched for an escape route. The cop cars rounded the intersection, sirens screaming.

My finger tightened on the trigger.

And that's when the golem dropped to his knees.

"Please, mister! I ain't done nothing wrong. I know what you people think of us golems. But I ain't like the others. You gotta believe me. You're my last chance. Someone done a terrible wrong and the cops think it's me, but it ain't. And if they take me away, whoever done it…they'll get clean away. And that ain't right. That ain't right at all. So, you see, you gotta help. You gotta find out who done it. You gotta put it right. And if you won't do it for me, you gotta do it for her!"

The golem stood up again. He flicked the lid off the garbage can. It crossed the room like a frisbee. Then the golem picked up the can and emptied its contents on the floor.

A girl came out. She was in pieces: sliced arms and diced legs, chunks of muscle and slops of gore that might have been lungs or liver or lights; spears of white bone like blank signposts poking out of the whole hideous mess. Handfuls of soft pale flesh slimed with crimson. Worst of all: a pretty face, unmarked except around its ragged edge, floating in a lake of blood.

I put my hand to my mouth. I'm no pussy when it comes to dead bodies, but this was messier than autopsy school.

Outside, six cop cars pulled up with screeching tyres.

The golem looked down at the girl's remains. At first I thought his face was melting. Then I saw he was crying.

Each cop car pumped four armed officers into the rain.

And, so help me, I put the water pistol down.

"Shut the door," I said.

"What?"

"You heard me."

The cops had drawn their weapons. They looked a lot nastier than my water pistol. The golem kicked the door shut with a heel the size of a labrador.

"Deadlocks!" I said.

The door obeyed. The room shook as the singularity bolts engaged.

"Will that keep them out?" said the golem.

"Not for ever," I replied. "Just long enough."

"Long enough for what?"

"For you to put down that axe and tell me what the hell is going on."

***

"I guess you don't like golems. Not many folks do. But we ain't all the same. There's different moulds."

The golem rocked from one foot to the other, twisting his muddy hands like a schoolgirl. His vast bulk obscured the mess on the carpet. That was no bad thing.

"Last time I ran into a golem," I said, "he grabbed my ankles and held me upside down over a cloud of toxic gas. Any wonder I'm cagey?"

"Lots of golems are like that. Bad clay. I should know—I have to work with them every day."

It figured. The yellow jacket and the garbage can were a giveaway: this golem was a municipal refuse collector. Garbage golems are dangerous like unstable cliffs: they're fine if you keep clear; get too close—they'll bury you. Literally.

"So what's different about you?"

"I got a name."

"A *name?*"

"It's Byron."

"Golems don't have names. They have numbers."

"I got something else too."

"What?"

"I got a soul."

***

A word about golems.

First, golems aren't born—they're manufactured, like crockery. Most anyone can knock up a golem: you just take a couple of tons of river silt and compress it into a mould. Then you scribble out a chunk of Hebrew binary code on a square of parchment and bury it in the golem's chest. Bingo: instant walking mountain. Golems are grumpy, slow-witted, and obedient. They have phenomenal memories and no conscience at all. They're ultra-loyal and ultra-violent in equal measure. They make great bodyguards and even better tax collectors.

But underneath they're just machines. Wet machines, but machines all the same.

So when a golem tells you he's got a *soul*, it's kind of hard to take.

Now, you ask a hundred different folk what a soul is, you get a hundred different answers. But there's one thing everyone agrees on: whatever a soul is, it's what a golem ain't got.

Except here's this golem, big as life, says he's just like me. Bigger collar size maybe. Thing is, if this golem thinks he's different, maybe they'll all start thinking they're different. Thinking they don't want to do the crappy jobs any more.

Thinking they've got rights. Who knows—maybe they do.

But if all the golems in the city start thinking that…that's a whole heap of angry clay to have on the loose.

***

I stood at the window and watched the cops pile sandbags in the rain. I'd silvered the glass so they couldn't see in.

"Let's forget the soul thing for now," I said. "Tell me about the garbage can. Tell me about the girl."

The golem—it was hard for me to think of him as *Byron*—sat on the couch. The couch broke. "I was on the morning shift. Down on the east side—you know, those old tenements?"

I nodded. I knew that part of town pretty well. Even the daylight keeps its distance. The tenements are old and mostly ruined. Some have fallen right over, but it doesn't stop folk living in them. Even the ones still boarded up from last year's plague.

"I didn't think the city bothered collecting garbage from the east side."

"We do it once a year. Looks good on the annual report."

"Figures."

"So there I was, collecting garbage, dragging it back to the truck. I like to go out ahead. The other golems stick together but I…well, I guess I'm a loner. So, I get to this big old brownstone. It's a dive, but there's still a garbage can out front. Funny—even trash throws out the trash." Byron paused. With one massive hand he smoothed his cheeks where the tears had melted them. The golem equivalent of drying his eyes. "So I pick up the can. Only I'm clumsy and the lid comes off. That's when I see what's inside."

"The girl? In pieces?"

"The girl in pieces, right. And the axe lying on top. All at once I'm scared. I dunno what to do. I pick up the axe—dunno why. Then the garbage truck is there, and there's the other golems. They ask me what's wrong. That's when I realise I've been standing there a couple of minutes, just frozen."

"What happened next?"

"Four-Oh-Seven-One—he's shift supervisor—he looks at the axe. Then he looks in the garbage can. He says, "What did you do to her, you freak?" Then they all back off and Two-Two-Eight-Six says, "I'm calling the cops!" and that's when I ran."

"Why run if you didn't do anything?"

"I dunno. I panicked. Anyway, I just ran."

"Why didn't you drop the garbage can? Or the axe, for that matter?"

"It's evidence, ain't it? I need it to prove my innocence."

I looked out at the cops. They'd finished piling the sandbags; now they were hunkered down, waiting. I looked at Byron the golem sitting forlorn in the wreckage of my couch. Whichever way you sliced it, this was a doozy of a mess.

Best thing I could do was open the door and let the cops do their thing.

I poured myself another coffee.

I forced myself to look at the girl's torn-up remains.

"This tenement on the east side," I said. "Where was it exactly?"

"Crucifix Lane. Does this mean you believe me? You're gonna help?"

"Don't get excited. I'm just curious. I think you and me should take a little stroll."

"But how are we gonna get out? We'll never get past the cops."

"The front door isn't the only door."

Byron looked at the four blank walls. He scratched his crotch. There was a lot of clay down there.

"You got a back door?"

\*\*\*

Everyone knows there's eleven dimensions. Most places you go, you only see three or four. Maybe five if it's late and the bar's still open. But there's some places where the dimensions…well, they get kind of crowded up together.

Think of a ball of yarn. However neat it looks, you start unravelling it, sooner or later you'll get a knot. Yarn gets snarled up—it's in its nature. Same with dimensions.

Take this city. It was built right on top of one mother of a cosmic knot. Mostly it looks like a city, but underneath it's got way too many dimensions for its own good. That's why it works the way it does. It's why the cops are all zombies and all the big crime lords are Titans. It's why time runs slower uptown than downtown and the mayor is a gangster-turned-goddess called Pallas Athene. It's why the skies are full of thunderbirds and the sewers have minds of their own. It's why nothing makes sense but everything hangs together. This city's like a knot all right, a knot in the middle of a great spider's web. Only the web's not made of silk, it's made of cosmic string. And whenever the string vibrates it sends all these echoes down into the web, into the knot, into this city. That's what this city is: it's all the sounds of the cosmos, all rolled into one.

Leastways, that's what it says on the tourist leaflet. Me, I just call it home.

The thing is, you also get knots within knots. Something to do with fractals—don't ask me, ask Mandelbrot. Which means that some places in this city get more tangled up than others. This block, for instance. Specifically, this office. This office is just full of dimensions.

And where you get lots of dimensions, you get lots of doors.

\*\*\*

Behind the bookcase there's a trapdoor. I pulled it open and shoved Byron down the cellar steps.

"You got a secret passage?" said the golem. He sounded like a small child with a large voice.

"Eighty-nine of them," I replied, "at the last count."

"It's dark. I don't like the dark."

"Stay there while I get my coat."

I went back up the stairs, grabbed my coat from the hook. I glanced outside and saw two unmarked automobiles scuttle up behind the barricade. Unlike the regular wheeled cop cars, these were the walking variety.

The first auto was a plain brown rust-bucket with stiff steel legs and a lamp hanging off. A wide-shouldered zombie climbed out of it holding a bull-roarer. A negotiator. So, as far as the cops were concerned, this was a siege.

The second was a Cadillac. It wasn't plain and it wasn't brown. It kissed the far kerb on expensive millipede feet. It was sleek as a whale and at least as big. A car for a giant. The screens were mirrored but the driver's window was open a crack. Through the crack, a pair of huge pink eyes stared right at me.

The zombie negotiator lifted the bull-roarer to what was left of his lips.

"SEND OUT THE MACERATOR! WE KNOW HE'S IN THERE! JUST CO-OPERATE AND YOU'LL BE FREE TO GO!"

Free to go. Right. Like I'd believe someone who has to hold his guts in with gaffer tape.

All the same: *the Macerator*. It explained why the cops were so keen to collar the golem.

\*\*\*

This city's seen its share of serial killers: Josey Doe, Doctor Eviscerate, the Scalpish Brothers. But they all had short careers. Serial killers get caught pretty quick here: zombies might suck at deduction (their brains are mostly soup) but they're hot on homicide forensics. Show a zombie a corpse, the first thing he does is sniff it. Next, he gives you the name and address of the killer.

But they couldn't catch the Macerator.

The first Macerator killing showed up behind the railhead last year. A male of debatable race was found spread over roughly three square miles of open ground. Since then, the Macerator's struck twenty more times. Each time the victim resembles casserole. And, no matter how much they sniff, the cops are in the dark.

I thought again about turning Byron in. Maybe the golem's story was candy-floss—maybe he *was* the Macerator. But golems only kill if they're programmed to. Which raised the question: Who wrote Byron's code?

I shook my head. Detective or not, I'm not much better at deduction than your average zombie cop.

Difference is, I play a mean hunch.

\*\*\*

I turned my coat inside-out three times until it was made of rubber and used it to scoop the remains of the girl back in the garbage can. I've done messier work, but nothing so pitiful. The worst part was picking up that peeled face. Her dead eyes looked like eggs. And it felt like they were watching me.

Soon there was nothing left but a crimson stain on the carpet. It's got a lot of stains, that carpet, and each one's got a story to tell.

I turned my blood-splattered coat inside-out five times until it was clean, then once more so it was back to moleskin. Then I hauled the garbage can down the cellar steps and took Byron's hand.

"It's still dark," he said. "What's that you dragged down here?"

"Never mind," I said. "Hold tight, big fella."

I squeezed the clay of Byron's hand until it squished between my fingers. Then I teased open a local spatial anomaly, rolled the golem into a ball the size of a tangerine and dropped him in my pocket. I made an origami scarf of the garbage can and threw it round my neck. Then I picked myself up, folded myself in half, and posted myself through the gap between the furnace and the coal chute.

There were the usual howls as I sliced my way through a pack of boundary wolves (you fold yourself in half, you get a sharp edge) but I soon left them behind. Boundary wolves think they're the protectors of the cosmos but they're just dumb animals. Soon I was between the strings. Time stopped for everything but me and for an instant—just an instant—I heard the distant silence of the still point.

"Jimmy," I whispered. "Are you there?"

Then the boundary was rushing at me again. I cut through another wolf-pack and slipped sideways through a fresh crack in reality's wall, all the while with a golem in my pocket and a girl in pieces round my neck.

I landed with a crash on a dust-covered floor and smelt rat droppings.

\*\*\*

*Why have you entered my domain?*

The voice came from the corner. It wasn't a room, just a dark place with corners. The corners moved. The voice bounced off a ceiling that wasn't a ceiling, just something soft and unspeakable hanging over our heads. The words were punctuated by wet thuds. Something dripping that sounded like jelly, but wasn't.

"I need a favour," I said into the darkness. Beside me, Byron trembled like a sack of plaster.

*Favour? Who are you that I owe you a favour?*

"Last summer, remember? The missing kid? Pornographic ransom notes and severed fingers in the mail? Cops thought it was you. I convinced them it wasn't."

*Ah, that favour. Tell me, was the poor little dear where I said he would be?*

"You know he was. Funny how you knew where to find all the pieces."

*I explained that at the time. I am not a killer. I am simply…attuned to those who kill.*

"Yeah, I know."

*You shudder?*

"A creep's a creep, innocent or not."

*Is it with such flattery that you seek a favour? I should turn you from here with your skin burned off and your tongue split in two!*

I felt Byron's clammy breath on my ear.

"What is this place," he whispered. "Who're you talking to?"

"Her name is…" I began. Then I addressed the voice. "Say, why don't you introduce yourself?"

The dark place got brighter. I saw the ceiling and wished I hadn't: it was made of rat-tails all woven together. Most still had the rats attached. It was like some crazy rodent jigsaw: tails strangling necks, tails plaited with drawn intestines, tails threaded through empty eye sockets. The mutilated rats dripped blood and pus on the dusty floor. And they squirmed.

A hunched figure stepped into the light. She was gaunt and yellow, wrapped in red rags. Filthy hair made syrupy trails down her sunken chest. She grinned and cackled, showing black crone's teeth; her breath was so rotten it ran down her chin like blackberry juice.

She scratched her cheek with nails like sewing needles.

*Greetings. My name is Arachne.*

The golem took a step forward. "Uh, pleased to meet you, Arachne. My name's Byron." Then, so help me, he stuck out his hand.

"Let's not waste time," I said, stepping in front of him. "Arachne, there's something I need you to do." Glancing at Byron, I hissed, "Don't let her touch you."

"Why not?" said Byron.

"Venom."

*Very well*, said Arachne. *Call in your favour and begone! Your company is already tiresome. Although, I am curious…this man of clay…does he grow hard when fired?*

I dragged the garbage can forward. Arachne stretched her scrawny neck and peered inside.

*Dead already. So sad. If she still breathed, I might help you find her killer. But you have left it too late.*

"No," I said. "There's something you can do. You know that."

Arachne's face turned black with surprise. She ran needle-claws through lank hair; giant fleas jumped like field-mice before the scythe.

*I am a weaver of silk, not miracles.*

"You telling me you can't do it?"

*I did not say that. But if I do what you ask, it is* you *who will owe* me *a favour.*

I thought about it. Arachne's not someone you want to be in debt to. On the other hand, she tends to stay home. I figured so long as I kept my distance, I'd never have to make good on the promise.

Of course, it didn't quite work out like that.

"All right," I said. "Do this and I'll owe you one."

"Do what?" said Byron.

\*\*\*

"So what's her story?" whispered Byron. "She gives me the creeps."

We'd retreated to a safe corner. Well, as safe as any corners are in Arachne's domain.

"Dirty tricks in the underwear underworld," I said. "Arachne used to run an illegal pantyhose sweatshop down by the river. The sweatshop was in direct competition with the shiny new factory Pallas Athene set up in the Diana's Glade Business Park. Now, as you know, Pallas Athene used to be queen of black market lingerie before she turned respectable and became mayor. These days, all PA's businesses are strictly legit. But Arachne never cleaned up her act. So, anyway, story goes Arachne was trying to undercut Pallas Athene on this wholesale lingerie deal. PA caught Arachne in the middle of the night handing over a truckload of bootleg silk teddies under the Green Knight Bridge. Now, PA might look like a doll and she might be mayor but she's got one hell of a temper. There's not many cross her and live to tell the tale. Arachne's one of the few."

"What did Pallas Athene do?"

"Turned Arachne into a spider, banished her into a self-reticulating semi-dimensional oubliette and revoked her weaver's licence."

"But…she don't look like a spider."

"That's just the oubliette at work. As long we're here our perceptions are regulated by Arachne's personal reality grid. Arachne *is* a spider but she still thinks of herself as a woman. So that's what we see."

Byron shuddered. "Don't like spiders."

"Who does?"

Arachne was waving her hands over the top of the garbage can. Her hands moved fast; as they moved, those needle-claws got longer. Soon the needles were longer than the fingers that held them.

Arachne plunged her hands in the garbage can. Her shoulders worked like pistons. Blood sprayed from the can, painting her face. Arachne's claws knitted the air with streaks of silver light; she looked like a crazed washer-woman up to her elbows in some ghastly laundry basket. The garbage can sang like a steel band. And all the while the patchwork rats looked down with sad eyes, because they knew exactly what was going on.

At last it was over. Arachne pulled her arms out. Her needle-claws were back to normal. Her arms were as red as the rags she wore. Her chin was black with condensed breath.

And the garbage can was shaking.

I took a cautious step towards the can. This time it was Byron who held me back.

"Don't wanna see," he whimpered.

Arachne lifted one scrawny leg and kicked the garbage can over. For the second time that day, the girl spilled out. Only this time she was all in one piece. Above my head, all the rats sighed in unison. Behind me, I heard a colossal thump as Byron fainted.

I had to admit, Arachne had done a beautiful job. Everything was in place, and the girl was a real peach: long legs and a tiny waist, and everything else responding nicely to gravity as she picked herself up. Not a drop of blood on her. Trouble was, good though the needlework was, you could see all the joins.

*Eleven thousand, three hundred and ninety-five discrete pieces*, said Arachne. *A triumph, even for me.*

I wondered if the girl would see it that way. It's one thing coming back from the dead. It's another finding you look like a patchwork quilt. I wondered if I'd done the right thing.

"I'm alive," said the girl. She held up her arm, examined the red, cross-stitched scars. She looked down at the rest of her naked body. It looked like a road atlas, each highway drawn in herringbone weave. "That's pretty neat," she said. "I always figured I'd get tattoos one day. A girl like me can earn ten times as much with tattoos. I just hate needles. But now it's done, and I didn't feel a thing. How cool is that?"

I shrugged off my coat, threw it round the girl's shoulders. Pretty as she was, I couldn't bear looking at those scars. At least on her face there was just the one—even if it did run all the way round the edge.

I kicked Byron until he woke up. When he saw the girl he nearly fainted again.

"Time to go, big fella," I said.

The girl turned to Arachne and beamed. "Thanks a bunch, old woman. What do I owe you?"

Arachne smiled too, but not at the girl.

*You* don't owe me anything, *young lady.*

"Come on," I muttered, grabbing a handful of clay and a handful of needle-work, "let's get out of here."

*Not so fast, gumshoe.*

Something slapped the back of my neck. I tried to bat it away but my hand stuck fast. I heard a scraping sound. I looked down: it was my shoes sliding across the floor.

With a glue-tipped rope of pure spider silk, Arachne reeled me in.

Three seconds later I was cocooned. Silk rigging upended me and buried my feet in the rat-tail ceiling. The rats gave way, squeaking in fury. And there I hung, blood filling up my head, watching Arachne stride towards me.

*I like my debts paid promptly*, she said, grinning to show her rotten teeth.

"All right." At least the cocoon didn't cover my mouth. "You got me. But let them go."

*They are free to leave whenever they please.*

"Uh," said Byron, "we don't know how."

"Come here," I said. Arachne watched with interest as the golem edged up to where I was hanging. "Collar pocket. There's a zipper."

Byron rummaged in my shirt and took out a grey cube the size of a craps die.

"What's this?"

"Spare dimensions. I keep them for emergencies. You got six to play with there—one per side. It's a one-shot thing though: you only get to use each side once."

"This will get us out of here?"

"Isn't that what I just said?"

"What about you?"

"I'll figure something out."

"No, I mean, how will we solve the case without you?"

"For a minute I thought you cared. Look, you got the girl back. Quiz her. Ask her what happened. Then...maybe *you'll* figure something out."

Byron stared at the dimension-die. It looked tiny in his huge, clay hands.

"Thanks," he said. His cheeks were going soft again. "I mean it. And I'll look after her."

"Get out of here, big fella," I said.

That's when Arachne set me spinning like a kebab. Through the blur, I saw Byron take the girl's hand. He rolled the die. There was a hollow pop and they were gone.

***

She let me spin long enough so I threw up. Trust me, when you're upside down, vomit lingers.

*How does it feel to be a prisoner?* Arachne said when I'd stopped spinning. I groaned. My sinuses had taken an acid bath and the whole world was doing the Peppermint Twist.

"Just...tell me...what you want," I managed to croak.

*It's very simple, gumshoe. I want out of this place.*

I closed my eyes. This was going to be bad.

"You know I can't do that. Only Pallas Athene can authorise your release. My hands are tied."

*In case you hadn't noticed, you're all tied. But that is academic. You can do it. You know you can. And...we made a deal.*

"So the only way to keep you sweet is by getting PA pissed? Where's the incentive? I'd rather cross you than her. No offence."

*None taken. Nevertheless, what you are failing to recognise is that 'getting PA pissed,' as you so delicately put it, is exactly the end result I wish to achieve. It is time someone taught our so-called mayor a lesson. Pallas Athene may think she's respectable now she wears that fancy shield, but I remember when she was a snot-nosed brat burning kittens with a magnifying glass. No wonder she thought it was a step up the career ladder when she started turning tricks in the back alley of the Hyperion Casino! How she became a public servant I shall never know! All I can say is, behind that porcelain skin and regal gaze lurks the mind of a monster!*

Arachne shivered, composed herself.

*All of which means that I understand completely your reluctance to set yourself up in opposition to a woman even the Titans cross the street to avoid. So let me put this simply…*

Arachne leaned close. The rags she wore fell away, exposing flesh like over-ripe Stilton. Instead of breasts, Arachne had a pair of twitching spinnerets. Silk oozed from them in milky strings. Crimson spider-legs dangled from her waist; they caressed her human thighs like eager schoolboys. The stench of her was unbearable.

*You will use your dimensional talents to release me from my prison. In return, I will give you my protection. From your point of view, it is a calculated risk. In making your calculation, I urge you to consider the alternative.*

Arachne stroked her spinnerets with her needle-claws. They spurted in unison. Clots of silk rolled down her belly like silver tumbleweeds. She squeezed the spinnerets harder and suddenly the silk was squirting into my face, my eyes. The silk crawled up my nose and into my tear ducts, scoured its way through to the skin of my brain where it latched on, and squeezed.

I felt a billion tiny spider eggs hose into my skull. I felt the eggs hatch. I felt Arachne's babies weave themselves into a living facsimile of my brain, each spiderling a synapse in the gestalt spider-mind. And every single thought the spider-mind had was a hot spear of pain. Then the spiderlings had babies, and the babies had more babies, and my brain swelled up until it was all that was left of me, and it was all made of spiders. But somewhere inside it was still me, and I was just one vast chattering web of pain.

Arachne pressed her spinnerets flat. The silk leaped back out of my head. My sinuses felt like they'd been shot-blasted. It was better when they were full of vomit. I swung there, retching. The rats gnawed at my shoes, lashing their tails in excitement.

*So,* said Arachne, *what is it to be? Will you risk the wrath of Pallas Athene? Or will you consign yourself to being a living host for the insane children of the spider woman?*

"Do I get a third option?"

Arachne gathered up her rags and stalked into the shadows.

*You have ten minutes to decide.*

\*\*\*

I wished I hadn't given my coat to the girl. That coat's got teeth. As soon as Arachne's silk hit the hem, the coat would have turned it to confetti. Still, someone had to cover her up.

But thinking about the coat gave me an idea.

I closed my eyes and tried an inter-brane trance. I'm not usually good at psychic connections, but this was my coat we were talking about. We went way back, my coat and me. It had to work.

At first all I could hear was the baying of the boundary wolves, forcing me back. I tried just running for it, but I couldn't get past them—Arachne's silk straight-jacket stopped me doing the moves. I was stuck here all right, just like Arachne.

But even though my body was trapped, some piece of my mind must have slipped through. Because suddenly I could hear a familiar sound. It started faint, in the distance, then it got loud and close.

The gurgle of a coffee pot. My coffee pot.

I tried opening my eyes. But I didn't have any.

I was a coat.

***

*I couldn't see, but I could smell…*

*… hot java, brewed just how I like it.*

*And I could touch…*

*… warm, soft, skin laced through with thousands of tiny ribbed carriageways. I felt a human pulse beating under pliable flesh, felt myself ride across intimate curves and bury myself in tantalising creases, felt the smooth slithering of me over a living, naked skin, which was her skin, of course: the skin of the resurrected girl.*

*I'm a coat, I thought.*

*And I was.*

*I let the sensations rule me. Inter-brane trances are fragile. You just have to relax. The more you immerse yourself, the stronger the link becomes. So I clung to the girl. It wasn't so bad.*

*And I could hear…*

*… their voices, Byron's and the girl's. The girl's name was Nancy. They were deep in discussion. I let my velvet lining slide over Nancy's scarred and sensual collarbone and listened in…*

***

"I was born on the east side," Nancy said. "I don't go back there much now. But this job came up and I knew the neighbourhood. It doesn't scare me down there, so I went."

"So what do you actually do?" said Byron.

"I work for Godiva Couriers. It's regular courier work, only I go on horseback and don't wear any clothes. I've got a licence."

"Oh. I see. Isn't that…dangerous?"

"I have several swords."

"Where do you hide them?"

"That would be telling."

"Oh. So, what happened then? When you made this delivery."

I felt Nancy shiver beneath me. "Well, I got a call to collect a package from this address on Crucifix Lane. Documents or something. The package was going all the way up to the mountain and the client wanted to make an impression. That's usually why people want to use Godiva."

"You sure do make an impression," mumbled Byron.

"Why, thank you. Anyway, I got to the address, railed my horse and knocked on the door. Nobody answered, so I pushed it open and went inside. Inside…it was odd. The building had, I don't know, maybe twelve floors. Or rather, it used to. Someone had gutted it, taken out all the floors so it was just one big space, floor to ceiling. Just a shell. It was wild, like walking into a giant's house. It was dark so I couldn't see if anyone was in there with me. So I called out. And that's when…"

"When what?"

"When something came out of the darkness and sliced me into a thousand pieces."

"Something? Or someone?"

"I don't know. But whatever it was, it was big and it had pink eyes…"

Nancy's voice grew faint. Suddenly I couldn't feel her under me any more. I was flapping like laundry on the line. Only the line was a silk thread, reeling me in. It dragged me back between the strings, back through the boundary where the cosmic wolves howl, back to where I was hanging upside-down from a ceiling made of rats.

I had time for one thought: *that golem makes a fair detective.* Then I hit my body like a slam-dunk and passed out.

∗∗∗

When I came to, Arachne was doing the spinneret thing again. I tried not to look.

"All right," I said. "I'll do it. I'll get you out of here. But on one condition."

*Another bargain? Is this to be our relationship, gumshoe? An ever-escalating sequence of deals and debts? Where will it end?*

"It ends here and now. This is the last deal I'll ever make with you. Take it or leave it."

Arachne closed her rags over her spinnerets and scowled. *What is it you want?*

"The girl."

The spider woman changed. Suddenly she wasn't a crone any more. She straightened up and smoothed out. Got beautiful. Her rags became a tiny red dress so tight it showed her pores. She looked like a loaded gun in a crimson holster.

*Well,* she said, seeing my surprise, *I'll need to look good if I'm going to be seen outside.*

"So that's a yes?"

Arachne started unslitting the cocoon. *You know the girl won't hold together. She was butchered, gumshoe. My needlework is good, but it cannot repair her soul. Her soul is in shreds and there is nothing I can do about that. Oh, sewing her up like that is a good trick…but it is just a trick. Give the girl a day or two, and she will start to come apart at the seams. Literally.*

"You think I don't know that?" I said.

*I just wanted to make sure you understand the small print.*

The last of the cocoon gave way. I dropped to the floor. Above me, the rat-ceiling sighed.

"I understand it," I said, massaging my arms. "So where d'you want to go?"

✳✳✳

"Hold your fire!" I shouted. "We're coming out!"

I unlatched the singularity bolts and led them out into the rain: Byron the golem, Nancy the stitched-up courier, and Arachne. Twenty-four zombie cops trained their guns on us. The zombie with the bull-roarer said:

"PUT DOWN YOUR WEAPONS!"

"We're not carrying," I said.

"PUT UP YOUR HANDS!"

"No need," I said. "The girl's okay. See for yourself."

Nancy came forward. When she stepped over the cellar vent, a jet of steam briefly lifted the coat above her shoulders. One of the zombie negotiator's eyes popped out and hit the street with a splat.

"MA'AM? ER, ARE YOU THE SAME NANCY LEE DONAHUE, FORMER EMPLOYEE OF GODIVA COURIERS, WHO WAS BRUTALLY HACKED TO PIECES AND HIDDEN IN A GARBAGE CAN OUTSIDE NUMBER EIGHT-EIGHT-SEVEN CRUCIFIX LANE, EAST SIDE?"

"One and the same," said Nancy. "Say—how come you know who I am? You never exactly got a chance to ID my body."

This confused the zombie. He lowered the bull-roarer and glanced across the street. Straight at the whale-sized Cadillac. The rest of the cops looked that way too. We all looked that way.

The door of the Cadillac swung open. A pair of shapely calves came out, each as big as a man. The calves belonged to a thirty-nine-foot goddess wearing a golden cloak. Hanging from her hip was a machete the size of a small ship's rudder. Her skin was white and her eyes were pink. On her breast was a shield with a gorgon's head in the middle.

Her flower-decked crown bore the initials: *PA.*

"Pallas Athene!" said Byron.

The goddess pulled the lens caps off the gorgon's eyes. Twenty-five zombies turned to stone. The rest of us were lucky: just as the gorgon's eyes came on Arachne jumped in front of us and dropped her disguise. A gigantic red spider burst out of that tiny dress like an eight-legged life-raft. It was so big it blotted out everything up to the skyline.

The spider advanced.

Pallas Athene snarled and puffed out her chest. Two of Arachne's legs had already turned to stone, but the gorgon shield was heavy and had a narrow angle of fire. Arachne was over the sandbags and ripping the shield from Pallas Athene's breast before the goddess could correct her aim. The shield landed two hundred yards down the street, facing up; seconds later it was crushed beneath a stone thunderbird with a surprised look on its face.

Then it was just a grappling match. Pallas Athene clawed Arachne's eyes—she had eight to choose from; Arachne wrapped her opponent's legs in silk and pulled them out from under her. To begin with, Pallas Athene was on top. But Arachne was mad—the kind of mad you only get from stewing in a self-reticulating semi-dimensional oubliette for seven years. She waved her spinnerets like a samurai waves his katana. Soon flowers were flying from Pallas Athene's crown. Once the goddess had dropped her machete she didn't stand a chance.

Last I saw, Arachne was headed for the docks with Pallas Athene cocooned on her back. Word is she's still down there, holed up in a derelict warehouse. One thing's for sure, she won't run short of food. When you string up a goddess by her feet and liquefy her insides, you get enough ambrosia for about a billion years.

As for me, I was just glad the debt was cleared.

Then I looked at Nancy, and remembered things weren't so good after all.

\*\*\*

"I feel peculiar," said Nancy. She sank to her knees, clamped her hands across her belly.

"Get her inside," I said to Byron. While he picked her up, I checked the street. The petrified zombies stared through the rain like museum exhibits. The stone thunderbird tipped over and broke a wing. Nothing else moved.

"What's wrong with her?" said Byron when I got back inside. He'd laid Nancy on the carpet. She was turning blue.

"I'm fine," groaned Nancy. "What the hell was that all about? Was I really murdered by the biggest goddess on the block?"

"Yeah. I put it together just before I brought Arachne out of the oubliette. But it was Byron who asked you all the right questions."

"I did?"

"How do you know what questions he asked me?" said Nancy. She winced, bit her lip, drew blood. But her eyes were bright: the girl was a fighter.

I figured she'd need to be.

"Long story," I said. "I'll tell it when there's more time. But you're right, Pallas Athene *was* the Macerator. She's always had a violent streak. Comes from her gangster roots—she used to go round wearing a Titan's skin, you know that? Anyway, going respectable must have cramped her style. When you're mayor you can't go around hacking people up any more. So she got herself a hobby."

"A *hobby?*"

"Some folk surf. Some paint toy soldiers. Pallas Athene—she took up serial killing."

"How come she never got caught?"

"When you're mayor, the cops tend to do what you say. Especially when you've got a gorgon on your chest."

Byron scratched his massive head. "But…if they knew it was her all along, why did they bother coming after me?"

"Who knows? Maybe PA figured it was time the Macerator retired. Maybe it was all a set-up—she did plant that axe with the body, after all. Probably knew a garbage collector would end up taking the heat. Nobody cares if a golem goes down. Tough but true. I figure you were just in the wrong place at the wrong time."

"Either way," said Nancy, "that bitch got what she deserved."

"Amen," said Byron.

Then Nancy started screaming. She writhed, tore off my coat, clutched at the scars on her arms and legs. It didn't take a medic to see what was up. Like Arachne said: the poor girl was coming apart at the seams.

"Didn't last as long as Arachne thought," I said.

"What?!" said Byron. "You mean…you knew this would happen? You got her all sewed up and you knew she'd come to pieces again?"

"If it's any consolation," I said, "I wish I hadn't. Seems you can stitch the body but you can't stitch the soul. Still, it got you off the hook."

"I'd rather be on the hook! What can we do?"

Nancy shrieked and snapped her back like a trout. She flipped on her front, landing exactly where she'd first landed when Byron poured her out of the garbage can. That time she'd been in pieces. Any minute now, she'd be in pieces again.

"There's something," I said. "But it's risky. And I've never seen it done. It's…well, call it a hunch."

"What is it!" said Byron. "I'll do anything!"

"You might not want to do this."

\*\*\*

He didn't hesitate. He didn't even ask me why. He just lay down and told me to get on with it.

Golems—you think you got them figured, but they just keep pulling surprises.

I'd grabbed Pallas Athene's machete from the street. I used it to cut a deep gouge in Byron's chest. It wasn't hard: there was nothing in there but orange river clay. I groped through silt and grit. I found a pretty shell, left it where it was. At last I found what I'd been looking for. I pulled it out.

A muddy square of parchment. Written on it, in Hebrew binary, was the code that made Byron tick.

"Do… it… quick… " croaked Byron. Without his code, his eyes were rolling. The floor shook as his system crashed.

I tore the parchment in half. Byron convulsed.

I put one half of the parchment back in Byron's open chest. His body went limp. I rolled Nancy on her back. She was blue all over; black fluid leaked from her scars. We were nearly out of time.

I bent over her, latched my fingers into one of the big scars on her chest. Then I peeled her open.

I didn't look inside. The stench of decay was appalling. That and the awful, liquid feel of her. She was going to pieces, fast. Eyes shut, I thrust the second half of the parchment under what was left of her ribs. Her lungs billowed over my knuckles; her heart drummed like a scared rabbit against my wrist. I let go the parchment, pulled my hands out, pressed the edges of the scar together. I opened my eyes, held my breath.

Nancy lay still. Her skin was one big bruise. Her scars looked like a black spider's web.

Then she convulsed, coughed up white froth, started breathing. Pink heat flooded her skin, she opened her eyes and pushed my hands away.

"Get your hands off my chest, pervert!" she said.

I looked over at Byron. He was resculpting his pectorals.

"You okay?" I said.

"I feel…just the same," he said.

"That's the thing with golem binary code," I said. "Ripping it up doesn't hurt it. It's neat technology. Especially since it shouldn't work at all, on account of the Hebrew numerical system not having any zeroes."

"Come again?"

"No zeroes. So they have to make the code nullatorily recursive."

"Huh?"

"It's simple: every phrase in the code points down to a smaller phrase buried in the previous line. And that smaller phrase points down to a smaller phrase still. The recursion is infinite, so even though there's no zeroes you get an infinite number of holes where a zero could fit. So the programmers just write the rest of the code around those holes and the SGOS—that's the standard golem operating system—fills in the gaps. It interpolates the places where the programmers want the zeroes to be and bingo—you get Hebrew binary. All of which is irrelevant."

"It is?"

"Yeah. But the side-effect isn't."

"What side-effect?"

"All that recursion means a golem's code parchment is like one big hologram. Every piece holds all the information contained by the whole. So you can rip a parchment in half and still have two complete pieces of golem code. It's a fractal thing—don't ask me, ask Mandelbrot."

"So…Nancy's running my code?"

"You got it."

"Doesn't mean we're engaged or anything," said Nancy. Then she fell, sobbing, into Byron's enormous clay arms.

***

They left hand in hand, like unmatched bookends. Without any books. I watched them disappear into the rain and tried to puzzle it out.

Did the shared code mean they were brother and sister now? Soul mates? Clones? But Nancy still had her memories, her personality. And Byron had his. They hadn't changed.

Which made me think back to what Arachne had said about Nancy:

*My needlework is good, but it cannot repair her soul.*

So if I'd managed to fix Nancy up with golem code, that could only mean one thing: by opening up Byron's chest I hadn't got my hands on a scrap of parchment at all.

I'd got my hands on a soul.

Byron was right after all.

I spent a while scrubbing the stains on the floor. The silt washed out okay. The gore took longer. Neither went completely. I wondered if I should get a new carpet. But, like I said, that old carpet's got a lot of stories to tell. And it goes with the drapes.

I closed the trapdoor, fixed myself a coffee. I slipped the dimension-die back in my collar. Good job I'd remembered to get it back. You never know when you'll need a spare dimension. Shame there were only five sides left.

Outside, a municipal garbage truck had arrived to clear away the petrified zombies. I watched the golems work in their yellow municipal jackets. They trudged and, where the rain lashed them, they went soft round the edges.

I wondered if I should tell them what I knew.

One of the golems bent to pick up something from the gutter. It was a flower from Pallas Athene's crown. The golem straightened the petals and tucked the flower in his jacket pocket. Then he went back to work.

I closed the drapes. They'd figure it out for themselves, sooner or later.

# IT WASHED UP

## JOE R. LANSDALE

In the moonlight, in the starlight, the churning waves seemed white with laundry soap. They crashed against the shore and the dark rocks there, and when they rolled back they left wads of seaweed and driftwood and all the tossed garbage and chunks of sewage that man had given the sea.

All the early night and into the midnight hour, the junk washed up, and then, a minute past one, when the sea rolled out and took its laundry soap waves with it, a wad of seaweed from which clinging water dripped like shiny pearls, moved. It moved and it stood up and the shiny pearls of water rolled over the seaweed, and the sewage clung tight and the thing took shape, and the shape was that of a man, featureless and dark and loose as the wind.

The seaweed and sewage man, gone shiny from the pearl drops of sea foam, walked toward town, and in the town it heard the clang and clatter of automobiles out on the brightly lit street, and it saw the street from its position in a dark alley, watched the cars zoom by and heard the people shout, and it chose to stick to the dark.

It went along the dark alley and turned down an even more narrow and darker alley, and walked squishing along that path until it came to the back of a theater where an old man with a harmonica and a worn-out hat sat on a flattened cardboard box and played a bluesy tune until he saw the thing from the ocean shuffle up.

The thing twisted its head when the music stopped, stood over the man, reached out and took the hat from the man's head and put it on its own. Startled, the man stood, and when he did, the thing from the ocean snatched his harmonica. The man broke and ran.

The thing put the harmonica in its mouth and blew, and out came a toneless sound, and then it blew again, and it was a better sound this time; it was the crash of the sea and the howl of the wind. It started walking away, blowing a

241

tune, moving its body to a boogie-woogie rhythm and a two-step slide, the moves belying the sound coming from the instrument, but soon sound and body fell in line, swaying to the music, blowing harder, blowing wilder. The notes swept through the city like bats in flight.

And out into the light went the thing from the ocean, and it played and it played, and the sound was so loud cars slammed together and people quit yelling, and pretty soon they were lining up behind the thing from the ocean, and the thing played even louder, and those that fell in line behind it moved as it moved, with a boogie-woogie rhythm and a two-step slide.

Those who could not walk pushed the wheels of their wheel chairs, or gave their electric throttles all the juice, and there were even cripples in alleyways who but minutes before had been begging for money, who bounced along on crutches, and there were some without crutches, and they began to crawl, and the dogs and the cats in the town followed suit, and soon all that was left in the town were those who could not move at all, the infants in their cribs, the terminally sick, and the deaf who couldn't hear the tune, and the thing from the ocean went on along and all of the townspeople managed after.

It went out of the town and down to the shore, and over the rocks and into the sea, and with its head above water, it rode the waves out, still playing its tune, and the people and animals from the town went in after, and it took hours for them to enter the ocean and go under and drown, but still the head of the thing from the sea bobbed above the waves and the strange music wailed, and soon all that had come from the town were drowned. They washed up on the beach and on the rocks, water swollen, or rock cut, and lay there in the same way that the garbage from the sea had lain.

And finally the thing from the sea was way out now and there was just the faint sound of the music it played, and in the houses the infants who had been left could hear it, and they didn't cry as the music played, and even those who could not move, and those in comas, heard or felt the music and were stirred internally. Only the deaf were immune. And then the music ceased.

The thing from the sea had come apart from the blast of the waves and had been spread throughout the great, deep waters, and some of the thing would wash up on the beach, and some of it would be carried far out to sea, and the harmonica sunk toward the bottom and was swallowed by a large fish thinking it was prey.

And in the town the infants died of starvation, and so did the sick ones who could not move, and the deaf, confused, ran away, and the lights of the town blared on through day and night and in some stores canned music played and TVs in houses talked, and so it would be for a very long time.

# THE THIRTEENTH HELL

## MIKE ALLEN

Her voice in my ear said, *look, look*.
Though I squeezed my eyelids shut,
hid my face in my hands, I could still see it.

I pressed my fingernails in,
hooked my thumbs and pulled,
like so many here before. And
she said, *look*, and I could still see it.

I crawled to the wall,
slammed my head on the stone,
found the cracks in the bone and clawed.
Her voice in my brain said, *look*,
and I could still see it.

I scrabbled at the ground
turned soft by my blood,
made a hole deep enough to force
my head in. She whispered from the earth,
*look, look*, and I could still see it.

The mud has swallowed me.
Things there feast on what's left
of what I used to be. And she
is one of them, her mouth moving
in my skull. *Look*, she breathes, *look*,
and I can still see it.

*for Laird Barron*

# THE GOOSLE

## MARGO LANAGAN

"There," said Grinnan as we cleared the trees. "Now, you keep your counsel, Hanny-boy."

Why, that is the mudwife's house, I thought. Dread thudded in me. Since two days ago among the older trees when I knew we were in my father's forest, I'd feared this.

The house looked just as it did in my memory: the crumbling, glittery yellow walls, the dreadful roof sealed with drippy white mud. My tongue rubbed the roof of my mouth just looking. It is crisp as wafer-biscuit on the outside, that mud. You bite through to a sweetish sand inside. You are frightened it will choke you, but you cannot stop eating.

The mudwife might be dead, I thought hopefully. So many are dead, after all, of the black.

But then came a convulsion in the house. A face passed the window-hole, and there she was at the door. Same squat body with a big face snarling above. Same clothing, even, after all these years, the dress trying for bluishness and the pinafore for brown through all the dirt. She looked just as strong. However much bigger *I'd* grown, it took all my strength to hold my bowels together.

"Don't come a step nearer." She held a red fire-banger in her hand, but it was so dusty—if I'd not known her I'd have laughed.

"Madam, I pray you," said Grinnan. "We are clean as clean—there's not a speck on us, not a blister. Humble travellers in need only of a pig-hut or a chicken-shed to shelter the night."

"Touch my stock and I'll have you," she says to all his smoothness. "I'll roast your head in a pot."

I tugged Grinnan's sleeve. It was all too sudden—one moment walking wondering, the next on the doorstep with the witch right there, talking heads in pots.

"We have pretties to trade," said Grinnan.

245

"You can put your pretties up your poink-hole where they belong."

"We have all the news of long travel. Are you not at all curious about the world and its woes?"

"Why would I live here, tuffet-head?" And she went inside and slammed her door and banged the shutter across her window.

"She is softening," said Grinnan. "She is curious. She can't help herself."

"I don't think so."

"You watch me. Get us a fire going, boy. There on that bit of bare ground."

"She will come and throw her bunger in it. She'll blind us, and then—"

"Just make and shut. I tell you, this one is as good as married to me. I have her heart in my hand like a rabbit-kitten."

I was sure he was mistaken, but I went to, because fire meant food and just the sight of the house had made me hungry. While I fed the fire its kindling I dug up a little stone from the flattened ground and sucked the dirt off it.

Grinnan had me make a smelly soup. Salt-fish, it had in it, and sea-celery and the yellow spice.

When the smell was strong, the door whumped open and there she was again. Ooh, she was so like in my dreams, with her suddenness and her ugly intentions that you can't guess. But it was me and Grinnan this time, not me and Kirtle. Grinnan was big and smart, and he had his own purposes. And I knew there was no magic in the world, just trickery on the innocent. Grinnan would never let anyone else trick me; he wanted that privilege all for himself.

"Take your smelly smells from my garden this instant!" the mudwife shouted.

Grinnan bowed as if she'd greeted him most civilly. "Madam, if you'd join us? There is plenty of this lovely bull-a-bess for you as well."

"I'd not touch my lips to such mess. What kind of foreign muck—"

Even I could hear the longing in her voice, that she was trying to shout down.

There before her he ladled out a bowlful—yellow, splashy, full of delicious lumps. Very humbly—he does humbleness well when he needs to, for such a big man—he took it to her. When she recoiled he placed it on the little table by the door, the one that I ran against in my clumsiness when escaping, so hard I still sometimes feel the bruise in my rib. I remember, I knocked it skittering out the door, and I flung it back meaning to trip up the mudwife. But instead I tripped up Kirtle, and the wife came out and plucked her up and bellowed after me and kicked the table onto the path, and ran out herself with Kirtle like a tortoise swimming from her fist and kicked the table aside again—

*Bang!* went the cottage door.

Grinnan came laughing quietly back to me.

"She is ours. Once they've et your food, Hanny, you're free to eat theirs. Fish and onion pie tonight, I'd say."

"Eugh."

"Jealous, are we? Don't like old Grinnan supping at other pots, hnh?"

"It's *not* that!" I glared at his laughing face. "She's so ugly, that's all. So old. I don't know how you can even think of—"

"Well, I am no primrose myself, golden boy," he says. "And I'm grateful for any flower that lets me pluck her."

I was not old and desperate enough to laugh at that joke. I pushed his soup-bowl at him.

"Ah, bull-a-bess," he said into the steam. "Food of gods and seducers."

\* \* \*

When the mudwife let us in, I looked straight to the corner, and the cage *was still there!* It had been repaired in places with fresh plaited withes, but it was still of the same pattern. Now there was an animal in it, but the cottage was so dim... a very thin cat, maybe, or a ferret. It rippled slowly around its borders, and flashed little eyes at us, and smelled as if its own piss were combed through its fur for pomade. I never smelled that bad when I lived in that cage. I ate well, I remember; I fattened. She took away my leavings in a little cup, on a little dish, but there was still plenty of me left.

So that when Kirtle freed me I *lumbered* away. As soon as I was out of sight of the mud-house I stopped in the forest and just stood there blowing from the effort of propelling myself, after all those weeks of sloth.

So that Grinnan when he first saw me said, *Here's a jubbly one. Here's a cheese cake. Wherever did you get the makings of those round cheeks?* And he fell on me like a starving man on a roasted mutton-leg. Before too long he had used me thin again, and thin I stayed thereafter.

He was busy at work on the mudwife now.

"Oh my, what an array of herbs! You must be a very knowledgeable woman. And hasn't she a lot of pots, Hansel! A pot for every occasion, I think."

*Oh yes,* I nearly said, *including head-boiling, remember?*

"Well, you are very comfortably set up here, indeed, Madam." He looked about him as if he'd found himself inside some kind of enchanted palace, instead of in a stinking hovel with a witch in the middle of it. "Now, I'm sure you told me your name—"

"I did not. My name's not for such as you to know." Her mouth was all pruny and she strutted around and banged things and shot him sharp looks, but I'd seen it. We were in here, weren't we? We'd made it this far.

"Ah, a guessing game!" says Grinnan delightedly. "Now, you'd have a good strong name, I'm sure. Bridda, maybe, or Gert. Or else something fiery and passionate, such as Rossavita, eh?"

He can afford to play her awhile. If the worst comes to the worst, he has the liquor, after all. The liquor has worked on me when nothing else would, when I've been ready to run, to some town's wilds where I could hide—to such as that farm-wife with the worried face who beat off Grinnan with a broom. The liquor had softened me and made me sleepy, made me give in to the old bugger's blandishments; next day it had stopped me thinking with its head-pain, further than to obey Grinnan's grunts and gestures.

* * *

*How does yours like it?* said Gadfly's red-haired boy viciously. *I've heard him call you "honey," like a girl-wife; does he do you like a girl, face-to-face and lots of kissing? Like your boy-bits, which they is so small, ain't even there, so squashed and ground in?*

He calls me Hanny, because Hanny is my name. Hansel.

*Honey is your name, eh?* said the black boy—a boy of black skin from natural-ness, not illness. *After your honey hair?*

Which they commenced patting and pulling and then held me down and chopped all away with Gadfly's good knife. When Grinnan saw me he went pale, but I'm pretty sure he was trying to cut some kind of deal with Gadfly to swap me for the red-hair (with the *skin like milk, like freckled milk,* he said), so the only thing it changed, he did not come after me for several nights until the hair had settled and I did not give off such an air of humiliation.

Then he whispered, *You were quite handsome under that thatch, weren't you? All along.* And things were bad as ever, and the next day he tidied off the strag-glier strands, as I sat on a stump with my poink-hole thumping and the other boys idled this way and that, watching, warping their faces at each other and snorting.

* * *

The first time Grinnan did me, I could imagine that it didn't happen. I thought, I had that big dump full of so much nervous earth and stones and some of them must have had sharp corners and cut me as I passed them, and the throbbing of the cuts gave me the dream, that the old man had done that to me. Because I was so fearful, you know, frightened of everything coming straight from the mudwife, and I put fear and pain together and made it up in my sleep. The first time I could trick myself, because it was so terrible and mortifying a thing, it could not be real. It could not.

I have watched Grinnan a long time now, in success and failure, in private and on show. At first I thought he was too smart for me, that I was trapped by his cleverness. And this is true. But I have seen others laugh at him, or walk away from his efforts easily, shaking their heads. Others are cleverer.

What he does to me, he waits till I am weak. Half-asleep, he waits till. I never have much fight in me, but dozing off I have even less.

Then what he does—it's so simple I'm ashamed. He bares the flesh of my back. He strokes my back as if that is all he is going to do. He goes straight to the very oldest memory I have—which, me never having told him, how does he know it?—of being sickly, of my first mother bringing me through the night, singing and stroking my back, the oldest and safest piece of my mind, and he puts me there, so that I am sodden with sweetness and longing and nearly-being-back-to-a-baby.

And then he proceeds. It often hurts—it *mostly* hurts. I often weep. But there is a kind of bargain goes on between us, you see. I pay for the first part with the second. The price of the journey to that safe, sweet-sodden place is being spiked in the arse and dragged kicking and biting my blanket back to the real and dangerous one.

\* \* \*

*Show me your boy-thing,* the mudwife would say. *Put it through the bars.*

*I won't.*

*Why not?*

*You will bite it off. You will cut it off with one of your knives. You will chop it with your axe.*

*Put it out. I will do no such thing. I only want to wash it.*

*Wash it when Kirtle is awake, if you so want me clean.*

*It will be nice, I promise you. I will give you a nice feeling, so warm, so wet. You'll feel good.*

But when I put it out, she exclaimed, *What am I supposed to do with that?*

*Wash it, like you said.*

*There's not enough of it even to wash! How would one get that little peepette dirty?*

I put it away, little shred, little scrap I was ashamed of.

And she flung around the room awhile, and then she sat, her face all red crags in the last little light of the banked-up fire. *I am going to have to keep you forever!* she said. *For years before you are any use to me. And you are expensive! You eat like a pig! I should just cook you up now and enjoy you while you are tender.*

I was all wounded pride and stupid. I didn't know what she was talking about. *I can do anything my sister can do, if you just let me out of this cage. And I'm a better wood-chopper.*

*Wood-chopper!* she said disgustedly. *As if I needed a wood-chopper!* And she went to the door and took the axe off the wall there, and tested the edge with one of her horny fingertips, and looked at me in a very *thoughtful* way that I did not much like.

\* \* \*

Sometimes he speaks as he strokes. *My Hanny,* he says, very gentle and loving like my mother, *my goosle, my gosling, sweet as apple, salt as sea.* And it feels as if we are united in yearning for my mother and her touch and voice.

She cannot have gone forever, can she, if I can remember this feeling so clearly? But, ah, to get back to her, so much would have to be undone! So much would have to un-happen: all of Grinnan's and my wanderings, all the witch-time, all the time of our second mother. That last night of our first mother, our real mother, and her awful writhing and the noises and our father begging, and Kirtle weeping and needing to be taken away—that would have to become a nightmare, from which my father would shake me awake with the news that the baby came out just as Kirtle and I did, just as easily. And our mother would rise from her bed with the baby; we would all rise into the baby's first morning, and begin.

* * *

It is very deep in the night. I have done my best to be invisible, to make no noise, but now the mudwife pants, *He's not asleep.*

*Of course he's asleep. Listen to his breathing.*

I do the asleep-breathing.

*Come*, says Grinnan. *I've done with these, bounteous as they are. I want to go below.* He has his ardent voice on now. He makes you think he is barely in control of himself, and somehow that makes you, somehow that flatters you enough to let him do what he wants.

After some uffing and puffing, *No*, she says, very firm, and there's a slap. *I want that boy out of here.*

*What, wake him so he can go and listen at the window?*

*Get him out*, she says. *Send him beyond the pigs and tell him to stay.*

*You're a nuisance*, he says. *You're a sexy nuisance. Look at this! I'm all misshapen and you want me herding children.*

*You do it*, she says, rearranging her clothing, *or you'll stay that shape.*

So he comes to me and I affect to be woken up and to resist being hauled out the door, but really it's a relief of course. I don't want to hear or see or know. None of that stuff I understand, why people want to sweat and pant and poke bits of themselves into each other, why anyone would want to do more than hold each other for comfort and stroke each other's back.

Moonlight. Pigs like slabs of moon, like long, fat fruit fallen off a moon-vine. The trees tall and brainy all around and above—*they* never sweat and pork; the most they do is sway in a breeze, or crash to the ground to make useful wood. The damp smell of night forest. My friends in the firmament, telling me where I am: two and a half days north of the ford with the knotty rope; four and a half days north and a bit west of "Devilstown," which Grinnan called it because someone made off in the night with all the spoils *we'd* made off with the night before.

*I'd thought we were the only ones not back in their beds!* he'd stormed on the road.

*They must have come very quiet*, I said. *They must have been accomplished thieves.*

*They must have been sprites or devils*, he spat, *that I didn't hear them, with* my ears.

We were seven and a half days north and very very west of Gadfly's camp, where we had, as Grinnan put it, *tried the cooperative life for a while*. But those boys, *they were a gang of no-goods,* Grinnan says now. Whatever deal he had tried to make for Freckled-Milk, they laughed him off, and Grinnan could not stand it there having been laughed at. He took me away before dawn one morning, and when we stopped by a stream in the first light he showed me the brass candlesticks that Gadfly had kept in a sack and been so proud of.

*And what'll you use those for?* I said foolishly, for we had managed up until then with moon and stars and our own wee fire.

*I did not take them to use them, Hanny-pot,* he said with glee. *I took them because he loved and polished them so.* And he flung them into the stream, and I gasped—and Grinnan laughed to hear me gasp—at the sight of them cutting through the foam and then gone into the dark cold irretrievable.

Anyway, it was new for me still, there beyond the mudwife's pigs, this knowing where we were—though I had lost count of the days since Ardblarthen when it had come to me how Grinnan looked *up* to find his way, not down among a million tree-roots that all looked the same, among twenty million grass-stalks, among twenty million million stones or sand-grains. It was even newer how the star-pattern and the moon movements had steadied out of their meaningless whirling and begun to tell me whereabouts I was in the wide world. All my life I had been stupid, trying to mark the things around me on the ground, leaving myself trails to get home by because every tree looked the same to me, every knoll and declivity, when all the time the directions were hammered hard into their system up there, pointing and changing-but-never-completely-changing.

So if we came at the cottage from this angle, whereas Kirtle and I came from the front, that means… but Kirtle and I wandered so many days, didn't we? I filled my stomach with earths, but Kirtle was piteous weeping all the way, so hungry. She would not touch the earth; she watched me eating it and wept. I remember, I told her, *No wonder you are thirsty! Look how much water you're wasting on those tears!* She had brown hair, I remember. I remember her pushing it out of her eyes so that she could see to sweep in the dark cottage—the cottage where the mudwife's voice is rising, like a saw through wood.

The house stands glittering and the sound comes out of it. My mouth waters; they wouldn't hear me over that noise, would they?

I creep in past the pigs to where the blobby roof-edge comes low. I break off a blob bigger than my hand; the wooden shingle it was holding slides off, and my other hand catches it soundlessly and leans it against the house. The mudwife howls; something is knocked over in there; she howls again and Grinnan is grunting with the effort of something. I run away from all those noises, the white mud in my hand like a hunk of cake. I run back to the trees where Grinnan told me to stay, where the woman's howls are like mouse-squeaks and I can't hear Grinnan, and I sit between two high roots and I bite in.

Once I've eaten the mud I'm ready to sleep. I try dozing, but it's not comfortable among the roots there, and there is still noise from the cottage—now it is Grinnan working himself up, calling her all the things he calls me, all the insults.

*You love it,* he says, with such deep disgust. *You filth, you filthy cunt.* And she *oh*'s below, not at all like me, but as if she really does love it. I lie quiet, thinking, Is it true, that she loves it? That I do? And if it's true, how is it that Grinnan knows, but I don't? She makes noise, she agrees with whatever he says. *Harder, harder,* she says. *Bang me till I burst. Harder!* On and on they go, until I give up waiting—they will never finish!

I get up and go around the pigsty and behind the chicken house. There is a poor field there, pumpkins gone wild in it, blackberry bushes foaming dark around the edges. At least the earth might be softer here. If I pile up enough of this floppy vine, if I gather enough pumpkins around me—

And then I am holding, not a pale baby pumpkin in my hand but a pale baby skull.

Grinnan and the mudwife bellow together in the house, and something else crashes broken.

The skull is the colour of white-mud, but hard, inedible—although when I turn it in the moonlight I find tooth-marks where someone has tried.

The shouts go up high—the witch's loud, Grinnan's whimpering.

I grab up a handful of earth to eat, but a bone comes with it, long, white, dry. I let the earth fall away from it.

I crouch there looking at the skull and the bone, as those two finish themselves off in the cottage.

They will sleep now—but I'm not sleepy any more. The stars in their map are nailed to the inside of my skull; my head is filled with dark clarity. When I am sure they are asleep, I scoop up a mouthful of earth, and start digging.

* * *

*Let me go and get the mudwife,* our father murmured. *Just for this once.*

*I've done it twice and I'll do it again. Don't you bring that woman here!* Our mother's voice was all constricted, as if the baby were trying to come up her throat, not out her nethers.

*But this is not* like *the others!* he said, desperate after the following pain. *They say she knows all about children. Delivers them all the time.*

*Delivers them? She* eats *them!* said our mother. *It's not just this one. I've two others might catch her eye, while I feed and doze. I'd rather die than have her near my house, that filthy hag.*

So die she did, and our new brother or sister died as well, still inside her. We didn't know whichever it was. *Will it be another little Kirtle-child?* our father had asked us, bright-eyed by the fire at night. *Or another baby woodcutter, like our Hans?* It had seemed so important to know. Even when the baby was dead, I wanted to know.

*But the whole reason!* our father sobbed. *Is that it could not come out, for us to see!* Which had shamed me quiet.

And then later, going into blackened towns where the only way you could tell man from woman was by the style of a cap, or a hair-ribbon draggling into the dirt beneath them, or a rotted pinafore, or worst by the amount of shrunken scrag between an unclothed person's legs—why, then I could see how small a thing it was not to know the little one's sex. I could see that it was not important at all.

\* \* \*

When I wake up, they are at it again with their sexing. My teeth are stuck to the inside of my cheeks and lips by two ridges of earth. I have to break the dirt away with my finger.

What was I thinking, last night? I sit up. The bones are in a pile beside me; the skulls are in a separate pile—for counting, I remember. What I thought was: Where did she *find* all these children? Kirtle and I walked for days, I'm sure. There was nothing in the world but trees and owls and foxes and that one deer. Kirtle was afraid of bats at night, but I never saw even one. And we never saw people—which was what we were looking for, which was why we were so unwise when we came upon the mudwife's house.

But what am I going to do? What was I planning, piling these up? I thought I was only looking for all Kirtle's bits. But then another skull turned up and I thought, Well, maybe this one is more Kirtle's size, and then skull after skull—I dug on, crunching earth and drooling and breathing through my nose, and the bones seemed to rise out of the earth at me, seeking out the moon the way a tree reaches for the light, pushing up thinly among the other trees until it finds light enough to spread into, seeking out *me*, as if they were thinking, Here, finally, is someone who can do something for us.

I pick up the nearest skull. Which of these is my sister's? Even if there were just a way to tell girls' skulls from boys'! Is hers even here? Maybe she's still buried, under the blackberries where I couldn't go for thorns.

Now I have a skull in either hand, like someone at a market weighing one cabbage against another. And the thought comes to me: Something is different. Listen.

The pigs. The mudwife, her noises very like the pigs'. There is no rhythm to them; they are random grunting and gasping. And I—

Silently I replace the skulls on the pile.

I haven't heard Grinnan this morning. Not a word, not a groan. Just the woman. The woman and the pigs.

The sunshine shows the cottage as the hovel it is, its saggy sides propped, its sloppy roofing patched with mud-splats simply thrown from the ground. The back door stands wide, and I creep up and stand right next to it, my back to the wall.

Wet slaps and stirrings sound inside. The mudwife grunts—she sounds muffled, desperate. Has he tied her up? Is he strangling her? There's not a gasp or word from him. That *thing* in the cage gives off a noise, though, a kind of low baying. It never stops to breathe. There is a strong smell of shit. Dawn is warming everything up; flies zoom in and out the doorway.

I press myself to the wall. There is a dip in the doorstep. Were I brave enough to walk in, that's where I would put my foot. And right at that place appears a drop of blood, running from inside. It slides into the dip, pauses modestly at being seen, then shyly hurries across the step and dives into hiding in the weeds below.

How long do I stand there, looking out over the pigsty and the chicken house to the forest, wishing I were there among the trees instead of here clamped to the house wall like one of those gargoyles on the monks' house in Devilstown, with each sound opening a new pocket of fear in my bowels? A fly flies into my gaping mouth and out again. A pebble in the wall digs a little chink in the back of my head, I'm pressed so hard there.

Finally, I have to know. I have to take one look before I run, otherwise I'll dream all the possibilities for nights to come. She's not a witch; she can't spell me back; I'm thin now and nimble; I can easily get away from her.

So I loosen my head, and the rest of me, from the wall. I bend one knee and straighten the other, pushing my big head, my popping eyes, around the door-post.

I only meant to glimpse and run. So ready am I for the running, I tip outward even when I see there's no need. I put out my foot to catch myself, and I stare.

She has her back to me, her bare, dirty white back, her baggy arse and thighs. If she weren't doing what she's doing, that would be horror enough, how everything is wet and withered and hung with hair, how everything shakes.

Grinnan is dead on the table. She has opened his legs wide and eaten a hole in him, in through his soft parts. She has pulled all his innards out onto the floor, and her bare bloody feet are trampling the shit out of them, her bare shaking legs are trying to brace themselves on the slippery carpet of them. I can smell the salt-fish in the shit; I can smell the yellow spice.

That devilish moan, up and down it wavers, somewhere between purr and battle-yowl. I thought it was me, but it's that shadow in the cage, curling over and over itself like a ruffle of black water, its eyes fixed on the mess, hungry, hungry.

The witch pulls her head out of Grinnan for air. Her head and shoulders are shiny red; her soaked hair drips; her purple-brown nipples point down into two hanging rubies. She snatches some air between her red teeth and plunges in again, her head inside Grinnan like the bulge of a dead baby, but higher, forcing higher, pummelling up inside him, *fighting* to be un-born.

In my travels I have seen many wrongnesses done, and heard many others told of with laughter or with awe around a fire. I have come upon horrors of all kinds, for these are horrible times. But never has a thing been laid out so obvious and ongoing in its evil before my eyes and under my nose and with the flies feasting even as it happens. And never has the means to end it hung as clearly in front of me as it hangs now, on the wall, in the smile of the mudwife's axe-edge, fine as the finest nail-paring, bright as the dawn sky, the only clean thing in this foul cottage.

* * *

I reach my father's house late in the afternoon. How I knew the way, when years ago you could put me twenty paces into the trees and I'd wander lost all day, I don't know; it just came to me. All the loops I took, all the mistakes I made, all laid themselves down in their places on the world, and I took the right way past them and came here straight, one sack on my back, the other in my arms.

When I dreamed of this house it was big and full of comforts; it hummed with safety; the spirit of my mother lit it from inside like a sacred candle. Kirtle was always here, running out to greet me all delight.

Now I can see the poor place for what it is, a plague-ruin like so many that Grinnan and I have found and plundered. And tiny—not even as big as the witch's cottage. It sits in its weedy quiet and the forest chirps around it. The only thing remarkable about it is that I am the first here; no one has touched the place. I note it on my star map—there *is* safety here, the safety of a distance greater than most robbers will venture.

A blackened boy-child sits on the step, his head against the doorpost as if only very tired. Inside, a second child lies in a cradle. My father and second-mother are in their bed, side by side just like that lord and lady on the stone tomb in Ardblarthen, only not so neatly carved or richly dressed. Everything else is exactly the same as Kirtle and I left it. So sparse and spare! There is nothing of value here. Grinnan would be angry. *Burn these bodies and beds, boy!* he'd say. *We'll take their rotten roof if that's all they have.*

"But Grinnan is not here, is he?" I say to the boy on the step, carrying the mattock out past him. "Grinnan is in the ground with his lady-love, under the pumpkins. And with a great big pumpkin inside him, too. And Mrs Pumpkin-Head in his arms, so that they can sex there underground forever."

I take a stick and mark out the graves: Father, Second-Mother, Brother, Sister—and a last big one for the two sacks of Kirtle-bones. There's plenty of time before sundown, and the moon is bright these nights, don't I know it. I can work all night if I have to; I am strong enough, and full enough still of disgust. I will dig and dig until this is done.

I tear off my shirt.

I spit in my hands and rub them together.

The mattock bites into the earth.

# BEACH HEAD

## DANIEL LEMOAL

"Are you still alive over there?"

Alvy's voice sounded weak, but it retained the bong-huffing tonality that had been his hallmark since he hit puberty. It grated at me almost as badly as the grains of sand coating my teeth. In my darkness, I could hear the sound of approaching water.

"C'mon Jim," he continued. "If you can't talk, just open your eyes for me."

I opened my eyes, and was immediately blinded by daylight. When my vision adjusted, I found myself staring at a stretch of deserted beach. The seemingly decapitated heads of Alvy and Mikey Burdy lay before me, propped up in the sand.

"What the fuck?" I croaked, as both of my crewmates blinked tiredly at me.

"It's about time you woke up," Alvy said. "We've been deep-sixed."

The ocean wind picked up suddenly, blowing more sand in my face. When I tried to raise my hands to shield my eyes, I found myself unable to move. I finally realized that my arms and legs were frozen in place, packed in sand that felt as heavy as concrete. Of course, I panicked.

"Save your energy," Alvy said, after watching me struggle for a while. "They probably tied your hands too."

"Don't fucking tell me," I groaned, feeling a sickness rising in my stomach. "Don't tell me it was Rody."

"The good news is that they buried us too far from the water," Alvy said. "The tide already came and went—fucking idiots."

The "they" that Alvy was referring to was likely our former trawler crew. For the better part of three years, we'd been running drugs, guns and assorted unmarked parcels for Colin Rody. It paid well, but Rody was taking the lion's share with little contribution on his part. I was sick of it, and Alvy was too.

We'd purchased our own cigarette boat less than four months prior, and had only used it for two freelance runs up the coast. Just a bit of cash on the side, while we kept up appearances with Rody. Neither run was a major haul, but someone obviously tipped him off.

My first suspect would have been Mikey Burdy. He was Rody's chief enforcer, a vicious prick who kept people looking the other way. He also policed the crew, in case anyone got too greedy or turned Fed. But there was only one problem with that theory: Burdy was buried up to his neck less than five feet away from me.

"Mikey," I began, choosing my words carefully. "Do you have any idea what this is all about?"

"Quite a few," Mikey said, pausing to spit sand out of his mouth. "You two are either feeding the cops… or you decided to become greedy fuckers. All the same to me. You're as good as dead."

"Fuck you, Mikey!" Alvy snapped. "Then what are you doing here, huh? Please tell us."

"Rody's made a major mistake," Mikey fumed, closing his eyes to another gust of wind. "He may as well have cut off his right hand."

"Well, it looks like you weren't all that indispensable," Alvy said.

I felt an overwhelming urge to laugh. Given our circumstances, Alvy and Mikey's tough posturing seemed ridiculous. They looked like a pair of obscene lawn ornaments.

"Let it go, Alvy," I interrupted. "Let's concentrate on getting out of here."

"We're not getting out on our own," Alvy said, looking more downcast. "I don't know about you, but I can't even feel my arms and legs anymore."

There were still sharp pains in my arms, but my legs could have been miles away. A friend of mine had once lain on his arm for an entire day in a heroin-induced stupor—he lost use of the limb entirely. Taking the moral of that story to heart, I made a mental note to try and flex my arm and leg muscles at regular intervals.

"Do you know where we are?" I said, scanning as much of the shoreline as I could. My forced line of sight only let me look in one direction down the beach; the other half of the shore lay hidden behind my head. The beach curved sharply towards the ocean, ending in a rocky point about a mile ahead; further inland, the white sand gave way to rocks, scrub brush and a wall of tall grass. "Were either of you awake when they dumped us here?"

"Nope. They must have put us under with something heavy-duty," Alvy said; he was buried facing me, enabling him to view the other half of the shoreline. Mikey was buried slightly further inland, facing the ocean. "The sand doesn't look anything like the mainland—too fine. Could be one of the Carrier Islands, maybe…"

"Wherever it is, it's off the main drags," Mikey Burdy said, barely audible over the waves. "I've been watching the water since I woke up, and I haven't seen one boat."

I tried to recall my last waking memory. Alvy, Mikey, Thornton, Swayne and I were readying Rody's trawler—the *Angelcake*—for a midnight run up the coast. The cargo was a few boxes of pills, nothing huge. So when Rody showed up right before our launch, I was immediately suspicious. But with Mikey and Thornton on board for "security," there was no chance of an easy exit.

I tried to stay on my toes during the run, but got distracted when Alvy came out of the hold with a large hypodermic needle sticking out of his neck. Before I could even react, Thornton's fist hit me in the temple. I was out before I hit the deck.

\* \* \*

As the sun climbed in the sky, we kept quiet. I was beyond thirsty, and didn't want to waste a breath until I saw a boat. Then I would scream louder than ever.

For a few hours, Alvy occasionally hollered, hoping to catch the attention of someone further inland. Every time he shouted, the entire situation seemed increasingly hopeless. With the roar of the water and the high wind, we were quickly out of earshot. Someone would have to trip over our heads to actually find us.

Meanwhile, Mikey appeared to be resting his eyes, or asleep. He was another worry. A shark's head is still capable of biting you, even after it's severed from the body; I half expected Mikey's ugly lid to roll across the sand and tear into me with its teeth. If Mikey found a way out before we did, Alvy and I were both in trouble.

And then there was another part of me that was actually afraid of being found—afraid of seeing Rody, Thornton and Swayne walking across that beach, ready to finish the job.

There was no point in getting emotional about it: we were fucked.

\* \* \*

The sun had reached its full height, heating the sand to a torturous temperature. I felt the skin on my nose and forehead slowly burn, and tasted nothing but sand on my tongue. Several death scenarios ran through my head: dehydration; blood clots; exposure during the night; or perhaps a drowning death after all, at the peak of a mid-summer storm.

"Jim," Alvy finally said, as he surveyed his half of the beach. "I don't believe it… HERE! OVER HERE!"

Mikey Burdy broke from his sleep, his eyes widening immediately. Although I couldn't see what had grabbed their attention, I saw hope in their eyes.

"Alvy," I said. "Someone's there?"

"Yes, yes… walking up the beach… HEY! HEY!"

Mikey Burdy and I both joined in with Alvy, screaming our lungs out with joy.

"It's okay," Alvy said. "He's coming, He's seen us."

At last, a long shadow drifted over the sand, covering my head in its cooling shade.

"My God, buddy, you have no idea how glad we are to see you," Alvy said, close to tears.

To my surprise, our rescuer stepped right over my head—a hairless set of legs in worn-out running shoes. It turned out that our stranger was no more than a boy, probably not even a teenager yet. His skin was baked brown from the sun, partially covered by a red bathing suit and a ratty old t-shirt. A mop of tangled brown hair obscured the top third of his face.

"Can you dig us out, little man?" I asked the boy. "Someone's played a nasty joke and left us out here."

"Dig me out first," Mikey suddenly jumped in. "My friends have sun stroke. I can help you dig faster."

"Don't listen to him kid—he's delirious," I snapped back. "Why don't you get one of us out? He needs medical attention."

"Christ you guys, be quiet," Alvy intervened, before trying a different tack. "My name's Alvy Fullerton. This is Jim Leach and Mike Burdy. What's your name?"

The boy didn't answer. Instead, he hovered over Alvy, staring down at him intently.

"Maybe he's French or something," I said.

"Kid, please, listen to me," Alvy said, ready to break down after an uncomfortable minute of silence. "We're close to dying here… dig us out."

The boy knelt in front of Alvy and picked up a handful of sand. Opening his fingers wide, he let the grains blow away in the ocean wind. Mikey Burdy had reached his limit.

"Are you fucking retarded?" he yelled, gnashing his teeth. "Stop fucking around and get me out of here. Now!"

The boy stood again, this time towering over Mikey's head. If the kid was scared or angry, I certainly couldn't tell. He was tough to read.

"I know you understand me, so I'll say this once," Mikey said, narrowing his eyes. "Use your hands, grab a stick or something. I don't care. Just know that if you don't start digging, I'm going to find you when I get out. I'll kill your family, and then I'll kill you. Very slowly."

Alvy and I were both dumbstruck by Mikey's stupidity. The boy casually walked away from us, disappearing in the tall grass behind the beach.

"Mikey, you fucking idiot!" Alvy shrieked, with an anger I'd never seen before. "If you've scared that kid off… HEY! COME BACK! WE'VE GOT MONEY… HEEEEEEEEEYYYYY!!!"

While Mikey boiled in his own blood, Alvy and I desperately scanned the scrub brush, searching for the boy. We continued to call out for help, hoping to coax the boy back to us, but to no avail. Alvy lost it.

"I don't blame him for taking off," he cried. "He's probably never seen such a bunch of rat-fucking-scumbags in his whole life."

"Alvy, relax," I said. Further down the beach, I could see the boy, emerging from the brush. "He's coming back. It looks like he's carrying something."

"It'd better be a shovel or a shovel-shaped stick," Mikey exploded. "Or I'll snap that kid's neck right on this fucking beach."

"No, no… it looks like… golf clubs."

\* \* \*

Mikey was still breathing, but in shallow gasps that were becoming less frequent. His head was an island, surrounded by a shallow pool of his own blood. Every once in a while, he would let another one of his teeth dribble down his misshapen jaw.

"Is he still here?" Alvy blurted, twisting his head several times in either direction. He seemed to be in deep shock, even though the boy hadn't laid a finger on either of us.

I hated Mikey Burdy. I'd seen him kill close to a dozen people, and had spent the last few months worrying that I would be next. But Alvy and I had both begged for Mikey's life, while a twelve-year-old kid beat his head to a living pulp. Through the entire ordeal, not a glimmer of emotion crossed the boy's face. When the deed was finished, he tossed the rusty clubs into the ocean and slid back into the cover of the tall grass.

"I think he's gone away for a while," I whispered, as the sun disappeared from view. Mikey Burdy wasn't breathing anymore.

\* \* \*

Whereas the sun was unbearably hot during the day, night on the beach was a hundred times worse. A deep chill entered every cell of my body, even before the wind grew stronger. I was so drained that I could have closed my eyes and never woken up. But Alvy and I both kept our eyes open, waiting for Mikey's young killer to return.

Hours passed without incident. It appeared more and more likely that the beach would take us after all.

"I have to shut my eyes, Jim," Alvy said, speaking for the first time in hours. "I just can't stay awake anymore."

"Go on then—I'll let you know if I see him," I said. Over the water, a full moon lit up a cloudless sky. A perfect evening for a midnight sail.

I stared at Alvy as he fell immediately into a deep sleep. I can't say I ever felt guilty very much in my life. But there it was, adding to every miserable second.

"*You're smart boys,*" my dad told Alvy and me once. "*But you're rotten to the core. You can have all the brains in the world—but if you don't got a heart, you may as well be stupid.*"

My dad was only half right. Alvy was a good person. His only mistake was following me around for most of his life. I'd finally gone and pulled him into the toilet with me. All we had left to do was to wait for someone to flush.

"I'm sorry, Alvy," I said, as loud as I could manage. If Alvy heard me, he didn't answer back.

\* \* \*

In what may have been several hours later, I woke to the thud of footsteps in the sand. All I could do was to react in the same way I would to a noise under my bed: I kept my eyes closed and tried to pass off the sound as imagination. Then I felt a wet towel engulf my face.

"Nooo!" I yelped, snapping my head backward. I opened my eyes and found myself staring into the face of a wide-eyed, runny-nosed little girl. She was wrapped in several beach towels, probably to insulate against the wind. My reaction had startled her.

"Don't go away… please," I rasped, as she took several steps back. "I need help."

My dehydrated voice cut out completely after that. I tried to speak, but no sound would come. To my relief, the girl came back to me. After all, I was only a foot tall and hardly much of a threat.

I watched the girl as she fumbled inside a small plastic cooler; she was probably only seven or so. A dark bob of hair topped her dirt-smeared face, while her legs were covered in scabs—the typical battle scars of summer.

The girl cleaned away the dried blood from my face with the damp towel before bottle-feeding me with a can of warm orange soda. As I guzzled the soda, I noticed she had already covered Mikey's head with a beach bag.

Once I had completely drained the can, I pointed towards Alvy with my lips: "Could you see if my friend's all right? You'll have to dig him out first—he's really sick."

The girl was padding toward Alvy when a noise distracted her; it had come from further down the beach. In the moon's luminescence, I saw a familiar tangle of hair and gangly legs. She saw him too. Her sarong of beach towels dropped to the sand. The boy had started to run.

"Get out of here," I barked at the girl. "Run and get help. Now!"

The girl didn't need to be told twice. She sped off towards the cover of the brush, kicking sand as she ran. Within seconds, the boy ran past me as well, silent except for a few measured breaths.

"Keep your fucking hands off her," I screamed. "I'm back here! I'm right here, you sick little fuck!"

But neither the boy nor the girl came back. I raged and struggled in my shallow grave, still unable to break free.

\* \* \*

The next time I woke up, I felt the heat of sunlight on my face. But the sun was screaming.

I opened my eyes and was nearly blinded by a bright ball of fire. It was as though the sun had dropped from the sky and landed on the beach in front of me. But it was night—and the screams were coming from Alvy. His head was rocking back and forth in a blanket of flames, his skin already blistered, black and hissing. A short distance behind Alvy, I saw the boy, illuminated by the fire. A small jerry can dangled from his fingers.

"No!" I tried to scream, but all that came out was a dry whisper. My lips continued moving in a silent, incoherent fit of obscenities.

As Alvy slowly died, I was overcome by the smoke and the stench of burning flesh. The boy stood and watched for some time. In the flickering light, I could detect his faint look of boredom—before that hateful face disappeared in a wall of black smoke.

\* \* \*

I wasn't sure how long I had passed out for—but when I awoke, the first signs of dawn were in the sky. I realized that I was facing heavenward; half of the sand had been pulled away from my living grave—and my hands were untied. To my right lay the girl, exhausted and clutching the hull of a broken toy boat.

As soon as she noticed that I was awake, the girl ran out of the small crater. In seconds, she returned with her tiny cooler, crammed full of juice cans and battered sandwiches. I wasn't able to eat the food, but swallowed the drinks she offered me. After a third can of pineapple juice, most of what I had drank came right back up again.

Despite the desperate look on the girl's face, we had to wait. She was in for a disappointment if she was expecting me to finish the digging. I was incredibly weak, and barely able to push the sand away from my legs.

Using the toy as a makeshift shovel, the girl resumed digging until I was free. Then all I could do was fumble on the sand, trying to coax the feeling back into my limbs. If our twelve-year-old sadist decided to return, I wouldn't have been able to defend either of us.

I tried to drink and eat a little more, as the girl and I stared out at the ocean. The sky above was overcast, but it glowed with a sickly yellow hue. Storm weather.

"Can you talk?" I eventually asked her. "Did he hurt you?"

I knew absolutely nothing about children. The girl could have been in shock or was simply unable to speak at all. The waves started to pick up, and she became agitated again, scanning the beach and the higher ground. When we finally locked eyes, I understood her immediately. *Let's move.*

Before we left the burial site, I armed myself with the jagged neck of a broken beer bottle and covered Alvy's head with a towel.

"I'll be back, Alvy," I told my oldest friend. "I won't leave you out here."

\* \* \*

Even though I was exhausted, I felt almost high. Minutes earlier, death had seemed to be just around the corner. Now I had a fighting chance. I would have to go into hiding, without a doubt—Rody had connections far and wide; and he wouldn't take kindly to me showing up alive somewhere.

Rather than risk being spotted on the beach, we walked under the cover of the tall grass, sticking to a well-worn path that snaked through the foliage. I let the girl lead, trying to keep up as best as I could. I was hesitant—and worried about being surprised along the trail.

Although the girl looked underfed, she had surprising energy, often running up the trail to make sure the coast was clear. When I lagged too far behind, she would run back to me and grab a firm hold of my index finger, pulling me up to speed.

At one point, while the girl was far ahead of me, the brush became more tangled. I ended up veering off the path, taking an artery from the main trail. Before I knew it, I was back on the beach. The unmistakable hum of countless flies filled the air. Closer to the water, there were three dark mounds, each obscured by a thick cloud of insects.

I only recognized one of the corpses; all of them were buried neck deep, in a far-too-familiar manner. Rody was immediately identifiable by his tattoo—an octopus on his neck. A bow saw was imbedded in the middle of his head—as though someone had given up halfway through the grisly task. The other bodies, I assumed, were Swayne and Thornton. Blood was everywhere, and I was immediately sick.

But I didn't say anything until I saw the wreck of the *Angelcake*. The main fragment of the ship was imbedded bow-first in the sand, like a jet that had taken a nosedive. Smaller pieces of the wreck were strewn across the beach—including our illicit cargo; red and white pills dotted the sand everywhere I looked.

Whatever had happened to us, Rody wasn't behind it. And I was getting the feeling that the competition wasn't involved either. There was no decent explanation for any of it.

"This isn't real," I told myself. But then I felt that small hand grabbing my pant leg; the girl's wide eyes pleaded to me once again, urging me to move onward.

\* \* \*

Back in the cover of the brush, we followed the trail up a steep incline. The grass and bushes started to give way to rocky terrain, with boulders the size of automobiles. Out of breath, I stopped and turned for a look back. From the higher vantage point, I saw that the "coast" was actually either the tail end of a narrow island, or perhaps a long strip of peninsula. The grassy ridge ran like a spine down the landmass, dividing two strips of beach. I had been a sailor for eight years along the East Coast, and none of this looked remotely familiar.

The girl's progress slowed considerably as she crept around the larger stones. The wind was stronger here, whirling between the boulders. As we came to the last cropping of rocks, I heard distant wailing; at first, I thought it was gulls. The girl immediately crouched down in a crevice of rock, motioning me to follow suit. The sound, on second thought, was too low-pitched to be birds.

"What is that?" I asked her, dropping to my knees. The girl put a filthy hand to my mouth; she was shaking, and wouldn't move an inch further. She pointed towards the opening at the end of the crevice. I crawled forward on my hands and knees, still unsure of what I was hiding from.

From this new vantage point, I could finally determine that we were on an island. The landscape declined sharply towards a rock-littered beach, much rougher terrain than where I had been imprisoned with Alvy and Mikey. The wailing had become much louder.

I looked more intently and realized I was staring at a crop of hundreds of human heads. It was the hair that confirmed everything; some of the people had longer locks that whipped in the ocean wind. Many of the prisoners kept their mouths open, in a constant wail; the others were either sleeping or dead.

"God," I exhaled, overwhelmed by the sight before me. Then I saw the boy.

He was at the edge of the island, walking between the rows of heads. His hands grasped a broken oar, which he used to absent-mindedly whack across the odd person who was in his path. Behind him, the waves were starting to roll in with greater force, submerging some of the screaming faces.

I climbed to my feet and balled my fingers into two weak fists. Immediately, the girl grabbed my arms and pulled me back into hiding. Far down along the shoreline, the boy had taken to the air.

At first, he floated several feet above the sand, discarding the broken oar and stretching his arms outward. As he climbed higher into the sky, seemingly invulnerable to the wind, the prisoners' moans grew louder. The waves became increasingly violent, and more of the prisoners disappeared underwater.

The boy was far above us now, as though touching the clouds; but he didn't appear to have noticed us. Instead, he cast his eyes out to the ocean. There, almost lost in the rolling waves, was a fishing boat that was only slightly larger than the *Angelcake*. It bobbed and spiraled in the water, drifting closer to a jag of half-submerged rock.

"I can't look," I told the girl, but found myself unable to turn away. The boat's erratic course made it appear as though the entire crew were asleep—perhaps as the crew of the *Angelcake* had been. Even if anyone on board had seen the rocks, they weren't able to stop the sickening collision that followed.

The boy had waited for the moment like a bird of prey. He rapidly descended to the surface of the water, where he retrieved a limp body in each hand.

Meanwhile, the storm was fading almost as fast as it had begun. As the waves subsided, the wreckage of several different boats rose to the water's surface. Amidst waterlogged boards, clothing and luggage, I saw the intact spine of an overturned lifeboat.

There wasn't much time. As the boy flew out for a second batch of victims, I scrambled down the rocky decline, pulling the girl's arm so hard that I thought it would come off in my hand. Thankfully, she followed without much protest, dragging her plastic cooler by its broken handle. I heard many voices as we ran across the beach. Some begged, some threatened, some wailed in defeat. I ignored them all.

With a minor struggle, I managed to upright the overturned lifeboat. Further down the beach, the boy had already accumulated a considerable pile of human beings. Some of the fishermen crawled weakly across the sand. The window of opportunity was closing.

I lost the girl for a moment; she was crouched beside the head of an elderly woman, who was miraculously still alive. The girl was digging madly with her bare hands. She may have been small, but that girl put up quite a struggle when I pulled her towards the lifeboat. I purposely avoided all eye contact with the old woman. The guilt nearly came back for a moment—but like so many other times in my life, I turned it off in seconds. Just like flicking a switch.

"There's no time, kid," I told the girl, who still flailed as I flipped her into the lifeboat with her cooler. "I'm sorry."

I pushed the boat until the water nearly reached my waist. As I pulled myself on board, I cast another glance down the beach. One of the fishermen was fighting back. After a brief struggle, the boy took to the air once again, grasping the fisherman by his neck.

"Row," I told the girl, as I removed one of the small oars from its clips and handed it to her. The boy was almost lost in the clouds before he dropped the fisherman to his death. I turned away before the body hit the beach and began to row as best as I could. The water was glass now, a photograph of a dead ocean. The effect was broken slightly by the wrecks accumulated along the rocks—several more fishing boats, and the barely submerged husk of a sizable yacht. Maybe the girl recognized one of the boats as her own.

I paused briefly to properly mount both oars, and then took over the rowing entirely. I never took my eyes off the boy after that. He likely saw us as well—but I think he had greater atrocities to commit that day. Even after the island disappeared from view, he still burned brightly in my mind.

\* \* \*

We've been at sea for over a day now, moving where the current takes us. Micheline spoke this morning—long enough to tell me her name and pass along one other bit of information: "I'm hungry."

I wish I could help her there. We should have taken more food. The little bit we did bring with us may have to last quite a while.

Neither of us has spoken since then; we should conserve every ounce of energy. So instead, I think about the beach, and try to decide what exactly I saw floating miles above the sand. But I won't get too philosophical about it. Angels, devils, police, criminals, they all have it in for me.

But they're going to have to wait.

# THE MAN FROM THE PEAK

## ADAM GOLASKI

The sun left tatters in shades of red across the sky; tatters that shriveled through purple, indigo—to black. The stars didn't come out. Instead, oil-gray clouds. I kept the car going, up, steering around the worst ruts and rocks in the road. I drove under the no trespassing sign, kept driving up. The forest around me was thick—the leaves had come in, hearty and wet: spring. I wondered if this would be the last time I'd make the drive up to Richard's. I thought so. Richard was leaving. Moving east. So, a farewell bash. Sarah would be there, too. With a sound like marbles clicking, or teeth, the wine bottle and the whisky bottle on the passenger seat bumped against each other.

Richard's house stood in the shadow of the mountain's peak. I turned off the car and sat, let my eyes adjust to the darkness, listened to cooling engine skitter. The walk to Richard's was lined with paper lanterns—no doubt Sarah's touch. I grabbed the bottles, set them on the roof of the car, lit a cigarette and looked up the peak. I heard people talking—some of the voices outside, from the hot tub, no doubt, and muted voices from the house. There were a dozen cars parked in front of my own. I opened the back door of the car and took out a small package—a book for Sarah, a collection of short stories she and I had talked about the last time the three of us—Richard, Sarah and I—had been together. I tucked the book under my arm, took the bottles and walked up to the house. I rang the bell and a woman wearing a bikini opened the door. She looked at me—looked me up and down as if I were wearing a bikini—laughed a little and brushed past me. As she passed, she asked, "Did you bring your suit?"

The house was long and narrow. To my left was the guest room, to my right a kitchen and a television room/bar. Michael, an old friend of Richard's who I'd come to like, was busy mixing drinks. He'd explained to me once that he took up the role of bartender at parties so he could get to know all the women. I approached the bar and said, "I'd say the hot tub is where you want to be tonight."

Michael nodded, ruefully. I handed Michael the bottles I'd brought. "Good stuff," he said. "Good to see you," he said. I shook his hand and patted his shoulder. "What'll you have?" he asked. "A glass of that whiskey," I said. He said, "Try this instead," and poured from an already open bottle. I put my cigarette out in a red-glass ashtray by the bar and had a sip. I nodded my appreciation. "I should announce myself," I said, and backed away.

The living room: a large, open space dominated by a fat couch and a grand piano (Richard didn't play). Sarah was on the couch drinking wine. When she saw me, she stood, crossed the room with a quick, woozy stride and put her arms around me.

"Watch the wine," I said.

She stepped back from me, a wounded expression on her face. I took her glass and rested it on the piano. She put her arms around me again and said, "I get so excited when you come. I always do. It's so silly. I always am so excited to see you."

"It's good to see you too." We kissed, as we did whenever we saw each other; I'm not sure how this greeting got started, but our kisses were long and on the lips; she'd been dating Richard as long as I'd known her.

"Have you seen Richard yet?" she asked.

"I just got here."

"Can I?" She tapped the cigarette box in my breast pocket. She slipped her fingers into the pocket and smiled at me. "You always have the best cigarettes." As she lit up, she eyed the wrapped package under my arm.

"It's for you," I said.

She unwrapped my gift, dropped the brown paper to the floor. "You found a copy," she said. She opened the book, careful with the spine, a delicate touch on the yellow edge of each page she turned over. "You're the only one who ever gets me books." She tapped her necklace: an elegant, expensive silver knot. "Richard always buys me jewelry," she said, with a frown.

We caught up, a little; a little about Richard's preparations for leaving, though we skirted the issue of whether or not she'd be going. We would have that conversation later. I needed to drink a little more, to meet everyone. I looked past Sarah, at the women on the couch. Sarah said, "That one's Carmilla—she's a stunning bore—and that's Kat—fun, fun, fun. They're friends of Richard's. From where, I do not know. Come, I need more wine." We left her glass on the piano, made our way up to the bar. She fell into a conversation with Michael. I walked off—I didn't feel like standing around while Sarah and Michael talked.

Richard was in the yard, beer in hand, talking with someone I didn't know. Just behind him was the hot tub. The woman who'd answered the door was in the tub with a couple of guys. Before Richard spotted me, the woman said, "You should come in, it's perfect, cold outside, warm in here." She giggled. One of the guys leaned over and whispered to her. She pushed him away.

"David, you made it," Richard said.

"I wouldn't miss it."

"Well I'm glad, you know."

He introduced me to his friend, and to the guys in the tub. He didn't know the woman's name and she didn't supply it. "Come on and sit," he said to me.

I sat on a cooler. Richard and his friend were talking about Boston, where Richard was moving. I'd never been to Boston, I told them, though I'd heard it was like San Francisco. We talked about San Francisco, Seattle, Portland.

The woman in the hot tub interrupted us and asked me to get her a beer. I got up to get a beer from the cooler. She stood. She was very thin, no hips, but gifted with significant breasts. She leaned forward—bent at the waist without bending her knees—and brought her bosom to my face. Freckles swirled into the dark line of her cleavage. "Thank you so much," she said, and took the beer. The guys in the tub were happily gazing up at her tiny bottom—those men were nothing to her, made to carry her bags and perform rudimentary tasks while she gazed off in other, more interesting directions. I'd met women like her many times before. "My name's Prudence," she said.

"Of course it is," I said.

"You really ought to join."

"You know I'm not going to."

She did know, too, and smiled a wide, long smile.

"But I'll be here all night," I said.

She settled back into her pool.

I lit a cigarette; for a moment, a flame cupped in my hand; I drew my hand away, and looked up to the peak. A man, briefly illuminated by moonlight before the clouds closed up, appeared at the top, moved toward the house. I said to Richard, "Does someone live up there?" Richard told me he didn't think so. I tried to point out the man—who I could still see, as a dark shape on a dark background—but Richard couldn't find him. "I'm going to go in, get a real drink," I said. Richard said he'd be in shortly. I shrugged and walked around to the front of the house—an eye on the man walking down the mountain.

Most of the people at Richard's party weren't attractive. They might be fit and many were dressed in expensive clothes, but most of his friends looked average and, upon getting to know them, were. The exceptions were notable. Michael, a transplant from the coast, a man of style; Kat and Carmilla—just beautiful; Prudence—a manipulator I appreciated; and Sarah. Kat and Carmilla were seated on a small couch in the guest room, surrounded by four or five guys and one unfortunate looking girl (pasty, a large, flat nose and hair forced into a strange shade of red). They were all watching a movie—Kat spotted me in the doorway, shifted on the couch, shoved at one of the guys, and gestured for me to sit beside her. They were watching *The Man Who Fell To Earth*, that beautiful David Bowie film—

I let myself get drawn into the movie. Kat ran her hand in a circle on my back. When the unfortunate girl sneezed, breaking my mood, I excused myself and walked down the hall to the bar. I passed the front door just as there was a knock; the door was answered and I heard, "What, you need a formal invitation? Sure come on in, you are welcome to come in." Sarah joined me at the bar and took my arm. We collected drinks and Michael and I went out onto the back patio. Mercifully, the three of us were there alone.

Sarah stole a cigarette and complained about Richard's friends—"Present company excluded."

Michael then brought up the subject Sarah and I had danced around once already: "What's in Boston for you? I mean, I know Richard has a great job, but what are you going to do?"

Sarah looked at the floor for a moment, took a drag and a drink and said, "That's just the thing, Michael."

I was eager to hear her explain to Michael just what that thing was—I thought I knew but I wanted her to say it—but instead she stared past Michael, back into the house. I turned and Michael turned and we all watched a very ugly man walk past the back patio door toward the bar.

"Who the hell was that?" I asked.

Sarah said, "I don't know, but—" then drifted past me into the hall. Michael and I looked at each other, then followed—I dropped my cigarette on the patio floor.

The ugly man wasn't at the bar by the time we stepped into the hall—no one was.

He was in the living room, behind the piano, playing the adagio from the *Moonlight Sonata* on Richard's out-of-tune grand—the result was not lulling or melancholic, as the adagio is, but dissonant and eerie.

No one else seemed to share my evaluation of the music. Everyone—the whole party except Prudence and her men—were gathered around the piano watching the ugly man play, laughing when he made an exaggerated flourish over the keyboard, but rapt, totally caught up—so that they all jumped when he moved into the more upbeat allegretto. I wanted to jump too—each out-of-tune note grated on my nerves.

I stared at the ugly man as he played. He was bald. His head was long and boney, his eyes lost in shadow. His skin was a dark brown—not like Michael's, no, he didn't look African—the ugly man was black all right, but his skin was waxy and all over there was a patina of green—the green of rotten beef. I couldn't help but imagine what it would be like to touch his skin—my finger, I was sure, would sink in, as it would in a pool of congealed fat. His ears were large and pointed. His mouth was small—pursed as he played—and his teeth were too large for his tiny mouth. His two front teeth were the worst: jagged, yellow, buck-teeth.

I was greatly relieved to see that Sarah did not appear to be under his spell. She stood in the corner watching not the ugly man, but the crowd—and Richard, who stood with a stupid open-mouthed expression on his face, clapping like a little girl every time the ugly man crossed his hands over the keyboard. I could hear, barely audible, David Bowie's voice in the guest room.

The ugly man stopped playing the piano then, and it dawned on me that he must be the man I'd seen coming down from the peak. He waved his hands in the air, and this seemed to release everyone. There was some applause, and people returned to what they had been doing. I watched Kat and Carmilla walk back toward the guest room, Michael made a bee-line for the bar, and Sarah and Richard walked over to me. I noticed the pasty girl with the bad dye-job standing next to the ugly man, looking down at him as he caressed her hand. The perfect couple, I thought. I led Sarah and Richard to the bar and insisted that Michael open the whisky I'd brought—a far better whisky than what he'd served me when I'd arrived.

I asked who the ugly man was.

Sarah said she didn't know. Michael and Richard acted as if I hadn't asked the question. I put my hand on Richard's arm and asked again, and he said, "Which ugly man?"

I took Richard's response to be a joke and gave him a forced, weak chuckle. My whisky was a relief. I needed a moment alone with Sarah—I wanted her to have a chance to finish what she'd been saying earlier, I wanted her to tell me that there was nothing for her in Boston, that she had no intention of ever joining Richard in Boston and was only pretending so as not to break his heart before his big trip.

I felt a hand on my shoulder. I was certain it was the ugly man's; I was surprised—relieved—that the hand belonged to Prudence. "I'm out of the tub," she whispered.

Sarah and Richard were talking; I asked Prudence what she wanted to drink and she held up a beer. "I'm all set in that department. Did you know they're watching a movie in the guest room?"

"Yes," I said. I followed Prudence down the hall. She'd put on a dress over her wet suit—somehow, with the bands of wet, clingy material around her waist and her chest, she seemed more naked than she had before. I'd catch up with Sarah later, catch her when Richard was off chatting up one of his boring friends.

Prudence and I entered the room—*The Man Who Fell to Earth* was still on— had Bowie yet revealed his alien identity? Kat and Carmilla were on the couch, and to my satisfaction, Kat shot Prudence a nasty look and beckoned me to a spot beside her. Prudence, first in the guest room, took that spot. Small as her hips were, there was no more room left on the couch. When she saw this, she slid off the couch, onto the floor, and offered me the spot Kat had already offered. Regardless of the outcome of my conversation with Sarah, I knew I would not leave the party alone; I considered, even, the possibility that Prudence and Kat's attentions would prove useful in gaining Sarah's attention.

Kat stroked my hair; Prudence my leg. The other men in the room couldn't help but glance away from the television to look first at the women, then at me, wishing themselves in my position.

Just before the movie ended—a sad, pale scene—I'd been lulled by all the petting—the ugly man, the man from the peak, walked past the guest room. I caught a glimpse of him, just as he walked out of sight. Except for Prudence, the people in the guest room left: the guys, Carmilla and Kat. Before I could dwell on this much, Prudence was on the couch beside me, hand on the inside of my thigh, mouth drifting toward my face. I knew that face, drifting sleepily, a drunk woman about to kiss me. I let her kiss me. We kissed. Her tongue darted in and out of my own mouth. Her open hand pressed against my erection. My hand on the damp cloth covering her right breast, my hand on the damp cloth at the small of her back.

I broke off our kissing. I said, "Let's get something more to drink." Though she gave me a petulant look, I knew she would do as I asked and I thought—for a moment—this woman actually knows what I'm doing, understands, would have ended the kiss herself, shortly, if I hadn't. In that moment I preferred Prudence to Sarah. The moment was fleeting.

The ugly man had been speaking—addressing the entire party, it seemed. When Prudence and I stepped into the living room, he waved his hand as he'd done before, and the crowd dispersed as it had before. Everyone left the room except for one person, one of the guys who'd been in the hot tub with Prudence—I watched her watch him talk to the ugly man and Prudence said, "I knew he was gay." I wasn't sure who she was referring to at first—I didn't think the ugly man was gay—and then I realized who she meant.

"Who is that man?" I asked.

"I don't know. I've been outside all night."

"Didn't you see him come down from the peak?"

"From the peak? There's nothing up there. I'm going to get another drink."

She left me. I lit a cigarette and went out onto the patio. Richard and Sarah were out there, though Richard was talking with one of his friends and Sarah was just standing around, looking bored. She brightened when she saw me. I gave her a cigarette.

"Why don't we go outside a while," Sarah said.

We left the enclosed patio. We heard voices, coming from the direction of the hot tub. We walked out into the dark yard, toward the woods.

"What was that guy talking about?" I asked.

"Which guy?"

"The ugly guy. They guy with the buck teeth."

Sarah turned up a confused expression. When she pulled on her cigarette, her face was illuminated. She had, I thought, the most perfect face. Between her eyebrows, just above the bridge of her nose was a circular patch of skin very smooth and brighter white than the rest of her face. I wanted to put my fingertip on that spot. I did. She scrunched her face up and giggled, brushing my finger away.

"So that's what that button does," I said. "So," I said. "You didn't finish what you were saying earlier."

She didn't answer me, but pointed, and I forgot what I'd asked when I saw what she was pointing out. The man from the peak walked across the lawn—on a line parallel with our own course, maybe twenty feet away—with the guy he'd been talking to in the living room. They walked toward the edge of the wood, where a woman—the woman with the bad dye-job—lay on the ground.

"What is going on over there?" Sarah asked.

I said, "I'm sure we don't want to know."

"Do you think she's all right?"

"She looks fine to me," I said, though there was no way I could actually judge, from where we stood. "We should leave them be," I said, but I asked, "Who is that guy anyhow? I saw him come down from the peak."

"Which guy?" Sarah asked.

"The bald guy." Right when I said that, he was out of sight, he'd stepped into a shadow that made him all but invisible. So I said never mind.

On the patio, we finished our drinks. Sarah took another cigarette. She looked around—there were other guests on the patio, but none we knew more than just in passing. Richard had gone inside. Sarah said, "I'm not putting any pressure on you, David, but I'm not going to Boston."

Sarah seemed like herself when she said that, more than she had all night, and I was glad, I'd known it, known she would leave Richard for me if I'd wanted, and I did want that, and I hadn't been wrong.

All the voices on the porch seemed to rise in volume—there was a scream—I decided from inside the house—but no one paid any attention.

Several hours later, I stood in front of Richard's house, trying to figure out why there were twelve cars, not including my own, in the driveway. The party had started to die about an hour before; people had slipped out one-by-one. I realized, as I stood in front of Richard's house smoking, sipping a cheap glass of whisky, that I hadn't heard a single car go. Even if people had carpooled, had designated a driver, there were still too many cars in the driveway.

My thoughts weren't adding up in any significant way. I was in a haze of drunk and sleepiness—not so far gone that I wouldn't be able to collect Sarah and leave soon, but dull enough that my lines of thought were short.

I stared for a while at the mountaintop. There were no houses, that I could see, higher than Richard's. If the man from the peak lived up there, he must have walked from the other side of the peak, and that looked to me like a hell of a walk.

I coughed, caught a coughing fit, felt a hand on my back.

"Prudence?" I managed, still bent over.

"No, not Prudence."

The voice was a voice I hadn't heard once that night, but I knew whose voice it was.

"Taking in the air?" the man from the peak asked.

I saw a laugh on his face; he was laughing at me.

"Smoke?" I asked. "Whisky?" I held out my drink and my cigarette.

He held up a hand—his fingers were long, his nails were long.

"You don't drink," I said.

He just grinned his stupid ugly grin, a set of teeth crooked and misshapen. That his speech wasn't impeded by his malformed mouth was a wonder—indeed, his voice was the most soothing voice I'd ever heard. "So who are you?" I asked.

He said, "I'm an invited guest," and I remembered what I'd overheard earlier that night.

I said, "I watched you come down from the peak. Are there houses up there?"

He looked at the peak, followed its upward rise with his head until he'd found the very tip and said, "No, there are no houses."

I thought maybe he lived in a tent or a trailer home and was just having fun with me, making me ask my questions just so. Normally, when I think someone's doing that, some cute girl who thinks she's coy or some clever boy trying to impress, I walk away without so much as a fuck you and that puts them out, and then they beg me for my attention. Normally, that's what I'd do. But I said, "But do you live on the peak? In a tent? In a trailer? In a mobile home?" I gave that ugly man from the peak all the options I could because I was desperate to hear his answer. For some reason: I was desperate to know.

He said, "I live in the peak."

I didn't know what he meant by "in the peak," but I smiled—I felt that dumb smile spread on my face—I smiled and nodded as if "in the peak" made all the sense in the world.

I asked, "So what is it you're doing in the backyard?"

He gave me a straight answer. An awful answer. And for a moment I could see him exactly as he was; all of a sudden I could see him, see that his clothes—from pant cuff to shirt collar—were drenched in blood and gore. Blood dripped off his shirt sleeves, blood was pooled around his feet, there was blood on the top of his bald head and there was blood all around his mouth. The blood around his mouth was the most horrible, smeared around like finger-paint. Before I became hysterical, I couldn't see the blood anymore. He looked ugly, but his clothes were clean. His pant cuffs flapped in the breeze. His bright white shirt sleeves were rolled up just below his elbows.

I wondered, if he could do that, why he didn't make himself look handsome to me. I think he knew my thought, because he said, "Charisma. You know what I mean."

I laughed. He walked back into the house. I stood shaking my head, enjoying for a moment the great joke. Then a wave of nausea passed through me and I vomited—all spit and whisky—and my head was clear. I rushed into the house—for Sarah, I thought, where is Sarah? The guest room was empty. No one was at the bar. Richard was seated on the piano bench next to the man from the peak, and they were playing "Heart and Soul." The man from the peak playing the chords, Richard plinking out the simple tune with a single finger, laughing like an idiot.

I ran into Prudence out on the patio. She was drunk, but when she looked at me I knew she was still in control: I'd known from the moment she brushed past me at the front door that the big breasts and the flirty girl-voice were all for show, plumage that got Prudence what she wanted. I'd known that she was like me in that way, and admired her for it. So instead of just ignoring her for Sarah I stopped and told her that we were all in a lot of trouble.

"I'd sort of picked up on that," she said, pointing with her thumb toward the backyard. Her calm was wrong, a part of all that was wrong that night. She said, "I was just leaving. My car's blocked though. I was trying to find someone—"

"So go out to my car—it's silver, it's the last one in the driveway. Go out to my car and wait for me. I'm going to get Sarah."

She said, "Sarah? Fuck Sarah. What do you need Sarah for?" I sensed her control was limited, or running low, and so she obeyed me, started toward the driveway. Better to do as I said, than to do what the man from the peak asked her to do. I went through the near-empty rooms, finally went into the backyard, where I knew everyone must be.

I tried not to understand too much of what I saw. Since there was no moonlight, no stars, I couldn't make out the exact details anyhow. But the yard was lined with bodies. Many stripped of their clothes, all flat on their back. The bodies, piled like sandbags, formed a wall along the edge of the woods. They were neatly stacked but for a few strays—I saw Michael's body, not five feet from where I stood.

And then I saw Sarah, on her feet, wandering in a daze. I became aware that "Heart and Soul" had stopped. I could hear Sarah's feet brush through the grass.

I couldn't speak—had no impulse to. I ran to Sarah, put my arm around her and guided her toward the side of the house, away from the patio door which was opening, away from Richard, who staggered out into the yard, singing, "Heart and Soul." He fell in love, he sang, "madly."

Prudence was not in the driveway, and I thought fine, if he has her, that'll buy me and Sarah some time, and I'm going to live, and Sarah, too. I pushed Sarah along the driveway, dragged her. I opened the car and put Sarah into the passenger seat, then started the car and backed up to turn around. In the headlights, the car still facing the wrong way, toward the house—I saw Prudence, on her back. Her body must have been just out of sight, just under the front bumper. She jerked, once. I couldn't help watching her breasts: a spray of freckles that vanished into her cleavage.

The mountain road was so rutted, I couldn't go fast, not without taking the chance of breaking an axle.

We were close. Very close to the bottom of the mountain when I heard the bang from the inside of the trunk. I jumped on the accelerator and I could feel a heavy weight shift. Sarah stared calmly ahead, as if we were on a day-trip. There was another bang, and the trunk burst open. I couldn't see anything out the rear-view mirror—just the silver trunk lid. I drove, swerving around boulders, bouncing in and out of pot holes, cursing each time the front end of the car ground into the dirt, until, incredibly, the man from the peak stared at me through the windshield. He clung to the hood on all fours, his arms and legs wide apart, face inches from the glass. He wasn't hiding himself: his teeth were bared and he was filthy with blood, dribbling blood onto the glass, foaming blood from his nostrils.

I felt, suddenly, quite serene. I brought the car to an easy stop. Sarah and I stepped out.

The man from the peak hid himself again. He hopped off the hood with a single, graceful flex of his legs. I heard stones crunch under his shoes as he walked up to Sarah. He looked at me while he put a hand on her right shoulder. And she relaxed completely—I wasn't sure what kept her from collapsing. He grabbed her hair and yanked, forcing her head to the side. She winked at me as if she were about to get a treat she'd been waiting for all day.

Did I make a move to stop him? No. His eyes locked onto mine. And any desire for survival I'd had, any wish for Sarah to live, just slipped away—was leeched from my thoughts. I reached into my breast pocket, slowly removed my cigarette pack, took a cigarette, tamped it against the box, lit it and smoked. I stood, smoked, watched as he tore a chunk of flesh from Sarah's throat with those stupid buck teeth of his and opened his mouth to the jet of blood that burst from her artery. I watched him and he watched me and was he grinning while he drank? Oh, surely he was and I smiled back at him, smiled and smoked my cigarette, smoked so hard the filter flared up before I finally dropped my cigarette and stamped it dead.

I looked up after watching my own foot twist a cigarette butt out on the dirt road and they were gone. He and Sarah were gone. I stared up at the top of the mountain. Stood for at least an hour. Finally, I was released. Trembling, I slid into the driver's seat and drove down off the mountain into Rattlesnake Valley, as blue light crept across the sky.

I listened to the radio for three days. I had the dial somewhere between stations. Sometimes one came in stronger, sometimes the other. I heard news, I heard a minister Bible-teaching, organ music, chants—when both stations grew weak I heard a murkier broadcast: two voices, disharmonious music, swamp-static. I'd ordered all my meals by delivery for the last few days. Greasy wax paper curled in on itself; half-eaten sandwiches, flat soda, Styrofoam. I spent the day in a leather arm chair. I slept there—I woke often to be sure that all my windows were fastened, that the bolts on the door had been shot—that I hadn't been careless after a delivery boy had come by, though, each time I closed the door on a delivery, I locked up, leaned against the door and double-checked the locks. I worried the skin around my fingers and smoked—I'd found a stale pack in my bedroom;

not my brand, someone else's cigarettes, some woman I'd brought here had left her cigarettes. I tried to think of ways that I could have stopped what happened from happening, but there was nothing I could've done. I could've done little things differently—not waited so long to take Sarah away (not sent Prudence on her own). Yet, even these small acts seemed out of the realm of possibility to me—that I couldn't have behaved any way other than the way I behaved. My own personality, my own desires, took on monstrous shapes in my mind.

On the third day I remembered the book that I gave to Sarah—that slim collection of short stories. An image of that book popped into my head, completely unbidden. And once that image was there, I couldn't shake it—try as I might. As if the image of that book were being broadcast directly into my head. The book must still have been at Richard's house. I could picture it in each room: on the bar next to a clear, empty bottle; in the guest room on the couch; etc. The book, then the empty room all around it. My thoughts returned incessantly to the book. The book as object. The book as icon. The book as literature—how did those stories tie in with the events of that night? At times, just as sleep would come over me, the stories in that book would seem clearly prophetic—how could I, having read the book, not have known what was going to happen at Richard's party?

I left my apartment to retrieve the book. A small part of my brain screamed at me not to, pointed out that going anywhere near Richard's house was lunacy. I drove up the mountain, tapped the steering wheel, chewed on the end of an unlit cigarette and drove under the no trespassing sign to Richard's. I would get the book and leave. I would have the book. The sun was high and bright, there was nothing at all to going into Richard's house and getting the book and then leaving with it, set on the passenger seat or, perhaps, on my lap. Once I had the book, I would be able to settle back into my rational life.

Prudence's body wasn't in the driveway. I remembered the wall of corpses the man from the peak had made.

I was glad there was still a mess from the party—bottles, ash trays full of butts, objects displaced, leftover dip, etc. If the man from the peak had taken the time to clean the house—that might have made me crazy—if the house had looked as it did on the occasions I'd come to visit Sarah when Richard was away, I'd've been greatly disturbed. There had been a party. The man from the peak had come.

The moment I touched the book I knew that I hadn't come for it after all, and that I hadn't come of my own will.

The peak was a black spike surrounded by sun. I climbed toward the peak. I sweated heavily in my dark clothes—if someone had stood at Richard's front door, would they have been able to see me at all? Just shy of the boulders that crowned the mountain, I found the crevasse I knew was home to the man from the peak. "I live in the peak," he'd said.

I sat down at the edge of the crevasse. A jagged, open crescent in the side of the mountain, as if a sliver of the moon had burned its impression onto the side of the mountain. When I leaned over, I felt a gust of wet air, like breath; it reeked of ammonia and dirt. I'd smoke until my cigarettes were gone and by then there wouldn't be much light left. I didn't want to be here but I found that it was impossible to leave.

# THE NARROWS

## SIMON BESTWICK

Except for the drip of distant water and the soft crying of the children, there is only silence.

Torches pick out brickwork, nearly two hundred years old and holding firm. Handmade bricks; nineteenth-century workmanship. Thank God for small mercies.

Ochre sludge clotted at the edges of the canal. The damp chill. The black, black water.

Jean's body presses close to mine in the small boat. We're well-wrapped. Thank God we're dressed for the winter; it's cold down here. Another small mercy. Despite that, I can feel her warmth, and something stirs in me; for the first time since I've known her, I think of her in a sexual way, what she might look like naked, and I feel sickened at myself.

Is she thinking of me the same way?

I think of Anya and force myself to concentrate on the tunnel ahead. The torches give us only a few yards visibility. I try not to think of how long they'll last.

We travel on down the canal. And the others follow.

And the only sound is the soft, occasional plash of our paddles in the water.

And the drip of water from the ceiling and the walls.

And the crying, the crying of the children.

My own is silent.

\* \* \*

When the sirens wailed, I took charge.

I don't know why that was. I wasn't the newest member of staff, but still far from long-serving. I'd only been at the school about a year.

But I took charge nonetheless.

279

I knew what the Headmaster, Mr Makin, was thinking. He was in his sixties, due to retire next year. All the years spent caring for others' kids, and none of his own—unless you counted a son who lived in Australia and never called or wrote. All those years, and all he'd wanted was to spend the last few with his wife.

"Ethel…" I heard him breathe in the stricken hush of the staff room.

Jean was as stunned as the rest. She was the Deputy Head and should have said something, but for the first time I could remember, she was at a loss. No one could think of what to say or do. No one but me.

I'd never been in serious danger before. Nearly had a car accident three years ago, avoided a collision by a hair—hardly in the same league. But they say a crisis shows you who you really are. I'd always assumed I'd fall short, feared I'd be weak or frightened.

But, come the moment, I wasn't. Even when Makin said his wife's name and sent Anya's face fluttering round my head like a moth round a light, I made it go away. She worked in the city centre; with a terrible coldness I realised there was nothing I could do for her.

I wish I'd at least called her on her mobile, said I loved her, said goodbye—but, no, I can't see that happening, can you? Switchboards have to be manned, after all. I wonder if anyone kept on mechanically doing their duty as the last few minutes ticked by.

Four minutes. That was all we had.

That endless moment broke and I was on my feet.

"The kids," I said. "Jean?"

She blinked at me. Outside, the playground had fallen silent.

"Get in the playground," I said. "Any kids live in the next couple streets, get home. Otherwise, get them down the basement."

"Basement?" She blinked again. It was a filthy place, not even used for storage anymore.

"Best chance we've got." I clapped my hands. "Come on! Everyone! Go! Go!"

Where did it come from, the sudden authority? I ask myself again and again, and have no clue. And then I stop asking, because I mustn't. The ball is rolling now, and I have to stay like this. Responsibility. It's like a millstone round your neck.

The staff ran out of the room. Except old Makin. He just sat there, blinking, old eyes full of tears.

I knew what I had to do. I reached across and touched his arm. "George?"

He stared at me.

"Go home, George. Be with your wife."

"I…" He wanted to, of course, but duty pulled him the other way. I absolved him.

"We'll be fine, sir," I said. "Just go. You deserve to…" I stopped.

He nodded once, rose. "Thank you, Paul," was all he said. His head was down and he couldn't look at me, but as he left the room, he began to run, surprisingly fast for a man his age.

A moment later, I was running too.

* * *

The tunnel, and the tunnel, and the tunnel. Endless, the brick arch, low above our heads, passing by. Coming out of darkness, yard by yard, coming towards us, passing overhead and back into the dark again.

The same, and the same, and the same. Again, and again, and again.

"Paul?" Jean's voice is a whisper. Her hand on my arm. "Where are we going?"

"I don't know," I say, and then remember I have to. I have to know something. "Not yet." I think. "There'll be a gallery soon, or a landing stage. Or something."

"What then?"

*How should I know?* I want to scream. But of course I can't. "We'll have to see, Jean. Might be fish here." I wouldn't bet on it, though. Rats in the tunnels? Did you get them down old coal mines? You get them everywhere, surely?

Worry about food later, I think to myself. Once you're underground and safe somewhere.

Safe? Where is safe?

I stop thinking that way. It may all be pointless, just delaying the inevitable, but what am I supposed to do? Just stop and wait to die, when the poison seeps down here into the mine and the canal? No. I can't. As much for me as anyone else. If I stop, you see, I'll think of Anya. And I mustn't. I mustn't do that.

* * *

Anya was… well, Anya was my girlfriend, of course. You must have worked that out for yourselves. Except that doesn't cover it. *Girlfriend* always sounds so casual, so teenage. And it wasn't like that.

We weren't married or engaged. Hadn't even talked about it. Weren't even living together, although we *had* talked about that. Just weren't sure where we'd live. Her poky flat, my poky flat, or somewhere new.

I first saw her in a bar in the city centre, near where she worked—I went over to her, to talk to her, of course, but I never thought I stood a chance. She was blonde, with blue eyes, a classic beauty. But she liked me. More than "liked" as it turned out

You see loads like that from the old Eastern Bloc countries. God knows why. I once joked that if Polish women looked like her, it was no wonder they kept getting invaded. She whacked me round the head with a pillow as I recall. But she was laughing when she did it.

She wasn't a dumb blonde. She was a student. A *mature* student, I should add. At twenty-eight, two years older than me. And me a teacher. She already had a degree, taken back in Poland. English Lit. She could hold her own in any discussion about poetry. Which was good. We had lots to talk about. Keats and John Donne, Wilfred Owen (her favourite) and R. S. Thomas (mine). She was taking a Business Studies degree at Manchester Uni.

We'd been together about a year. Around the same time, give or take, as I got the teaching post at the school. A good little school, a small suburb with small classes, a plum job. I had that and Anya. I was so lucky. So bloody lucky.

I ought to have known it couldn't last.

She would've been working. She was in her final year, had two or three days free each week, so she'd taken an office job to pay the bills. Right in the city centre. Practically at Ground Zero, I'm guessing. She wouldn't have stood a chance.

I tell myself it must have been quick.

\* \* \*

The caretaker, Mr Rutter, forced the basement door open, then stumbled away. Never saw him again. Well, I did, but I wouldn't have recognised him if not for his shoes. Old brown brogues, they were. He never wore anything else. All that was left intact of him.

He stumbled away. I have no idea where he thought he was going. I had other things to worry about.

We herded the kids down the stairs and into the basement, slammed doors shut behind us.

"Lie down," I shouted over the scared babble, then shouted it again, louder. "Lie down. Everybody. Shut your eyes. Put your hands over your ears and open your mouths." As far as I remembered, that was how you prepared yourself for the blast. I'd seen it in an old war movie, somewhere.

"Paul-" Jean's face was scared. She was about ten years older than me, competent and attractive, but didn't look much older than the kids, now. I wondered what I looked like.

"Yeah."

"What are we going to do?" she asked.

"Lie down," I told her, clambering to the floor myself. "And if we—"

That was when the bomb hit.

Brilliant light blazed, outlining the door at the top of the stairs. I looked away fast. Someone screamed—they hadn't, not in time.

A heat equal to that of the sun was consuming—had consumed—the centre of Manchester. The CIS tower, the Arndale Centre, the Lowry Hotel—all gone.

And Anya. Among all the rest, Anya too.

Then there was a distant rumbling. The sound was coming. The sound and the blast.

"Hands over your ears! Mouths open! Shut your eyes!"

And then, as I followed my own advice, the blast wave struck the school.

\* \* \*

I've almost forgotten I'm in a tunnel. It's like watching a visual effect, a bit like one of those fractals you get on a computer, or the light effects a computer screen can create if you play a CD on it.

*Got* on a computer. The light effects a screen *created*. If you *played* a CD. It's all past tense now. I have to get used to the idea. All past tense.

Someone once asked Einstein, what would be the weapons of the Third World War? He said he didn't know. But that the weapons of the Fourth World War would be stones and clubs.

If anyone's left in a hundred years, and they read this—will they even understand what I'm talking about? So many reference points I took for granted, and they'll mean nothing to whoever—whatever?—survives, landmarks and signposts of a world long gone.

Christ, in a hundred years, will they still even *read?*

We used to bandy that one round the staff room, but then we were worried about literacy declining because the kids'd rather play on their Playstations and cruise porn sites on the internet. Reading? Who needs it if you can get rich and famous making a dick of yourself on a reality TV show?

Old Byerscough, the History master—he said it was capitalism's final and cleverest game to keep the working class in its place. Time was, you couldn't get an education if you were poor. Now? Now, they convince you education's for nancy-boys. Books? Being clever? Bollocks to that. Just get pissed or E'd up and have fun. And you think that's the best way, when you're just being kept happy and docile and stupid.

Past tense again. Byerscough too. He was close to retirement as well, and lived nearby, just like Makin, but he never thought about leaving. His wife had died a few years before. He died at the school. Not in the blast, but after when—

\* \* \*

"Paul! Paul, wake up!"

Anya was shaking me. I must've slept through the alarm. But she'd be the one running late, wouldn't she? She had to get up before me. Neither of us could afford a place in the village where the school was, but I lived closer to it than to the city.

"Paul!" Desperation, terror. I smelt smoke. Not the alarm. A fire. The house was burning.

"Paul!" Not Anya's voice. Who was she? The bomb'd set the house on fire.

The Bomb. And I remembered where I was, and Anya—

"Paul!"

"Alright!" I sat up. My brain seemed to slosh around in my skull, water in a bowl. Fingers gripped my shoulders. Jean.

I could see light through the ceiling. The sky glowed. Sunset already? No, a fire.

Fire.

The school was gone. And the ceiling with it. Well, mostly. Some had blown away. The rest had fallen into the basement. And was burning. I was lucky; I'd been under the bit that'd blown away.

The air was full of screams. Kids and staff, trapped and burning.

And the sky—

I knew if I looked, I'd see the mushroom cloud, over the city, full of ashes and dust. Some of those ashes would be Anya's. And in a few minutes, she'd rain down on me.

And she'd be bringing the bomb with her.

"Everybody out!" I shouted. Things cracked and crackled all around me. And screamed.

We got up the stairs. Byerscough stopped at the top, then turned back, starting back down.

"Alf!" I shouted. "What're you—"

He turned wild eyes on me. "There's kids still down there, man!"

And he ran back down, even though the smoke was billowing and choking.

He stumbled back up, a few seconds later, smoke-grimed, red-eyed, coughing and choking, one of the girls in his arms. He set her down, ran back into the smoke. He never came back out.

Jean knelt by the little girl. When she looked up, she was crying. She shook her head.

"What do we do?" she said. "Oh God, what do we do now?"

Three of the staff were still alive: me, Jean and Frank Emerson, the Physics teacher. About a dozen kids. They were all looking at me.

"I've got an idea," I said.

\* \* \*

The tunnel changes at last. A fork. The water laps around a big central column. The canal, going off in two directions. "Which way now?" Jean whispers.

Have to choose. Which way now? Have to pick. But what leads where? Where does each go? Which is better? Safer? Is there meaning to either word now?

"That way," I say, pointing right.

So we veer to the right. It only occurs to me later that veering to the right was what got us into this mess in the first place.

Minutes pass. I haven't looked at my watch in—not since before the bomb fell. Does it have any meaning anymore, anyway?

Then one of the kids screams.

"What is it?" I shout, trying to keep panic out of my own voice.

It's one of the boys, one of the younger ones. "A man," he shouts. "A man in the water."

I flick the torch-beam over the black surface. "There's no one there."

"He was there, Mr Forrester, sir. He *was*."

"What'd he look like?" A drowned miner? But no one's been down here in years. There'd only be bones by now.

"White," the boy sobs. "White."

A chill up my back, and it's not just being down here. The boy's hallucinating. Who can blame him? I'm surprised I'm not. Will I sleep later? And will I dream? God, please not.

"Let's keep going," I say.

* * *

We stumbled through the remains of the school. Passed what was left of Mr Rutter on the way. "Don't look," I told the kids. Bile crept into my throat. The smell of roast, charred pork.

To get where we were going, we had to pass the Physics lab. It was, for God knows what reason, the only part of the building left more or less intact. Frank Emerson let out a shout. "Wait up!" he yelled, and dashed into the lab.

"Frank!" I yelled. "We haven't time—"

"Trust me." He forced the store room door open and came out again seconds later, clutching what looked like a metal box with a microphone attached.

"What—"

He clicked the "microphone" on and there was a soft crackling, ticking sound. "Geiger counter," he said.

I was about to ask where that'd come from—not exactly standard-issue in schools these days—but it didn't matter. Never look a gift horse in the mouth and so on. "You're a genius," I said. "Come on."

* * *

Worsley village—now it's a posh, desirable residence sort of place (*was, then*; past tense once more, Mr Forrester) but in the Industrial Revolution it'd've been anything but. The Bridgewater and Liverpool/Manchester canals all met here, and the whole area was a big coalfield, bringing up about 10,000 tons of coal a day.

Why do I mention this?

Because of the Delph, where we were heading.

There was next to nothing left above ground. The houses were gone, and where most of them had been there was only fire. There was nowhere to hide from the dust that would soon be falling.

It might already be too late, of course. I'd been to the Imperial War Museum up at the Quays the year before; one of the exhibits had been an atom bomb. Deactivated, I presumed. Beside it had been a diagram, a sequence of concentric circles marking out distances from the blast, and a table showing what would happen within them.

Nothing would be left for a mile or so around the blast site. Anya was dust, again. But where Worsley was:

*All those not killed by the blast would be dead of radiation poisoning within hours.*

Were we dead already? How long would be a fatal exposure? I didn't know, but I couldn't just stop, couldn't just quit. Easy to do so; easy to stop and spend the last of my time railing at the sky and the mad, sick bastards who'd done this to us. The politicians on both sides...

I'd grown up in the shadow of the Cold War; when it'd ended, I'd been in my teens, but I knew enough by then to have felt some of the dread that my parents—who would also be dead now—must've spent most of their adulthood under. And a weight had lifted. One less worry. Or so I'd thought.

Now...

Beside the Delph was a shed, belonging to the local boating club. We smashed the doors down. Inside, boats. Dinghies and open-topped canoes. And paddles. We took what we needed.

And torches, too. We were lucky. There were half a dozen, and a box or two of batteries. We took them as well, and then scrabbled over the fences, lifting boats and children, and headed down into the Delph.

"Delph" simply means a delved place. Delved; dug. An old sandstone quarry, half-filled with orangey-coloured water. The canals round Worsley are full of it—iron oxides from all the heavy industry.

If you go into the Delph, you'll find a hole, a tunnel entrance. Gated up. We forced the lock—me, Jean and Frank Emerson, chest-deep in that water. And then we climbed into the boats and paddled through, into the dark.

You see, the Delph is an entrance, to one of the biggest engineering feats of the Industrial Revolution.

I said the whole area had been a big coalfield. The coal had to be transported. And what was the main means of transport in those days?

Canals.

Entered, via the Delph, are forty-six miles of underground canal. Extending down on four levels, deep and deep and deep. To the galleries of the mines.

That was where we were headed. Deep underground, the one safe place I could think of.

If you're so clever, tell me where else we could have gone.

I knew the Delph had been closed off because of carbon monoxide seeping up from the old mines. I could only hope it'd dispersed by now. But even if it hadn't, it beat radiation sickness. Carbon monoxide, you got groggy, disorientated, queasy, yes, but in the end you just drifted off. That had to be better than the alternative.

And so we paddled, and soon the light died and we used one of the torches to destroy a tiny portion of the dark ahead, so we could see where the hell we were going.

\* \* \*

I tried looking at my watch a moment ago. Blank. Of course. It was a digital.

EMP: electromagnetic pulse from the blast. Wiped it out. Thank God the Geiger counter still works. I wonder if anyone here has an analogue watch. Only chance of keeping track. Mobile phones might have clocks but they'll have likely gone the same way as the digital watches.

There's no way of gauging the time. The same unending tunnel, after the brief variation of the fork, in unending repetition. It just goes on. Perhaps it'll be like this forever. Perhaps we're all already dead. Perhaps we died in the school, or on the way to the Delph, or at some point on this journey and this is all the last hallucinatory moment of dying, stretching on out forever…

No good thinking that way. I force myself to keep paddling. My hands are numb. The damp chill of the air, a nip at first, but like a swarm of soldier ants eating through to the bone bite by tiny bite.

The air is stale and foul. An olfactory memory skitters across my nerves; the summer just gone, walking in a meadow, the smell of fresh-cut grass, flowers breathing perfume into air, soft, clean, clear air.

Treasure that memory, Paul. You aren't likely to have another like it.

Cold. The air stinks. My teeth have begun to chatter. What it must be like for the children, back in the smaller boats, I don't like to think. Is Frank Emerson alright back there? I ought to shout at him but I can't seem to. My jaw won't let me, refuses to let me waste the energy.

"Paul?" It's Jean. She's been crying. So have I, silently. I can feel the burn of the dried salt on my cheeks. Anya.

I'm wandering, vague, keep greying out. Radiation sickness? Or carbon monoxide? Or just going cold and tired? Be ironic that, if it's hypothermia and exhaustion that finishes the job. Maybe a kind of bleak triumph there, a bitter laugh at the death that thought it'd've have us.

"Paul?" Jean again. Her voice is cracked. She's been thinking about her husband, must've been with all this time on our hands, just paddling—well, the endless tunnel can sort of hypnotise you. Better if it does, in a way. If not, your mind begins to wander. I'd've been thinking about Anya so so much if not for that lucky effect. But Jean—

I met her husband once. A small, quiet man, balding and moustached. Bespectacled. Smoked a pipe. Scottish, like her. Glaswegian, or was he from Edinburgh? Sipped a Britvic orange in the pub at the staff do last Christmas while Jean got tipsy on Dubonnet. Did he work? From home, I think she said. What was he? An accountant, I think. They lived in the village. His—their—house was—

Can't remember. Burned to ashes anyway. Doubt he'd've had a chance. But at least, with Anya, I can be sure she's dead. Horrible, how easy you can accept that, the fact that the person you love the most in the world is gone. Oh, my heart's been ripped out of my chest. Well, there it is. There you go. Never mind.

Except I *do* mind, but what to do? It's keep going or stop and die. Some instinct or drive, something in me, won't just let me lie down and quit. It's not the responsibility for the kids that keeps me going. That's getting it backwards.

*That's* why I seized control when the sirens went. It was my excuse for living. Anya would have approved.

"*Just because I'm dead, Paul, doesn't mean you can give up.*"

No ma'am. I know that, darling.

"*Keep going. We'll be together again one day.*"

Yeah, right. Now I know that's my imagination. Anya would never have said anything so trite, so twee, not even to motivate me. She'd been raised a Catholic, but lapsed long ago.

She was the most honest person I knew. *When you're dead,* she'd told me bluntly, once, *you're dead, that's it. You're a match that flares in the dark. You burn a few seconds and then you go out.* A little poetic, but it was the small hours of one morning and we'd been smashed on bisongrass vodka and a couple of joints. In vodka veritas. *You have seconds in the dark. Out of the dark and back into it. You have to use it while you can. Don't waste it.*

It would be nice to think of my survival as my tribute to Anya, that I'm doing it for her, but—

"Paul?"

God *damnit.* I turn to Jean. "What?" My voice is gravel.

Her teeth are chattering too. Hard to tell in the gloomy backspill of light from the torch, but I think her lips are bluing from the cold.

"We can't keep going much longer," she whispers. "Look at us. We're nearly all in. The kids must be finished. I don't know how they keep going."

"Yeah. I know."

"We're gonna have to stop soon."

"I know." But where? That's the big question, isn't it?

I'm about to confess I have nothing left, no ideas, when I become aware of something. A current in the sluggish water, pulling the boat sideways.

"What—"

I flash the torch. There's a sound too, a new one—I've missed it from being so lulled by the repetitive journey. It's water, rushing. I flick the torch-beam ahead. It skates along the wall on the left, and then plunges through into darkness.

"What's th—"

Something's punched a hole in the tunnel wall, or it's caved in. What could do that? I don't know. But water's draining through the hole, pouring through.

We draw level, and I use an oar to brace us, stop us sliding through till I know.

I shine the torch through the hole.

Water slides down in a low black gleaming slope, into a deep pool—no, not a pool, a small *lake,* on the floor of a great big fucking cavern.

I let out a shout. There are yells down the tunnel; the kids, startled.

"Paul," says Jean.

"Sorry." I shine the beam around. A big chamber. A natural cavern. A high ceiling. Stalactites. Stalagmites. And around the pool, a shore of crumbled stone. Dry land. A place to rest.

"Is it safe?" asks Jean.

I laugh. "God knows," I tell her. "What's safe?" I turn back to the others. "Through here," I call.

* * *

We pull the boats onto the blessed dry land and stumble on up, legs weak and shaky. A couple of the younger kids, deathly tired, have to be carried ashore.

We sit and take stock. Frank Emerson stares at the clinker on the ground and grubs through it, picks up a lump of something black and brittle. A grin spreads across his cadaverous face; not a pleasant sight.

"What?" I ask.

He grins the wider. "Coal!"

Of course. We grub together a heap of it. Thank God for my lighter. Anya used to nag me about my smoking, but thank God for it now.

What'll we do, I wonder, when its fuel is all gone?

The fire smoulders into life and we switch off the torches as a little puddle of heat and light spreads and gathers round.

We're all tired. Time to sleep. No strength to consider what other dangers there might be down here. If we don't wake up, so be it. We're too tired to care now, after all we've been through.

We have no blankets. I'm shivering—of course, we all were standing in that water—God, so cold. How have I held out this long? I'm lucky to still be alive. Thank God for the coal heat.

We huddle together for warmth as we sleep. Jean on one side of me, one of the younger boys on the other. Yesterday I'd've run a mile before being in this kind of proximity to one of the kids. Inappropriate contact. Now it's irrelevant; now it's about survival.

*Anya*, I think, and then, thank God, I drift off to sleep before I can think anymore.

* * *

I dream of fire. A room of fire. In the middle of it, a table. Anya sips coffee there, putting another cup in front of me.

"Thanks," I say.

"It's alright."

"No, I mean it. Specially with you being dead and all."

She snorts and flaps a hand, the way she always used to when she thought I was being silly. She keeps the left side of her face turned to me. The right side is eyeless and black, charcoal, the skull beneath half-bared. Grins at me whenever she turns without thinking. "Are you alright, Paul?"

"I think so. Relatively speaking."

"Relatively speaking."

"Well, you're dead."

"Don't go on about it."

"And the world's ended."

"Don't be so dramatic. The world's still there. It's just the people that are gone."

"Of course. I forgot."

"Don't worry about it. You've a lot on your plate right now. Just be careful."

"Of what?"

"Of everything, Paul." Her hair catches fire, her clothes. I don't. I remain unscathed, just watching as the flames crawl over her and the rest of her face blackens and her one blue eye melts and trickles down her charcoal cheek like a tear. "Of everything."

* * *

I wake up. Jean's gone. Sound nearby.

I rise, looking round. Jean squats nearby, gathering up more coal. The fire's almost dead, smouldering. How can I see down here? The darkness should be total. Then I see dull green patches of luminescence smeared on the rock. "What's that?"

"Fungus of some kind, I should think." She isn't shocked by my sudden whisper. She's almost glacially calm. "Are you alright?"

My joints are a little creaky and I've a banging headache, but otherwise I feel fine. "Just hungry. And thirsty."

"You think that water's safe to drink?"

"We may have to chance it. We could try boiling it."

"Aye." She heaps coal on the embers of the fire, watches it start to smoulder. "Alan probably looks like that now."

"Alan?" I realise she means her husband.

"Aye. He has to be, doesn't he? I mean, no way he could've survived."

I don't know if that's true as yet—he might've got into the cellar, if she had one. I don't know if he did, and it doesn't matter. Things like that she doesn't need or want to hear. "No," I tell her, "no way."

"Anya worked in the city centre, didn't she?"

"Yes. She wouldn't have had a chance either."

"No." She sits beside me, huddles close, takes my hand. Is it just warmth she wants, companionship? I can't see myself having anything else to give, but I seem to—I feel my body stirring in her presence. It never has before today. But we never so narrowly escaped death, losing so much in the process, before.

It might be good for us, or it might not. I can't tell and I won't risk it. Not so soon. I squeeze her hand, and when she puts the other on my knee I gently but firmly remove it, but don't let it go.

Her sigh's a warm breath in my ear. "OK," she says. "For now."

We settle back down to sleep once more.

This time I don't dream.

* * *

The next—day?—God knows. There is neither time nor light down here, save the light we make. But I have to call it something. The next day, we explore the cavern.

Big, roomy. Plenty of coal, big chunks of it in the walls. We can hack bits loose with rocks. We won't freeze. We might starve or die of thirst, but we won't freeze.

Thank God, in one of the boats, someone had stored a kettle. I don't know what for. One more piece of luck, like the torches and the Geiger counter and the whole ceiling of the basement not falling in on us. Blind chance, saving us all.

Well, the fifteen of us, anyway.

Me, Jean and Frank Emerson are the only adults. The rest: eight boys, four girls. Most of the kids are the older ones, between fourteen and sixteen years of age. Two ten-year-old boys, one nine-year-old girl. The older kids—stronger, more grown-up, more independent. They were the ones who fought their way out of the basement. The younger ones—scared, huddled, either frozen where they were or running around in hopeless panic—never had a chance. All the little ones… I think of Alf Byerscough going back down there, never coming back. There was a brave man. A hero.

And dead. Better a live coward… or is it? Look where it's got me: a hole in the ground. But still alive.

Frank heats water in the kettle, lets the steam collect in the upturned hull of a boat, angled so it trickles down and collects in a corner. There's a tin cup too. A small water ration for everybody.

Food is a more pressing concern, at least until one of the younger boys yells and points at the water—the same one thought he saw a man in the canal yesterday. But he's seen something this time, something big and white and floundering. A fish, a big one. I whack the water hard with an oar—it flops to the surface, stunned.

"Bream," pronounces Frank, who used to go fishing. It's white and eyeless. "They tend to go for muddy water."

Muddy isn't the word for this water, but I'm grateful nonetheless. It's a big fish, but among fifteen people it doesn't go far. We need more.

"There might be rats," says one of the boys. Jeff Tomlinson. Sporty, practical, goes camping a lot, reads books on wilderness survival. Should've known he'd make it. "We could eat them."

"If we can catch them," says Frank.

"Maybe the rats'll be blind too," says Jeff.

"Have hearing like a bat."

I wonder if there'll be any of those down here too.

"Mr Forrester." It's one of the girls. Jane Routledge. She's at the end of the cavern, pointing.

"Look at this, sir." She's a scarily calm girl. A kind of brittle shock, a shell around her.

At the end of the cavern, the path branches off down channels, streams disappearing into holes in the walls. Small narrow caves, winding. I could just about get down one if I was hunched over like Quasimodo. Looking round I see others in the walls. Some are draining off the water. Others are dry, dusty. Off into the mine. Or maybe not. Was this cavern part of the mine? I doubt it somehow.

I venture a few feet into the nearest cave. Not far. Something about it makes my scalp prickle. I touch the walls. They feel—ribbed. These are not natural. These have been dug.

I say nothing about it, but something about the caves draws the kids.

By what I guess to be the end of the day, they're going into them, but not far, never out of sight of the main cavern, on my instructions. Last thing we need is any of them getting lost.

Also, by the end of the day, the caves have been given a name.

The children call them the narrows.

\* \* \*

"Like a big worm's been through them," Jean whispers. "Isn't it?"

I give her hand a squeeze. "Don't."

We're at the far end of the cavern. It's late, as we reckon time now. The children and Frank are asleep around the dying fire. Jean and I… we're warm enough and restless enough to pull away. I shine a torch down one of the narrows. It glances off the ribbed, irregular stone. I can see about ten yards down it, before it bends right and is lost to view.

"They're weird, aren't they," she whispers.

"Yeah." We move to the neighbouring entrance. "The kids seem to like them, though. Gives 'em something to occupy themselves with."

"Aye, well. Just don't let them go playing in it. Bloody easy to get lost or stuck, place like this."

"Mm." I shine the torch again, then frown. "Hang on."

"What?"

"Look." I cross back to the first cave. "See that?"

"Bends right. Aye. So?"

"Look." I step to the right and shine the torch down its neighbour. "See?"

The neighbouring tunnel extends in a straight line for longer than the first—fifteen, twenty yards, easily—before veering off and up. Its walls are smooth and unbroken, right the way through.

"That can't be," says Jean.

"I know."

We cross back to the first one and look again. "Must be a dead end," Jean says.

"Mm. Hang on." I venture down the tunnel, shining the light.

"Paul!" she hisses.

"It's okay. I'll be right back. Just…"

I trail off; I've reached the bend in the first narrow. No dead end; the torch picks out another long low tunnel, stretching away from me.

I can't see a break in its walls either. But there must be. Some trick of light and shadow the composition of the walls lends itself to somehow. Must be. An optical illusion, that makes the entrance invisible.

"Paul?"

"There's a tunnel," I say. "It must… Jean?"

"Aye?"

"Go to the next narrow," I say. "Just hang about there."

"But—"

"Just try it."

Muttering, she does. I start down the cave, stooped, flashing the torch side to side. This narrow and the second are about five yards apart, if that. A yard; that's about a pace for me. I count my steps: one, two, three, four… "Jean?"

"Paul?" Her voice is faint.

"Jean?" I shout a little. "Can you hear me?"

"Where are you?"

I shine the torch around. The walls are unbroken. I flash the beam ahead. "Can you see that?"

"See what?"

"The torch light. Is it coming through into your narrow?"

"No, it bloody isn't, Paul, and it's bloody dark out here. Will you come back now, please?"

"Okay." I feel a beading film of sweat on my forehead. The narrow looks straight and level but it must go under or over the neighbouring one. It's the only explanation.

I backtrack to the bend in the narrow. Shine the torch around—

This isn't right.

I left a long straight tunnel, with the main cavern at the end to my left, but where the main cavern and Jean ought to be there's just a flat wall of black and yellow stone, the narrow branching left and right. And to my right, where there was a dead end, the narrow now extends on for as far as I can see and there are very visible openings in it—two on the left and one on the right—where other narrows branch off.

Panic squirms low down in my belly. I turn back towards the T-junction. "Jean?" I shout, and I can't quite keep my voice level.

"Paul?"

It's coming from behind me, down the mysteriously extended narrow. "Jean!"

"What?" She sounds pissed off. "Where are you?"

Good question. "Jean, just keep shouting to me, alright? I'm sort of— lost here."

"Lost? How the hell are you—"

"Jean, just do it!" I yell. First time I've really lost it since we got down here. Since the bomb, in fact.

"Okay. Okay. Can you hear me?"

"Yes, just about. Keep talking."

"Talking? More like shouting."

"Just keep it up."

I head towards her voice. My hand is shaking on the torch.

"What should I say?"

"Anything. Sing if you want."

"Sing? I canna sing for toffee."

"It doesn't have to be tuneful."

She breaks into a halting rendition of "Scotland the Brave." I can see what she meant. At least it's not "You Canna Shove Yer Granny Aff the Bus." Small mercies again.

It rings in the narrow. I pass the first of the entrances on my left. When I reach the second, I realise her singing's coming from there.

There's no guarantee that sound's a reliable indicator of location, as everything else I'd normally rely on has gone screwy, but what else can I do? I start down this new narrow. It slopes steeply upward, but I follow it.

The singing gets louder. Water splashes around my ankles. Something white and blind wriggles past on its way down. I keep on climbing. The water flowing down this narrow is fast and cold and quite deep. Why didn't any of it spill out into the other, longer one I've left behind?

The singing stops. "Jean?" I shout.

"Alright, alright." I hear her coughing. Then she starts again, the *Mingulay Boat Song* this time.

*"Heel ya ho, boys, let her go, boys, sailing homewards to Mingulay…"*

Where is Mingulay anyway? The Hebrides? Orkneys? Shetlands? I'm pretty sure it's an island of some kind anyway.

The singing's good and loud, at least. The narrow steepens till it's almost vertical. I clamp the torch between my teeth and use my hands to climb.

At last, I reach the top. Been climbing too long. Flat floor, water gushing across it, and I can hear Jean's voice, loud and clear, close to. I look up; the narrow has a mouth and water glistens beyond it. It opens out. I hear voices, too.

Someone shouts as the beam of my torch flashes from the narrow-mouth and I stumble out, almost falling headlong into the lake. Across the water on the bank, Jean and Frank and the others spin from the mouth of the narrow I entered and stare at me dumbfounded.

* * *

"No one goes in there," I say later, huddled round a fresh fire some way from the circle of children, sharing its warmth with Jean and Frank. "No one."

Frank looks at me doubtfully. "Paul, I know you've had a shock, but—"

"No buts," I say. "I didn't imagine what happened in there."

"Are you sure?" he asks gently.

I glare at him. "Frank—"

"Paul, all I'm saying is we've all been through a hell of a lot. You especially. You've been responsible for all of us. It'd be unbelievable if you didn't feel the strain somehow. And you have to keep everything so bottled up and reined in, it's not surprising if-"

"Are you a psychoanalyst now?" I know I'm overreacting, taking it out on Frank, but I can't stop myself. Luckily he seems to understand that too.

"No, Paul, I'm not. All I'm trying to say is this: stress, lack of sleep, grief, trauma, all those things, they can cause you to hallucinate. As can simply being underground, in the dark, in tunnels. I've been caving once or twice You'd be surprised what… look. All I mean is this. What you saw down there is physically impossible. Right?"

"I know that." I rub my face. "But I saw it."

"I'm not questioning that." I look up. "All I'm questioning is whether it was *objectively real*. Be honest. What's the most likely explanation? Either the tunnels really did shift and change around like you say, or you experienced a hallucination brought on by your emotional state and the conditions down here. And I don't doubt the narrows themselves could be disorientating too, once you got out of sight of the main cavern. You obviously lost your bearings and were lucky to find your way out again. But out of those two explanations, which makes more sense? Which is more probable? That's all I'm saying."

I bow my head. I have to admit he's right on that one. But that's what *really* frightens me. Because if you can't trust your own senses, the evidence of your own eyes, what *can* you trust?

*In the cold light of day*… I've had the occasional weird experience in my time, and most could be put down to hallucinations, like Frank says about this, or something more mundane. But it helps when you can get away from the place where you saw the weird thing or heard the weird sounds and go somewhere normal, four-square, the land of Starbucks and McDonald's, busy city streets and cars, brand names and day jobs. *The cold light of day*.

Except that it might still be cold back up there, but light? I think of all the predictions I heard and read, the nuclear winter, the great clouds of smoke and ash blotting out the sun and plunging the world into a new Ice Age. And even if we could get back up there, even forgetting that the radiation would kill us in hours, the world of Starbucks and McDonalds, busy city streets and brand names—it's all gone. The day job, the worries about bills and rent and mortgages, shopping at Morrisons or the local market—*it's all gone*. There *is* no normal anymore. The world is what's around us now, wherever we're clinging on to life a bit longer. The world is this cave. And reality... *what's* reality? Frank's right. We can't trust what we hear or see—with everything we've been through, it'd be a miracle if we didn't see or hear things that weren't there. And it isn't safe to be here. Nowhere is, anymore.

Panic wells up; I fight it down. I know that if I give into it once, that'll be it, nothing will ever make sense anymore and I'll either curl up catatonic or run screaming into the water till I drown to escape the knowledge, or not believe a real danger till it kills me or run to my death from an imaginary one.

So I push it down and instead I let myself realise the magnitude of our loss. Not just Anya, but Poland is gone. Not just the school, the village, Manchester and Salford, but Britain itself in any meaningful sense. America, too? Or—what if the bombs only fell on Manchester? If there weren't any others? It's impossible to say. And impossible to believe.

It's all gone. Names fly past, already robbed of meaning: Adidas, Reebok, Microsoft, BBC, ITV, Sky TV, Sony—all the brand names, all the twenty-first-century totems. They mean nothing now. Will mean nothing to anybody till whatever archaeologists of the future there might be dig them up and mount them in museums, try to decipher what they meant to us.

I can't get a handle on it. Only think of Anya, imagine her there in front of me. And there she is, sitting beside me, whole and unharmed, unmarked. Not burnt up like in my dream, but the Anya I kissed goodbye the morning before the bomb fell. There are now four of us round the fire: me, Jean, Frank and Anya. Jean holds my left hand, Anya my right. She looks at Jean's hand on mine, then up at me, raises an eyebrow. I pull my hand free of Jean's, embarrassed, caught out, almost caught cheating.

"Paul?"

I blink, and Anya's gone. But I can still feel the warmth of her hand where it held mine. Jean. Jean drove her away. I turn to shout at her, then stop myself. She was never there. Never here. It wasn't real, however real it was.

"Paul, are you okay?"

"Yes." I nod, but I'm not. God, how could I be? Come that close to raving and shouting over *something that wasn't there*. I'm crazy. Or going crazy. But what's crazy? What's not? What's mad and what isn't? How much more food will we find down here? And if there isn't enough to eat—how long before we start eye-ing each other like that? Before we're killing each other, smashing each other's heads in with lumps of rock, roasting pieces of each other in our coal fires?

I try not to think about it, but I can't stop. What criteria will we use, to choose who lives or dies? The smaller children are of least use. Will we eat them first? But there's less meat on a nine-year-old kid than on a grown man or woman. Will it be the biggest of us, to go the furthest, last the longest, before we have to do it again? Me? Frank? Jean? Or are we of more value? In what way? We've as little idea as anyone else of what to do next. Hell, Jeff Tomlinson probably has more idea. And we're adults, we're authority, the powers that be, as far as the kids are concerned, who killed Mum and Dad and their friends and brought them down here to this. How long will the shreds and threads of our authority as teachers last? How long before they realise there are more of them than there are of us and like any who hold power, we only do so because they allow it? I see myself, my torso and an arm, all that's left, lying by the fire, flies crawling across my glazed eyes, the gnawed bones of the rest of me in the embers of the fire. Kids' famished faces, eager and greedy and animal, smeared with my blood and grease.

When are you insane? When you think about this? When you imagine it? Plan it? Or when you do it? Or is it insanity, will it be when it comes, or will it be only necessity, need, do or die? Will the mad ones be the ones who won't do it, clinging to an outmoded way, as mad in this time as worshipping the Sun God would be to the people we were last week?

Oh God.

Oh. God.

I can smell the roast pork stink that came off Mr Rutter's corpse, and saliva fills my mouth.

I'm crying. Softly. Again.

"Paul, it's alright." Jean's arms are around me. "It's alright. We've all been through so much. It's alright."

I nod, squeeze her hand. I look at Frank. "Get some sleep," he says. "You'll be okay."

We both know that's a lie. For all of us. "Frank," I say.

"Yes?"

"I still think—the kids mustn't go into the narrows again. Whatever it was in there. If it happened to me…"

"Then it could happen to anyone else." He nods. "Yes. I thought of that too. I just wanted to make sure."

*That I knew it wasn't real.* I nod. But, of course, I don't know. None of us can, anymore.

* * *

Taking Frank's advice, I get some sleep. It's deep and dark and blessedly silent. I wake once, and in the dim emberlight of the waning fire, someone tall is standing over me.

"Wh—"

"Sh." Anya kneels by my head. Warm light glows on her face. She strokes my forehead, my matted hair. "Sh. It's alright, Paul."

"Anya."

"Sh." She bends and kisses me: my forehead, my eyes, my cheeks, my nose, my mouth. The last, long and deep.

At last, she squeezes down next to me and huddles close, kisses me again. "It's alright, Paul. Sleep now."

*Polish women,* I think, *are so beautiful.*

And I sleep again.

In what passes for the morning, when some vague consensus of reality is established by enough of us all being awake at once, I have no idea if I was dreaming or not.

\* \* \*

When we were journeying, searching, at least we had some momentum, a purpose, a goal, a quest. Now—now all we have is an increasingly desultory routine, with too little in it to fill the aching gaps of time in these days that aren't days and nights that aren't nights.

We hunt the lake for fish, catch two more blind bream. We consider the greenish fungus on the cave walls, and can't be sure if we dare eat it or not. Soon we'll have no choice.

Jeff T sees a rat skitter across the cavern floor and chases it, but it bolts into one of the narrows and is gone. "No," I shout as he makes to follow.

"But sir—"

"*No,* Jeff. It's dangerous in there."

He looks at me with a smirk playing round his lips, a smirk that says *coward, weakling,* but more, worse, *nutter.* And he was one of the good kids, respectful, obedient, yes sir no sir. Now it's a direct challenge, open insolence, and I have nothing to back me up, I daren't meet it. It could be the blow that shatters all discipline, all balance.

I look away. Jeff wanders off. He mutters something. There is muffled laughter in response. I look up, fists clenching. Jeff and a couple others smirk back at me. Jean takes my arm and draws me aside.

We catch two more bream in the lake. Have to take one of the boats out on it to find the second; only one's dumb enough to come close to shore. How many does the lake hold? And what will we do when they're all gone?

We cook and eat the fish. Hunger rumbles in us. Fish are low-calorie. We're getting weak, tireder quicker. At least it makes for an early night.

I sleep—

And am shaken awake. A boy, crying. "Sir! Sir!"

"Wh—" I sit up. Everyone's awake. "What? What?"

"It's Jeff, sir, Jeff and Mike."

Mike? Mike Rawlins, one of the smirkers. This was the other one—James? No. Jason. Jason Stanton. *Not so cocky now,* I think. His face is grimy and cut and he's soaking wet. Tears have cut clean streaks down through the black coal dust on his face and his eyes are red.

"What about them? What happened?" I look around. No sign of the boys in question. Torches are lit, flashed around the cavern. "Where are they?" I demand.

For answer, Jason Stanton points a trembling hand towards the back of the cavern, and the black mouths of the narrows.

\* \* \*

Jeff said I was crazy, apparently. A nutter, fruitcake, a screwball, a patient. And other things too. A stupid cunt, for one.

Kids, eh?

He reckoned we could catch rats for food. Not a bad plan. Good source of protein. Reckoned we could get lucky in the narrows. Asked for volunteers. Jason and Mike stepped up straight off the bat.

Jeff, of course, was the man with a plan. He had a ball of string; tied one end around a rocky outcropping near the mouth of the narrow they used. They took a torch and two of the "spears" we'd made lashing sharpened rocks to the hafts of oars. And they went a-hunting. Stupid, stupid kids.

But I can't deny a sneaking, ugly relief; the first challenger to my authority, to ours, that of the adults, is gone. The most capable. The one who sneered. Major challenge removed and an object lesson in daddy knows best. Adults are always right, because we say so. It's a lie and I've always known that, but right now I've never been so grateful for it.

The three of them went in, paying out the string as they went. They'd go a distance, wait. Listen. Switch off the torch at times. Listen. No sound. Any rats there were silent.

So they moved on. And paid out a little more string as they went.

Time passed. And in the end they started to get bored. And tired. And fed-up. And low on confidence.

See, Jeff? It's not so easy, is it, being in charge? Wait till you have the responsibility. Easy to criticise, from the sidelines. When it isn't you.

And yes, I realise, thinking that even to myself, how like the politicians I always most despised I sound. *Wait till you see what I've seen, then you'll know I'm right.* Oh God. All the things happening to me that I can't bear. Is this the price of survival? How much of myself will I give up to stay alive, of what I was?

So they retraced their steps, following the string, and then they found—

The string was lying in the middle of a narrow, the tied end frayed and unravelled.

Shouted recriminations, near-panic, quelled by Jeff's fists—Jason has the split lip to prove it. Jeff taking charge. They headed back up the narrow. The string couldn't have trailed far. They can follow their tracks in the dust of the narrow's floor. Retrace their steps to the cavern. If they stay calm.

They follow the marks in the dust.

To a fork they don't remember.

And the dust of each branching narrow's floor is disturbed (by what?) and it's impossible to tell which is which, which they might have come down.

Panic in the air again; Jeff quells it. They go right. More narrows branching off. *Which way?*

At last they hear the trickle of water. We go towards that, Jeff tells them. It'll be runoff from the cavern. See? We'll be okay. Forrester found his way out like that, didn't he?

Not quite, Jeff. But it was worth a try.

They keep going and they find the water, alright. But it's not the cavern. Oh, it's *a* cavern, yes. But not the one they were looking for. A small chamber, almost wall to wall water, running down from a narrow high up in the cavern wall.

Mike yelping, shouting that he saw something in the water. Big, white, moving. Not a fish. Jeff slaps him into silence, the crack of flesh on flesh ringing in the wet, trickling dark. He saw nothing. Imagining things, seeing things that aren't there. Like that puff Forrester did.

They climb the wall to the narrow the water's coming through, none of them admitting what they know; the torch's beam is starting to dim.

They follow the stream that trickles down the narrow's floor, praying for the cavern that's hearth and home in their mind's eye now.

And it opens out into another cavern. The floor awash to ankle or maybe even knee height with fresh water. They don't check the depth in this cavern. There are houses there.

("What?" "Houses?" "What're you—" "Sh. Go on, Jason.")

Not like houses you'd see up top, Jason says. Crude ones. Can't even call them huts. Just stacks of rocks, heaped up drystone, covered over with big heavy flat pieces, slabs. No windows, but a hole that might be a door. Jason reckons he counted about a dozen of them.

And the cave is not silent. Things are moving around. Inside the houses. Slithering and shifting, slumping and flopping around. And there are other noises too. Not noises a fish or even a very big fucking rat could make.

The boys start to go back the way they came, and then—more sounds, the same as from the houses, coming up the narrow, towards them. The dying torch shines: shadows flick across the wall.

They have to go round the edge of the water, past the houses, towards the only other narrow they can see. The noise from the houses grows louder; none of them look back at the sound of splashing in the water.

The torch goes out a few yards into the narrow.

Jason breaks and runs. He's screaming, but he thinks they aren't the only ones he hears.

He runs on—in the dark, cannoning into walls, scrabbling on, feeling ahead with his hands, terrified of what his fingers might touch.

But somehow—by pure, blind, lucky chance, it can only be—he finds himself crashing headlong into our own little lake. Screaming, splashing, blundering, and then he sees the dim distant glow of the fire, catches its gleam off the upturned hulls of boats, flounders and staggers to the shore and shakes me awake, all believing in Mr Forrester now, wanting answers, wanting someone to make it alright.

* * *

"This is why I warned everyone not to go into the narrows," I say. "As soon as you get out of sight of this cavern—they can start playing tricks with your head. It's very easy to get lost in there. We don't know where they all go."

Jason cries like a baby, and no-one blames him. Jean holds him tight, rocking him. All the kids' eyes are wide.

"Sir-" it's one of the little ones. "Sir—what about the monsters?"

"There aren't any," I say.

"There are," sobs Jason.

"No," I say. "Jason, listen. That place—the narrows—they play tricks on you, remember? They—" I look up, catch Frank's eye. He nods.

Frank Emerson—one thing about him, he can explain anything. Always had the highest pass rates in the school; he could make anything crystal clear and easy to understand. I've never been so grateful for that as now.

Hallucinations, Frank explains. It happened to Mr Forrester too, though not as badly because he didn't go as far in, wasn't so badly lost. Jeff and Mike are still in there somewhere, but there's nothing we can do. We can't go in there or we could end up lost as well. The best we can do is call them, shout down the narrows, hope they hear and find us that way.

The kids are wide-eyed. We're just leaving Jeff and Mike in there. Teachers don't do that, abandon their charges. But it's different now. The rules have changed. I used to despise people who said that too.

And so we try. In relays, groups of us, all through that night that is not a night, screaming ourselves hoarse.

But from the narrows, there isn't a sound.

* * *

Waking in the 'morning,' the mood's sullen and still, scared. We know they're dead. If they're lucky. My big fear was that we'd hear them but not be able to call them home. We'd have to listen to them dying slowly. At least it looks like they're doing that out of earshot.

Unless the things in the houses that don't exist got them.

Otherwise—we try not to think of them, still hopelessly lost, starving, dying by inches in there, wandering around.

As we are, will be. Jeff and Mike are just us in fast forward.

Jason has slept the night in Jean's comforting, maternal embrace. She releases him, comes over, leans against me.

I feel her weariness, her need, and I know I will sleep with her tonight.

We catch a bream. It's all we eat today. We've all lost weight; I've tightened my belt as far as I can, but my trousers still keep threatening to slip down.

We go to sleep still hungry.

No one goes near the narrows today.

\* \* \*

Jean and I wait till the others are asleep. Then she crawls to me, takes my hand, draws me to my feet, and we head off to as quiet a part of the cavern as we can. There's little in the way of privacy here—we have a corner for purposes of nature, but even that's not very private. And we'd hardly go there. Inside one of the narrows might be private, but we'd fuck in the middle of a circle of the kids before we did that.

We kiss and fumble with each other's clothes. In the dark, I fondle the pale blurs of her breasts, rub at her cunt till it's wet enough to push my fingers inside. She moans into my neck, muffling her cries in my flesh, rubbing my cock. She moans with Anya's Polish accent.

We fuck on the gritty floor, taking turns on top. In flickers of chancy firelight, I see Anya looking down as she rides me.

I wonder if Jean sees Alan.

\* \* \*

Our fragile, glass-brittle equilibrium, such as it is, shatters for good and all the next day.

At first it looks lucky. A dead bream bobs in the shallows when we wake, wafts to shore. An easy breakfast.

It's only later that Frank takes my arm.

"Paul, we've got a problem."

"What's that?"

For answer, he picks up the Geiger counter and walks towards the shore. I look round. Jean and the remaining ten children are further down, towards the top end of the cavern. We're up near the narrows; everyone else is, understandably, giving them the widest possible berth.

Frank switches the microphone on. A moment later, the Geiger counter begins to crackle and tick. Before he switches it off, it's risen almost to a screech.

"It's bad, isn't it?" I ask. Foolishly.

"You know it is." Frank nods towards the breach in the tunnel wall, the one we came through. "The radiation's seeping down here."

I sag. This doesn't end. It just doesn't end. "Oh shit."

"Yeah. Yeah."

"What can we do?"

"Get away from it," Frank says, simply. "Go deeper in. It's the only way."

I turn and look unwillingly at the narrows.

"Look—Paul. I know it's freaky in there. But if we just keep going—"

"Are you mad?"

"No. Look—most of the disorientation was about trying to find your way back. We won't be. We can survive: we know there's water in the narrows."

Water and what else, Frank? Low, crude houses? White things that flop and grunt and hiss in the water?

"We don't know where any of them go anyway," he says. "So we can't get lost as such. It's as good a chance as any of finding somewhere safer."

"What about…" I point back towards the breach in the wall. "We could head on down the canal."

"And go where?"

I shrug. "We don't know what else could be there. Might be something better than this place. And whatever you say about *that*—" I point at the narrows "—I don't want to go back in there. I know—" he opens his mouth "—it's not about what I want. But it's bad in there, Frank. You talk about it but you don't know what it's like."

"I've got an inkling," he said. "I heard what Jason said, like everyone else."

"That stuff, about the houses…"

He spreads his hands. "Let's not go there, mate."

"But that's the point. We'll have to."

"Alright. Maybe the houses were real. Maybe some people got trapped down here back in the day one time and had to rough it, or they were used for storage. Or something. Doesn't mean they've got something out of a midnight movie living in them."

I find myself wishing he hadn't put it into words. "I don't like the idea of putting the kids in there."

"I know." He chews his lip.

"If we tried the canal," I say, "at least we'd know where the hell we were."

"Yeah. Yeah."

In the end, a compromise is reached. Frank and two of the older boys—volunteers, one of whom is Jason Stanton, unsurprisingly up for anything that poses an alternative to the narrows—will head down the canal in one of the boats. I can see why Frank's reluctant—we spent hours—even days, it felt like—heading down the canal before we found the cavern, and that was sheer luck. By the time we give up and turn back, the radiation might've seeped so far down we can't get to the narrows at all.

But that's no loss to me; Frank doesn't understand. He can't. He hasn't been in there.

They row the boat off. Jean and I stay with the rest of the children and the Geiger counter. Frank told me what to look for. When the radiation gets too high, keep moving away from the water's edge, and if you have to, head into the narrows.

*I'll die first,* I think.

The plash of oars recedes. Long silence falls. Jean sits beside me. We haven't spoken since we fucked last night. Don't know what to say to each other. I try to pretend it didn't happen. I saw Anya while I fucked her. I'll call it a dream. In this blurred twilight place that comes easy.

"Do you think they'll find anything?" she asks at last. Perhaps she's made the same decision as me.

"I hope so." But I doubt it. It's almost as if Frank wants to go into the narrows. Maybe he does, because he never has; he wants to experience it for himself.

*That's crazy,* I tell myself. But we'd all be crazy *not* to be crazy, in one way or another, down here. I know my own madness pretty damn well by now. But Frank's? He seems so together, so calm and controlled. But that could only make him the craziest one of all, just waiting to—

Then the screaming starts.

Jason. I know that voice. Howling, pleas and promises and threats. "No! No! Please! I'll—no! You fucker, I'll kill y—"

And Frank screams too, and the other boy. Terror or rage, I can't tell.

The water thrashing and churning. Who's fighting who, or what?

At last, silence falls.

Much later, a broken oar drifts over the lip of the breach and bobs slowly across the lake to the shore. I pick it up. Its blade is smudged red, and cracked.

After a time, I remember to switch on the Geiger counter.

The screech is piercing. I turn it off. But they're all looking at me now. All but the youngest kids understand what it means.

Jean looks to me for a lead. No help, no decision there. Once again, it's all down to me.

\* \* \*

"Alright," I say. "Now. Whatever happens, you stay close to me. Hang on to the person in front of you. Do *not* stop unless everyone else does. Understand?"

"Yes, Mr Forrester."

I meet Jean's eyes. She's pale, close to welling up.

Torches, batteries. No food. There isn't any. We've brought what coal we can, stuffed in our pockets, tied up in an old jacket.

I flick the torch into the mouth of one of the narrows, and then another. Where do you start? Which do you pick? It's all *terra incognita.*

In the end, I pick the longest narrow in sight. It extends a good fifty yards without a bend. This one.

"Alright," I say. "Let's go."

We start down it, torches shining ahead. A small hand is hooked into the back of my belt. It's the same all the way down the line.

*I'll die first.* That's what I thought. But—what was it pushed me on? The same refusal to die that drove me down here? Or was that what it was, after all? Was it something else? Did something call me down here, lead me into this? A secret love of the dark, a curiosity about places like this? If so, the narrows are the logical conclusion. Was it really a struggle to avoid going back in or a struggle against what kept me out?

Everything's coming apart; even my own motivations. I can't be sure what I want anymore, who I am, what makes me tick.

Or maybe it was simpler. Maybe I could've faced dying, but the kids—the kids and Jean—I know enough about radiation sickness, read and seen enough to know it's a bad death, maybe the worst. Could I have even put myself through it? In the end I couldn't put the children through it. Couldn't watch them die like that because of me.

Or… I just don't know anymore. It feels as if everything's been pushing us—me—towards the narrows. The radiation, whatever happened to Frank. Sooner or later, I had to give way.

What *did* happen to Frank and the others? Something in the water? Something like what Jason heard in the narrows? Or did Frank decide it was a non-starter? Was the tunnel blocked further down? Was he going to turn back and the fight was between him and Jason?

We'll never know. No-one was going to chance trying it again. Maybe we should have.

Too late now.

"Paul?"

"What?" I snap out of the reverie. Snap being the operative word. I look back. Jean, scared face above a line of others like hers.

"I—sorry—Paul. If we go any further we'll be out of sight of the cavern."

She's right. We're about at the first bend. When we round that, the real narrows begin.

"Okay," I say. "Let's stop. Everybody sit down. No-one go anywhere. Not even to pee."

We sit. I can just see the rocks and the glimmer of the lake. Now we're so close to leaving it behind for good, I feel a pang of loss. Like it's home we're leaving.

This is the furthest we can go and hope to turn back. But of course we can't. The radiation…

After a while, I switch on the Geiger counter. It ticks and it crackles, but it's not too loud. Not yet. I switch it off again.

One of the girls, one of the older ones—Laura, Laura Rodgers—is crying quietly. I can find nothing to say to her.

Time passes. I switch on the counter again. It screeches in the narrow like a wounded bat. I switch it off. My eyes meet Jean's.

I force myself to stand. "Alright, everybody," I say. "Let's go."

\* \* \*

The tunnel is endless.

Yard after yard. It stretches on forever.

A torch gives out. Dead batteries fall to the floor. New ones are pushed into place.

They will not last forever.

We keep walking.

Laura Rodgers keeps crying.

Finally we reach a fork. Left or right? I pick the left. We've gone right enough times now, and look where it's got us.

We've stopped twice. The first time, I waited till the Geiger counter screamed at me to move. The second time, I didn't even switch it on.

I just keep walking, leading the children on. Like a Pied Piper, going into the magic mountain. Hushabye. No trees sprouting candy canes here. My stomach growls. I don't think about it. Something scurries, small, somewhere. I can't see it. A rat. *Food.* No. Don't go looking. You'll get lost and you'll never find your way back. Back to what?

I keep walking. And walking. And walking.

Laura Rodgers keeps on crying. It gets harsh, worse. I should tell her to stop, but I can't seem to. All I can do is put one foot in front of the other.

Her breath starts hitching. It's building. To a scream.

*Stop her. Calm her down.*

But even as I think it, she shrieks.

Yelps, cries of alarm, a struggle, blows.

"No! No!" She screeches, and breaks out of the line and blunders back down the narrow. She's not a big girl, only about fifteen and hardly tall for her age, but she knocks Jean aside like a puppet when she tries to hold Laura back. She runs off, still screaming.

"Laura!" I shout. "*Laura!*"

But she's gone. Running back down the narrow towards the cavern. Except of course it won't be there. Still screaming, all the way.

The shrieks and sobs die, echoing into silence. And Laura's gone. We wait for a last screech, the sound of her meeting some final doom, but it doesn't come. She just recedes. Disappears. Is gone. Swallowed up.

The kids are crying. The three little ones, back at the far end with Jean, are almost in hysterics. She holds them tight.

"Everybody stay still!" I shout. I flash the torch, do a quick head count. Everybody here. Except one. Laura Rodgers. The first of us to go.

Me. Jean. And seven kids now.

"Everyone grab on to the person in front of you," I say hoarsely.

And we move on.

* * *

We stop again for a rest. I switch on the Geiger counter, remembering this time. A faint crackling murmur. Safe. For now.

We're all tired. And hopeless.

But this has to end somewhere. Doesn't it? There has to be a place where the narrows end.

Yeah. Maybe a blank wall.

An hour—?—later, I switch the counter back on. It's louder. Much louder. Too loud.

"Come on," I say, and stand.

* * *

We walk, and walk, and walk.

New narrows everywhere now. Gaping in the walls, beckoning us down them, like sellers in a bazaar. *Come this way. No, this way. No, that. That. The other.*

"Shut up!"

"What? Paul?"

God I've spoken aloud. Cracking up. "Nothing," I say. "Sorry."

We keep going. "Rest stop," I gasp. We sit. I do a head count and—

"Jean?"

"What?"

"Someone's missing."

One of the boys. Danny Harper. "Where's Danny?" I say. "Where did he go?" No-one seems to know.

"Who was behind him?"

A hand goes up. Lisa Fowler. "Where did he go?"

"I don't know, sir. I didn't see. I was just holding on to him. Whoever was in front of me."

"Did you let go? Even for a moment?"

"I… I don't know, sir." But her eyes are downcast.

I glare at Jean. "Didn't you see anything?"

"We're all tired, Paul," she snaps. "Can barely focus on whoever's in front of us. Don't start—"

"For Christ's sake! We've lost another one!"

The shout fades to silence. Pale faces stare at me, angry and frightened.

I can say nothing to them. He must have slipped down one of the narrows. Saw something, or thought he did. Heard something, or thought he did. And now he's gone.

Let's go.

* * *

Further on up, the narrow begins to twist and turn. Like we're riding a snake that's realised we're there and is trying to shake us off.

It bends cruelly, sharply, pinching almost too narrow to climb through at all. And for one boy, it is.

Toby Thwaites. His panicked scream explodes like a bomb. "*Mr Forrester!*"

I stumble to a halt. Turn back.

"I'm stuck! I'm stuck!"

Toby, halfway down the line, is wedged solid. Stuck behind him, Jean and the three little ones. Leaving me with the two girls, Lisa Fowler and

Jane Routledge.

Jean and I stare at each other, past Toby's shoulder.

We try everything we can to move him, but it's no go.

"Don't leave me," sobs Toby. He's fifteen years old. "Don't leave me."

"We won't, Toby," I promise him. "We won't."

But we all know it's a lie.

So we wait, and eventually he falls asleep.

"What do we do?" whispers Jean.

"Have to try and go around," I say dully. "Meet up again. We can't stay."

No. We have to keep going. Have to try and find a way out. Even though we know now we never will.

Jean reaches through and clasps my hand.

"Good luck," I say. We know we'll never see each other again.

And we don't.

I watch Jean and the kids go back down the narrow, back the way they came, into the dark, and gone.

"Come on," I say to the girls.

The narrow straightens out again soon enough after that. It's done what it set out to do. We all hope we'll be out of earshot before Toby wakes up and starts screaming at us to come back.

We aren't.

\* \* \*

Further down, the voices start.

First one is Laura Rodgers. "Mr Forrester? Mr Forrester?" Crying, desperately. "Please. *Please.*"

We keep walking.

"Help! Help! Hello? *Hello?*" I know that voice. It's Jeff Tomlinson.

"Can anyone hear us?" A stripped, hysterical scream: I think it's Mike Rawlins.

"Paul? Paul? Are you there?" It's Jean. I shout her name. She shouts mine. But she only gets further away.

Until she's gone.

\* \* \*

The last set of batteries for the last of the torches. I'm stumbling, shuffling. So are Jane and Lisa. We press close, link hands; I lead them on. My left hand holds Lisa's right; her left holds Jane's.

"Listen." It's Jane. Her voice is a croak. "Can you hear it?"

"Hear what?" asks Lisa.

"Water. Listen."

Yes. It's there. Trickling. I realise how swollen my mouth and tongue are. How dry.

"Keep going," I manage.

The trickling seems to get louder and louder.

"Keep g—"

There's suddenly less weight on my left hand. I turn. Lisa stares back at me, then looks round to stare down an empty narrow. A few yards behind us, the sound of water echoes from a hole in the wall.

We go to it. A narrow, extending for maybe five yards, then branching off into three new ones.

"Jane? Jane!"

But there's no reply.

\* \* \*

Walking on. So tired. Sounds of things moving in the darkness beyond. Big things. Heavy things. A hissing sound, close by. Lisa gasps, clutches my arm. A grunt from behind us. We walk faster.

Water, trickling.

\* \* \*

At last, too tired to keep on. We need a place to stop, but the endless narrows—there's nowhere.

But at last, the narrow opens out. Only briefly, two new ones beyond, but it's a small chamber.

We lie down. I curl up; Lisa huddles against my back.

I sleep. No dreams. I wake once; I hear Lisa, crying. "Mum?" she calls. Her voice cracks with terror and relief. "Mum? Mum, is that you? Where are you?"

I should wake up and stop her. But I'm so, so tired. I go back to sleep.

I wake up alone.

\* \* \*

I've been walking a long time now.

The beam of the torch is faint and flickery. I don't have the Geiger counter anymore. I don't know when or where I left it behind.

Voices. All around me. Calling my name. Pleading. Praying. Damning me.

Jean.

Lisa

Jane

Danny

Laura

Toby, poor Toby,

The little ones

Jean.

\* \* \*

The torch goes out.

I shake and rattle and bang it, but it's good and dead this time. At last, I let it fall.

The darkness is total.

I walk into it, hands in front of me.

Dreading what they might touch.

\* \* \*

Can barely walk now. So tired. So hungry. So thirsty. Oh. God.

Plod. Plod. Stumble. Shuffle.

Hit a wall. Ow. Feel at it. Push myself clear. Arms out to either side, then in front. To the sides again. And out front. And so on. And on.

Something stings my eyes. What..?

Light. It's light. It's been so long since I saw it.

Where is it?

Up ahead. I can see it now. There's a bend in the narrow. I stumble towards it. An exit, at last?

I round the corner. And stop.

Anya steps out; she is in silhouette and her outline looks thinner than I remember, but it's her. "Hi, Paul."

A noise comes out of my throat. I want to believe this, but—

"Paul?" She takes a step forward; a slow, dragging step. I stumble backwards. "Darling?"

I backpedal faster. Then, with a horrible crack, my ankle goes as a lump of rock gives underfoot. I fall down, crying out.

"Sh. Baby. Sh." She's holding out her arms. "It's alright."

I cover my face as her dragging footsteps approach. "It's alright."

I pray for death to reach me before her.

But it doesn't.

# HONORABLE MENTIONS

Allan, Nina
—"Ryman's Suitcase," *A Thread of Truth.*
Allen, Mike
—"deathmask," *Helix: A Speculative Fiction Quarterly*, winter.
Avery, Simon
—"101 Ways to Leave Paris," *Crimewave, Now You See Me* 10.
Barron, Laird
—"The Occultation," *Clockwork Phoenix.*
Bear, Elizabeth and Monette, Sarah
—"Boojum," *Fast Ships, Black Sails.*
Bestwick, Simon
—"The School House," (novella) *Houses on the Borderland.*
Bird, Allyson
—"The Bone Grinder," *Bull Running for Girls.*
Block, Lawrence
—"Keller the Dogkiller," *EQMM*, May.
Bobet, Leah
—"Bell, Book, and Candle," *Clockwork Phoenix.*
Bulkin, Nadia
—"Intertropical Convergence Zone," *ChiZine* 37.
Campbell, Ramsey
—"Double Room," *The New Uncanny.*
Campbell, Ramsey
—"The Long Way," PS Publishing chapbook.
Cowdrey, Albert E.
—"The Overseer," (novella) *The Magazine of Fantasy & Science Fiction*, March.
Dowling, Terry
—"The Fooly," *Dreaming Again.*

Duffy, Steve
—"The Oram County Whoosit," *Shades of Darkness.*
Emshwiller, Carol
—"Wilmer or Wesley," *Asimov's Science Fiction*, August.
Ferris, Joshua
—"The Dinner Party," *The New Yorker*, August 11&18.
Finch, Paul
—"The Pumping Station," *We Fade to Grey.*
Grant, Helen
—"Grauer Hans," *Shades of Darkness.*
Grant, John
—"Will the Real Veronica LeBarr Stand Down," *Postscripts* 16.
Haines, Paul
—"Taniwha, Swim with Me," *Midnight Echo* 1.
Harland, Richard
—"A Guided Tour in the Kingdom of the Dead," *Dreaming Again.*
Hirshberg, Glen
—"Like Lick em Sticks, Like Tina Fey," *KRDR.*
Kiernan, Caitlín R.
—"The Steam Dancer (1896)," *Subterranean.*
King, Stephen
—"N." *Just After Sunset.*
—"The New York Times at Special Bargain Rates," *The Magazine of Fantasy & Science Fiction*, Oct/Nov.
Kirk, John
—"The Talion Moth," *Weird Tales* 349, March/April.
Kosmatka, Ted
—"The Art of Alchemy," *The Magazine of Fantasy and Science Fiction*, June.
Laidlaw, Marc
—"Childrun," *The Magazine of Fantasy & Science Fiction*, August.
Lake, Jay
—"America, Such as She Is," (novella) *Alembical.*
Lane, Joel
—"A Mouth to Feed," *Shades of Darkness.*
Lane, Joel
—"Even the Pawn," *Crimewave* 10.
Langan, Sarah
—"The Agathas," *Unspeakable Horror.*
Llewellyn, Livia
—"The Engine of Desire," *Unspeakable Horror.*
Ludwigsen, Will
—"In Search Of," *Alfred Hitchcock Mystery Magazine*, June.
Lynch, Mark Patrick
—"The Apartment of Bryony Hartwood," *Shades of Darkness.*

MacLeod, Ian R.
—"The Hob Carpet," (novella) *Asimov's Science Fiction*, June.
McDermott, Kirstyn
—"Painlessness," *GUD* 2.
McHugh, Ian
—"Bitter Dreams," *Writers of the Future volume XXIV*.
Meloy, Paul
—"All Mouth," *Black Static* 6.
Monette, Sarah
—"The World Without Sleep," *Postscripts* 14.
Pile, Rog
—"The Pit," *The Second Black Book of Horror*.
Pinborough, Sarah
—"Our Man in the Sudan," *The Second Humdrumming Book of Horror*.
Probert, John Llewellyn
—"Don't Look Back," *Coffin Nails*.
Rickert, M.
—"Traitor," *The Magazine of Fantasy & Science Fiction*, May.
Roden, Barbara
—"Endless Night," *Exotic Gothic*.
Samphire, Patrick
—"At the Gates," *Black Static* 8.
Schweitzer, Darrell
—"Living with the Dead," (novella) PS Publishing chapbook.
Strantzas, Simon
—"Under the Overpass," *Shades of Darkness*.
Thomas, Jonathan
—"Into Your Tenement I'll Creep," *Studies in the Fantastic* 1.
Travis, Tia V.
—"No Need of Wings," *Subterranean* online winter 08.
Valentine, Genevieve
—"The Red Shoes (Continued),"*Journal of Mythic Arts* final issue.
VanderMeer, Jeff
—"The Situation," (novella) PS Publishing chapbook.
Weiss, Ernst
—"The Rat Ship," (novella) *A Public Space* 5.
Williams, Conrad
—"68° 07' 15"N, 31° 36' 44"W," *Fast Ships, Black Sails*.

# ABOUT THE AUTHORS

Mike Allen lives in Roanoke, Va. with his wife Anita, a demonic cat, and a comical dog. By day he covers arts and theater for the city's daily newspaper; in his spare time the hats he wears include editor of the poetry journal *Mythic Delirium* and the anthology series *Clockwork Phoenix*. He's a semi-regular performer in the local improv venue and a three-time winner of the Rhysling Award for poetry. *The Philadelphia Inquirer* called his work "poetry for goths of all ages." His latest fiction includes horror tales in *Tales of the Talisman* and *Cabinet des Fées*, as well as *Follow the Wounded One*, a dark fantasy chapbook from the publishers of *Not One of Us* magazine. His short horror story "The Button Bin" was a finalist for the 2008 Nebula Awards.

Laird Barron's work has appeared in places such as *The Magazine of Fantasy & Science Fiction, SCI FICTION, Inferno: New Tales of Terror and the Supernatural, Poe,* and *The Del Rey Book of Science Fiction and Fantasy*. It has also been reprinted in numerous year's best anthologies. His debut collection, *The Imago Sequence & Other Stories*, was recently published by Night Shade Books. Mr. Barron is an expatriate Alaskan currently at large in Washington State.

Simon Bestwick lives in Lancashire. Since 1997, he has had in excess of one hundred pieces of fiction published in Britain, the US, and Canada, including appearances in the award-winning anthologies *Inferno* and *Acquainted with the Night*. His first story collection, *A Hazy Shade of Winter,* was published in 2004 and the title story was reprinted in *The Year's Best Fantasy and Horror #18*. His second collection, *Pictures of the Dark,* and his first novel, *Tide Of Souls*, were published in 2009.

Richard Bowes has written five novels, the most recent of which is the Nebula Award-nominated *From the Files of the Time Rangers*. His most recent short fiction collection is *Streetcar Dreams and Other Midnight Fancies* from PS Publishing. He has won the World Fantasy, Lambda, International Horror Guild, and Million Writers awards.

Recent and forthcoming stories appear in *The Magazine of Fantasy & Science Fiction*, *Electric Velocipede*, *Clarkesworld*, and *Fantasy* magazines and in the *Del Rey Book of Science Fiction and Fantasy*, *Year's Best Gay Stories 2008*, *Best Science Fiction and Fantasy*, *The Beastly Bride*, *Haunted Legends*, *Fantasy Best of the Year 2009*, *Year's Best Fantasy*, and *Naked City* anthologies . Several of these stories are chapters in his novel in progress, *Dust Devil on a Quiet Street*.

Steve Duffy's short stories have appeared in numerous magazines and anthologies in Europe and North America. His forthcoming collection, *The Moment of Panic*, will be his third, and includes the International Horror Guild Award-winning tale "The Rag-and-Bone Men." He lives in North Wales.

Graham Edwards, after spending rather too much of his life messing about with graphic design, animation, and pretty pictures, decided to write instead. The rest, as they say, is alternative history. His fantasy novels include *Dragoncharm* and its sequels, and *Stone & Sky*, which kicks off a time-travel adventure trilogy.

His short fiction has been published in *Realms of Fantasy* and *Jim Baen's Universe*. He exists as part of the usual set of physical dimensions in an English city called Nottingham.

Adam Golaski is the author of the fiction collections *Worse Than Myself* and *Color Plates*. He edits the journal *New Genre* and is cofounder of Flim Forum Press. The publication of "Green," his translation of *Sir Gawain & the Green Knight*, is ongoing in the critical journal *Open Letters*. Golaski's work has appeared in numerous journals and anthologies, including: *McSweeney's*, *Supernatural Tales*, *Conjunctions*, *Haunted Histories*, *Exotic Gothic II*, *Torpedo*, and *The Lifted Brow*.

Euan Harvey teaches writing and linguistics at Mahidol University International College in Thailand. He lives in the suburbs of Bangkok with his long-suffering wife and three children, where he leads a life of sun-drenched tropical indolence. (At least, that's what he planned when he moved to Thailand; so far, things haven't quite worked out that way.) His fiction has been published in *Semaphore*, *Byzarium*, *Black Gate*, and several times in *Realms of Fantasy*.

Trent Hergenrader is a Ph.D. student in Creative Writing at the University of Wisconsin-Milwaukee. His short stories have appeared in *The Magazine* of Fantasy & Science Fiction, Realms of Fantasy, Weird Tales, Black Static, and the anthology Federations, among other places. Hergenrader is also a graduate of the 2004 Clarion Writers Workshop. He lives in Madison, WI.

Glen Hirshberg's first two collections, American Morons and The Two Sams each won the International Horror Guild Award and were selected by Locus as one of the best books of the year. He is also the author of a novel, The Snowman's Children, and a five-time World Fantasy Award finalist. With Dennis Etchison and Peter Atkins, he cofounded the Rolling Darkness Revue, a traveling ghost story performance troupe that tours the West Coast of the United States each October. His fiction has appeared in numerous magazines and anthologies, including multiple appearances in The Year's Best Fantasy and Horror, The Mammoth Book of Best New Horror, Inferno, The Dark, Dark Terrors 6, Trampoline, and Cemetery Dance. He lives in the Los Angeles area with his wife and children.

Daniel Kaysen's short dark fiction has appeared online at ChiZine and Strange Horizons, and in print in Interzone and Crimewave, among other venues. "The Rising River" was his first publication in Black Static. He has since appeared there several more times. He lives in England, near London.

Margo Lanagan lives in Sydney, Australia, and works as a contract technical writer. She has published three collections of speculative short stories: White Time, Black Juice, and Red Spikes, and a novel, Tender Morsels. Her stories have won two World Fantasy Awards, two Ditmar Awards, four Aurealis Awards, and two Michael L. Printz Honors, and have been shortlisted for many other awards, including a Nebula, a Hugo and the James Tiptree Jr. Award. Lanagan taught at Clarion South in 2005, 2007, and 2009. She has also published poetry, and fiction for junior readers and teenagers.

Joe R. Lansdale has been a freelance writer since 1973, and a full time writer since 1981. He is the author of thirty novels and eighteen short story collections and has received the Edgar Award, seven Bram Stoker Awards, the British Fantasy Award, and Italy's Grinzani Prize for Literature, among others. As obvious from his awards, he writes in several different genres and is proficient in them all.

The novella "Bubba Ho-Tep" was filmed by Don Coscarelli and is now considered a cult classic, and his story "Incident On and Off a Mountain Road" was filmed for Showtime's Masters of Horror.

He has written for film, television, comics, and is the author of numerous essays and columns. His most recent work is the collection Sanctified and Chicken Fried, The Portable Lansdale, and Vanilla Ride, his latest in the Hap Collins, Leonard Pine mystery series.

Daniel LeMoal is a writer and communications assistant based in Winnipeg, Manitoba, Canada. His fiction has appeared in the pages of genre publications such as *On Spec* and *Apex Science Fiction & Horror Digest*, while his journalism has run in local dailies including the *Winnipeg Free Press*, the *Winnipeg Sun* and the *Portage la Prairie Daily Graphic*. He also once worked on the kill floor of a slaughterhouse. To this day, people still ask him what wieners are really made out of. They never like the answer.

E. Michael Lewis studied creative writing at the University of Puget Sound in Tacoma, Wa. He is a lifelong native of the Pacific Northwest, where he raised two sons who routinely make him proud. His work can be found in *All Hallows*, *Shadowed Realms*, and *The Harrow*.

Margaret Ronald's fiction has appeared in such venues as *Fantasy Magazine*, *Strange Horizons*, *Realms of Fantasy*, *Baen's Universe*, and *Clarkesworld* magazine. Her debut novel, *Spiral Hunt*, was published in early 2009. She is an alum of the Viable Paradise workshop and a member of BRAWL. Originally from rural Indiana, she now lives outside Boston.

Nicholas Royle, born in Manchester in 1963, is the author of five novels —including *Counterparts*, *The Director's Cut*, and *Antwerp*—and two novellas—*The Appetite* and *The Enigma of Departure*. He has published around 120 short stories, twenty of which are collected in *Mortality*. Widely published as a journalist, with regular appearances in *Time Out* and the *Independent*, he has also edited thirteen original anthologies, including two *Darklands* volumes and *The Tiger Garden: A Book of Writers' Dreams*. The winner of three British Fantasy Awards, he teaches creative writing at Manchester Metropolitan University.

R. B. Russell's first collection of strange fiction, *Putting the Pieces in Place*, was published in January 2009, and his second collection, *Literary Remains*, will be published in late 2009. He runs Tartarus Press with his wife, Rosalie Parker, and also writes music and poetry and occasionally draws illustrations for dust jackets.

Miranda Siemienowicz lives in Melbourne, Australia. Her work has appeared in literary and speculative magazines including *Overland*, *Island*, and *Aurealis*, and been reprinted in *Australian Dark Fantasy and Horror Volume 3* (Brimstone Press).

William Browning Spencer is the author of four novels and two collections of short stories. Spencer's satirical horror novel *Résumé with Monsters* describes a corporate America in which Lovecraftian monsters haunt the workplace. The novel won the International Horror Award for best novel.

Various creatures from Lovecraft also inhabit his novel *Irrational Fears*, in which alcoholics are discovered to be the progeny of an ancient underground tribe who worship Tsathoggua.

His short stories have been included in *The Year's Best Science Fiction* and *The Year's Best Fantasy and Horror* and have been finalists for the Bram Stoker, World Fantasy, and Shirley Jackson awards. He currently lives in Austin, Texas, and is completing his novel *My Sister Natalie: Snake Goddess of the Amazon*, which will be published by Subterranean Press.

JoSelle Vanderhooft is the critically acclaimed author of poetry collections *The Minotaur's Last Letter to His Mother*, the 2007 Stoker Award-nominated *Ossuary, Desert Songs, The Handless Maiden and Other Tales Twice-Told, Fathers, Daughters, Ghosts & Monsters, The Memory Palace*, and *Death Masks*; the novels *The Tale of the Miller's Daughter*, and *Owl Skin*; and *Ugly Things*, a collection of short stories. She is currently at work on a series of novels. Her poetry and fiction has been published online and in print in a number of publications, including *Cabinet des Fees, Star\*Line, Mythic Delirium, MYTHIC, Jabberwocky, Helix, The Seventh Quarry*.

An assistant editor of a gay and lesbian newspaper by day, she lives in Salt Lake City, Utah.

# Night Shade Books Is an Independent Publisher of Quality SF, Fantasy and Horror

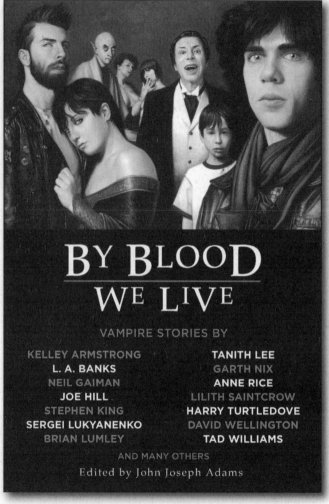

BY BLOOD
WE LIVE

VAMPIRE STORIES BY

KELLEY ARMSTRONG     TANITH LEE
L. A. BANKS     GARTH NIX
NEIL GAIMAN     ANNE RICE
JOE HILL     LILITH SAINTCROW
STEPHEN KING     HARRY TURTLEDOVE
SERGEI LUKYANENKO     DAVID WELLINGTON
BRIAN LUMLEY     TAD WILLIAMS

AND MANY OTHERS
Edited by John Joseph Adams

ISBN 978-1-59780-156-0, Trade Paperback; $15.95

From Dracula to Buffy the Vampire Slayer; from Castlevania to True Blood, the romance between popular culture and vampires hearkens back to humanity's darkest, deepest fears, flowing through our very blood, fears of death, and life, and insatiable hunger. And yet, there is an attraction, undeniable, to the vampire archetype, whether the pale, wan European count, impeccably dressed and coldly masculine, yet strangely ambiguous, ready to sink his sharp teeth deep into his victims' necks, draining or converting them, or the vamp, the count's feminine counterpart, villain and victim in one, using her wiles and icy sexuality to corrupt man and woman alike...

Gathering together the best vampire literature of the last three decades from many of today's most renowned authors of fantasy, speculative fiction, and horror. *By Blood We Live* will satisfy your darkest cravings...

# Night Shade Books Is an Independent Publisher of Quality SF, Fantasy and Horror

FEATURING STORIES BY

JOAN AIKEN
PAOLO BACIGALUPI
STEPHEN BAXTER
PETER S. BEAGLE
ELIZABETH BEAR
HOLLY BLACK
TED CHIANG
GREG EGAN
KIJ JOHNSON
STEPHEN KING
MARGO LANAGAN
KELLY LINK
MICHAEL SWANWICK
AND MANY OTHERS

THE BEST
SCIENCE FICTION
AND FANTASY
OF THE YEAR
VOLUME THREE

EDITED BY JONATHAN STRAHAN

ISBN 978-1-59780-149-2, Trade Paperback; $19.95

An alien world with an argon atmosphere serves as the stage for the ultimate self-examination; an African-American scientist dissects a Lovecraftian slave race while fascism rears its head on the other side of the world; an elderly Jewish artist attracts a celestial muse; a doomed village of scavengers discovers the scattered pieces of a metal man; a stalwart reporter gambles on an interview with the power to alter the world; a steel monkey defends a young girl from a rival family's assassins; two girls discover that the cruel social rituals of adolescence apply differently in fact than fiction...

The depth and breadth of science fiction and fantasy fiction continues to change with every passing year. The twenty-eight stories chosen for this book by award-winning anthologist Jonathan Strahan carefully map this evolution, giving readers a captivating and always-entertaining look at the very best the genre has to offer.

# Night Shade Books Is an Independent Publisher of Quality SF, Fantasy and Horror

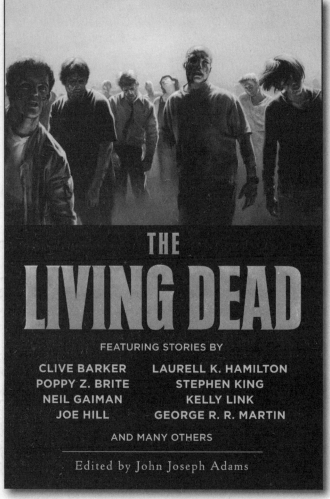

ISBN 978-1-59780-143-0, Trade Paperback; $15.95

From *White Zombie* to *Dawn of the Dead*; from *Resident Evil* to *World War Z*, zombies have invaded popular culture, becoming the monsters that best express the fears and anxieties of the modern west.

Gathering together the best zombie literature of the last three decades from many of today's most renowned authors of fantasy, speculative fiction, and horror, *The Living Dead* covers the broad spectrum of zombie fiction, from Romero-style zombies to reanimated corpses to voodoo zombies and beyond.

"When there's no more room in hell, the dead will walk the earth."

# Night Shade Books Is an Independent Publisher of Quality SF, Fantasy and Horror

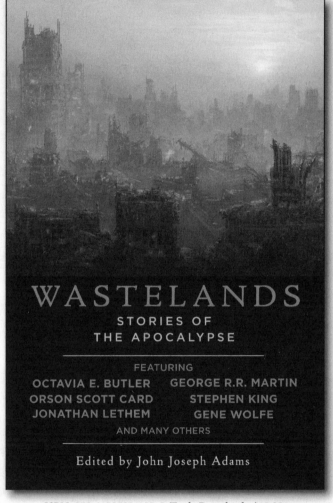

## WASTELANDS
### STORIES OF THE APOCALYPSE

FEATURING

**OCTAVIA E. BUTLER**     **GEORGE R.R. MARTIN**
**ORSON SCOTT CARD**          **STEPHEN KING**
**JONATHAN LETHEM**            **GENE WOLFE**
AND MANY OTHERS

Edited by John Joseph Adams

ISBN 978-1-59780-105-8, Trade Paperback; $15.95

Famine, Death, War, and Pestilence: The Four Horsemen of the Apocalypse, the harbingers of Armageddon—these are our guides through the Wastelands.

Gathering together the best post-apocalyptic literature of the last two decades from many of today's most renowned authors of speculative fiction, including George R. R. Martin, Gene Wolfe, Orson Scott Card, Carol Emshwiller, Jonathan Lethem, Octavia E. Butler, and Stephen King, *Wastelands* explores the scientific, psychological, and philosophical questions of what it means to remain human in the wake of Armageddon. Whether the end of the world comes through nuclear war, ecological disaster, or cosmological cataclysm, these are tales of survivors, in some cases struggling to rebuild the society that was, in others, merely surviving, scrounging for food in depopulated ruins and defending themselves against monsters, mutants, and marauders.

Ellen Datlow has been editing science fiction, fantasy, and horror short stories for almost thirty years. She was co-editor of *The Year's Best Fantasy and Horror* and has edited or co-edited many other anthologies, most recently *The Coyote Road* and *Troll's Eye View* (with Terri Windling), *Inferno, The Del Rey Book of Science Fiction and Fantasy, Nebula Award Showcase 2009, Poe: 19 New Tales Inspired by Edgar Allan Poe,* and *Lovecraft Unbound.*

Forthcoming are, *Digital Domains: A Decade of Science Fiction and Fantasy, Darkness: Two Decades of Modern Horror, Naked City: New Tales of Urban Fantasy, Best Horror of the Year, Volume 2, Haunted Legends* (with Nick Mamatas), and *The Beastly Bride* (with Terri Windling).

She has won multiple awards for her editing, including the World Fantasy, Locus, Hugo, International Horror Guild, Shirley Jackson, and Stoker awards. She was named recipient of the 2007 Karl Edward Wagner Award for "outstanding contribution to the genre."

For more information, visit her website at www.datlow.com.